NIMBUS

Other Books by
Alexander Jablokov

CARVE THE SKY
A DEEPER SEA

NIMBUS

ALEXANDER JABLOKOV

An AvoNova Book

William Morrow and Company, Inc.
New York

AVON BOOKS
A division of
The Hearst Corporation
1350 Avenue of the Americas
New York, New York 10019

Copyright © 1993 by Alexander Jablokov
Published by arrangement with the author
ISBN: 0-688-11114-9

Printed in the U.S.A.

To Mary,
who is marrying a writer,
and knows what that means.

Acknowledgments

As always, to the Cambridge Science Fiction Workshop: Jon Burrowes, Steve Caine, Pete Chvany, Margaret Flinn, James Patrick Kelly, Steve Popkes, David Smith, Sarah Smith, and Paul Tumey.

- 1 -

I CHOKED AND FOUND MYSELF AWAKE. I BREATHED SLOWLY AND LET THE dark images of sleep slide from my mind like drops of rain down a night window. The ceiling was vaguely lit from somewhere below. The sheets, as usual, had wrapped themselves, sweat-damp and sticky, around my legs. I extracted myself slowly from them, a tired, still-unmetamorphosed caterpillar, and sat up on the edge of the bed. I rubbed sleep gunk from my eyes.

A body lay sprawled face down amid the dirty laundry that covered the floor, one hand under a pair of boxer shorts. It glowed with a soft internal light. I blinked at it, wondering if I'd left the TV on when I went to sleep. I didn't think so. I'd been in the operating room most of the night.

I waved my hand to raise the volume. " . . . estimates time of death as 8:00 P.M. 18 October 2030—forty-eight hours before the body was found by the apartment manager." The glowing dead man wore pajamas that looked cleaner than mine. His head was an opaque black sphere.

"According to Chicago police, the victim was strangled. Specifics have been retained pending investigation."

Alphanumerics pulsed above the body: "REWARD N$10." Decent amount, ten nudes. "Specifics." Sounded like the police were concealing some fine murdering style. Maybe it was another forward-shock skein death with some ridiculously detailed form of mutilation. Not my field of interest. So why had the set called it up?

I snapped the set off, tripped across to the window, and pulled the curtains, letting the sun struggle in through the greasy panes and dusty air. I squinted against the light and looked around the room. The breath I drew in next burned in my throat.

During the night my decorating ralfies had redone my bedroom to look like a teenager's room from the 1950s. College pennants decorated the walls. The furniture was much-scuffed imitation colonial. Exuberantly but inexpertly painted models of ships and animals filled the shelves, and model airplanes dangled from a string across the ceiling, diving on strafing runs. The bedside lamp was shaped like a binnacle and had a blue sailboat on the shade. The clothes on the floor, immune from the ralfies' ministrations, were still my own, no grass-stained baseball uniforms or worn cords with slingshots in the back pocket among them.

"God *damn* it!" The ralfies had disguised themselves as WWII soldiers—chubby ones, like drafted gingerbread men, standing earnestly at attention on the desk amid pencils and graffiti-covered blue three-ring binders.

I tried to grab the football lying on the headboard shelf so I could knock the miserable gadgets over with it, but it was synthetic, about as massive as cotton candy, and shredded in my hands. The ralfies sucked the foam from some bioreactor in the house walls that made it out of god-knew-what.

In a fury I punched and pounded the headboard, made of a synthetic a little harder than the football, feeling it shatter satisfyingly. But it was built on a real frame and I smashed the side of my hand against it, nearly dislocating my little finger. I shouted a stream of obscenities and stumbled around the room. Clothes grabbed anxiously at my feet.

A narrow shelf by the window held trophies in the shape of the busts of famous composers. I picked up a head of Robert Schumann. "Sylvanus West High School Regional Piano Competition—2nd Place, January 2019. Theo Bronkman." I stared at Schumann's ivory nineteenth century romantic face. He'd died mad, but looked sternly normal, disapproving of my lack of control.

Schumann flew across the room and slapped face first into the wall. He was followed by Beethoven, Stravinsky, and the rest. Theo Bronkman. I hadn't seen that name in years. It had once been my own. How had the ralfies gotten a hold of it?

I stood, massaging my throbbing little finger, and struggled to catch my breath. I had no idea why I was so furious. It seemed that there were things coiled up in the recesses of my mind that I still had not managed to find and root out. After a minute the tight, hot band across my chest relaxed enough for me to talk without screaming.

"That's what I get for buying cheap." The ralfies didn't react, programmed to respond only to a limited set of commands. "Redo," I said. "Back to zero and restart. Give me something different." I thought a moment. "Louis the Sixteenth, maybe?" I'd seen a TV special on old furniture a few weeks ago. It was the first thing I could think of. "Do it."

The ralfies twitched and rolled off the desk, already ceasing to look like soldiers, features running like melted crayons. Was that the trace of a periwig on the last one? They lived and charged themselves inside the walls like hitech mice. I could hear them scurrying there, getting programmed by the decorator-style data base and then waiting for me to leave so that they could get to work. I picked clothes up at random and put them on, feeling sagging, sticky, and foul. I cursed the damn TV for having woken me up, even though I had work to do downstairs.

The hallway was dark. I'd always meant to put more lights in it. It felt like it was underground. I crept down the stairs, already ashamed of my anger, though no one had seen it. The house was silent, holding its breath.

As I passed through the kitchen door, I looked up, a reflex I thought I had suppressed long ago. Nothing waited to drop on me from above, nothing but a stained ceiling. I was normally paranoid, but this was getting extreme. Why would there be a bloodhound waiting for me in my own house, so many years after? The place was surrounded by a security system that informed me of every field mouse and squirrel that scampered across my property, giving me nice, if completely meaningless, frequency histograms for nocturnal activities of Rodentia.

I sat down in a wood kitchen chair and stared up at the pots and pans hanging over the stove. Their copper bottoms gleamed. My kitchen, at least, looked like a decent person lived here. I'd thrown out everything Corinne had put in. Her taste in kitchens had not matched mine. A terra cotta pizza stone rested near the double sink. I'd made and—Jesus—eaten an entire sausage and pepper pizza the previous night, in between work sessions in the operating room. Maybe that was behind my paranoia. I prodded my bulging belly. Damn pizza was screwing up my blood chemistry, altering neurotransmitter secretion, whatever. Cheese is full of tryptophan, a serotonin precursor. That must be it.

For some reason, I'd left the windows open. A cold wind blew in. I reached across the sink and pulled them shut. As I did so, I brushed against a big, scummy cup of something on the counter. I frowned, and tasted it. It had once been hot chocolate. A disgusting mate to pizza, I thought. Whatever had possessed me? I didn't even remember owning any cocoa. Probably left over since Corinne's time. I poured it down the sink and vigorously scrubbed the counter.

But I couldn't delay any longer. I had to force myself to look out the window. I was afraid I would see the eroded hills of Bessarabia, Carpathians bulking at the horizon. It was hard to turn my head, as if I was twisting it into a knife blade whose point rested against my temple. It's an old and absurd game, pushing in the direction of maximum resistance for no better reason than because it is there. I did it. All I could see was my tree-choked backyard. The ground between the trunks was covered with several years' worth of dead leaves. The maple leaves were changing color.

Bessarabia. I stood up, got coffee beans out of the freezer, and ground them with a cast-iron hand grinder, adding some cardamom seeds, hoping the familiar ritual would exorcise the memories. I'd obviously tripped some memory cascade and they were spilling out like junk from an overstuffed closet. I poured the grounds into a filter and let almost-boiling springwater seep through them.

Bessarabia. Anthony Watkins had given me the originals of those trophies upstairs, a half-hostile, half-loving joke as I struggled with the piano in the old barracks at Camp Fitzwater. The originals were long well lost. Watkins had been with me in Bessarabia. They all had. The entire Group. It was suddenly as if all my old comrades were standing on an until-now invisible horizon and a rising sun had suddenly pushed their shadows across the miles to me. Get a hold of yourself, Ambrose. That was years ago, all vanished now, just like the trophies. Just like bloodhounds. Peter Ambrose, that was my *name*, not that old handle, Theo Bronkman. That had been forgotten with everything else.

I took a gulp of coffee, then pretended to myself that I hadn't just burned my lips and tongue. I sucked cool air.

Bessarabia. Screw Bessarabia.

I felt queasy. My skin felt like the congealed surface of last night's pizza. I should go see my client, downstairs. I'd delayed long enough.

I went into the bathroom off the kitchen and scrubbed my face and hands. Gritty pumice soap, steaming water from the fine silver taps. Again. A rough towel. My sagging face was a pink blob in the steamed-up circular mirror, but I didn't feel any cleaner.

Grabbing my coffee, I went through the self-sealing door at the base of the stairs. It sucked shut behind me. This was the true heart of my dwelling, hidden inside the sagging suburban house. Surfaces flowed together smoothly without a hint of corner. Precipitators and filters kept the air absolutely clean. Power and environmental support were separate from the rest of the house.

This functional core had once been the emergency survival system of an interplanetary spacecraft, now long obsolete. I'd bought it in a huge industrial recycling center piled on what had once been a residential subdivision in the Florida panhandle, near Eglin Air Force Base. I could have bought turbofan engines or low-orbital boosters, or any other Near-Earth-Orbit military stuff useless after the end of the Wars of Devolution. This survival module had come from a Ukrainian observation platform. I'd never learned to read the insistent Cyrillic notices printed everywhere.

The harsh sterilizing light of the operating room beat down on the naked body of a middle-aged blond man that lay prone on the table, spread-eagled legs higher than his head. He was going just soft around the edges, belly and upper arms, the way all of our bodies do, life pressing down on us like a thumb on a gumdrop. Thousands of fine electrodes sprouted along his spine from sacrum to occiput like a silver pelt. His official name was Thomas Francis Inman and he'd come in here the afternoon before for his final implantation session.

Then, dressed in a silk Malaysian suit with a filigree gold clip holding the calculated drapery of his embroidered neckpiece, Inman had been every inch the confident, demanding executive. Now, head down and naked in the insolently revealing blue-white light, he looked like he had been buggered by aliens from Betelgeuse and dumped by a roadside. I tried not to find the image amusing. He was my client, after all.

I gave the command to retract the sacral probe whose infomycelia innervated the lower part of his spinal cord, cranked his legs shut, leveled him, and initiated wake-up.

The space was crowded with round-cornered plia-black cabinets, their liquid-crystal display screens blinking excessive data about blood pH, skin conductivity, and leukocyte counts. Their texture was that of human skin. Running a hand across a cabinet's optical fiber plugs could be a disturbingly erotic experience.

Inman began to regain some basic neural function. I restarted his heart and lungs. I did a final set of system checks, nerve velocities, data transfers into his cortex. Yesterday, Inman had been tense, almost angry, as if something was wrong with what I had done with him. But everything was smooth. I'd installed the last virts in his brain, each one marked by its manufacturer with six interlocking circles, a corporate logo I was unfamiliar with, and checked his neural functions a dozen times.

Right now, lying on my operating table, he was nothing more than a mass of highly organized matter full of propagating action potentials, bursting vesicles of neurotransmitters, flickering sodium and potassium gates. Once I pressed a few spots on my control panel, he would, with the same potentials, neurotransmitters, and ions, become Thomas Francis Inman, a heo of a company called Transcendental Transition. It always seemed that there should be more of a difference between those two states.

I settled back and waited for him to exist. And to wonder why the TV had decided to dump the image of a murder victim onto my bedroom floor.

-2-

"**H**OW DO YOU FEEL?" I ASKED.

Inman, sitting on a living room armchair, considered the question. As he had been careful to arrange the night before, he wore a silk lounging suit more suited to a sunny deck facing the busy waters of the Sea of Siam than a cool fall living room outside of Chicago, Illinois. Inman had brought several changes of clothing in two pigskin suitcases. They were large enough that I wondered if they also contained a scarlet riding outfit and a formal jellaba.

"You spend all night analyzing my every nerve impulse and you ask me how I feel?" Inman's voice was more curious than irritated. "Don't you know?"

I blinked at him. There was a lazy authority in his voice that hit me in a nervous place. I took refuge in technical expertise, and felt like a datadork even as I did it. "I know how mathematical data from the net enters your conscious mind through the supramarginal gyrus. I know how the auxiliary processor in the ventral posterior nucleus of your thalamus is working. I don't know how you feel. And I do want to know. It's important."

"I feel fine." He brought his hand up to run it over his head and seemed startled to find his curling brown hair. He wound a lock around a finger. "It's just that . . . it doesn't make sense at all." He squinted into the morning sunlight, then lifted his weight and tugged his armchair out of its place in the living room arrangement until its back was to the front window. "I'm worried. I've been coming here for . . . what? Three weeks now? All sorts of things have been going on in my head. I don't feel right."

"See?" I said. "That's why I asked you. In what way don't you feel right?"

"I don't know. I'm not an installer. Like I'm being pulled in different directions. Like I'm having different thoughts. Is everything working

7

right? All the brain modifications—you call them virts, don't you?—are they all operational?" He took a sip of his coffee, pleased at knowing some craniac slang.

"Technically, it's perfect, Mr. Inman." I didn't allow myself to sound impatient.

"Are you absolutely sure about that?" he demanded.

"I'm sure." I was cool. Clients often got arrogant after their operations, suspecting that I saw their brains as just so much complex gray oatmeal. That suspicion was correct. "You can check if you want. The built-in contract monitor in your temporal lobe gives you direct access to all test results. Just think about it and remember."

He blew out his lips, looking suddenly like a small boy. Data flowed into his mind like long-forgotten memories of lessons he'd learned in third grade. He thought about it, and looked annoyed. "Perfect. Everything is according to contract. But I don't feel . . ."

He hunched forward over the cherry wood coffee table. He tugged at a cookie package I had put there to comfort him on his return to consciousness. The delicate Japanese-inspired packing unwove and he was left holding a thin ribbon. He picked up a ginger cookie and stared at it. "I'm not sure that I can remember everything right. Everything that I need to." He looked lost.

"Your contract did not allow me to remember any of it for you."

"I know, I know."

Inman's brain was lousy with mindblocks guarding proprietary information. A number of new ones had been inserted just prior to his coming to me, in case I was in the pay of one of Transcendental Transition's competitors and would try to yank them out by tapping associative pathways. Right now, Inman's own thoughts were encrypted. I hoped he'd be able to find his way home. It was a devil's bargain, working for a curling-edge company like Tran^2, but there were many who made the deal. Having his own thoughts be on loan to him was something Inman took in stride.

Of course, "Thomas Inman" was just a label. I didn't know his real name, the name his friends, relatives, children called him, and it would have been a contract violation for me to have tried to find out. Like many corporate heos he had a professional personality, maintained for optimal efficiency: focused, calm, undistracted. But he wasn't being professional now. He looked genuinely scared.

"If you suspect there's something wrong, you should tell me," I said. "If you are at all dissatisfied with my work—"

"No, no. You're the best. I know that. That's why I hired you." He

smiled at me, crinkling at the corners of his eyes. He looked quite lov-
able. I hadn't checked whether the dermal keratin around his eyes had
been massaged by a microsurgeon into a pattern called "Powerful-But-
Sensitive-High-Executive-Officer," but if that's what it was, he was pretty
sophisticated. Most men, particularly heos, go for facial microsurgery
that makes their faces as suspiciously smooth as processed high school
graduation pictures. "I was told by someone whose opinion I trust."

"Nice of them." I took a ginger cookie myself. Crisp and spicy. It made
sense, in a way that Inman didn't. I'd done a final check of everything
I'd installed in his nervous system over the previous three weeks, every
auxiliary processor, the netlink in the sacral segment of his spinal cord,
the fatigue suppressions, coordination enhancements, everything. There
was nothing wrong with any of it. "Your mind wasn't made for what has
happened to the brain underneath it. If you remember, we discussed it all
before—"

"I know all that. I know!" His eyes darted from side to side. "I just didn't
know that I would feel so lost. It's so big out there. I feel it sucking at me.
At me. And I'm not any different."

I sighed. This was an old ritual with me. "I know it's hard to get used
to. All of us do though, finally. The results don't match our expectations.
They can't. Having instantaneous access to terabytes of data, fast internal
processing, and increased association doesn't make you happy. It doesn't
force the universe to make sense. It doesn't make you a better human
being. Just a more efficient one. We live with that. It's all we can do."

"That better not be all you can do. It's gigashit, is all, gigashit." Again,
he brought his hand to his head, and again seemed startled by the hair, as
if he'd expected to wake up with a bare cranium. He yanked at it. "I can't
stand that."

I was getting worried. "Mr. Inman, you can calm yourself through
inhibitory amygdaloid stimulation, if you wish. As contracted, you have
the ability to—"

"I don't want to goddamn calm myself! I want to figure out where you
fucked up." He stood, bumping the table and knocking the stack of cookies
to the floor. I only just stopped myself from kneeling immediately to pick
them up and put them neatly back on the table. But there was spilled coffee
all over the cherry wood. If it stained, Corinne . . . damn it, he was really
getting on my nerves.

"I need more than you've given me, Ambrose." Inman sucked in a
breath. "A lot more." He towered over me. His face disappeared in the
light from the windows behind him. For a moment, I felt fear.

"Mr. Inman! Please relax. Use your amygdala, use your common sense, use whatever. But *stop it*. This won't get us anywhere. Please."

He stared at me, pupils dilated, breathing hard. His anger was his prize dog. He wanted to feel it growling and straining against its leash, not vanishing as the result of a neurotransmitter surge.

Without waiting to see what he did next, I went into the kitchen, got a sponge and the coffeepot, and came back. I poured him another cup and wiped the table. It, like the rest of the furniture, was that sharp-edged Mission-influenced cherry-and-ash style known as Solar Mission. Classically unfashionable, and it reminded me of her, but I did need somewhere to sit. My calmly domestic actions abashed him, as far as that was possible. It was stupid of me to have suggested his god damned amygdala anyway. Who wouldn't have burned? No excuse for me to have said it. I wondered what it was about him that annoyed me so much.

"OK, OK. Sorry." Inman sat back down and sipped coffee, for all the world as if he hadn't just been yelling at me. Maybe he'd used his amygdala after all. "You put cardamom in it. That's a Yemeni habit, isn't it?"

I sipped my own coffee placidly. Yemen was precisely where I *hadn't* been, which was why I cultivated habits from there. Some patterned rugs, some beaten brass ornaments, and anyone with any suspicions would be baying full speed in the wrong direction, I hoped.

"I had friends who died there." Inman was thoughtful. "Did you serve?"

"Here and there," I answered, in the evasive way of Devo War vets. "It's all over now."

"Yeah." He laughed. "We always think things are over." He grinned smugly at me.

He was really making my butt itch. I wanted him out of my house. "Mr. Inman, I can't help you unless you give me some specific—"

"Corinne Zamm told me you were good. You wanted to ask who had recommended you, but you didn't. I wonder why? You used to be married to her, didn't you? She gave you a good report. Ex-wives don't usually do that, so I figured it meant something."

I couldn't speak. Corinne had sent this guy to me? Whatever for?

I hadn't seen or communicated with Corinne in years. I had seen her once, completely by accident, climbing into a long electric car on Michigan Avenue with a load of Christmas packages. A light snow was coming down, Christmas lights glowed on the bare trees, and she looked dazzling, light brown hair spilling out from under her hat, yellow gloves tight over her precise fingers. She handed the packages in and slid gracefully into the dark car. I'd stood frozen in the slush and tried to see who was driving it. I'd deliberately refused to learn anything about her new life, but at that moment had wanted to know very much how she lived.

And now she was sending me clients? As far as I knew, Corinne didn't have the vaguest idea of what I now did for a living. When we'd parted, I'd just been a musician. A musician with a lot of secrets.

It wasn't like her. She was severe, but she'd never been cruel.

Before I could speak, Inman shook his head. "That was rude of me." He gave me a tight little smile. "Forgive me. I need to go home." He hunched his shoulders. My company was suddenly making him uncomfortable. He had said more than he intended, probably, I realized, startled, because he found *me* annoying.

"Mr. Inman," I said. "I want you to understand. You're not yourself. We'll need to do a follow-up, perhaps several, before you are completely in control of your own central nervous system. We can schedule—"

"I'm busy from now on. Maybe we'll run into each other at some point." He looked up as an alarm indicated a car coming into the driveway. "That will be Priscilla. It's later than I thought. Excuse me, will you? That's a very nice piece you've made there." And, with perfect grace, he walked off to the changing room off the kitchen. I looked down at my hands. Unconsciously, I had grabbed the cookie ribbon and woven it back around what we had left of the cookies. Damn. I never liked for clients to see my compulsive habits. I got up to answer the door.

Streams of blinding sunlight came through the thinning trees, and their bright landing places, textured with fallen leaves and bent-over drying grass, broke up my field of vision so that nothing looked familiar. Vertical tree trunks vanished, sliced by light, and the front of my dilapidated suburban split-level seemed a wall of massive light and dark boulders. I felt dissolved myself, from the light in my lungs.

A pair of high-heeled pumps, shiny patent leather, stood on the cracking concrete of the front porch. They were new enough that the gold label at the instep was still unworn. I stared uncomprehendingly at them.

A rustle of leaves. "Don't you ever take care of your lawn, Mr.—or is it Doctor?—Ambrose? I thought everyone did, in the suburbs."

A wind blew the trees and a woman emerged from the dappled sundrops like a suddenly clarified optical illusion. She stood on the grass in her stockings, curling her toes amid the leaves. She kicked a few into the air. She had dark satin skin, a high forehead, and oddly stubby fingers, like a small girl's.

"Those suburbs are somewhere else," I said. She took my arm to step onto the porch, inclining her head to acknowledge my assistance. She touched the inside of my arm with cat's-paw pressure, delicate but insistent. "Around here, the, ah, Sons of Glen Canyon prefer wildness. Enforce it, actually."

She looked amused, an expression perfect for her mobile lips and wide, brown eyes. "This isn't an oak-grass savanna. Or a high-grass prairie. I'm no botanist but . . . it's just a mess. A real mess." She laughed. "Not that I mind. The world can get too neat. Or worse, deliberately messy." She stepped back into her shoes and gave me her hand. "My name is Priscilla McThornly." Then she winced and wiggled her toes in her shoes, something they were not made for. If she kept that up, she'd put creases in the smooth leather. "Now my stockings are wet."

"Peter Ambrose." We shook with exaggerated formality. Her grip had the same insistent gentle pressure as her pull on my arm. "But you knew that . . . it's Mister, not Doctor."

"I don't know much about you. Tom has been so mysterious about it all. He's a businessman. They don't get enough mystery in their lives." The way she said his name confirmed my suspicion that it was false, put on for the occasion.

"Few of us do."

She smiled as if I'd said something genuinely clever, rather than party-chatter obvious.

"Then we owe it to each other to provide it."

McThornly wore a close-cut dark coat against the fall chill. It was buttoned and strapped, hugging the curve of her hips and breasts, and I looked at it, trying to figure out how I would help her out of it, if I had the opportunity.

"I'm afraid I don't have much mystery to provide." I gestured at my house. "You see it all, here."

"You stick your fingers into people's skulls and you have no mysteries of your own? Isn't that dangerous?" She reached up and, with a distracted air, undid the top three straps of her coat. The dress she wore underneath was high-collared, austere. I could smell her in the still air and was surprised by the vividness of the scent.

"Yes," I said. "It is." Sunlight came through my head.

She smiled and put her arm through mine, as if we were walking down the street after an evening at a restaurant. An expensive restaurant. It was a pressure so subtle it was impossible to resist, and I found myself being guided around the side of my house.

"Besides," she said. "You're lying to me, aren't you? A mad scientist's lab in the basement, and a piano to soothe the beasts you create there . . . no mysteries, Peter?"

The path by the house was cracked concrete, long in disrepair. She stepped precisely over the shifted blocks in her heels, pulling me past the untrimmed bushes and the rusting chain link fence that divided my property from that of the dark red brick house next door, whose inhabitants I had never seen. Forgotten trash littered the dead ground by the foundation.

I had not put on a coat. The air trapped between the earth and the sky was colder than I had expected, despite the bright sun, and I found myself shivering. Dried and curled remnants of summer's weeds crackled and broke as we stepped through them, and covered my pants and her coat with countless cleverly spiked geometric seeds. She didn't seem to notice.

"What do you know about my piano?" I asked, suddenly suspicious. The basement studio was my private place, and no one ever went there. There were a lot of doors between it and the outside.

She laughed. "You're a musician, a pianist. You play clubs, right out in the open where everyone can see you. Not bad, too, from what I hear. You're a real musician, and real musicians play when no one else can hear them. So you have a piano."

"But how do you know it's in the basement?"

She pursed her lips in annoyance at my persistence. "Because Thomas couldn't find one anywhere else. I had him look around your house."

"Why?"

"Because I was curious about who was screwing around with Thomas's open skull." She grabbed an overhanging yew branch and shook it. Dew showered down on us, sparking in the sun. "And I find it's a man with a secret piano."

"It's not so secret." I felt grumpy, like a child with a treasure in a beat-up cigar box that's just been revealed as something excruciatingly common.

"Then why are you so pissed off that I'm asking about it?" She looked piercingly intent, a suddenly funny expression.

I let out a breath that turned into a laugh. "Don't know. It's just something private."

"That's good," she said, suddenly contrite. "We all need things like that. I'm sorry I pestered you about it. God, Peter, this mess is even worse. Or better."

We'd turned into the backyard. Beyond the adolescent trees sprouting through the former back lawn was the burnt and twisted ruin of the house that had once stood on the other side of the block. No one had lived there for over a decade. I owned that lot and the ruin formed the outer edge of my defensive perimeter.

A plump cherub lay in the dry birdbath by the back door, the supposed centerpiece of a purely hypothetical perennial bed, looking coyly at me, his charm undiminished by the droppings of frustrated, unbathed birds.

"I guess I should get out here and rake some leaves," I said.

"Despite the Sons of Glen Canyon?"

"To hell with them." I was bold. "I'll thwack them with my rake." I looked around vaguely. "If I can find it, that is."

She laughed again.

A dim figure appeared at the kitchen window. Inman, looking out at us. He leaned across the table and put his hand on the glass. Pressed flat, it was white and bigger than his head, looking like something that lived under water.

"Looks like Thomas wants—what's wrong?" Priscilla took my arm. "See a ghost?"

I found myself staring with goggle-eyed intensity at the kitchen window, not really seeing anything. I blinked, but Inman was gone. "Who is he?"

Her face went blank. "You've been all through his brain. Half of what's in there is stuff you put in yourself. You must know better than anyone."

"No, I . . . it's just that I have no idea of who he is. His real name. It isn't Thomas. I can tell just by the way you say it. What he does. Who he's . . . married to."

"As I recall, you signed a contract stating that these things were of no interest to you." Her voice was suddenly professionally cool.

"I signed a contract that said I wouldn't probe his mind to find them out. It didn't say I couldn't ask someone."

"Well, Peter, I have my own contracts. Let's get back out. *Thomas* will be anxious to go." Her hand on my elbow was more forceful this time. I found myself resisting. She dropped her hand, and I followed her back out to the front.

Thomas Inman stepped out of the door and Priscilla McThornly moved close to him. This morning his neckpiece was a silver-plated precision gear, an homage to our nation's powerful industrial past. His collar was edged in gold, based on the contact slots of old-time computer boards. The outfit was a little too forward-shock for him. It was an outfit that took a chance. Men like Inman didn't dress to take chances. The way McThornly's childlike hand held on to the sleeve let me know that she had chosen it for him. I don't know why that interested me so much. I just like drawing utterly useless conclusions about people who have nothing to do with me.

"Be sure to call me," I said. "I'll need to see you again." I felt jowly, paunchy, needing a starched white collar to keep my head from drooping off my neck like an autumn sunflower. I resisted the urge to rub my eyes, stick my pinkies in my ears to scratch out wax.

Inman just stared impassively at me, eyes blank blue marbles, then let McThornly lead him down to her sleek car. She moved fluidly next to him, a dozen components of motion in each step, while he walked with the joint-rattling stolidity of a former college athlete whose muscles have calcified. She smiled back at me over one shoulder and gave me an elaborate hand wave, each finger independent. She had marvelous legs, I could see now, dark stocking seam mathematically precise along each calf. They vanished into the glaring reflector glass of the car. I squinted and turned away. I went back into the house, and climbed the stairs down into the basement.

- 3 -

HAD BUILT A MUSIC STUDIO HERE, WHERE I COULD PRACTICE WITHOUT being heard in the rest of the house. This no longer mattered, of course, which was probably why I had not replaced the sound-absorbing panels that had fallen away from the concrete wall. I stood, one hand on my piano, and looked up at the stretch of exposed concrete. There was a black crack, and a dark, looming stain that stretched up to the ceiling. It looked disquieting, as if the supports of the house itself were about to collapse, but I knew it looked a lot worse than it actually was. The damage was largely cosmetic.

The other half of the basement had once been Corinne's dance studio, where she had occasionally taught small classes. Reluctantly, I opened the door to it and walked in. The sprung floor still bounced under my feet without a creak. No cracks or leaks here, of course. Corinne would never have tolerated it, and it seemed that her rule still ran.

The dusty mirror was a bank of fog, my reflected figure a dim navigation hazard. I brushed at it. Pieces of me appeared in the clear streaks. I blinked at myself. My sleeve was worn at the wrist and my pants sagged at the crotch. Usually such things were a matter of little concern, but this was how Priscilla McThornly had seen me, as an efficient but sloppy suburban operator. I felt a pang of dismay.

My thin blond hair, too long uncut, stood above my scalp like wheat abandoned by a dead farmer. Even my eyelashes were blond, giving me a dopey look. I rubbed my face—unshaven, I saw now. Actually, since I was big and bulky, with a flat wide face, I looked like the stupid school bully who waited, guffawing to himself, for smaller kids to take the shortcut home through the alley. I'd picked the face: who suspects someone ugly of having had cosmetic surgery? But it seemed that I looked worse than I ever had. I'd looked better when I was that strong young pianist the Melinsky Studio had hired to play Tchaikovsky on the

17

piano for an introductory ballet class taught by Miss Corinne Zamm. I had to have.

I was a professional jazz musician in those days, and was lucky to find some musical way to eke out my income. The Melinsky Studio had an old Hallet Davis, a marvelous instrument sadly strained by the dry radiator air. I have wide hands, more than an octave, and flexible fingers. I had my first serious discussion with Corinne when I discovered that my boogie-woogie improvisations on the Dance of the Cygnets were not exactly what she wanted for her petit allegro. "A good musician should be able to play any kind of music," she told me. So I went back to straight Delibes and Tchaikovsky, and did the job I was getting paid for.

But she asked me to stay with her after class and play more variations for her. It was a challenge. She saw me as a wiseass and wanted to show me something. As I seesawed through the ancient boogie-woogie eight-to-the-bar rhythms of piano blues from the 1920s, she danced her own set of variations to it. I had always heard that a good jazz dancer is just as much a lyrical improviser as a good musician, but had never believed it. Like most musicians, I did not have much respect for the intelligence of dancers, any more than I did for that of professional wrestlers.

I'd always had the opinion that people who followed dance were those who were too stupid to understand a play and too unimaginative to listen to music without something to look at. But Corinne was in the music, not on top of it. Most dancers like to turn musicians into accompanists. We were a duet, neither part making sense without the other. When we finished we were both soaked with sweat and the Melinsky Studio's night janitor was standing at the door impatiently with his mop and bucket. And the bastard wasn't even tapping his foot.

Dammit, Inman had really set me off. Thinking this much about Corinne was a bad sign. I turned away from her mirror and went back into my own studio.

I knelt and rummaged in a wall cabinet. Sheet music was piled up there in random stacks. I sneezed at the dust that rose up as I dug. I refused to be distracted by the fascinating music I had forgotten completely about, the Victorian music hall songs, the popular 1920s sheet music, the Szymanowski, the Reger, and finally found what I was looking for: a copy of Beethoven's 17th Piano Sonata, the D minor. The yellow cover had been torn and Scotch-taped at some time in the past and the tape adhesive had dissolved and aged the paper under it. It almost came apart in my hands.

I put it on the piano, sat down, and played a little of the opening movement. It had been a long time. I couldn't even remember how long.

The notes themselves felt dry and dusty. My notes hit a hard chord and I stopped there, my heart pounding in inexplicable panic. A corner in the upper hallway of my grandmother's house had given me a feeling like that. The hall took a kink just before the bathroom and there, on the wall, was a mysterious dark stain just visible underneath the flower-print wallpaper. No matter how often the paper was changed, the stain bled through. The hallway always smelled the same, too, of licorice and burnt oil, a smell that always reminded me of my grandmother. But the stain, the stain never became completely visible, never revealed to me what it was trying to be.

In an age of mental modification, a sudden irresistible urge is always suspicious. Perhaps it rises from the writhings of the archaic lizard mid-brain in the roiled swamps of the surrounding limbic system, sucking up flows of memory, or perhaps it is the calculated result of an implanted microscopic processor that artificially stimulates neurotransmitter release at carefully calculated synapses. Sitting there at my piano, sucking the cold air of the studio, I could have no idea of which it was.

I did a detailed check of my central nervous system on a weekly basis, the way some people wax their antique cars. I had yet to find any evidence of post-service tampering. Leaving the sheet music there, I got up and walked slowly into Corinne's space.

I counted boards away from the back wall and pressed a wood peg. A trapdoor swung neatly open. Corinne had never known it was there, only one of many secrets I had kept from her. She and her students had chasséd and pas-de-bourréed over my secrets for years, prodding them with their toe shoes.

A crawl passage below, smelling of damp and forgetfulness, led to underground electronics access. It was a good place to hide things, but I hadn't hidden anything there. My secrets lay directly inside the wood of the trapdoor itself. It was a good thing that I had narrow secrets. The box I finally slid out was a foot square, but only three inches thick. I hadn't looked inside it for ten years.

So why should I look now? Why had a TV body appeared on the floor of my bedroom? I put the box on the floor. The Group was in there, what I had of them. And that was it. The Group. Long ago, I had decided to forget them, and backed that decision up with mental and neurochemical blocks. But forgetting without being able to remember was dangerous. I'd set defenses, warnings, wards—and they had come to life. Last night. The Group, somehow, was back.

I clicked open the top of the box. It was filled with small objects: a fine-textured Japanese sword guard, a child's marble the color of a full

Earth as seen from orbit, a heavy automotive ratchet wrench, an antique
scalpel with a bone handle, a soft leather glove and—I pulled it out and
draped its silk over my arm—a blue-green formal neckpiece hand painted
with vaguely Indonesian figures. I wadded the neckpiece up, shoved it
back in, and slammed the box shut, heart pounding. Charlie Geraldino.
I remembered him suddenly, vividly, an ineffectually smiling figure with
a love for weak beer. The wrinkles of his face had always looked like
they had white powder deep in them. His hobby had been hand-painting
neckpieces, as mine had been the piano. Anything to pass the time at Camp
Fitzwater. Charlie was dead. Not years ago. What had the announcer said?
Forty-eight hours before last night. Murdered.

I ran up the stairs, box under my arm. The door of my bedroom opened
on Versailles crossed with K-Mart. The ralfies, in their uncritical way,
had been busy. Gone was the 1950s boy's room with its incriminating
and mind-jogging trophies, replaced by what looked like acres of carved
simulated wood, an embroidered bed canopy that seemed to be made of
cobwebs, and a fancy little desk that would have collapsed into dust if I
had so much as brushed against it. The ralfies stood in a row under the
window, dressed in court costume with periwigs.

I called up the image of the murdered man. The TV demon was
smarter than me and had stored it, according to instructions I could
no longer remember having given it, instructions from years ago. The
body reappeared on my floor. With a little coaxing, the TV disgorged
the detailed holoimage of the victim's apartment. My own room faded.
The dead man had lived in a fair-sized apartment, generically furnished
and decorated in the obsolete hotech of a decade ago. I wandered through
the scene, checking details like the half-empty bowl of breakfast cereal on
the table, cereal box facing it in the way some people have of endlessly
rereading the back of the box while eating breakfast.

Pictures were askew, a chair overturned. The body was wearing only one
slipper and the bottom of his foot was dirty. Just above one outstretched
hand was a carefully arranged rack of neckpieces, hand-painted ones with
colorful patterns. A simple hobby for a Group veteran. The man dead on
the floor was Charles Geraldino, and he had once been as close to me as
a brother, which meant that I had sometimes hated him and often wished
that I would never see him again.

The police had an update: the body had been identified as that of Morris
Lanting, an inhabitant of Avondale. But there was nothing else. My old
colleague had already receded to the status of a routine murder, under
an assumed name and identity, no one who truly knew him to mourn his

passing. Maybe it was just that. Routine, a random death that happened to have caught a former Group member without caring that that's what he was. I didn't believe it. The cold chilling wind of the past on the back of my neck didn't let me believe it.

A ponderous old armchair with worn upholstery, completely out of place amid the sleek and easily cleaned furniture of the rest of the apartment, stood with the light of the window behind it, like a throne. It had been jerked out of its usual place in front of the TV, as the throw rug bunched up against its leg showed. It would have been an excellent place to sit and watch Charlie Geraldino die.

I felt sick. I had blocked it, blocked everything. After the end of the Devolution Wars, the Group had split up and we had all gone our separate ways, secure in the knowledge that no one would ever find us again. Someone had found Charlie Geraldino. My system had dumped his corpse right on the floor in front of me and I had ignored it, spending the morning arguing instead with an insolent client. If the screens I had put up around that time in my memory were preventing me from seeing real threats, then it was time to get rid of them, painful though that might be.

And I needed Corinne for that. No wonder my thoughts had been swirling around her like water funneling down a drain. She had a key to a lock in my brain that I didn't. I had given it to her, thinking I had to, when I loved her, and had not ever gotten it back. I never thought I would need it.

Distracting myself from that thought, I wandered farther through Geraldino's apartment. Three pictures hung on the wall. One was a deep forest glade, seemingly cut out of a travel magazine. One was a photograph of Michelangelo's *David,* in an elaborate frame that mimicked the look of marble. And one, tilted, was a photograph of a group of men and women. I zoomed in on it.

There were seven people in the photograph, five men and two women. They stood, somewhat self-consciously, in front of a lab table. The clothes marked the picture as at least ten years old. No one had worn extended shoulders like that since 2019 at the latest.

It was probably the occurrence of this image that had alerted my household security system, pulling the body into my bedroom and setting the ralfies on their mad fake-nostalgic building spree. The security system was certainly able to identify these people, by the programming I had put into it long ago.

I knew them, all the faces, the sober, dark-skinned Karin Crawford, already semimechanical Hank Rush, blocky Gene Michaud, sly Anthony

Watkins, Lori Inversato in a grease monkey's coverall, and sad Charlie Geraldino. I had spent the years of my youth with them. The seventh face was one I no longer knew, an intelligent, somewhat haughty face with a strong jaw and a high forehead, the face of a young man who has not yet realized the limitations of possibility. He was called Theo Bronkman then. The name and face are different now, but I knew him.

That was me.

-4-

"**H**ELLO? WHO IS—" CORINNE PAUSED AND DREW IN A BREATH. "PETER. Hello."

I stared at her image for a moment and cleared my throat. I should have done that before I called. "Hi, Corinne. I'm sorry that I had to call like this, but . . . I have a question. It's pretty important."

Her image was processed so that she was a silvery madonna in half-light. Her skin was satin. Her serene face didn't give anything away. I stared intently, as if I could clear away her home system's image manipulation by looking hard enough.

"I know," she said. "You wouldn't call unless you needed something very badly."

"Corinne, that's not fair, I . . ." A tactical error. I sounded like a petulant child wanting a bigger piece of pie than his brother. "Thomas Inman. You know him?"

She looked startled. "Peter, I don't see what—" She thought for a long moment. "Yes, I know him."

"Why did you send him to me?" The question sounded peremptory, because it wasn't the one I wanted to ask. Thomas Inman, whoever the hell he was, was a peripheral issue. I needed to ask Corinne to unlock my mind. I had to see her.

Her face didn't change. The image's eyes were vivid blue marbles, without pupils. Had the pupils been there when she answered? I hadn't noticed. "Me? I didn't send Thomas to you, Peter. Though I know you have a business he was interested in." A note of puzzlement entered her voice. "At first I wasn't even sure it was you. Taking brains apart? What *have* you been up to, Peter?"

Despite myself, I smiled. The quizzical perplexity in her voice made me feel close to her. "A long story. This isn't the time to tell it."

"Well, don't call me to tell me what you won't tell me. And leave Thomas Inman out of it."

Damn these phone processors. I couldn't read her expression. But her last statement distracted me from my goal. "Why should I?" I challenged. "Who is he, Corinne? Tell me."

The madonna's eyes flashed, flaring the face with red. "I don't want to tell you anything, Peter. You know that." She paused. "But that's not fair, is it? You should have pointed that out. You always did." She took a deep breath. "Thomas Francis Inman is the corporanym of my husband, Gideon Farley." She stopped and stared, gauging my reaction.

It startled me less than it might have, because I'd half-suspected it from the first. Her husband. Why not? It made as much sense as anything else.

"Have I answered your questions?" she said. "Do you have what you want?" I could hear the anger in her voice, though the face stayed impassive.

"Wait!" I didn't have to fake desperation. "What did I say? It was natural that I should want to know. What else could you expect? That's all. I'm sorry! I don't understand. . . ." What she saw was my real face, panicked and sweating. I was leaving myself open. Did she understand that?

She shook her head. It looked like a marble portrait bust rotating on a turntable. "There isn't anything you need to know about me, Peter. Nothing at all. I'm sorry if I was, even indirectly, involved in Gideon's coming to you."

"But I need . . ." My voice stuck. I need my head. I need my soul. You have it, all of it. You just don't know it. But I didn't say any of that. "I'm sorry."

The madonna image melted and, for a moment, Corinne's real face peered through. Her hair was in a turban and her smooth skin was pink with bath heat. She wore no makeup and there were lines at the corner of her eyes that hadn't been there the last time I saw her. Her short lashes made her eyes look vulnerable. It was a private face, one that wouldn't normally go out over the phone. She was leaving herself open too. "That's all right. Remember, I had to get used to figuring out what you wish you meant." Her smile was tired. "Maybe I'm just a little out of practice. I'm sure you'll find what you need. Good-bye, Peter." The phone cube went blank.

I bent over and put my shoes on. I pulled the laces as tight as I could, until they squeezed my feet hard. As I always had, I put the conversation with Corinne aside in my head, like spent reactor fuel rods in a cooling pond, until I could stand to handle it.

Charlie Geraldino was dead. Of any number of possible facts in the world, that, right now, was the important one. He had been murdered. His body lay in the cold room at the Cook County Morgue, part of Atman Medical. I had to go to him, to stare down at his dead face and see if he would tell me anything. I'd abandoned him, as I had abandoned everyone, when the Group broke up. Maybe now I could make my peace with him. I didn't have anyone else left.

Corinne was married to the so-called Inman, the man I had just operated on, just talked to. The son of a bitch had sat in my living room, on Corinne's old, uncomfortable chair, chatted amiably, and never told me.

AN AUTOMATED GURNEY SLID BY ME ON SILENT WHEELS, OMINOUSLY intent on its business. Its body container was an older model, a satin-textured hexagonal prism. Newer ones, in keeping with organiform aesthetic, resembled giant insect egg cases.

I followed the gurney down the hospital hallway like an anonymous mourner, and it took me onto the glass-walled platform overlooking the cold room of the Cook County Morgue—Cook County Dead, Sister Death, as those of us in the business usually called it. A receptionist's desk stood to one side.

The cold room was an impressive pharaonic construction. It seemed about an acre in extent at the floor, far below. The walls, ranks of preservation modules, rose and slanted inward, like the interior of a pyramid, but the light above was too strong to see if they ever joined. The gurney passed through a security checkpoint, rolled onto the spidery elevator, and descended to the appropriate module. The module slid open and the gurney deposited its contents, all untouched by human hands and unseen by human eyes. The doors did not open for me. It was not a place in which living human beings were welcome.

The cold room was beneath several layers of environmental and security seal and lock. A craniac's brain might be protected by the infectious and deadly fast kuru. Cutting through the chest wall for an autopsy might combine a binary nerve toxin sequestered in the sternum and kill everyone in the operating room. On at least one occasion an undetected network of contractile analomycin fibers operated by a postmortem module in the corpse's brainstem set a dead and partially dissected body to dancing, dropping loose organs on the floor.

An organiform gurney linked to the pyramid wall. It stood there for a moment, obscurely puzzling, then withdrew a transparent cube containing a human liver. Pleased with its acquisition, it sped along the unrailed balcony and vanished into a distant tunnel. All autopsy results were stored in suspension there since video and computer records were subject to manipulation.

It was a vision of the world after the end. The machines could use human bodies and parts as currency, trading them back and forth in exchange for electric charges and data.

Doors to my left opened out onto the ambulance dock. A sleek ambulance stood there, two orderlies leaning on it, smoking desultorily. The autumn sun glowed sweetly on the oil-streaked asphalt.

The reception desk, a dark-green veined organiform growth, was occupied by a round-faced woman with flared-back gray hair. She wore severely precise makeup, suitable for a sitting judge, which brought out her cheekbones. She had a stocky, strong-looking figure, that of a woman who could shoulder sacks of cement, and looked like she was about fifty. It seemed to be my day to notice women, of whatever sort. I was glad I had changed my clothes. There was something harshly exact about her. I tugged at my lapel and hoped my suit had not been completely left behind by the curling edge.

"Excuse me," I said.

She turned and looked at me, a disturbingly piercing glance. Then she smiled professionally. "Yes? May I help you?" Her voice was low and husky.

"I'm here to perform an identification on a body . . . a friend of mine. There's no next of kin. It's a necessary formality, I understand. It should all be arranged."

She looked sadly sympathetic. "Ah. Who is it?"

"Name of Morris Lanting." I'd gotten everything I could on Charlie Geraldino's cover identity as Lanting. He'd been a neurotransmitter architect for Daemon-Harmonetics, specializing in monoamine neurotransmitters. That gave me a plausible professional contact with him, should anyone prove curious.

"Let's see." She looked down at her panel. "Lanting . . . how sad. What's your name?"

"Ambrose. Peter Ambrose."

"Did you go to school together? Serve in the Army?"

"Ah?" That last was too close for comfort. "We worked together."

She smiled gently. "Didn't mean to pry. You go down to room . . . oh, damn." She stared down at her panel, then up at me. "Damn." She had a high forehead and a forward-jutting chin. Her eyes squinted sleepily, so it was hard to guess their color. "We've had an accident. Toxic disease release—it might even be fast kuru. Neural sliming agent. Shamble, maybe." She said the terms with relish. "No one is allowed in to the secure areas until it's neutralized. I'm afraid you'll have to wait. It shouldn't be long." A beep. "Excuse me." She answered and began chatting animatedly.

Outside the doors, a tired-looking mechanic wearing coveralls and a Cubs cap approached the orderlies, waving a pink sheet. He looked like a boy playing repairman. They exchanged a puzzled glance, then shrugged and moved away from the ambulance. His tool kit contacted the vehicle's processor and it jacked itself up for inspection. He slid underneath.

The receptionist's toxic release story didn't ring true. I didn't see decon crews in sealsuits scrambling to take care of it, and a dropped petri dish of cold virus would have brought them out. Everything around was completely calm. It had the air of a quickly improvised delay tactic. I looked at her, but she continued to gossip, wide gestures sliding heavy bracelets up and down her solid wrists, her words hidden behind a privacy sound screen. I thought about turning and running. The dead Charlie Geraldino suddenly seemed like the bait in a trap. But if it was a trap, they would have thought up a better cover story. . . .

A gurney left the cold room through the security point and slid slowly past me, out to the waiting ambulance. The mechanic dodged it as he left, his repair job quickly done. He was a tall lanky man who didn't maintain enough tension over his joints. He waved good-bye to the orderlies and swung off with his tool kit, whistling, ready to play some other game. As he left the field of view of the doors, another orderly, a tall woman, appeared.

"It was kind of you to come in, Mr. Ambrose," the receptionist said, hanging up the phone, "but, fortunately, your identification is no longer required."

"No longer required? Why?"

She shrugged. "I guess we found some next of kin. All the formalities have been dealt with. I'm sorry you went through so much trouble."

I felt a moment of intolerable frustration. Suddenly Charlie's strangled corpse was the most important thing in the world, as if I could put my hands on his contused neck and understand how and why he died. He had no goddam next of kin. None closer than me.

The receptionist's eyes flicked past my shoulder. I turned. The gurney was depositing its body into the ambulance and the orderlies were climbing in. They glanced nervously at the woman who had just arrived. She was dressed as a hospital orderly, but didn't look a bit like one. A sober and muscular woman with close-cropped hair, she had eyes that looked around in a scanning pattern, missing nothing. The double-sphere at her belt might have contained emergency diagnostic equipment and drugs, but I didn't think so. It more likely held a gun. Everything about her, the relaxed leg-spread pose, the knotted jaw muscles, the nonhospital street shoes, said *cop*.

I watched the body container slide into the ambulance, feeling the receptionist's eyes on me. That ambulance contained the body of Charlie Geraldino. I was suddenly sure of it. Not knowing what I was doing, I started toward it, as if just getting near it would help me.

Before I had gone two steps, the ambulance exploded.

-5-

THE DOORS GLOWED ORANGE AND SHATTERED. THE HOT BLAST SMASHED into my face. I ducked and rolled, covering my head with my arms. Flames roared, tugging at my clothes, and then were gone, leaving burnt stink behind them. Alarm bells shrieked.

I found myself crawling through the remains of crumbled ceiling tiles. "Keep your head *down*, Charlie," I muttered. Free Moldavian troops had lobbed rockets into our research compound along the Byk River, above Kishinyov, and blown up what had once been a massive, industrial chicken coop. Chicken shit burned hot.

Strong hands grabbed my shoulders and rolled me over. I found myself looking up into the sharp dark eyes of the receptionist. If the blast had affected her, she didn't show it. Her skin was tight over the prominent bones of her face and glowed in the firelight as if always meant to be displayed in that way.

"Are you all right?" she asked, tone calmly urgent.

I coughed. "Yes. What—?"

But she was already gone, running out into the flaming street.

I couldn't see out of my right eye. I ran my hand across my face and brought it back red. Despite the gallons of blood I'd spilled across my operating table, I felt sick. I stuck a finger into what I feared would be a scorched and empty socket and poked my eyeball, causing more pain than the original explosion had. I wiped the blood from my forehead, and could see.

The flexible glass of the doors hung in shreds and garbage was strewn across the reception area. A gurney bumped cautiously across the suddenly uneven floor, ignoring the commotion around it. But the cold room doors, cautious of contamination, refused it entry. Disconsolate, it turned down the hall labeled DECON.

I pushed myself to my feet. The receptionist had square, no-nonsense

29

hips and a wide back. She had kicked off her shoes and was yelling
something into the smoke-concealed noise beyond. The shorthaired police
disguised as an orderly struggled to her feet. Blood was vivid against her
hospital green. Her left arm hung limply, torn to shreds. She grabbed
at her belt and came up with a gun, more as a reflex than because she
remembered what to do with it. The two women looked at each other for
a moment, silhouetted by the flames, half-concealed by swirls of smoke,
then the receptionist took the gun and vanished. The police dropped to her
knees and stared at the ground as if playing some sort of child's game and
concentrating on her next move. Then she fell forward on her face.

My sturdy receptionist was a cop too, of what sort I couldn't yet decide.
I could just hear her voice shouting angry commands. I had to get out of
there. The doors I had entered through refused to open for me. The cold
room doors did not recognize my existence. The only set left, the only
escape from the reception area that had suddenly become a trap, faced
the burning ambulance. I brushed back my hair with both hands, cleaned
crumbled ceiling tile from my belly, and strolled out.

Uniformed police were in the process of blocking off the bottom of the
ambulance ramp, which curved up to us in a broad sweep from the street.
A crowd was gathering there, attracted by the commotion. Bug-helmeted
fire fighters sprayed fire-suppressant foam onto the ambulance, covering
it with whipped cream. Light flickered inside for a moment, then died.
Rescuers picked up the injured police and bundled her into a stretcher,
leaving a red stain on the pavement. The two orderlies in the ambulance
were burned hideously black. Hospital crew stuck IV's into them, sprayed
tissue-seal over their wounds, and hauled them off.

Bessarabia had been a war, though not our war. The Group had had other
business, business that went on only inside people's skulls. But the war
was always there. I'd seen lines of bodies lying against a wall by a bus
stop, bare feet sticking out from under worn synthetic sheets, their shoes
stolen. Living people lined up for the bus right parallel to them. I did too.
There was no other way to get around Kishinyov.

I found myself shaking. It's easy to get distracted by dramatic things like
exploding ambulances and gun-toting receptionists. But the thing hadn't
exploded because an orderly tipped his cigarette ash into the hydrogen
sponge. It had exploded because the mechanic with the Cubs cap had
put a bomb under it. That much seemed pretty clear. That damn game-
playing, insolently slouching mechanic, never actually seeming serious
while secretly taking everything dead-seriously—I almost stopped walking
as his identity hit me.

The black, thick smoke was vanishing into the clear sky. Foam, job done, was sucked up by wide-nozzled recycling devices pulling harnessed enameled tanks. One of them slid over the bloodstain and that was gone too. Shiny-coated fire fighters opened the back of the ambulance with carbon-composite pry bars, supervised by the tensely poised figure of my gray-haired receptionist, authoritative despite her impractical jacket and jewelry. She jabbed a precise finger as smoke boiled out of the ambulance's rear. A fire fighter gave it a couple of quick blasts with an extinguisher, then scrambled in. A moment later, she turned and shrugged. There was nothing left back there. Charlie Geraldino's body had been cremated, ashes to ashes, dust to—

And Anthony Watkins had done it. I should have recognized that long-armed, gibbon-walking-erect posture immediately. He hadn't changed from the days of the Group. Hadn't changed a bit. Still his old playful self. When the last trumpet sounds, all the dead rise together.

I moved as quickly down the ramp as I could. My heart pounded painfully against my ribs and I wished I'd kept at least some voluntary autonomic nervous system control from my Group days. I'd gotten rid of everything when we disbanded, not knowing which features were a trap. Nothing was under my control any more. My body felt sticky. The police cordon had not been briefed and were only interested in keeping people away from the scene. They were blind from the other side, my side, the only side that mattered. I slid out onto the crowded, hotly curious street, and ran to my car.

GONE WAS MY ONE GOAL, GERALDINO'S BODY, MEANINGLESS THOUGH THAT might have been. I'd gotten right up to it, only to find police swarming around it like flies. A few of them were bound to settle on me now. They'd rub their little black feet and get happy on my skin. After all, I'd come right up and given my name. Son of a bitch. I picked at the steering wheel cover with my fingernails, trying to figure out how I could get out of all this.

I had to find Watkins. He was now my only link to things, the only one who might have some idea of what was going on. Of course, he could have been the one who killed poor Charlie in the first place. In which case, I reflected, he was still my best source of information.

I called up the location of Morris Lanting's apartment in the car's navigator. That was all that was left for me. The apartment was behind a police cordon now, all its details downloaded into an investigatory data base, but there was no other landmark on the horizon to aim at. Besides, I knew how thorough Watkins was. He wasn't about to just leave that place sitting there, full of evidence, things that could be reexamined weeks or months later in the light of new understanding. Lanting/Geraldino's apartment was in Avondale, on the Near West Side. I requested a slot on the Kennedy. Traffic was light this time of day, so I whipped along the upper deck, too tense to enjoy the view it gave me of the city, and was spit out at Diversey.

I was late again. A block from the Lanting apartment another police cordon blocked the street. Beyond it were more fire trucks, sun-glittering mist rising up from their nozzles and vanishing into the smoke that billowed from one line of apartment windows, four floors up. A braided stream flowed quickly down the gutter, swirling dried leaves, and dived into a drain. A police with a glowing baton directed traffic up another street.

It wasn't even worth stopping and getting out of the car. Watkins *had* been thorough here as well. It was nice that my perceptions were still so acute. A pity they were still so slow.

The metal frames of the apartment windows were twisted outward. Shattered glass gleamed on the sidewalk. A precise takeout, probably by a shoulder-launched Frisbee of vapor-vortex explosive. Wonderful stuff, vavoom. Microscopic crystals sublime into air. The energy liberated by the sublimation starts a vortex. The crystals ignite. More energy, the vortex spins supersonic, and you have a precisely calculated explosive lens, all in a fraction of a second. I've seen a twisted I beam in the rubble of a demolished building with the saboteur's signature incised on it by the explosion. There was nothing left in the apartment—while on the floor above there wasn't so much as a cracked china saucer.

Lacking any better plan of action, I allowed myself to be directed by the police's glowing baton, then drove up and down the surrounding streets, trying to look as if I was searching for a parking place. It was a tiny chance, but my only one—Watkins couldn't have been too far ahead of me, and he had just spent at least a few minutes destroying Geraldino's apartment.

I saw him on the third street I searched. He was just getting into a beat-up gas turbine van, DOMESTIC HYDRODYNAMICS on the side in obsolete swirling hololetters. His posture was slumped, completely uninterested in what was going on around him. Apartments might explode into the clear October sky, but that was none of his business. He'd fixed whatever he'd come to fix and now was going home. With a smooth swing of his shoulder he slung his tool kit onto the seat next to him and pulled himself into the van.

I watched him with fascination. Whatever Tony Watkins did, he still looked like he was playing rather than being, enjoying himself just a bit too much. Just now he was playing at handyman. He'd given me those composer trophies at Fitzwater—another game for him. The van backed and pulled out of the space. Cover story taking over from true intent, I started to park in it. I tromped the brake before I succeeded.

Anthony Watkins. He'd just seriously injured three people, probably killing two of them, and destroyed Charles Geraldino's body and apartment. What was his game now?

I pulled into traffic and followed him.

-6-

HE VAN SLID SMOOTHLY INTO TRAFFIC, FOR ALL THE WORLD AS IF he didn't give a damn whether anyone was following or not. That was Watkins too. He'd always walked, whether down a hospital hallway or through the collapsing streets of Kishinyov, as if everything was packed up and put away as soon as he was past it.

I first met Anthony Watkins in that shoddy mobile-home park the military had labeled Camp Fitzwater. I never did figure out where Camp Fitz was—somewhere in the dry lands of eastern Oregon, I thought, but that may just have been a calculated delusion. Life was full of those.

We were just researchers then, those of us in the Group, balancing the promise of research money and technical support against the threat of the vital-needs conscription that could leave our expensively educated brains spread across the rocks of some miserable splinter republic. The VN draft cleared out a lot of academic deadwood during the Devo Wars, an unintended positive side effect.

We ended up in Project Nimbus. Not In My Butt You Sucker, as Watkins had instantly put it. Butt rather than Brain, which would probably have been more appropriate, but that was the way he thought. Dr. Anthony Watkins, MD-PhD, Johns Hopkins. Watkins from Hopkins. I'd liked him when I met him. We were officially independent contractors, lost somewhere in the scientific feudalism of the wartime government. The world was transforming itself and we were one of the forward-chewing teeth of the future as it bit through the delicate, blushing skin of the present. The past, now, it was. Camp Fitzwater, Nimbus, the Group, were the past. Or had been.

Images floated into my consciousness. Karin Crawford, a long-limbed black woman with silver-tipped braids, pointing triumphantly at a holo shot of a nerve tract hanging in the air in front of her. Hank Rush displayed a weirdly malfunctioning mechanical arm, all hydraulic tubes and pistons leaking smoking lubricant, laughed as it squealed and shuddered spasmodically, and showed teeth that were themselves half glass stumps, like ancient vacuum tubes. Gene Michaud stood, one thick leg on the tire of an APC, talking to a suspicious-but-willing-to-deal Army Major in a razor-pressed uniform, negotiating God-only-knew what piece of military skullduggery. Light glared in my eyes, so bright in the past that I squinted my eyes in the present, not seeing the street in front of me. A dark form appeared in the light, a smooth head staring down at me. . . .

I jerked back from running over a middle-aged woman in an expensive sudoskin coat covered with Japanese-style tattoos. She stood in the crosswalk and shouted an obscenity at me, waving a fish-scaled umbrella. It was a gutsy act: wearing sudoskin based on the dermis of another race can lead to . . . hostility, let us say, though the wickedly shining hook at the umbrella tip indicated that this lady knew how to protect herself from comelanists who took umbrage. I hit the accelerator and kept going.

The van slowed and pulled into a commercial lot in an abandoned-looking industrial area. I drove slowly past, catching a glimpse of Watkins, the tired mechanic, slouching down out of his cab.

AN HOUR LATER I WALKED SLOWLY THROUGH PARACELSUS SQUARE, SOCIAL center of a neocultural area called Thothville. Watkins walked ahead of me.

Paracelsus Square was a large, brick-surfaced area with spindly, accelerated-growth oak trees rising above it. The sky had turned dark and a single snowflake, unrectifiable error of some overenthusiastic weather sprite, drifted through the halo of light around a wrought-aluminum streetlamp. Windows glowed yellow in the high-shouldered buildings that surrounded the square. A child ran past me in pursuit of an erratically bouncing ball with some randomly changing balance mechanism inside it. The child enjoyed the game, squealing every time the ball evaded her, finally falling, weak with laughter, on her little butt. A parent scooped her up.

The square was crowded enough with evening pedestrians that I was not conspicuous, though I did feel out of place: everyone else seemed to know how to dress. The man and woman sitting on the lion-footed park bench, for example, were razorslick, he in a clinging scale-patterned snakehyde that provided rumors of muscles he did not have, she in a black wool coat that on second look was infected with nebular colonies of bioluminescent fungi, turning her into something seen through a telescope. They held hands, she tracing out a pattern on his palm with her finger, and talked quietly, sadly.

It wasn't anything like the packed, collapsing city of Kishinyov, full of refugees during the height of the Bessarabian conflict. Hysterical local terrorists had sought to commandeer buses, irrationally hoping to commute to some better world. Satellite lasers cooked random areas like a small child picking frantically at chicken pox. I remembered it most of all with my nose, the smell of crushed-together unwashed people, the stink of open sewers, the stomach-turn of bodies decaying beneath the tilted concrete slabs of an apartment block collapsed through missile attack.

It was the anthropoid figure of Tony Watkins that made me remember Kishinyov. The Group had been stationed in the ruins of an old collective farm along the Byk River, tentatively realigning the neural systems of chosen revolutionaries, but Watkins had always insisted on his little expeditions for local color. I remembered seeing him loping ahead in our journeys through the doomed city.

Watkins vanished into a bar called the Discreet Event. It filled the bottom of an old three-flat that backed up against the high wall that separated this neocultural area from the next. Two exterior corkscrew escalators carried people to and from the glowing tents that covered the roof. I blinked at it. I didn't recognize where I was. I felt that I stood in a place cut loose from history, a bubble from some other universe. I took a deep breath of the ever-colder night air. The hell with it. If I was going to keep track of Watkins, I'd do it from inside a warm bar where I could get a drink.

This bar was crowded. Lighting came from odd angles, emphasizing abnormal parts of people's faces. Cult figures stood in wall niches, sculpted, austere: Miriam Tarant, Hector del Annas, Barclai, Elvis Holly III. Watkins was just settling down to a beer.

My bladder was full, a problem the detectives I'd read about in books never seemed to have. If I stood at the bar, I'd have to order a drink, and that would kill me for sure. I pushed my way through the crowd and out the back door. Watkins would have to sit at his beer for a couple of minutes. The men's room was in the basement, at the end of a long hallway, behind the cleaning supplies. The hum of conversation faded. I did my business. As I pushed the door to leave, I sensed a flicker of movement just at the periphery of my vision. I dropped instantly. The blow brushed past my cheek and pain blossomed in my shoulder.

I rolled and bounced off the wall at my attacker, reacting through ingrained reflex. It was Watkins. My response caught him by surprise and he caromed off cleaning equipment, knocking down mops and brooms. I pursued. My mistake—I should just have run, like a sensible person.

He swung himself up on a couple of shelves and slammed me back with his legs. I rolled off the floor and back at him. I was quick, considering. He was quicker. I took his next blow in my kidney. In rewiring myself I'd cut out my pain blocks. I doubled over. He pressed his advantage, knocked my legs out from under me, and pressed his forearm into my throat. I struggled to suck air and stared into his excitement-distended face.

-7-

"WHY, THEO BRONKMAN, YOU SON OF A BITCH." WATKINS STARED down at me in amused surprise.

I felt the concrete of the floor on my shoulder blades and his weight on my chest and the slap of my old name in my face. I could barely breathe.

"Excuse me, I'm afraid I don't—"

That annoyed him. He held my razorslick lapels and knocked my head against the floor, not hard, but in a communicative way. My head rang like a gong.

"You know who I am, Theo. You've been following me. You have a new face, but sit behind a new face long enough, and it starts to look like the old one."

When had he noticed me? That was the question that determined how much I could get away with.

"The name's not Theo, Tony. It's Franklin, Hen—"

He grinned. "Peter Ambrose. You shouldn't get well-known in your profession if you want to stay anonymous. But it's not Tony. My name's . . . Stephen Underhill." He sat back and yanked me off the floor. He had my new real name, but I had no way to check his. "Sorry I bashed you. Getting jumpy in my old age."

"So . . . how's life been treating you, Stephen?" I asked.

"Not too bad." He peered at me as if no longer sure of who I was. "We have shit to discuss."

"I suppose we do at that."

"You guys done with the bathroom?" An elegantly dressed man stood diffidently on the stairs, looking down at us. He peered at the scattered mops and solvent bottles, not knowing what to make of it.

"Yeah, yeah, no problem." Watkins looked ominous. "Go right in, don't mind us."

"Right," I said. "The latch on the door doesn't work but that shouldn't bother you too much. We'll hold it closed for you."

The man's eyes widened and he backed up the stairs. He muttered something about getting back to his seat and was gone.

Watkins and I looked at each other and laughed. Briefly. Even a rotten older brother is still a brother, and we had our old family games. No one else knew how to play them. "Let's go," he said. I didn't even think of refusing.

He led me out of the back door into an alley. I wasn't afraid, even though a murder would be much more reasonable out here than in the bar hallway. Watkins obviously had other things on his mind.

Overheads zebra-striped the alley with light. It was lined by the massive forms of restaurant fermenters and composters. The air was sweet with their decay by-products, and the bubbling of their contents was just audible.

We walked a distance along the brick wall until we came to a large metal door. Watkins manipulated some controls and the door rumbled open.

"Garbage disposal access," he explained. "The only connection between the neocults and the rest of the world. I won't lecture you on the appropriateness of that." We stepped through.

Though we'd only gone a couple of meters, we were now in a different world. We stood on a sidewalk of high-impact mesh, garbage stuck immovably in it by the passage of countless feet. Flaring pinspots hanging high overhead in their cages cast crisp, soul-stealing shadows across the noisy, auto-crowded roadway.

On the other side of the road were the giant egg cases of warehouses. The faint high note of their sour stink came across the road. Poorly maintained, they bulged out of their flimsy retaining cages and pushed flaccidly onto the sidewalk. Huddled against the rightmost one, ready to be absorbed, was an older warehouse of bent and corroded metal. The sign above the door said BAR.

We ran across the road and through the heavy bar door. As we walked in, Watkins—Underhill, though I found I couldn't think of him that way— glanced up. He had the same reflexive tic I'd woken up with that morning. Had we learned it ourselves, through experience, or had it been inserted directly into our nervous systems? I'd spent years searching my brain for things like that, but never found this one.

Inside was vast and dark. The tables were far apart on the high-friction grip floor, each with its own light source hanging from the distant ceiling.

Machinery bulked in the murk around the tiny alcoholic oases, silhouetted by the occasional glow of dangling caged incandescent plugged into the power strips that ran in a grid along the floor. Clattery, nondescript music played somewhere overhead. Most of the bar crowd was young, and couples periodically wandered off into the lubricant-and-electric-transformer-smelling expanses to screw on the hydraulic lifts. Their skins must have been gritty-slick with old oil, with a few burn scars from spilled battery acid. Silicon grease as a sexual lubricant. Lubrication nipples as sex aids. A shop manual for a 1998 Chevy as an industrial *Kama Sutra*. The old industrial age exercised its undoubted attractions, but this was one I'd never shared.

We took a table at the edge of the darkness. Watkins went to the bar and returned with two water-beaded long-necked brown bottles. The place, monument to archaic technologies that it was, had no bioreactor and so I could enjoy an honest beer. With an old friend, no less.

"So, Peter Ambrose." He tasted the name. "Suits you somehow. You never were a Theo." He looked at me with interest. "It's been a long time. I won't lie and claim you haven't changed a bit."

"That's the cruelest thing old friends say to each other anyway. But it's bad luck to count the years."

"Or the dead." He raised his bottle to me in salute and drank half of it down with one swallow. I sipped more sedately. Bitter and good. Picking bars was one talent Watkins still had.

"You're back in the brain whiz biz, Theo . . . I mean, Petey?" Watkins was antic, gray-blue eyes flashing. "I remember that stuff—like being a hitech wasp, laying eggs in people's heads. Fun, I guess. Sneaky-snakey, slithering down those convolutions. What brought you to Thothville? Looking for fresh mushminds who want to remember second-order Bessel functions and the Merovingian kings of France without needing to learn them?"

"Business is business, even still." I attempted to be airy.

"That it is, that it is . . . will you cut that out?"

The temperature in the bar was just warm enough that the condensation had loosened the beer label. Unconsciously, I had been picking at it and almost gotten it off complete, a rare prize.

"Sure . . . Stephen. Mr. Underhill. If it bothers you so much."

"God, Pete—I like that name, I do—you're a mess, you know that? Unless you had cosmetic surgery to give yourself bad skin, make yourself overweight, and lower your jowls, you've let life treat you hard. You're as twitchy as a Tourette's victim."

I looked at him, hard. His hair was bristle-cut over a lumpy skull that looked like it had been opened and crudely rewelded. A muscle twitched just perceptibly under his left eye, cruelly mocking his words. "You don't look so great yourself, buddy."

He laughed. "Damn right, there. It's been a rough few years. A few squabbles in the committee, up here." He tapped his skull. "Street's lousy with stuff that makes what we did at ol' Camp Fitz look like a few warm Buds sucked down in the backseat of Dad's car. I learned a few things. Twisted a few things my way. Old skills, you know."

"I know all about it. I keep up with the literature." I examined him clinically. "A bit too much Elysion at one time, looks like. It's always a temptation. A few psychotomimetic virts too, I'll bet. Those are popular among you vitrified-and-subducted types. You spend some time carrying one of those lust-paranoia jobs? I don't install them, but you can always find someone to do it. You know, where everything and everyone is following you, watching you, wanting to rub you, to *fuck* you, the world's hard and pulsing, bush juice dripping out of the kitchen cabinets—"

"Fuck you too, fat ass."

It was my turn to laugh. That was the first control I'd gained over the conversation. Watkins had always been able to keep me off balance. "Drop it, Tony. Didn't you keep a record, your old soul in matrix, so you could pull it out and check your decay? We can all see what we used to be. . . ."

"The EEG of Dorian Gray?" He laughed. "I should have thought of it. We're all wrecks. Look at you, you can't even sit still. Maybe you've been doing a little obsessive-compulsive work on yourself. Eh? Lets you spend an entire afternoon rinsing one glass, I hear. Convenient for the unimaginative. And—" he suddenly spoke more quietly, as he reached out to touch my face. "You've gotten clumsy. How'd you get all these cuts? You look like you walked through a window."

I jerked back. "I was working on my car. The rear battery pack—"

"You'd wear goggles working on your car. You're not stupid. That ambulance had a rear battery pack. I saw it while I was crawling underneath. That might have been what hit you. What do you think?"

"I—when did you spot me?" There was nothing for it but to fess up.

"Right there near Geraldino's apartment. Smart, finding me there. I didn't expect anyone until a lot later, when I'd had time to lay a nice trail. Don't feel bad about it. Your tracking was actually pretty good, and I found I could rely on your smarts. Besides, I was looking for you."

"For me?"

"Not you exactly, but . . . one of us. Some one of us." The mania left him and he slumped, like an inflatable doll with a leak. "One of the Group. We're in trouble, Peter. Trouble. We can't stay apart any longer. Don't you agree?"

"I might. If I knew more."

"You probably know more than you think." He reached out a long leg and pushed the extra chair at our table out, as if waiting for someone to sit in it. "Certainly more than you'll admit." I couldn't keep my eyes off the empty chair. Something about it, standing on that grimy floor, gave it a palpable sense of absence, as if the person *not sitting* in it was realer than we were.

"Do you remember Director Straussman?" he asked.

I choked. My throat contracted and I could—not—breathe. Watkins held his beer bottle in both hands and watched me dispassionately. I could hear the footsteps in the hallway. Cordovan oxfords, smooth leather soles on the warped wood of the temporary building. He always came when you didn't expect him. Except I always expected him, always. The steps stopped at the door. My head was clamped to the armature and I couldn't turn it to look. Only the three degrees or so in the center of our vision is detailed and in focus. It's a physiological fact normally concealed from us because our eyes dart constantly around. Freeze that saccading and most of the world becomes a blur. I couldn't *see*. I couldn't see anything but the empty chair set right in front of me, the pool of light behind it silhouetting the curves of its back.

"Straussman is dead," I managed.

Watkins looked sour. "Well, so I'd always thought."

"He's *dead*, Tony. How else would we be here? How else would we have gotten out?"

"I said, *I know*. And my name isn't Tony. It's Stephen. Right, *Peter?*"

"Right. His plane, Stephen. It crashed in northern Alberta. Flying alone. He always flew alone. A ravine near Mt. May, a hundred miles from anywhere. I've looked it up on a map."

"Right. And someone had filed a phony flight plan for him. By the time anyone could get to the wreckage, the wolves had eaten the body and carried off most of the bones. It had been a cold winter and they were hungry. There really wasn't anything left of him."

"What are you saying?" I felt a chill, as if from that Albertan winter wind.

"Figure it out. Do you remember Straussman?"

"What did I just say?"

"You said you knew where his plane crashed. Gave me lots of circumstantial detail. Do you remember him?"

The chair was still empty. "No, I don't. And I don't have to. He's dead."

Watkins looked at me. Walked off to the bar to get another couple of beers. Came back. Sat down and stared. His eyes looked loose in their orbits, as if ready to fall out.

"I think Linden Straussman murdered Charlie Geraldino."

For some reason, that shook me a lot less. Maybe because it made no sense. I sipped my beer, wondering if Watkins really *was* crazy. A damned careless thing for a Group member to let happen to himself. "You're the one who crawled through a security screen, planted a bomb under him, and blew him up. You burned up two orderlies and blew the arm off a police. They might all be dead." The orderlies' bodies had been burned shiny, like bug carapaces.

Watkins waved a hand, dismissing this concern. "Best place to injure someone is right in front of a hospital. Nice of me, eh? There's a war on, Peter. Remember war? You tried to ignore it, but it was always there. It will be always there. You should be glad I blew all that up, or IntraCranial would be all over your butt by now. Charlie was sloppy with his skull, you remember. His brain was full of mods going all the way back to Camp Fitzwater. He never replaced them, just clamped around, kludged it. If I'd just left him be, an IC neuropath team would be teasing his cortex apart right now and finding out that the Group existed after all, that it wasn't just some loony netwank made up by some overamped, understimulated datadork. Cranial archeology. They'd find bits and pieces of us in there. Psychopotsherds. They're experts at reconstructing the vanished civilizations of the mind."

That receptionist . . . a luke from IntraCranial? It made sense, of a sort. But only of a sort. How would IC have known that there was anything important about Geraldino's body before they actually autopsied it?

"That's real poetic, but do you have any good reason for thinking this?" I asked. "Have you seen him? Had a beer with him?" I stopped myself from picking at the label on my bottle.

"No, I haven't." His voice was short.

"Any evidence that he is anything other than . . . absent?" Even as I spoke, I wondered at my own vehemence, as if convincing Watkins would make everything all right. Geraldino was dead. It might just have been regular old housebreaker having a little late-night fun. Coincidence, in other words. I was running scared for no good reason. No—not for no good reason. I had the reason sitting right in front of me. Watkins hadn't killed Geraldino. But he'd covered up the evidence for whoever had. There was a lot he wasn't telling me.

If he could screw with my head, I could screw with his. "Are you sure Geraldino's body was in there?"

"What do you mean?"

"I mean you blew up an ambulance. What was inside of it, Stephen? We saw a gurney slide out there—but we have no idea what was inside it. Might have been someone else entirely. . . ."

"Bullshit." I'd found something he hadn't thought of. "If you want to go back into Sister Death to look for him, go right ahead. Poor Charlie. He's starting to seem more interesting dead than he ever was, alive."

"Charlie's dead." I hadn't seen him for years, but I suddenly missed him, missed seeing his figure hunched intently as he painted a neckpiece. He'd purse his lips and whistle opera arias. At least that's what he told me they were. I had no way of knowing. "No reason to pee on his corpse."

"Something's out there, Ambrose. I've known it for months." Watkins held his hand out in front of him. A little shivery, but well within normal tolerances. "That's why I'm clean. Because I'm going to get that son of a bitch. I've always wondered why I survived this long. Now I know. For him. For him. And I need you. I need every fragment of data you have, if we're going to find him." He was energized, even his hair seeming to stand up straighter. "I trolled you out and now you have to help me. Let's head to your place right now, suck up those data bases." He grabbed my hand in a tight grip. "Fix me up a spare bed. It'll be like old times. There's probably something you don't even know you know, something that could let us get him, something—"

I yanked my hand out of his grip. "Get the hell away from me, Watkins—Underhill—whatever you call yourself now." I stood up. He just sat there looking at me. "I escaped the Group. We planned it, we executed it, we did it. We're free, all of us. Free from each other. There's no goddamn way I'm letting you suck me back in again, do you understand me?" My voice had risen loud enough that people at other tables were looking at us.

"Don't be an idiot, Peter," Watkins said. "He's out there. You can't escape him."

"I can't believe I just spent the entire afternoon chasing after a lunatic. You stay away from me." I was shaking. Watkins watched me with interest. "If you so much as show your face, I'll make sure someone finds out who blew up that ambulance. It stays a secret otherwise. Do you understand that?"

"I understand that you have a problem, Peter." He did not get up from his seat. "It won't be long before you find out what that problem is. Take my card."

"I don't—" I pulled my flexicard out of my wallet. It was now transparent, with the simple legend "Gregory Zis" on it in black letters, and an access code. " 'Gregory Zis'?"

"A nom de rete. A netname. What other kind should we have? Good night, Peter Ambrose. Sleep well." He turned his attention to his beer.

And that was the final indignity. He wouldn't even let me storm out in a rage, him calling after me. He just dismissed me. But I wasn't about to sit down at that madman's table again. I had other things to worry about.

- 8 -

"YEAH, PETER, YEAH, I'M MAKING A DROP SOON." SHELDON SHUT off a bank of ultrasonic cleaners and a subliminal hum disappeared. He downchecked the circuits, his face serious. "In a coupla minutes, as a fact." He gestured at a pile of gold-edged gray envelopes on a clothes-folding table. "Wait that long, can you?"

"Ah, yes, Sheldon. I just need to send a message. That's all."

"That's all any of us can do with our entire lives, fact. Don't *know* if anybody's listening. Don't *know* if there's an audience. Don't *know*, send anyway."

We stopped by an immensely fat woman wearing layers and layers of coats and shawls. Surrounded by masses of laundry, she was the last customer in the laundromat and didn't seem particularly interested in leaving and going out into the sleety cold.

"I'm working on it, Sheldon," she said. "Can't believe this much piles up over a week. Can you?"

"Well, no, Marga*reet*. I just can't. You stealing other people's laundry again?"

"Now you know that's not true, not true at all! It was that bitch Lana," she said—"

Sheldon chuckled and picked up a huge orange blouse. "Well, Marga*reet*, let's just get you going here. Help out, Peter?" Sheldon was long-chinned blend of Asian and African and, with his bony forehead, resembled a praying mantis. He was a mean trombonist, which was how I knew him.

I sat down and started folding ballooning underwear. At least it gave me something to do. The laundromat was bright-lit and silent. Sheldon, who lived above it and managed it, had hauled in all sorts of cast-off furniture to give it a homey feel. The plan backfired because much of his clientele liked being there more than they liked going home. Like Margarethe.

Information. That was what I needed more than anything, and what Watkins had stubbornly refused to give me, spouting nonsensical and obviously false theories about risen dead men instead. I needed to know about Watkins. I also—my thoughts circled like disturbed starlings—needed to get to Corinne. That might have been the most important thing of all.

I shouldn't have limited myself to the two beers with Watkins. They weren't enough to soften the edges of the thoughts that cut their way through my head.

"You know what I got upstairs?" Sheldon was conspiratorial. "Two of Chester Donato's reeds."

"Chester—?"

Sheldon's face lit up at having caught me. And he had, because I knew we'd discussed Donato. "He used to play sax with the Bremmer Boys, out Philly way. Early Eighties. I got some old discs of them, you want to hear. You got to hear their version of 'Why Do You Do.' "

"Sure thing." I was starting to remember our discussion. "Chester Donato . . . he ever play with Calvin Minsenger?"

"Nah. Tried once. A pickup club date. Couldn't stand each other. But then, who *could* stand Minsenger?"

Neither Chester Donato, the notorious Calvin Minsenger, nor the Bremmer Boys had actually existed, not in our world, at any rate. They were a complete creation of Sheldon's imagination, though I had no doubt the reeds were real. Many products of Sheldon's imagination were real.

He had, with some help from me, come up with an entire alternate history, which separated from ours at about the time Chuck Berry and Fats Domino came on the scene. In his history, the failed experiment of rock had never occurred. Instead, jazz had continued to evolve uninterrupted from bebop clear into the twenty-first century. Sheldon's history was dense with nonexistent clubs, stars, arrests, fights, and romantic incidents. He had them all backed up with programs, photographs, memorabilia like hats, lucky bow ties, and Chester Donato's cracked reeds, even recorded interviews with nonexistent musicians. I'd seen some of those things created, but now they were real. The truth of a Duke Ellington top hat was indistinguishable from that of a Rory Barilleau pith helmet.

Back behind Sheldon was a world that worked, and even though I had contributed to it, I couldn't share it. His history was so much more vivid than the one that actually happened. Sheldon's past made *sense*.

Something crossed my mind and I spoke without considering. "But I thought Chester Donato was a longtime Calvin Minsenger band member. Donato left after they had a fight at a Studebaker car show in South Bend,

Indiana. Remember? They were playing at the premier of the new model. What was it called? . . . the Consul, I think. Late Seventies. Minsenger slammed Donato in the head with a tire iron or something. . . ."

I stopped when I saw the look on Sheldon's face, that of a skater who's just heard the ice crack. He'd told me that story, in great detail, a few months ago, but had forgotten it. I could hear his breathing in the silent laundromat, above the subvocal mumbling of Margarethe as she folded.

I thought as fast as I could. Sheldon was astonishingly vulnerable with his universe, as if it would all crumble into nothing at the first hint of contradiction. His world wanted robustness. It needed another witness to give it dimension. Ambiguity is a sign of reality, as broken symmetries are in the physical universe. I thought I could give it to him.

"That's the story everybody tells, anyway," I said. "I think you did too. Shame on you, Sheldon, repeating without checking. I don't think Chester Donato was ever *in* South Bend. But Leatherlips McKonnachie was. You remember him."

"Yeah." Sheldon brightened. "Trumpet player. Troublemaker."

"*Exactly*. He got on the wrong side of Brock Stolier—"

"When they were playing with Phaedrus's Follies, Minsenger's band. Of *course*. Bad place to *be,* Candy Ass Baboon's wrong side. Don't know he had a *right* one." I could see Sheldon's mind sail. "Donato gets the story 'cause no one's *heard* of McKonnachie. Hell, I seen his name spelled three four different ways in the same book. Never in any of the pictures. 'Cept one, of course." He looked thoughtful. "Even *looks* like Donato in that one."

"Could be brothers."

"Maybe *were*. Donato's ma was a traveling gal. Dropped babies across the lower forty-eight. Regular Johnny Ovumseed." Sheldon grinned. "Played a mean piano herself. Like you. Come up and play now. Got some people coming over. Late-night jam. The best kind. Don't need sun. Jazz ain't roses."

"I really should—"

"You got something better? Come on. We miss you, you're not there."

"Thanks, Sheldon." I got a warm flush at the idea that someone would miss me somewhere. "I'll do that."

"Hey, Mister, quit folding that brassiere like that. It ain't no piece of origamey. Give it here."

I handed Margarethe her gargantuan bra.

I had to get in contact with Sal Tigranes. I could roam the nets for weeks and not get the information I could from him over a cup of tea. He might know about Watkins . . . or Stephen Underhill—or, hell, Gregory Zis. He might even know if IntraCranial was sniffing around Atman for traces of what happened to Charles Geraldino. He might be able to strike a match in the darkness that seemed to surround me.

I had come to Sheldon because he was the only one I knew who could get in touch with Tigranes on short notice. Those envelopes on the table were going on tonight via Tigranes's special messenger service.

"Here he comes," Sheldon said.

I looked up from Margarethe's overalls. We were almost done folding.

A tall man with an extravagant feathered cap slid into the laundromat. He wore complex, woven-pattern silk robes of no historical period. They had been designed by a computer program similar to the one that had done my ribbon cookie containers: packing for a human being who needed to eat, shit and piss, connect into computer networks, sleep, engage in hand-to-hand combat, make love, climb buildings, and, for all I knew, harpoon whales and dance Odette/Odile in *Swan Lake*. Perhaps, with Sheldon's ultrasonic cleaning system, he never needed to take them off at all, and a simple press-seal on the back opened and allowed the robes to become a shroud. I considered recommending the technique to Margarethe.

He walked quickly across the floor, saying nothing, and scooped the pile of envelopes into a huge leather bag, like an old-time postman's. In an instant he would be gone. I stood.

He turned and froze, examining me carefully. He had high-arched, supercilious eyebrows, probably the result of surgery. I had to be careful how I spoke to him: if the message was not correctly formed, he would ignore it even as he understood me, like an infuriating Parisian. It was damnable decadent formalism, but the metaphor was strict. In any communications system, format is important.

I had come here prepared. I reached carefully into my breast pocket. A wrong breath and my hand could have been pinned to my chest by a spring knife. Street-and-mall types like to give the Messengers a rough time. They have learned to take care of themselves.

I pulled a packet out with two fingers, opened it, and slid a dried plant root out to him. Dirt was still stuck to it, and scattered across the table. Across the dirt I laid a bundle of silvery null-g–manufactured monofilaments.

"For him himself?" the Messenger finally asked, in a voice low and sweet, like that of a child molester.

"His very self."

These symbols did not come from history, at least, not from the history I knew. They were from a self-contained system of signs and symbols, one known, supposedly, only to initiates, though popular magazines and netgabs kept "revealing" them—always with some grotesque errors that would have caused amusement, perhaps rage, not communication. The whole thing was impossibly arch, and I suspected depths of secret behind it. I used it, but I did not understand it.

From another pocket of my suit I pulled a piece of dark paper. As the Messenger watched solemnly, I wrote: "Sal. I need a meeting. Please let me know as soon as possible. Peter Ambrose." I folded it in a complex figure and handed it to him. He immediately turned and left the laundromat.

Sheldon gazed after him. "Woo. They human under those coats, you think? Moves like he's on roller skates." He peered at me curiously. "Business with them?"

"Something of the sort." I didn't want to discuss it.

Sheldon waved his hands in front of him. "Sorry, forgive. That's *outside,* in quiet. Don't mix with *my* notes."

"That's all right, Sheldon." I sat down, feeling incredibly tired. The night weighed me down. I had brought the box with the Group memories with me from the car. I could feel its sharp edges in my bag.

Finally, with grunts and groans, Margarethe waddled out of the laundromat with her bags and bags of clothing, her own ample figure almost invisible under it all.

Sheldon gazed after her. "She'll be back next week, same stuff. Not even dirty, most of it." He shook his head. "Must be better places to go. Why a laundry?"

"Maybe because you're here," I said. "I at least have the excuse of the music."

His dark skin flushed and he smiled, not looking at me. "Don't you start flirting with me, Peter. I'll have to tell Arnie."

"Arnie knows I'm a pussycat." I thought a moment. "Can you do something for me, Sheldon? It's professional."

He straightened and put on what he thought was a professional demeanor. "Sure thing."

I pulled out Charlie Geraldino's crumpled-up neckpiece. "Can you flatten this out for me? Without hurting it? It's silk."

"I know silk." Now I'd affronted his professional dignity. He smiled to show that he forgave me, took it, and walked over to a small pressing machine. A moment later, he was back, with the neckpiece pristine and crisp.

I folded it carefully until it was shaped like a flower and put it back in the box. Charlie was dead. It was one of the few things in this world left of him. I closed the box and sat looking at it.

Sheldon looked concerned, rubbed his hand on my shoulder. "Coming up?"

I wanted it so bad it felt like a fire inside, a fire only music could quench. "Let's go."

I WAS ABOVE MY AVERAGE THAT NIGHT, WHICH DIDN'T SURPRISE ME, because the people Sheldon had over—Wynans, Elzbeth, Lars the bassoonist—were genuinely good. Elzbeth had a high-stacked sense of rhythm and being able to bounce around her syncopations was exhilarating.

We paused for a break, toward morning. The apartment, dense-packed with jazz memorabilia from Sheldon's alternate universe, seemed to vibrate with the music we'd been pouring into it. Sheldon's lover, Arnie, lay in a corner under an elaborately draped pile of satin sheets. I couldn't tell if he was listening because he never moved, except once in a while to drink distilled water from a tube. He looked, with his bare chest and long, curling hair, as if he was posing for a painter of huge historical scenes.

I sat at the piano and wiped my sweat from the keys. The others walked around and gossiped, getting beer from the kitchen refrigerator, but I had too much to think about. They sensed that, and no one approached me, save through the music.

I opened my box and looked at the objects inside.

The blue marble. I held it out at arm's length, seeing it glow. The full Earth seen from somewhere out in space. Anthony Watkins. It had been his, part of his huge collection of childhood games, most of them obsolete. Watkins had played mumblety-peg with real verve. I flipped it up from my thumb and caught it in my palm.

The bone-handled scalpel, once part of a collection from a Victorian doctor's black leather satchel, along with bone-cutters, saws, a gallstone cracker. They had given Karin Crawford a feeling that her science was old and extended back over the centuries, though it was actually an invention of the late nineteenth century. Before then, the word "medicine" had meant torment and superstition.

The automobile ratchet wrench. I turned it, hearing it click. A simple thing, still covered with a thin film of ancient motor oil. Lori Inversato had changed the plugs on an old car with it, then left it lying on the concrete of the garage, where I had picked it up. A grease-stained incarnation for her and, I think, her favorite.

The soft leather glove. I picked it up and started to slip it over my hand. Sharp pinpricks stopped me. I held the glove up and looked inside. Its lining was all metal needle points, gleaming in the dim light. One of my fingers welled a drop of blood. I sucked it. It was Hank Rush's little joke, one of many. He'd worn it on a synthetic hand, feeling the needle points as a soft, massaging lining.

The hand-painted neckpiece folded like a flower.

And a four-lobed piece of fine-textured red-patinaed metal with a long, triangular slot in the middle. On it, in gold, were two phoenixes. It was a seventeenth-century Japanese sword guard by the school of Kaneiye, an object called a *tsuba*. Gene Michaud had always been a frustrated military man and had collected military memorabilia to link himself with the science of creative destruction. I'd taken the tsuba just when we escaped from Camp Fitzwater, after the death of . . .

I emptied the box, turned it over. Nothing in it but those six objects, one for each member of the Group, my link with them. There was nothing whatsoever in it from Linden Straussman.

I shuddered and put everything back. I learned something about myself every time I played. It grounded me. I was already sorry I had blown up at Watkins. He'd always had a gift for that, though. He'd get me mad then sit back and watch what I did. I'd have to find him again. Him and the others. I had already started.

During a previous break I had checked the net markets for Japanese military collectibles—and let out a specific for-information signal about this one. It was a one-of-a-kind. Gene Michaud would definitely notice it. I would have to wait to find out what he did about it. As I remembered, he was an impulsive man. He'd do something, fast.

"Oh no, Sheldon," I heard a complaining voice behind me say. "Not another one of your Nonexistent Jazz Greats."

"You bet," Sheldon said. "Famous guy, you should know him. This photo's from a little commercial gig in 1978. The main Studebaker showroom in South Bend, Indiana. There's where the notorious air horn incident occurred."

That got my attention. I turned around. Wynans, a plump lawyer who played a beautiful tenor sax, had slapped his hand to his forehead and was looking up at the ceiling in a mute appeal to God. He looked at me and shook his head. "Crazy. His brain and this universe are out of rhythm." In contrast to his instrument, his voice was squeaky.

Sheldon ignored Wynan's lack of interest, grinned at me, and shoved an 8 × 10 photograph at him. I edged over and took a peek.

A jazz sextet, *Phaedrus's Follies* in red letters on the bass drum, played on a small stage above a crowd of dancers. Behind the band was a semicircle of new, showroom cars. Spotlights caught their shining enamel paint. The one in the middle had dramatic gull-wing doors that opened upward.

The men had ridiculous sideburns, the women wore short skirts. It *looked* like the Seventies, our Seventies, I mean, the real one, if any Seventies can be said to be real. The saxophonist was blowing for all he was worth. His eyes weren't closed, though. He looked icily at the photographer, as if his body was playing the instrument but his mind was focused elsewhere. He was a powerful black man with a complex bald skull marked with scars, almost tribal cicatrices.

Sheldon tapped the photograph. "Brock Stolier," he said reverently. "Called himself Candy Ass Baboon. Born Baton Rouge, Louisiana, in 1952. One of the great tenors, Wynans, never heard of him? Could have lifted Bird out of his grave, this one."

"If he'd ever existed," Wynans snorted. "But he didn't."

Sheldon shrugged, not interested in Wynans's skepticism. "At that time Stolier was heavily into a neo-African jazz called TseTse."

"Why? Because it put you to sleep?" Wynans was pleased at being clever.

Sheldon sighed. "You really want to be playing a dead art for all your life?"

"Dead? It's not dead, Sheldon."

"Sure looks that way to me."

I looked at the arrogant face of Brock Stolier, his lips firm on the mouthpiece of his tenor sax. When had Sheldon managed to make this photograph? It was a product of his image-generation system, which filled most of a room. Looking at it, I was sure that no amount of technical analysis could demonstrate that the photograph was invented. I was also sure that he'd created it as a result of our earlier discussion. During a coffee break? Sheldon knew how to work fast.

"This is when it happened." Sheldon pointed to the trumpet player, who stood behind Stolier, looking straight ahead, horn under his arm, a fat boy with loose hair and the facial expression of the class troublemaker. "The night before, Leatherlips McKonnachie had stolen Brock Stolier's sax and taken it to an all-night welding shop. They cut it open and installed an air horn. An E-flat air horn that would blow only when Stolier hit that note and no other. Before the Studebaker show, Leatherlips got Stolier drunk, and so he didn't notice anything wrong until he started to play. The first

E-flat he hit, he almost dropped the thing." Sheldon laughed as if he'd been there in the audience. "The rest of the band was in on it and played as if there wasn't a damn thing wrong."

"So what happened?" I asked. "A riot? A new musical style?"

"What?" Sheldon looked puzzled. "It's a pretty famous story, actually. Stolier decoyed Leatherlips back to look at the car, this one in the middle. Then he bashed him on the head with the gull-wing door, right in front of everybody. Managers didn't like it, made the car seem unsafe. A Regent, it was called. Phaedrus's Follies weren't even much popular, ever. Good, real good, but not popular. Broke up in 1982, in Tacoma, after a bad tour. Had a bitch of a bandleader, guy name of Calvin Minsenger." He smiled at me.

I smiled back. "Funny thing about McKonnachie. He's the spitting image of Chester Donato."

"Funny damn thing." Sheldon laughed.

Sheldon and Wynans, argument forgotten, started talking about a club date. Sheldon, aside from being the laundry king of the Near North Side, also ran an odd interactive nomadic jazz club called the Club Le Moustier. He used Tigranes's Messengers to send invitations to those people he had selected. Those were the gold-edged gray envelopes I had seen the night before. Sheldon knew that most people didn't understand music at all. His special invitations were an attempt to create a culture that did, a culture that understood *his* musical history, a culture where rock and roll was a curiosity about as important as Gregorian chants. I wished him luck.

Lars the bassoonist started to play, a catchy little tango-rhythm tune. It wasn't until I put my fingers to the keys that I realized how tricky that tango was. Damn bassoonists. They rarely get to play, so they spend too much of their time thinking. I'd never met one who wasn't a troublemaker.

I started to play, giving the bassoonist room for his loony improvisations. We played until morning knocked on the window.

OUT ON THE STREET, AN OWL SAT ON THE HOOD OF MY CAR. EVERYTHING was crisp and unforgiven in the morning light, the gutter-wash of garbage around my car tires eye-hurting in a hundred glaring colors. The street was asleep with its mouth open, snoring. Only the owl moved, fluffing out its feathers and sidestepping across the hood. I recognized it. It belonged to Tigranes. The owl blinked and swiveled its head toward me. I stopped and watched. It flattened its feet and infomycelia grew out of its claws, almost-invisible shining fibers. Its two eyes were different, the right natural, the left a folded-optic viewer that was probably transmitting an image of me directly onto Tigranes's desk. I waved.

The owl's infomycelia crawled through the interstices of my car's information system, inductively tickling its memories. A navigation program to Tigranes's house got fed in.

The owl shook itself, recovered its infomycelia, and, with a sweep of its wide wings, launched itself from the hood. I watched it vanish into the bright sky. Damn thing. It was broad daylight. Didn't it know that it was supposed to be asleep, hanging upside down in a closet? No, wait, that was bats, I thought. I never pretended to be a naturalist. I got into the car.

-9-

THE WROUGHT-IRON GATE IN THE HIGH WALL SLID OPEN AT MY APPROACH and shut behind me. A speed restriction slowed the car as if it was hitting a wall of suddenly thick air. Substantial dull houses stood proudly on their lawns, happy to be far away from the city. Tigranes's new house had originally been a brick-faced French chateau in no way different from its neighbors, but he'd already added a huge greenhouse that stretched around the side of the house. I could see the fugitive glow of brightly colored jungle flowers amid the dense greenery. New dormers stuck out of the house's high black roof, marking newly added rooms.

The house had its own gate, which also slid aside and then retained me. I reached a brick parking place under a hedge. My engine stopped. The door lock clicked and my door swung open. I looked around as I got out, searching for gun emplacements and laser target locators. I couldn't find anything but a hummingbird feeder and a birdbath. Unlike mine, this one had water in it. I walked up the sidewalk. The lion-headed knocker rapped once and the door opened.

In the dark front hall a floor clock textured the shagreen of sharkskin, obsidian teeth in a circle at the top marking the devoured hours, bonged secretly deep within itself. The owl sat atop it, its head turned back at me, blinking as if wondering what had taken me so long.

"Back here, Peter." A french door opened to a bright garden at the end of the hall. Outside, Sal Tigranes, wearing a wide sun hat despite the unpromisingly cloudy sky, kneeled at the rosebushes he was protecting from the encroaching winter. Insulating crystals sprouted on the thorns as he sprayed them, turning the roses into rock candy. His white beard spilled down his overalls like a glacier. His pale fingernails were outlined with dirt.

Tigranes looked up at me and grinned, his dark face a mass of wrinkles. "Glad you could make it, Peter." He stood up slowly, first one foot, then the other, wiping his hands on a rag. He hung the sprayer in the garage, near the hoe and a gleaming antique pruning hook from Victorian England.

I looked around the yard which, aside from the rosebushes huddled against the house, was a patchy grass lawn stretching out to a chain link fence. "This doesn't look too promising, Sal."

"Nothing much here now," he said. "Old-time suburban monoculture. But just wait until summer. Then you'll see something." He took me on a walk through an imaginary garden, full of perennial beds, cleverly bent shrubs, aromatic ground covers, moss-covered rocks. As he pointed out the nonexistent features, I started to see them myself. He did all that despite the fact that he knew any place he lived was purely temporary and that he would have to leave it all behind.

He dug his fingers into the dirt between two patches of grass. It was packed hard and resisted. "This was farmland, once. Good farmland, before they spilled most of it into the Mississippi. Savannah before that. Glacial till, alluvial deposits over it. Imagine spending all your time growing this weird Eurasian ground cover that can't take the heat of an Illinois summer."

"You mean the grass? I thought that was from . . . Kentucky, or somewhere." I squatted down next to him, though I could see nothing but grass and dirt.

He crinkled his eyes at me. "Jesus, Peter. Haven't you been paying attention? What would the Sons of the Canyon say if they could hear you?"

" 'Fertilizer.' " I imitated what I imagined of a clipped Canyonite voice giving a command and, despite myself, felt a chill.

Tigranes laughed. "Not in my garden. You'd make the soil too acidic. Thanks for the offer." Of all the things he did, and they were many, Tigranes was most proud of being a gardener, of making things grow. Or rather, of changing things into some other possible aspect of themselves, a gardener's true job.

"Where does the tree go?"

"That corner, by the garage. A bur oak." No matter where he stayed, and for how long, Tigranes always planted a tree, usually a thick-barked bur oak, a standard tree in northern Illinois. I didn't know when he started, but I knew he'd been doing it for years.

"How big do you suppose your oldest one is?"

I had hit a bad spot in Tigranes's memory. He looked momentarily bleak. "I've managed to forget that one." He stood and stretched his back.

He was a slender man, in much better shape than I was. "Let its shade fall on someone else."

As we walked, I thought about that first tree, imagining it standing alone, in a field, next to a crumbling city apartment, in a suburban backyard, just a tree, just a tree. I didn't believe it was just a tree. I wanted to find it, climb its branches, and ask it its secrets. What had the young Tigranes been thinking as he planted it? I snuck a glance at old Tigranes's sober, bent-over head. What a wonderful thing, to have your tragedy in the form of an oak. That way it at least *did* something.

Two people, a man and a woman, now lounged in the front hall. They wore the same long, elaborate, woven-silk robes as my Chicago Messenger. Their eyes flicked across me negligently, classifying and then dismissing me. Here in the house they did not wear anything on their heads and the elaborate structure of their hairless skulls was clear in the blue glow of the overhead gas sconces. It was, in theory, some sort of embryological neoteny-suppression, a demonstration of the heaviness of anthropoid bone allowed to grow to full development, though I knew it was actually shims of foamed chrome steel fastened through the cranium. Tigranes's people had carried the fashion for alternate history to ludicrous extremes—they were actually supposed to be distant descendants of *Australopithecus robustus,* or something like that.

Past them, I could see into the living room. The furniture was a serious and slow organiform. A bulking armoire gleamed with the dark iridescence of butterfly wings in a twilit jungle. The bright teardrop-ready-to-fall of a desk light was supported by a curving skeletal neck with elongated cervical vertebrae. The two rib-skulled and robed Messengers, silently trading tiny symbols on an inlaid chessboard in some obscure and involved game, looked like just another pair of collectibles.

We sat down in a corner nook in the kitchen. He poured me a glass of lemonade. Tigranes would have been famous for his lemonade, if he'd been the kind of guy who let more than a very few people know anything about him. I could just smell his work-sweated body, an odor of moss and long-stored suitcases.

He put his chin on his hands, sticking his beard out at me. "Well, Peter. What seems to be the problem?" He had taken off the sun hat, revealing his bald head. "It's been a long time since I got such a formal message from you."

I was suddenly shy. Tigranes was my friend, but in a dangerous way, because he was useful to me. He supplied my high-end virts. Though I liked to think I was a good neurosurgeon and cognitive psychologist, my skill as an underworld operator wouldn't have gotten me through an Elysion purchase in a schoolyard.

I got up and opened the window. Then I picked up my glass and clinked the ice cubes in it. The sound was relaxing, as if there were absolutely no problems in the world. "I need information, Sal."

"Ah." He nodded, his bald head ponderously thoughtful with its long beard. "What sort of information?"

I'd thought about it a lot. Tigranes didn't give information for free, even if sometimes I didn't like the prices he charged: if I paid for information, the rest of what we did was safe, untainted. Outside of that exchange, we could be friends.

"Some easy," I said. "Some hard."

"Let me be the judge of what's easy. What's the first thing?"

"I need some information about someone. As much as you have. He goes by several names. Stephen Underhill and Gregory Zis are two of them. Let me transfer his card data. . . ."

Tigranes examined the display that flipped out from the wall. "Okay. What else?"

"I want to find out if someone is a luke from IntraCranial, and if so, what her mission is."

That one gave Tigranes pause. He frowned his big white eyebrows and looked away from me, out through a window at his winter-ready garden, where a little compressed vista led to a statue of a nude muscular woman who was either stringing a bow or breaking a large bundle of spaghetti.

"An icy luke? Is she after you?"

"Not that I know of. I ran into her by accident—I think. She was masquerading as a receptionist at Sister Death. Someone I know got himself killed under unpleasant circumstances. She is investigating the killing—once again, I think."

He rubbed his forehead. "I've been hearing things . . . nothing definite, but then IC is always a mystery. They're never after us small-timers. But it always behooves us to pay attention, because we may get stepped on in the process. Let me see what I can dig up."

"And what do *you* want?" I asked. "As fee." That could not be avoided.

Tigranes didn't hesitate. "I need you to help break into the Atman Medical Center with me to recover something a contact has left there for me."

I like to think I'm pretty glib, but Tigranes's statement left me completely speechless. I just blinked at him and tried to make what he said mean something else.

"Now, Peter, it's not so bad. Just a big hospital, after all."

"Be serious, Sal. Atman's security makes the Putarana Plateau holocaust gene store look like it could be broken into with a bent paper clip. I know, I've dealt with the place. Besides, why would you want to use me? I'm no secure-penetration expert."

"You know more about it than you think."

"People keep telling me that about everything. I suppose it's true."

"It *is* true."

The two game-playing Messengers from the front hall had left, but another, an immensely tall woman, silently put a bowl of watery soup full of greens in front of me. I tasted it. It was bitter, without a trace of salt. The Messengers were skilled at symbolic communication and the maintenance of Tigranes's illicit empire, but not a one of them could cook. It was a symbology they did not care to understand. Or perhaps the message they were trying to convey was simply not one I wanted to receive.

"So what *do* I know about it?" I asked.

"You know Franklin Sanderson, in the County Morgue division. Old business associate, right?"

"Right," I said reluctantly. "I know Slip. Same way everyone knows my business."

"We need to make a deal with him. He's got partial access through bottom-level Atman security. It just happens to be a part of the puzzle that I don't have. You know how to contact him. I'm not saying he trusts you—he doesn't trust anyone. A wise man. But you can convince him. You know the kind of things he wants."

The hell of it was, I did. I'd known Slip Sanderson years before, when we were sliding illegal virts in and out of Sister Death together, Sanderson as Mr. Inside, me as Mr. Outside. We hadn't liked each other much even then.

But I did know what Slip was after, what he wanted, what made him salivate or lose his water. Just as he knew the same things about me. With Tigranes's resources, I could bribe him, persuade him. I didn't want to. I didn't ever want to see Slip Sanderson again.

"What are you after, Sal?"

"I need to get something out. I have a contact in a high-security area. She's spooked, just phase-balanced, ready to tip."

"What about?"

"That Atman Security you are, so sensibly, worried about. She's a heo in research there, high-end quantum transition virts. She's been one of my best sources, sliding the stuff out to me, but she thinks they're on to her.

The pressure's been going up faster than her prices and she's about to close up shop. She's been collecting money for something—to get away, I think. To escape. She wants to get a few last things out to me. Stratocost gadgets."

"How strato?"

He turned his long nose toward me. "Each of the devices in her stasis box would bring, at a minimum, five thousand nudes on the market."

Five thousand new dollars in a world where dinner at L'Angoulême, with wine, cost upwards of ten, was a good fraction of my annual income. Five thousand megabucks or five billion dollars in old-time greenback currency. Currency reform had made calculations much easier and given us back nickel beer. It all goes back to beer, finally, I'd been told. I had a friend who was an economist.

I glanced at Tigranes. He sat staring out of the window, his nose as sharp as a hawk's.

"All right," I said finally. "That I'll do. Access to Atman through Slip Sanderson. But that's it."

He looked annoyed. "What do you mean, that's it?"

It was hard to deny Tigranes, my friend, but I had to. "I mean I'll get to Slip Sanderson and get your access, but I'm not assaulting the goddam medical center. I have a lot going on, Sal. Too much. I didn't come to you for information because I was just curious. I *need to know*. But I can't spend my time and effort breaking into Atman. *I can't*."

He sat silently for a long moment. "All right, Peter. I'll see what I can do."

"The Zis information is more important right now than the—"

He raised a hand to silence me. "Besides, you know that I'll have to get the IC info even if you don't want it. *I* can't afford not to know that."

"Now, Sal—"

"Don't bullshit me, Peter." His voice was severe. "Go on upstairs. I'll talk to you later."

I SAT IN THE MIDDLE OF AN EMPTY UPSTAIRS BEDROOM, ON A FLOOR SO polished it felt frictionless. Light came from overhead gas jets. I was in the secret upper parts of the house. Wherever Tigranes lived, there were large areas that remained mysterious to me, as blank as the blacked-out areas on Charlie Geraldino's TV body. Outside the dormer window I could see the lights of other houses glowing securely in the night.

A Messenger handed me a woven bento box like a giant cocoon, its synthetic silk fibers pliable until pressed, when they became rigid. I could feel the chambered food inside of it, but it took me a good fifteen minutes to figure out how it opened. The dumplings inside tasted as if they were filled with warmed library paste. I was starving, and ate them anyway.

Tigranes, now robed like his employees, slid in and dimmed a gas jet. He didn't use that technology out of romantic temperament. It was sheerest paranoia. He avoided any unnecessary contact with the power net, fearing security penetration. Who knew what parasitic signals could come through, concealed in power line noise? I recognized the fear. That it was paranoid didn't make it irrational.

The last time I had visited Tigranes he had been living in an old woodpile of a house in Lake Forest, on a bluff looking out over Lake Michigan. Pilot drills had dug into the walls, dragging fiber-optic cables through the old oak beams and hollowing spaces out for processors in the attic rafters, an infestation of information termites. That house had been compromised some months ago, and abandoned complete, as if a curse had been put on it. The house was still the same, with its venerable shingles and wraparound porch, but its digital spirits were now perverted and owed their allegiance to darker forces. So Tigranes had moved here.

He laid a pouch on the table. Crystals, dried leaves, and tiny metal figures spilled out of it—the morphemes of his peculiar communications system. He played moodily with them for a moment, setting up patterns and then destroying them. He'd let me sit up here alone for long enough to feel guilty about refusing to help him.

"Who is your contact?" I asked.

He ran a thumb around his lips, and the silence stretched. "Really, Peter. If you're not going to participate, I don't think you need to know that." He thought for a minute. "But maybe you should know something about it. It might be of interest to you. Because you have a link. My contact was always concerned with finding the proper home for the virts she designs in her lab, the ones I'm trying to get out. It was a precise obsession with her. She refused to deal unless I guaranteed obedience to her instructions." He looked at me. "Once she came to me with a virt and said, 'I think this should be installed by a musician.'"

The cold blade of an ancient trepanning blade dug from a tumulus caressed the back of my skull. "A musician?"

"Yes. Isn't that odd? 'Only the best, Sal, only the best musician you can find. This is a complex and, more importantly, an ambiguous device. Only a musician will be able to understand it. An improviser, not a classical violinist or something like that. A jazzman. Do you suppose there are any left in this world?' She does that a lot, listing requirements that should be regarded as . . . shall we say, nontechnical. How someone wears his hat, whether it seems that they are religious. Virts are complex, interactive. Who's to say her requirements are irrelevant? Well, in this case I did know of a good musician."

Someone out there knew who I was. She'd set up a smoke screen, but I was sure of it. His contact. A woman, no name. I needed to know who it was, up in Atman.

"Yes, Sal. I'm probably the only one you know."

"That's right."

The angle of the light had changed and suddenly everything looked completely different. Atman was no longer an irrelevant sideshow, but a hole in my knowledge, a blind spot in my vision from which something could strike me. I had to shine a light there to see what was hiding.

I cleared my throat. "Sal."

He raised his eyebrows. "Yes?"

"I've changed my mind. I'll . . . I'll dive into Atman with you. If you still want me to."

"All right." And that was that. If he connected my sudden acquiescence with his information about his contact, he didn't reveal it. He clicked his tongue thoughtfully. "I tracked down your Gregory Zis—whose name is actually Mack Salvucci."

"Mack Salvucci?" That was a new one.

"That's right. Until a few months ago he was a mallside mess, a real user. Regular outlet scum. Now he's clean, as near as I can tell. A modern miracle. He should appear on talk shows." He peered suspiciously at me. "Who the hell is Mack Salvucci?"

"Someone I had dealings with, years ago. He's reemerged, clean, as you say. Claims I slid something out on him, that he was cheated. He's on my ass. I want to get him off."

"For a little extra, I know people—"

"He's my business. No one else's. I just needed to find him."

Tigranes had many sources of information, many of them out-of-Net. Some real netheads don't believe in such things, thinking that anything worth knowing comes in bit-mapped form. This comes from all that direct-perception junk we've installed into people's otherwise vestigial brains. I should know. I've installed a fair amount of it myself.

"And as for your icy luke . . ." He looked thoughtful. "Easier to get data than I thought. Name, Amanda TerAlst. Married, husband now dead—a firefight with an armed gang. Made a good account of himself. Two children, couldn't find ages or places of schooling. *That's* secure. She defends them. Lives up on the North Side, regular old place. She's an Inherent Potentialist ... which means she rejects our work completely."

"Some kind of primitivist philosophy, right?"

"Don't brush it aside so blithely, friend. IP's are tough and smart. They know how to use the brains they have, better than anyone. Most importantly, they know who they are. It may not be someone you or I would want to be, but they're solid. I'd watch her, Peter. Watch her close. The rest of the data on those two is now in your system."

"Thank you, Sal."

"Now, for our project. Subject's made the arrangements. It's a direct drop, but it has to look like a penetration and extraction."

"Can't look like an inside job."

"No way. I guaranteed that. You'll need this." He handed me a datacrisp.

I stared down at the dried cockroach body in my hand.

"It's a security screening system for penetrating Atman's data bases."

"What is—"

"There's nothing I can describe to you, Peter. It's all high-level software. Algorithms, procedures, coding schemes, branching chains of increasingly unlikely possibilities. It's just a key, that's all."

"Just a key." The crisp in my hand had the computing power to run an industrial chemical plant. There was, indeed, no way for me to understand it. It was a captive sprite, an enchanted sword, a magic key handed me by a sorcerer. I could retire to a monastery for the rest of my life, dedicate myself to studying its intricacies, and never have a hope of understanding anything about it. I put it in a pocket.

"So you go to Sanderson. I'll pay high, if I can. But I suspect he won't go for it. You'll have to squeeze him. You must have some way to do that. I need you to get a handle on him."

"I'll do my best." I thought a moment. "Sal. There's more to it than I've said."

"I know." He peered out of the window at the anonymous lights of his neighbors, not looking at me.

"There's a past I have ... I've managed to forget most of it. But it's still there."

"The back of your head doesn't disappear just because you can't see it."

"Um, right. But it's come up, all of a sudden. A long-lost brother ... like that. Sal, it's difficult."

He reached over and took my shoulder. I don't think he'd ever touched me before. His hand was strong and hard. I could see why plants would grow under its care.

"That past's a hard place because we can't ever do anything to change it. The least we can do is remember it correctly."

"That's right. And I don't. I have to."

He finally turned and looked at me. "Did you ever wonder how I got into this line of work?"

"Of course," I said.

"Polite of you never to ask."

"Prudent, I'd say."

He looked closely at me, unsure how far I was joking. I don't think he understood how much he frightened me sometimes. "My daughter got me into this business." He placed a piece of broken glass on a basil leaf and pushed. The sharp edge cut through and I smelled the herb in the close room.

Tigranes had never mentioned any family, not wife, not parents, not children. As far as I knew he'd grown himself from a bean.

"It was an accident—I think. One never knows, there are so many plans in the world. Shira was just . . . five or six, I think. Funny, I can't remember, though I could look it up if I wanted. A bright child, but then, all our children are bright. Perhaps I should say normal. Her mother was driving her to a ballet class, I think. On manual. A multisegment truck hit them and folded the car up. Shira's mother died instantly. Shira . . . lived, the left side of her body crushed. And the left side of her brain shredded. Aphasia, somatic distortion, defects in foresight and judgment, stuff ripped from the prefrontal to the parietal lobes. There was still an intelligent being in there somewhere, I could feel it, but you couldn't detect it in the babbling, slobbering thing that lay in the hospital bed, tubes stuck into it." Tigranes's tone was detached, as he held the memory away from himself on fire tongs. I realized that, among other things, I would never learn the name of his wife. She had vanished along with the rest of his old life.

"I acquired an early speech/math processor. It was a spin-off of some secret military project. All I ever learned was the name: Project Nimbus." If he'd been looking at me, he might have seen me blanch, but he was once again staring out the dark window. "The device was . . . strange, and had a lot of drawbacks. For example it let her write, gesture, manipulate symbols, but not speak. It didn't have the motor control function for that. But she could communicate, in her own way. So, for a few years, I had a rational, if silent daughter. But the changes weren't enough. Some years later, she died."

He looked at me, his eyes appraising. "Not everything we deal in is useless, Peter."

"I never thought so," I said.

-10-

THE NEXT MORNING, AFTER A DEAD SLEEP ON TIGRANES'S WOOD FLOOR, I pushed my way through the doors of the Mall of the Mysteries. I had information to get before I could confront Slip Sanderson and the Mysteries was the best place to get it.

The Mall of Dreadful Night was packed dense with people. It was hot, too hot, and smelly—spicy, rank, and sweet. The inside was huge and brightly lit, with arching walkways and multilevel shops, their once marble-paneled entranceways now fallen into desperate and not-at-all-charming decay.

Food sellers squatted over their grills and tandoor ovens, families gathered around, fuel-cell–powered coolers full of lamb haunches and sausages humming behind them. One of them had a stack of military stores, devices meant to be buried in desert sands for ten years and then dug up, their personal-sized Thanksgiving turkey, stuffing, and yam dinners heating on opening. Smoke swirled up into the upper reaches of the Mall, blackening the balconies and coating the domed ceiling with soot.

I sauntered and window-shopped. Going directly after information rarely worked. Information often acts like the quarter you are trying to pull out from behind the sofa cushion—the closer you get to it, the more it retreats, until you get nothing but a handful of lint. There was plenty of lint here at the Mall Heureux, the Mall of Broken Dreams. But if you wanted to find something rare and valuable, this was often the only place, because you could pretend that you were looking for something else entirely.

A huge hologram of a human brain hung over the Mall's central atrium, flickering with energy. Various functional areas—basal ganglia, speech centers, the limbic system—flashed into focus and vanished, leaving behind them a mass of blocky Japanese ideograms and kabbalistic diagrams. This eidolon marked the place of the fortune-tellers. Modern seers used the complex tracts of the CNS as previous generations had used tea leaves, *I ching,* and tarot cards, a pseudorandom pattern from which prophetic information was extracted. Their booths, made of obsolete hotech surgical steel and quantum-energy-drop alloy glowing with vague internal light, were crowded with those unable to afford actual brain modification.

One of the prophets, a bearded man with his head wrapped in symbolically bloodied surgical bandages, raised the curtain to his booth and I saw a fat, middle-aged woman in a green hospital gown just lying down in his bootleg positron-emission tomographic scanner, handing her empty glass of radioisotope-containing orange juice to the attendant. The prophet would ask her questions and then tell her fortune from the intricate pattern of responding active areas in her brain.

I walked into Reve Tokaido, the weavemesh noodle parlor on the third level, to catch the foam. I could have caught it at home, of course—the curling edge bubbles out of every datalink indifferently, an informational hologram whose every part contains the whole—but like anyone, I prefer to sit down on a cracked plastic chair, rub real physical elbows with some disreputable colleagues, and slurp some noodles while I listen to the latest rumors.

I ordered chow fun with gumbo filé, and a flask of Saijito Black. The white-powder–faced waitress pursed her lips in disapproval, since black sake is long behind the crest, but a lot of old craniacs drink it, so Reve Tokaido lowers itself for its customers. I suspect it would like to offer them some remedial fashion therapy.

The place was a maze of pressed-plastic beams lit by pinspots. Each of the noodle parlor's cracked plastic chairs was different, but matched exactly one each in every other Reve Tokaido in the country. There were at least two hundred parlors identical, in every respect, to this one, and all were connected by high-capacity leased lines in a proprietary wideband network. All of them dissolved in the same information space like so many sugar cubes in a vat of boiling water. That is the societal congruence of a weavemesh establishment.

The wizened form of a game addict spun in a vortex bubble above us like a fetus in its amnion, playing some idiotic game, challenging an entirely nonexistent universe. He was probably famous internationally among people similarly brain damaged. He stopped dead for a moment, his wide-pupiled eyes watching the flare of a nova sterilizing its planets. His body hung slack, mere appendage to his eyes. Then he yelped in pleasure and was spinning again.

As I ate my noodles, holographic versions of diners in other Reve Tokaidos flickered past me and exchanged rumors, the basic currency of the nets. Netwanks. Some long-ago theorists had expected network linkages to increase information transfer. If it does, it's buried so deep under layers and layers of misinformation, misinterpretation, slanted views, partial truths, and outright lies that it's impossible to extract. Rumors, however . . . Netwanks we got.

Most I'd heard before. "Remember Kalmbach? Used to run hard-memory embossers for Sebong out through Brunei. Big guy, no imagination, a plus in dealing there . . . Got nailed by a datagrub—ate his mind right out of his head, left him a phosphorescent tuber . . . No, I don't think datagrubs are AIs, that's just wanky, but maybe they propagate through the net incorporating memory structures and so have *past* consciousness if not *present* . . . What do you mean, absurd? How else do you explain . . . ?"

Forces were trying to take over the net, the net was trying to take over people's minds, artificial intelligences dwelled somewhere in the net. The usual nonsense.

I thought about Charlie Geraldino, living alone, dying alone. Alone, that is, except for the company of his murderer. There hadn't been overturned furniture, or signs of struggle. Charlie had never struggled.

I remembered him fumbling for his wallet and grinning uncertainly at a screaming prostitute in a feces-smelling Kishinyov apartment courtyard. She was wearing a piece of old carpet as a stole, a Byelorussian military hat with the brim torn off, and had purple nails like knife blades. When I found him there I thought, for sure, that he was one of those quiet violent sex offenders, a "but he was such a *nice* boy" type who had just ripped somebody's throat out. Instead, it turned out he'd let the prostitute inveigle him into some deal involving smuggling some cheap bioreactor-made whiskey across the border into Free Moldavia, a deal that had then gone as sour as the gut-buster whiskey . . . or something, I never really got it clear. All I knew was that it ended up costing us both a lot of money to keep Charlie out of the hands of whichever police were in charge of Kishinyov that week. To show there were no hard feelings, the prostitute gave us a gallon jug of the whiskey. Charlie and I drank the foul stuff until our throats burned, and laughed and howled at the Moon, now too poor to afford anything else.

Charlie had let his killer in. There had been no sign of forced entry. Let him in while still wearing his pajamas, still eating his meager breakfast. Let him in and sat down to chat and then been knocked from the chair and strangled. . . .

I sat at that table in Reve Tokaido and, for the first time, felt a sense of my own desolation. I was alone, and none of the eager voices babbling in my ears could disguise that fact.

I felt something touch my back. With a flare of cold panic, I dropped to the side, grabbed the offending arm, and hauled.

"Hey!" A figure tripped to the floor. I followed, on him immediately, wrist in his throat. I found myself looking into the startled face of Newton Pavlichuk. "What gives?" he said. "Let me up."

I could feel his breath heaving in his chest. He was a fine-featured man with broad, muscular shoulders that I could now feel were artificial. His hair was long and fluffy, not the usual datadork greasy. I released my weight and he stood up, examining himself elaborately.

"I was just trying to give you a little style help, Peter. You don't have to get so pissy about it." He held up an adhesive 3D poster that showed a complex of neurons glittering like ice crystals on a sunlit window, and the legend NEURAL LIBERATION FRONT. The poster was startling, though uninformative. "Particularly since you, Peter Ambrose, are one of the main oppressors of neural tissue." He was stern.

We sat down at the table. There wasn't much else I could do, so I poured him a cup of steaming black sake. He took it in both hands, bowed with mock-graciousness, and drank it.

"I want to talk to you about the NLF." His voice was as sober as an insurance salesman's. "You are familiar with our work, of course."

I sighed. Dig for data and come up with dorks. An old story. Pavlichuk was a small-time tapper, selling dribs and drabs of spilled or stolen data. He existed on the edge of bigger things, like those birds that follow rhinoceroses and eat the bugs the huge things stir up.

He leaned toward me earnestly. "Artificial intervention in the brain is essentially a technocratic enslavement of naturally free brain tissue. It's a decision the conscious mind, a mere epiphenomenon of synaptic interactions, does not have the right to make. We, the NLF, speak for the neuron."

"But isn't your group itself just an epiphenomenon of consciousness?" If he could be difficult, so could I. "That puts you at two removes from your constituency."

"We're very reductionist," he said confidingly. "Not to mention fractally scale-independent. The NLF faithfully reflects specifically neuronal concerns."

Pavlichuk rubbed his hands together like a rug merchant, which, inexplicably, chilled me. It seemed that I had seen that gesture somewhere before. I couldn't remember where. "My life is taking a turn for the better, Peter," he said, as if we were old friends.

"At least someone's is." I couldn't resist a touch of self-indulgent bleakness. But what did I want? Pavlichuk to feel sorry for me? That was ridiculous.

"You have to look at things right. That's all there is to it." Pavlichuk did look happier than I'd ever seen him. He was typical of those who indulged in the edge-diving soulstyle, surfing with their toes over the curling edge, dealing, hustling, betraying, being betrayed—because he really didn't seem to be enjoying it much. Playing 52 Card Pickup as your only game can get dull after a while. And in his world, getting bored meant getting dead. "Someone's come back into my life who I thought I had lost." Looked like Pavlichuk had found another game to play.

"You've lost people in your life, haven't you, Peter? Lost them and thought you'd never get them back?" Pavlichuk's head jerked back and forth as if on a ratchet. It made me uncomfortable to watch it.

Painfully and unwillingly, I remembered Corinne. A streak of sweat down the back of her T-shirt, she stood on tiptoe to hand something up to me as I sat on a ladder, working on the basement studio. Light came down the stairs from the kitchen and through her light-brown hair as it floated around her shoulders. Try as I might, I could not remember what she was handing me. A hammer, a sandwich, a box of nails. It remained a blur. She held me tight, strong arm around my neck, as I pulled a splinter out of the dancer's callus on the sole of her foot. We sat at the bottom of a weathered wooden stairway leading down a dune in Indiana. Her tanned legs were smooth and long under her sundress. One of her knees was scraped and taped. Like many dancers, she fell down a lot, forgetting that the world was not a dance floor. I could smell her, I thought, her desert perfume, overlaid by the oily smell of suntan lotion. Did I really remember that? She walked the garden, early in the morning, blue delphiniums and darker-blue monkshood behind her, gravid tomatoes beyond. Her head was down, neck arched to show the vertebrae and the fine gold hair there. There was no way I could see that hair from the kitchen window where I sat, holding my breath. I remembered it anyway. Summer was ending. She'd gotten up early, not waking me, sliding out from between the sheets like a spirit. When I woke up, it looked as if no one had slept next to me. We'd had a fight, a bad one, the night before. She'd wanted to know what I wasn't telling her. And there was a good reason I wasn't telling her. I couldn't even tell her what the reason was.

As I watched, she looked off through the trees and her shoulders rose in decision.

"Yes," I said to Pavlichuk. "I've lost people in my life. And *known* I wouldn't get them back. That's how you learn to live."

"Well then, you know what I'm talking about." He pushed his hand through the hair on the back of his head as if to fluff it, a gesture more characteristic of a hairdresser than a datadork.

He rubbed his broken nose thoughtfully. "You're doing a job for Sal Tigranes, aren't you, Peter? Crazy boy. Plays things too close to the edge."

"Where did you hear that?"

"Come on. You hear, you hear. There's so much foam you can't suck it all down. Can't even try. Am I getting wanked?"

"Did you hear that President Gombrovich was assassinated by aliens from Rigel?"

"Rigel's too young to have inhabited planets." Pavlichuk frowned as if the issue were still a vital one. It had been hissing foam a few months ago. "But I'm just trying to help out. Don't core *my* spine."

"All right," I said. "Why should you be interested?"

"I worked with Sal for a while. Swollen skull, the works." Pavlichuk palpated his scalp. "Gives you strong neck muscles, that's for sure. And that weird symbol system of his. Interesting thing about that."

"What?"

He smiled conspiratorially. "It's got links way back, Peter. Way back. There were projects during the Devo Wars. All sorts. Early virt technology, some of them. Strange stuff, never became standard. Tigranes gets his out of one of those, don't know the name. You know who'd know? Lemuel, down at The Penitentes. He's got a handle on everything."

Now, Lemuel . . . That was a good idea, and I'd already been considering him. I needed something, anything, on Slip Sanderson, to act as a lever, and if anyone had it, it would be Lemuel.

"Thanks, Newt."

"Sure, sure," he said vaguely. He stared up at the vortex bubble. "Hey. He's done. My turn now."

Without another word, he got up and walked over to the now-empty Spiral Death game. Its previous inhabitant lay sprawled on the floor having a nasal stimulant administered by the waitress. Attendants at game parlors are required to have emergency medical training. I've seen guys hauled away bleeding from the ears. And those were the winners.

Pavlichuk climbed into the game and spun it up. He favored one leg, as if he'd injured it. I was in a heightened state of awareness where every irrelevant detail seemed significant. I had to shake it, because otherwise I'd never be able to pick out anything that really *was* significant. I paid my count and headed down to The Penitentes.

-11-

LEMUEL WAS SITTING AT THE BACK OF THE PENITENTES, A PURPORTEDLY high-class operation that displayed its memory interfaces spotlit on black velvet hands left over from some long-defunct jewelry store.

He was a jowly, sad-faced man. I found him staring sourly at a flush of teenagers who were learnedly debating the merits of various memory modules, as if these garbled visions of sexual encounters beneath the Taj Mahal by moonlight or on a table during a meeting of the Senate Subcommittee on farm price supports were works of high art.

Lemuel was not happy to see me. He was never happy about anything, true, but I still thought I detected a hesitation in his manner, as if he had expected to see me but had hoped that he wouldn't.

"Ambrose," he said. "Haven't seen you in a while." He looked resentful.

"I was beginning to feel out of touch." I wondered how I would get him to tell if he had anything on Slip Sanderson. He loved to gossip, but he also loved getting full value for it. "I hear Scamman's got a whole load of myoaugments he can't unload." I pulled out a foam fleck I'd just collected upstairs. Some of its bubbles hadn't popped yet, maybe.

Lemuel should have smirked. He always felt superior to such cortex-stripped business decisions. Instead he shrugged. "Could happen. Unpredictable business advances. He'll be able to sell them downmarket. High school athletes, that sort of . . . customer." He jerked his lip in contempt. Installing obsolete technology in your body was an evolutionary regression in his eyes, like developing beetling brow ridges and an occipital crest.

"I need some information, Lemuel. I—"

"Not today, Peter." Lemuel was solid. "Sold all I got and haven't got a fresh shipment in. Sorry."

This was completely unlike him. "But Lemuel, it's actually kind of interesting. I have an old friend—"

"We all do. Most of them aren't friends at all. Will there be anything else?"

I stared at him. "I just want a little—"

She appeared then, my cop-receptionist from Atman, as serene as a woman showing her ancestral home to a respectful historian. Her face seemed older than it had before, at the hospital. She was dressed in a conservative, almost uniform-like dress. I froze.

Lemuel scuttled back from his counter. I shook my head sadly at him. "Ah, Lemuel, that's a poor way to do business. A damn poor way."

"Look, Peter," he began. "I couldn't—"

"He had no choice," the cop-receptionist said, her voice as cold and smooth as an iced vodka.

"And do I?" I looked at her, suppressing my fear. She looked solemnly at me. Lack of fear did not impress her, any more than its presence would have excited either her pity or her contempt.

"No, Mr. Ambrose, you do not. Please—this way." I preceded her into the back room.

She hadn't traced me here to the Mall Half As Old As Time because I hadn't known I was going to be here until I found myself driving into the parking lot. She must have been doing the same thing as I was, trolling for information where it schooled most richly. But she had set a trap out, just in case—that bastard Pavlichuk. He'd fingered me. I was certain of it. Diatoms like him always flowed with the current.

Lemuel, for some reason, had acquired only one lonely ralfie. As if that wasn't enough, he would never let the poor thing finish decorating before he ordered it to do something else. We sat down in two chairs, armatures protruding through half-finished Chippendale legs. The ralfie was glumly dissolving a purple classical pilaster stuck in the middle of the concrete wall, and vomiting the waste into a gurgling nozzle caked with spilled foam.

An alcove to one side was occupied by what must have been someone's eccentric doctoral project in servomotor control. There were half a dozen complex moving soft sculptures of old *Playboy* centerfolds, each of them using the more-or-less random props that had always been supplied in those photographs. One was riding a bicycle, another endlessly swinging a club at an invisible golf ball, a third busily climbing an endless cliff, little Tyrolean hat perched on her head. Their oversized breasts bounced as they moved. Internal flickering lights revealed the complex of servos and circuits concealed beneath their silky skin. With a frown of annoyance, TerAlst spent a few moments figuring out how to turn them off.

"Perhaps you want to know who I am," she said as she tested switches on the desk.

I pulled out my flexicard and looked at it. Her photos appeared on it, front and sides like a mug shot, no makeup, no earrings. It identified her as a duty police detective with the Chicago Police Department, name Amanda TerAlst. The name was right, but the employer was wrong. I knew she was IntraCranial. I knew a lot about her that she didn't know I knew. I tried to get that to relax me. The card went blank, having given me as much information as I had a legal right to.

In a long-forgotten piece of promotional material, some flack had decided to compare IC officers to leukocytes. That hadn't lasted long, but we still called them lukes. Their jurisdiction was where the inside universe intersected with the outside. The hard covering of the nervous system is called the dura mater, which gave some of them another nickname. And from the looks of things, Ms. TerAlst was a dura mama indeed.

"You already know who I am," I said.

"Maybe I do, Mr. Ambrose. I'm not sure." She tapped an entirely functionless pen against her teeth. There was no pad for her to write on. She was probably recording my words on some slushware memory. Was a hippocampus-linked synthetic memory store a recording or an eyewitness report? Courts were still trying to decide.

"Can you tell me what you were doing at Atman Medical on the afternoon of the twenty-first of October?"

"You mean yesterday."

"That is correct."

"I told you, I think, when I saw you there. I came to identify the body of Mr. Morris Lanting. I knew him, vaguely, just to have a few beers with, you know, and thought it was too bad that he had to lie there, ID'd only by a gene trace. It may be just a formality, but it's an important one. It's important that we not die unremembered."

"Very nice, Mr. Ambrose. How did you know no one had already come to identify him?" Every question from her was a trap.

"I called and asked because I suspected that might be the case," I said, inventing quickly. "Someone at the office, a sympathetic sort, told me. I didn't get his name."

"Ah. Quite commendable. And where were you on the night of the eighteenth of October? That's four days ago, Wednesday."

"I was in a meeting with client, Kukrit Premasad, president of a Bangkok-registered company called Amaryllis, from six in the evening until midnight, after which I went home to bed, drunk as a weasel. We were discussing a basic labor-netlink for their plants in Borneo and Sulawesi—"

"I am familiar with Thai business practices, Mr. Ambrose." TerAlst's voice was coolly hostile. "They are not at issue here." The Thais were notorious for their cortex-suppressed labor, human beings working like battery chicken farms. There were plenty of jobs, even in the twenty-first century, where consciousness is not a positive labor feature.

I raised my eyebrows. "I assure you, Ms. TerAlst, I am not in violation of any techexport restrictions."

"I'm sure you aren't."

That meeting with Premasad was lucky, and not just financially. Most nights I just sat around and watched TV and ate . . . sausages, chocolate-covered potato chips, veal scaloppine, whatever. When I woke up in the morning I couldn't remember what I had watched or what I had eaten. That certainly wouldn't have made much of an alibi, even if absolutely true.

TerAlst couldn't link me to the murder and, try as she might, she wouldn't be able to link me to the destruction of the body, either. In other words, I wasn't guilty of any crime she might be interested in. So why did she scare me so much? Maybe she put the same intensity into every routine witness interrogation. I didn't think so.

"I see that you also have a rather cozy business arrangement with . . . what's the absurd name . . . Transcendental Transition."

That one brought me up short. Inman's company. What the hell did that have to do with anything? "What? I don't have any sort of association with them."

"You have had . . . dealings with one of its high executive officers, Mr. Ambrose. Thomas Francis Inman is his corporanym. In his day-to-day identity, he is married to your ex-wife." She looked at me as if expecting the information to make me jump out of my chair. If Corinne hadn't already told me her husband's name, I *would* have.

"My contacts are with the individuals concerned, not with the corporation per se." I hoped that was prim enough.

It was. TerAlst looked irritated. "A nice distinction."

"Law, as I understand it, is made up entirely of nice distinctions."

Instead of further angering her, this seemed to soothe, even amuse her. "True enough." She examined me. "I'm not sure you understand how true. You puzzle me, Mr. Ambrose."

"I puzzle myself."

Her flash of good mood vanished. "A simple symbol-parsing algorithm can come up with a response like that. And be just as honest."

She was obviously not taken with me. A pity, because suddenly I very much wanted her to like me. I had the feeling her respect was not easily earned. Under her drooping lids her eyes were not brown at all, but a blue so dark it verged on brown. Perhaps it was also the weight of intelligence behind them that made them seem so dark. They glittered at me like a scalpel. One glance and you wished they would look somewhere else.

"You wander into a murder investigation, witness the destruction of the body and the ambulance, and then vanish, not waiting to answer any questions. Why did you do that?" Now she seemed idly curious, making conversation.

"I was afraid." That was an honest answer, as far as it went. "I didn't know a damn thing about it and I didn't want to get involved. I'm sorry that made you think I had done it."

"Let me decide whether you know anything about it. You may have seen something significant and not realized it. Do you remember what the weather was like outside that day?"

I met her eyes. "Sunny, bright, cold."

"Could you see the sunlight through the doors?"

And that was the way it went. She ran me through every detail of the minutes leading up to the destruction of the ambulance and what happened after. I felt like I was riding a roller coaster made of razor blades. What details would I have seen? Which would I have missed? I wasn't about to tell her I had seen Watkins. It's a true art, the imaginary garden made up to explain the presence of the real toad, and I wasn't very good at it. When she stopped I was sticky again.

"Whew," TerAlst said, and her posture changed from erect to more relaxed. The relaxation took a visible effort. Her body was stocky, too muscular to be motherly. Her hands were wide and spadelike, with close-cropped fingernails. Two children, Tigranes had said. Almost college-aged, probably. "There," she said. "That wasn't so hard, was it?" She leaned forward, suddenly intense again. "We *need* this kind of information, Peter. We don't have a lot to go on, and we need it to catch the killer of your friend Morris Lanting. Does that make sense to you?" Her dark-blue eyes sought mine out.

For a moment I felt guilty. What if she was just a homicide cop doing an honest, dirty job? In that case I was merely an incidental witness, of no real interest. But she wasn't. I knew that. She was after something else. Poor dead Charlie Geraldino was just a signpost to her, something that pointed to what she was really after. I wondered what that was.

"I understand," I said.

"Good. I wouldn't want you to think that I was just slamming you around to have a good time." Before I could respond to this apology, if that's what it was, she stood. "If you get more information, you know how to contact me."

She escorted me out past the sagging Lemuel, who ignored us, and out into the tangle of the Mall. As we walked out of The Penitentes I glanced up into the overhead lights.

And saw a familiar shadow high up on the wall.

A black spot detached itself and fell toward us, almost invisible against the glare. I hit TerAlst hard with my shoulder and flicked the thing with the back of my hand. I felt the prickle. A simple, casual way of brushing past instant death.

It hit the floor and scuttled. It looked like a spider, moving with mechanical purposefulness. My world narrowed down to the crawling thing on the filthy floor. Olfactorily targeted, it was still perfectly capable of killing. I finally succeeded in crushing it with my heel.

When I pulled my foot off, it vanished, subliming into the air. There was nothing left to indicate it had ever been there.

"LOOK, AMBROSE, I HAD TO DO IT." THE MOMENT HE SAW ME COME BACK into his store, Lemuel raised his hands in front of his face. "You know I did. I even kept you from dilating your pharynx and spitting up your guts. Remember? You kept trying to—"

"Yeah, yeah." My head was still buzzing from death's running its fingers through my hair. I pushed past him. "Let's go. There's stuff I need to know."

"But—"

"Let's *go*."

In the back room, the ralfie had finished devouring the pilaster and was dangling from the ceiling, producing some sort of elaborate molding at the wall. With a wave of his hand, Lemuel turned it off, leaving it hanging there as if executed.

He sat down behind a hotech granite-slab desk with several 3D computer displays inset in it. It floated above the steel cylinders of its legs on superconducting magnetic fields. A desk light of interlocking dendritic crystals threw an intense light over the smooth stone surface of the desk. It was a dowdy old thing, typical of Lemuel's glassy-swell style. He gazed in puzzlement at his now-still centerfold girls and turned them back on. Their pneumatic movement seemed to relax him.

"She wasn't looking for you, I don't think," he said.

"How did she find me then?"

He shrugged. "I don't know anything about police procedure."

Lemuel had been arrested at least half a dozen times for violating various neural statutes, but I let it pass.

"Never mind that," I said. "I have something else I'm interested in. I think you might be able to help me."

I outlined my need for putting pressure on Slip Sanderson, without explaining why I had to do it. As I had expected, Lemuel was anxious enough to get back in my good graces that he did a little extra to help me out. In some ways, Lemuel was an idiot oracle: he knew almost everything, but had no idea what he knew. It didn't help that *I* had no idea what I was looking for.

From past experience, however, I knew the kind of compromising stuff that was likely to come out of Slip's office at CCD. And, what do you know, we found it: three bootleg aggression/attack circuits, aggatts, obviously popped out of autopsies at the morgue by someone who really should have known better.

"I don't even know why I picked the damn things up," Lemuel said, putting them back in their case. "Kind of a collector's thing, I guess. These things are Iron Age."

"Sure, Lemuel. See you around."

"Try not to drag the cops in with you next time."

-12-

"I'M OVER HERE!" CORINNE'S VOICE CALLED FROM SOMEWHERE BE-
yond. "Through the doors on your left. Be sure to put on some slippers."
Her voice was so comfortable that, for an instant, I imagined that she was
calling me from somewhere in my own house. One look at the patterned
lizard-scale organiform walls of her foyer dispelled that particular illusion.
I took off my shoes and put on some embroidered house slippers from a
basket by the door.

The rooms around me were filled with many-drawered wood furniture
that looked carved from living tree trunks. I edged past a redwood-bole
armoire that had its doors cunningly pushed open by an avalanche of
patterned silk kimonos.

Despite the expensive clutter, Corinne's place was incredibly neat. The
randomly dangling kimono sleeves were actually artfully arranged, held,
I saw on closer examination, by long silver pins with carved coral and
ivory heads. In a moment of malicious glee, I pulled a bunch of them
out, flopped the sleeves around, and stuck the pins back in.

I then did a slipper-shuffle step across the parquet floor into the warm-
lit kitchen. High windows looked out over the Chicago River, flanked
by gleaming yellow vases grown from six-foot-long fused flower petals, their bases resting in fish-filled pools of water. In witty restate-
ment of organiform aesthetics, the flower-petal vases held sprays of
null-g–manufactured iron and quartz crystals.

Corinne herself sat at the table in a dark-blue robe. She regarded me
solemnly, head tilted down, chin on thumb. There was a breakfast plate in
front of her, one on the table's other side. A glass of clear red juice stood at
her elbow. Cherry? Cranberry? In restaurants, she'd always ordered juice
by color.

"Good morning, Peter." She smiled, perfectly friendly. "You know that I didn't want you to come here."

"I know. But I had to. I had to." I stood, resting the fingertips of one hand on the table, shifting my weight from side to side.

Her face grew serious. She examined my face, her eyes large. "Sit down. Want some coffee?"

I lowered myself into the chair with a grunt, as if dropping a huge load, and pushed aside the plate. Gideon Farley's, I presumed. He had eaten well. I could see the remains of eggs, bacon, hash browns, toast, and orange marmalade. I'd always hated orange marmalade.

"Coffee. Sure."

She jumped up, glad of something to do. "Black? You haven't changed that, have you?"

"I usually put motor oil in it now, for a postindustrial taste. 10W-40, if you have it."

"Hmm." The silence was now awkward, strained by my poor attempt at a joke. I remembered how easy it had been to talk once. Sleepily in the morning, with her leg slung over my hip and her breasts just kissing my shoulder. Sitting in an evening-darkened park on a red-and-white checked tablecloth, our picnic now many hours past, me wearing a garland of dandelions she had made, she making some important point by gesturing with the empty champagne bottle. And way back to my first memories of her, me sitting at my piano, affecting care in packing my music just so and she, sweaty and sweet-sour–smelling from exercise, leaning over me, her silky hair escaping loose from her elastic and pouring down her shoulders, and mine. I couldn't remember a single thing we had ever talked about, just the sound of our voices, like wind through the trees.

The only thing I could remember now was the things we had never talked about. A small category. It just included everything important.

She placed a cup in front of me. She still wore the same perfume, a smell of desert flowers and sun-washed citrus trees beneath a warm stone wall. "Peter. You're in my *home*. I never wanted you here. I don't know why you should want to be here. And you show up right at my door . . . is it because of Gideon?" Her eyes searched my face. "He told me only after he had been to you. *I didn't send him to you.* Do you believe me?"

"I don't know. It seems a bit much to ascribe to coincidence."

" 'Ascribe'?" The corners of her eyes crinkled. "Come on, Peter, who the hell do you think you're talking to?"

"I'm not sure." I felt, and sounded, sullen.

"Don't be tiresome." She sat down with an exaggerated movement, clearly exasperated, and stared out the window. I stared with her. The apartment was in an old limestone warehouse that stood over the clean waters of the river. A sober red-brick neighborhood stood on the other side, dominated by the double, green-copper–capped towers of a Catholic church. Brown reeds pushed against the worn wood fences of the backyards. A fluttering line of laundry indicated someone who was not a customer of Sheldon's. A neon-garbed bicyclist forged along the riverside path, his magenta image reflected in the ebony water. He was the only other living person I could see.

"I talked about you, of course." She didn't look at me as she spoke. "Not at first, but later, when we trusted each other. *He* had information about you. About what you were doing. You'd become a man who opened other people's skulls and rewove what was inside."

"Something I learned—"

"It wasn't something you *learned,* Peter." At last she looked at me. A despairingly angry look, the same one I always earned for sliding away from explaining something. "It was something you *knew.* Something you knew all along, all the time we were together. Wasn't it?"

"It was." I took a breath. "I'm sorry, Corinne."

"You already said that." She brushed her hair back from her face. "If it had been just me, I would have told Gideon that you were a musician. A wonderful musician, hot and cool all at once, like burning ice. Clichés, right? But you were the best. I wouldn't have suggested he go to you to have his brain rewired. I did tell him one thing about you. I told him that, no matter what, he could trust you."

"Thank you."

"I don't think you should. I'm sorry I said it. You don't know how much." Her voice snapped. "What do you want here, Peter? To see if I'm happy? I am. I don't know what you got from looking at the convolutions of my husband's brain, but I'm here, alive like I never was. Is that enough for you?"

"That's not why I came here." I drank my coffee, trying to look calm as it turned to battery acid in my stomach. I possessed the unwelcome knowledge that her husband kept a professional mistress. I couldn't imagine a fight serious enough to force me to reveal that, but I did wonder what was really behind her life. "I was in the old studio a few days ago. It's all dusty."

She wrinkled her brow but didn't otherwise react. "Is that so unusual? It's in your own basement."

I shrugged. "I don't go there much."

She stared at me, her look, I thought, a trifle pitying.

"Do you have a studio here?" I asked.

A slight change in her posture indicated her wariness. "I do. Gideon put one in for me."

"May I see it?"

Her hand wandered up to her bare throat. "Is there a reason for this?"

"There is."

She led me down a long hall, doors opening out to either side. I tried not to peek, but found myself craning my head into each room we passed. Two guest bedrooms, one austere and crystalline, one heavy with mahogany and plump feather beds. Gideon Farley's masculine office, unmasculinely neat. A jungle-filled bathroom. And a small, empty peach-colored room with a door leading to the master bedroom. Its ceiling was painted with puffy cumulus clouds. I blinked at it.

With quiet firmness, Corinne pulled shut the door. "Don't be so nosy, Peter." She sounded more tired than annoyed.

"Corinne," I said. "If we'd had a daughter, what would you have named her?"

"Melissa." She didn't hesitate. "I've always liked that name. I would have let her hair grow long and brushed it for her."

"So why haven't you and Gideon had any children?"

"Damn it, Peter!" She rounded on me.

"Is he too busy, or are you?"

"It's not a matter of busy." She leaned against the wall, as if we were standing together on the street somewhere, just talking. "Although things do seem to move too fast. It's just that . . . Gideon doesn't feel that we are in a safe place to have children."

I looked down the long hallway. "Where in the world would be safe?"

"Not here, Peter." Her voice was matter of fact. "Certainly not here. That's our world." She straightened and pushed herself away from the wall. "But this is none of your business."

"You're right." We kept walking.

The studio was a large room with a polished wood floor. The front and one side were mirrors, while the back had high false windows with a view of slowly tumbling clouds lit from below, as by a burning city. It looked more like a place to perform some sort of philosophical physics experiment than a dance studio.

She watched me carefully as I walked across the springy floor to the piano in the corner. I pulled out the bench and sat on it. I ran my fingers across the textured, vat-grown ivory keys. They were as responsive as living things.

"You kept it," I said.

She shrugged. "You insisted I take it, remember? It's a good piano. Don't read too much into it."

"I won't." I leaned back and looked at myself in the mirror. Burning clouds boiled above my head, looking like obscene thought balloons in a comic. This was my piano, the one I'd played for all the years of our marriage. When we split I found I couldn't imagine playing it anymore, and forced it on a reluctant Corinne along with a lot of other stuff, a hell of a half-ton keepsake. I'd missed it immediately, but had never called her.

"Corinne, I—" My throat felt clogged with dust, as if I had been buried for a long time and had only just been exhumed by indifferent archaeologists.

I began to play, just some light piano-bar tunes, nothing that occupied much of my mind. I could drink a margarita, flirt with the waitress, and talk personal tragedies to several customers while playing their requests, wondering the whole time if they were any more honest than I was. A damnable skill, it sometimes made me feel like a player piano that had developed intelligence for no good purpose.

"Corinne, I came here because I need your help." The notes flowed out from under my fingers. Without them to skate my words on, I would fall through into the freezing darkness that lay beneath the music.

"What do you want from me?" Her voice was anguished, the same tone she had always reached late at night, after futile attempts to reach for whatever it was that I wasn't telling her. I glanced at her, quickly and away. She stood with her forehead against the mirror, like a small child trying to communicate with the image she saw there, the image of the only person who had a chance of understanding her. Her fingers slid along, seeking human flesh and finding nothing but cold glass.

"I need you to tell me who I am." Cole Porter, there, now *that* made sense. I almost found myself paying attention to it. Paying attention to anything, except—

It was hard as turning my head to look at the backyard had been, the other morning. Reality seemed soft, until you pushed it and found it had sharp points. I lowered myself onto them.

"I never told you . . . anything," I said. "And guess what, Corinne? I still won't. I just hope I can tell you enough to make you understand. Understand enough to help me."

She slid her back down the mirror, legs spread out wide in second position, feet pointed, until her behind touched the floor. She leaned her weight forward on her elbows, back perfectly straight. I could see that

she wore dancer's tights under her robe. She walked her elbows over
to her right leg to stretch. Hair cascaded over her knee. Despite myself,
I felt a surge of desire. I shook my head to clear it. She wasn't my wife
any more.

"*Let* me understand, Peter. Don't make me. You can't. You can't make
me do anything."

"Ain't that the truth." I didn't try to laugh. "Before we met I came from
a bad place. I won't tell you anything about it except that it was a project
involved in the Wars of Devolution."

"You never—"

"I never *told you*. I know." I found myself attempting a Chopin Noc-
turne, an absolutely ridiculous thing to do, and sounded like dinner plates
being thrown down the basement stairs. I switched to a medley of pop hits
from the Eighties and Nineties. I couldn't remember a single one of their
names. I didn't think anyone could. "I came out of there, met you, and
decided that the best thing I could ever do was forget that. Forget what
I had been through, forget my family, forget . . . everything. Start over."

"Your family. . . ." Her voice was musing, her hair now over her left
knee. I could see the clean definition of the muscles of her calf and inner
thigh. She hadn't lost anything there.

"Not a biological family. But who assorts genetically anymore? It
was the only family I ever really knew. They found us, through some
winnowing paradigm, damaged children, veterans of a dozen foster homes,
deserters from those vicious wars fought between domestic walls, and
gave us something we had never had. A home. All I remember of my
childhood, my real childhood, is a haze of television and refrigerator doors.
I remember a few magnets shaped like fruit. . . ."

"You poor children! No one should bring children into a situation like
that." Her voice came from under her hair. "It's not fair. They have no
way to defend themselves." I looked at her, and wondered who it was,
between her and Gideon, who refused to have children.

"We were crazy, I guess, all of us. We lived in abandoned barracks
somewhere in the Oregon desert. The furniture looked like something a
college fraternity had thrown out. Dust got all over everything. And we
sat around and had late-night technical bull sessions instead of bedtime
stories. That was my family."

"Peter, are you all right?" Corinne shook my shoulder. My claw-tight
fingers held the keyboard in a cacophonous chord, the sustain pedal
making sure it dangled slowly as it died. I pulled my fingers back and
dropped them in my lap. The piano was silent.

"I'm all right." She kept her hand on my shoulder. "I made sure I forgot it all." I looked up at her. "I locked it away, piece by piece, until there wasn't anything left. It was dangerous. We'd been involved in things that should have never seen the light of day."

There were tears in her eyes. She blinked, and I could see her annoyance at herself. Never cry over ex-husbands. It was a sensible rule. "Why are you telling all this to me now?"

"Because I have to. My family is back. One of them is dead. Murdered. I can't keep that stuff locked away any more. And you have it. I used you as the key."

She dropped her hand and moved away, drifting like a ghost. "You used me." Perhaps she'd suspected it all along. And suppressed it as the paranoid suspicion of a wronged wife.

I spun around on the bench. "Your movements. I used them to key in the memory suppressions. I had to . . . I had to use something I loved to do it. It was the only thing strong enough."

"You watched me dance so that you would forget."

"Yes."

"Is that why I felt the man beside me in bed get hollow, as if something was eating him away from inside? Because of what I was doing? Because of what I loved?"

"It wasn't because of what you were doing. It was because of what I wanted. Needed. I thought forgetting would make me whole."

She shook her head. "You always were such a fucking idiot, Peter." Her tone was contemplative, not angry. "A telescope with its end stuck in the dirt."

"That's me." I listened to my tone. "Oh, damn it, Corinne, I don't mean to be flip. Don't . . . get mad at me. I just . . ." I wanted to go over to her, take her into my arms, feel her breath against me. I wanted to be able to fly. "I've come to you for help. I tied my memory to you, without telling you. It was a way of . . . tying us together. A stupid way. Just as soon give you control of a valve in my aorta so that you will love me. You don't have to give it back to me. That's what it was about, wasn't it? Free choice. But I'm asking. I'm asking you to help me." Meaningless words jostled each other on my tongue. I wanted to say everything at once, and ended up saying nothing.

She didn't speak. She just reached down and pulled her robe off over her head. Underneath she wore a turquoise leotard. She'd been ready to dance, then, when I showed up. She'd been sitting in her kitchen, grabbing a last cup of coffee before getting to work. Sometimes I'd wondered if she'd quit, if being married to a wealthy man had made her give it up. I should have known better.

She took an elastic band from a speaker and tied her hair back. "Let's get to work then."

We'd worked on a lot of pieces together over the years, from the experimental to the frankly archaic. And in them, tied to the music and the movement, were the keys to my memories.

We worked through the afternoon. She remembered almost every movement flawlessly. And *she* had to remember them. I couldn't, any more than a lock can generate its own key. She slid across that polished floor and twisted in the air, each movement tearing across my vision like a lightning bolt. I played better than I ever had alone. The piano seemed to flex under my fingers.

When it was done, when she had gone through our entire repertoire, she slumped down against the mirror. Her back was soaked with sweat, her hair was wet, she gasped in great breaths.

"Are we done?" she said, forehead against the glass.

"We're done. Corinne—"

"Then get out. You know where the door is."

I didn't say anything else. I slid down the long hallway to find my shoes.

-13-

LAY IN MY BED, LISTENING TO THE FREEZING RAIN TICKING AGAINST THE trees outside, and looked up at the already-shredding canopy of my Louis the Sixteenth bed. Ralfies labored diligently somewhere in my peripheral vision.

Linden Straussman had always had carefully manicured nails, his only physical vanity. His fingers would not leave prints; they slid frictionlessly across things. I tried to imagine them white-knuckled on the ends of a rope around Charlie Geraldino's meager neck. It didn't make sense. Straussman had never done anything for himself. He was just a deformation in psychological space who caused things to happen without acting himself.

I could easily imagine him in that armchair pulled over by the window though, dabbing at his forehead with a handkerchief as he watched his old employee get choked.

He'd always come to see us after our operations. I remembered sitting in a sacrum-to-cranium brace, my skull healing, while he talked to me. He sat to one side, talking, and I couldn't turn to look at him. All I could see, out of the corner of one eye, was his hand. I thought it was his hand, anyway. Peripheral vision is much fuzzier than most people think. His hand lay on a table and I got the feeling he was looking at it too as he spoke.

If I strained my eyes in the other direction, I could see his shadow, thrown on the doorway by the reading light behind him. It was cold in the room, a winter high-desert cold, because the windows were open. Straussman loved to breathe, loved his fresh air, and would have flung open windows in the Antarctic.

He was telling me about our planned expedition to Kishinyov. "Proof of concept," he called it. Volunteer revolutionaries would have their "elective affinities" modified, their allegiances shifted, their understanding of who they were transformed. Sometimes I thought Straussman believed that ethnic identity resided in some specific location in the brain. He wrote some of the key words down on a little scrap of paper, a habit of his. As he spoke, I entertained myself by determining the nonfactorability of twelve-digit prime numbers. I got bored quickly. Even the surgically installed ability to perform mathematics didn't make me love it.

That sort of thing came later.

Finally giving up on sleep, I swung my legs out of bed and sat up. I felt like the room had shifted, but I hadn't moved. Straussman hadn't appeared in that photograph on Geraldino's wall. Where had he been that day? I clicked on the TV and called up the image of that photograph. Suddenly, as clearly as if I had been thinking about it the entire time, I remembered how it had been taken.

I'd been lying on a lumpy sofa in a corner of the east lab, lazily watching the exploded schematic of an experimental language processor as it hung over my head. It was Karin Crawford's design, characteristically idiosyncratic, resembling not at all the operations of Wernicke's and Broca's areas of the brain, the normal speech-processing cycle. She was trying to persuade a skeptical Anthony Watkins of some abstruse point about symbol parsing, one I didn't understand. I liked watching the unfolding diagrams, though, each of them marked with six interlocked circles, symbols of some other level of thought.

Gene Michaud hunched at a lab bench, examining an experimental aggression/attack circuit, an aggatt. It served as a new part of the ancient limbic system, between the amygdala and the hypothalamus, allowing for semivoluntary control of anger and fear. A print of the Emperor Napoleon was on the wall above him.

Lori Inversato, in this incarnation a startlingly blond African woman, had the skin-creme-and-ammonia smell of a hair salon, and wore a pink uniform with the name "Margie" sewn above the right breast. She'd just returned from giving manicures in town and was demonstrating to Michaud how to stimulate nerve growth into his contraption. Michaud was resentfully interested.

Hank Rush stood on the other side of the bench, his hand in the aggatt assembly. He'd recently replaced the little finger of his left hand with a laser scalpel and micromanipulator assembly, suitable for performing surgery on tree shrews. It had nothing to do with his supposed job as a digital encoding and deciphering expert, but it had proved useful.

Then Charlie Geraldino had wandered in with a camera he'd gotten somewhere, quite against regulations.

"A family shot. How nice." Watkins was contemptuous, but somehow had gotten up and stood with the rest of us, his shoulder leaning against mine, while the camera timed a photograph. Lori Inversato, reaching from somewhere behind, had tickled my ribs, causing my face's exaggeratedly pompous expression.

Lori Inversato. I pulled in close to her face. She had a lumpy nose, broken in some childhood accident. No matter what identity she switched to, she kept it—son of a bitch. Son of a *bitch*. Newton Pavlichuk. I blanked the screen and remembered talking to him yesterday morning. Fine-featured face . . . and broken nose. And he'd rubbed his hands, Armenian-rug-merchant style, just as Lori always had.

I brought her image back up. The face overlapped Pavlichuk's in my memory.

She'd been mocking me the entire time she was talking to me, knowing that I was somehow blocked from perceiving her for who she was. How many times had her path crossed mine since Bessarabia? I had vague impressions of other faces, all hers, stretching back over the years.

I took my box out from under my bed, opened it, and pulled out the ratchet wrench. The crosshatched handle was still slick with residual oil. I clicked it around, flipped the switch, clicked it in the other direction. I tried to remember what she had once really looked like, but couldn't. In her obsessive bodily modification, Lori only actualized what we saw on our phones every day. I remembered a stocky, strong-faced woman with a lumpy nose. A broken nose was an odd thing to pick as the single stable way point in a chaotic universe, but that was Lori's way.

How, in the ridiculous churning world of datadorks, was I going to find Newton Pavlichuk again? Answer: I wasn't. Lori Inversato could never be found if she didn't want to be.

I had to get her to find me. I slid into the nets and called up Pavlichuk's mailbox. I could just leave her a message and let her—the system informed me that no such entity existed.

Pavlichuk's box was marked DEACTIVATED-DECEASED.

I called up a condolence bulletin board and put out a brief message: "From the family of Newton Pavlichuk. If the shoe fits, water it. We need to talk." Let her demon spot it and spit it out to her.

I got dressed without turning on the lights. Ralfies cannot make torches; I had asked them more than once. The flames would consume them and all their works, and so it is not in their repertoire. In our old farm headquarters in Bessarabia we used torches at night, partially to avoid observation by spotting planes and partially to conserve generator power. It seemed romantic, but then, most of the villages around used torches and candles by necessity, their power grids having been knocked out by bombing. We could see them glimmering in the darkness, a vision sometimes brightened by a burning roof accidentally ignited by sparks.

I remembered one night at that old estate along the Byk River . . . or it might have been a succession of nights, all blurred together by lazy memory, which never remembers something new if something old can be modified to fit. Our dining room was in the center of a bombed-out old building with elaborate window frames. You could see them going up three stories, because the floors in the main part of the house had been blown out. When everyone was quiet you could just hear the rumble of the river below the bank. Torches left black streaks up the flowered wallpaper. A transparent tensile tent made the roof, as if we were an ant farm for some student's observation. The stars shone down at me as I sat at the table.

Watkins and Michaud came in all dusty from their golf game. They had had a pitch-and-putt course at Camp Fitzwater that had looked more suitable to the surface of the Moon. Here they had greenery, between the river and the labs, though a slice to the left would put the ball in the exhaust stack of the sewage fermenter.

"Lucky shot, that last one," Watkins said.

"Funny how skill improves your luck," Michaud answered. "As Clausewitz pointed out."

"Clausewitz was a wiseass."

They sat down on either side of me, grimy as little boys, coated with cow-smelling dust. The dirt around our buildings was half undecayed cow manure and made us cough on dry, windy days. Watkins wiped his face, smearing the dirt around.

"Those dorks are ready," Watkins said. "Desperate, even. Hell, if they could, they'd peel their own scalps off, give us ivory-handled spoons to eat their convolutions with."

"They want power," Karin Crawford said from the other side of the table. She'd been sitting there quietly with a book and I'd almost forgotten that she was there. "What's that worth?"

"Not your brain," Watkins said, though he no longer sounded sure. Perhaps he was remembering how much each of us had given up to be where we were. He looked thoughtful. "Not even mine."

"The Emperor Gaius faked epilepsy because he believed that all great military leaders had it," Michaud said deliberately. "If we could really have given him epilepsy, I'm sure he would have demanded it." He pulled off one of his boots and wiggled his toes under the table. The bench creaked. He always seemed more massive than his size indicated. "And showed his generals his EEGs."

"Gaius?" Watkins said, annoyed.

"Maybe you know him better as Caligula."

"If you *mean* Caligula, say so. Don't be so pedantic, Gene. It's not an attractive trait."

I had no idea who Caligula was, so did not contribute to the discussion. I thought about our Moldavian revolutionaries, now sedated in the old workers' barracks, anxious to become something other than what they were, their fragmented brains flapping like shredding sails in a high wind. I had originally feared that we would need to kidnap people as they scythed grain in the fields, tie them down with big leather straps around their heads, crack their craniums with brass mallets, but they flocked to us, eager to be someone other than who they were.

"The cooks have outdone themselves tonight," Charlie Geraldino said, as he wheeled in the food cart. "They seem happier than usual." He took the lid off a pot and started ladling stew into bowls. He rattled the lid. "Hank. This handle is loose. Could you . . . ?"

Hank Rush squatted down next to the cart. A bright flare illuminated his thoughtful face, right eyeball a gleaming nightfighter attachment, as he welded the handle back on with his little finger.

"The Ruthenian Hetmanate has been releasing hostages from northern Transylvania as part of the June 5 cease-fire agreement," Michaud, always aware of every detail of the incredibly complex politico-military situation, said. "Must be family. Worth a celebration."

"If feeding us is a celebration," I said.

Most of the kitchen cooks were Transylvanian, a vast improvement over the Wallachians we'd had the previous year, who had used food as an instrument of terror. I spooned a thick dumpling out of the stew into my mouth. The taste made me wish I'd grown up Transylvanian, so that at least my childhood would have been full of good food, if nothing else.

"Food is always a celebration," said Hank Rush, who rarely ate. Charlie reached for it, and Hank held it away. "It's still too hot to touch. Be careful. You don't want to lose all the skin on your fingertips."

"Thank you, Hank," Charlie said.

Lori Inversato swooped in from the night outside, laughing. She was dressed as a gypsy, and her rings and bracelets clattered as she sat down at the table and deposited a wooden box in front of her. She had a heavy, jowly face with a blotchy complexion and a noticeable mustache. A fortune-teller's scarf was wrapped dramatically around her hair. She always chose faces and bodies that discouraged sexual interest, at least from men. Perhaps that was what enabled her to wander through the blasted villages and return unharmed.

"Okay," Karin said. "You want me to ask, so I will. What's in the box?" She leaned forward, interested.

Lori laughed again. "I found it in the cellar of a building. Well, I guess there was a building there before, otherwise why would there have been a cellar?"

"Brilliant," Watkins muttered through a mouthful of stew.

"But then, if they blew the building up, how did these stay whole?" She flipped the lid off the box with her thumb and pulled out a gleaming crystal goblet.

There was a moment of silence. The goblet combined the torchlight and the starlight brilliantly, and seemed brighter than either. "They must be old," Lori said, "and waiting a long time for someone to look at them."

"None of them broke?" Charlie hunched over the box and peered into it. He wore a dark-red neckpiece tied elaborately around his neck. It looked like a Persian carpet. His face was pale above it.

"Not a one." She pulled them out, scattering excelsior all over the table. I had to fish some of it out of my stew before I could finish eating. "And there are eight of them. One for each of us," she placed a goblet at each of our places, "and one for the Director." She put Straussman's at the end of the table, precariously near the edge.

High above us was a door with a ponderous lintel, which supported the shattered coat of arms of whatever noble family had once lived in this house. The door itself, heavy wood clamped with elaborate cast-iron hinges, had somehow survived the bombing unscarred. It opened out on nothing, its floor blown away. Or almost nothing: the stubs of a stone stairway led down from it, clinging to the peeling-plaster wall.

Watkins, suddenly boisterous, uncorked several bottles of strong, leather-shod Hungarian red wine, and filled our glasses. With a casual tilt, he also filled Straussman's goblet, and the ruby liquid glowed with torchlight.

The door above us swung open silently, casting a huge shadow like a bat's wing up into the abandoned third floor. A figure appeared at it and looked down at us.

"Director Straussman!" Charlie Geraldino straightened and raised his glass in a toast. Suddenly we were all standing, shouting his name. "Linden, come down! The food's good tonight. Bravo, Director! We'll have this war won in no time."

As he descended the stairs we jostled each other, raising our wine up to him, shouting as if on a parade ground. We were tired, we had been working too hard, our eyes hurt, our minds jangled against the simultaneous tearing up of entire cities and the micromanipulation of nerve tracts, but we stood with joy, laboring in a common cause for a man we respected, even—

I turned on every light I could, bringing my poor housekeeping into cruel relief. I kicked dirty clothes as I stumbled across the floor. My heart felt like it was fibrillating, close to not beating at all. A breath was something too big and hot to pull into my lungs. I leaned against a doorjamb and willed the muscles in my chest and abdomen to relax.

The phone rang.

I managed a shaky breath. "Hello."

"Peter. Theo." An almost-familiar voice. "Which do you prefer? I'm glad you finally got in touch with me. It's been a little . . . frustrating talking to you, you know."

"Lori," I said. "How are you?"

"Never better, Peter. I'll call you that, since you answered to it the last time we talked."

"When you were Newton Pavlichuk."

"Dear, dead Newton. You just looked at him with your shiny little button eyes and didn't see a thing. And you guys always got down on me for fucking with my head. And body." I could hear the rain where she was too. And an irregular clanking, tinkling sound, metal against metal. "Damn rain. It's blowing right in. But we need the fresh air, right? It's good to breathe fresh air."

"Lori, I have to see you."

"You've been seeing me for years." She giggled. "All right, Peter. Since you asked so nice. Meet me near Benton Harbor, at the lake, tomorrow morning, bright and early. Say, seven? We'll get some coffee, talk over old times."

"Lori—"

"Ta-ta. See you then." She hung up. My system displayed her phone number, but there was no way I could tell where she was physically, except that it was somewhere in the city of Chicago.

I lay down on my floor amid my dirty laundry and looked up at the ceiling, examining it carefully, inch by inch, for a dangling bloodhound. A bloodhound can drop on you from out of nowhere and blow you to pieces. It happened to one of our support staff while riding a crowded bus in Kishinyov. Not even the people pressed up against him figured out what happened to him until they reached the next stop and the crowd thinned out enough for him to fall over. And no one ever figured out why him, why that particular inoffensive Macedonian plumber. Perhaps it was personal, and not political at all, though Watkins insisted that there was nothing in politics that wasn't personal.

TerAlst had reacted to the attack with aplomb, and thanked me graciously for reacting so quickly. And then she had left me there, for all the world as if I had just stopped her from stepping off the curb in front of a speeding car.

Gene Michaud had dropped that bloodhound. I was sure of it. I had a sudden image of him, stern, blocky, determined, stainless steel glasses gleaming like sword blades. Had it been a response to my tsuba advertisement? If so, he wasn't trying to kill *me*. He wouldn't do it until he had it back, something I was counting on to protect me. If he was trying to kill TerAlst, it meant that both he and she knew more about what was going on than I did. And that meant I had to find him. Or he had to find me.

-14-

LAKE MICHIGAN WAS HEMMED IN BY SEVERAL RANKS OF HUGE CON-
crete blocks. They had tilted in the years since they were put in and
ridged, rusted lengths of iron bar emerged from them like the fossils
of ancient worms. We walked quickly along them, leaving the forlorn,
winter-shuttered municipal beach house where we had met far behind.
The lazy waves of the lake slapped the concrete below us.

The lakeshore curved away behind us, to where the towers of the Loop
shadowed the morning sun. Far out in the water were what looked like
stranded stone ships, the vessels of accursed mariners. These cribs, actually
stone walls protecting water intake pipes, had served as mysterious symbols for generations of Chicago schoolchildren.

I had no trouble in recognizing her this time. She was back to her
original appearance, as far as I could remember it: a strong-featured
woman with thin, sandy hair. She must have had to dye it to get back
to that color—her follicles had long ago been reprogrammed to produce
hair completely without pigment, so that coloring it would be easy.

She had her broken nose. She had shape-modifiable sacs on the bones
underneath her facial muscles and extensions on the muscles themselves.
Her zygomatic arch had been replaced by an articulated assembly that
could change its shape. She could quickly change the conformation of
her face, raising or lowering her cheekbones, beetling her brows, swelling or shrinking her chin and jawline. But she always had the same
broken nose.

"Lori," I said, touching its tip with my finger. "How did this happen?"

She flinched away as if my finger was Hank Rush's welding apparatus.

"I don't remember."

"Then why do you always keep it? Aren't you afraid it will give you
away?"

"Give me away." She laughed. "You've never recognized me, have you? Not in all these years."

"That's right, Lori," I said, irritated with her little tricks. "I know you've been everyone I've met since Fitzwater."

"Near enough." She looked thoughtful. "Remember, three years ago, sharing a cab from the airport with a dealer in used slaughterhouse equipment? Black guy, gray hair, mustache? He built ship models in his basement, though you never talked about that. His hobby. Slave ships, mostly. You could slide the decks aside and see all the tiny people crammed in there. He worked late into the night. He just did it, never talked about it with anybody."

"You?" I remembered him, lumpy nose and all. A reasonable guy, weirdly familiar somehow. His heavy arms and stomach had been sacs beneath her skin that filled with a substance mimicking the resilience of body fat. She had almost-invisible valves in her navel, elbows, and shoulders. We'd had a beer afterward. We never talked about our hobbies.

"Me. And that woman you slept with a few months after your marriage broke up? She was a divinity student at Chicago. Angelic sort. She came up and told you what a mean piano you played? You always were a sucker for that sort of thing."

"I was. You were Hispanic then. . . ."

"Guatemalan. I explained it all to you. Do you forget things about women so quickly?"

"You confused me because your accent was more Honduran."

She laughed. "Screw you, Peter. I do my research. I was perfect—born in a village in the mountains around Quetzaltenango, spoke Quechua and Spanish. The accent was real—English was only my third language. Speech-center processing has progressed since our days in the business. I wonder if Karin is still into it. And I got to wear that great mestizo skin. Which you greatly admired, as I recall."

"I did." She had artificial pigment cells in the basal layer of her epidermis, which could secrete or absorb a melanin analog within the hair follicles and lower epidermal layers. The shade of her skin could change drastically overnight, under control of a circuit near her pineal gland. I knew that, because I'd installed it myself. "Do you remember being her?"

"Carina Maria? Not really. She's just part of my family tree, now. I don't think she enjoyed the experience, sorry to tell you. She was gay. Ashamed of it. Loved music, though, really a lot. That was kind of fun. I do remember that. She wanted to do you a favor. Carina Maria did that all the time. Kind of a sexual St. Francis."

"You deliberately came up with a personality that wouldn't enjoy what it was doing?" Carina Maria had had wonderful, and, I now knew, at-least-partly artificial breasts.

"Hey, it's an experience. Besides, faked orgasm is the origin of all religious ritual. Carina Maria was writing a paper on it."

That time I laughed. "Glad to help out with the research."

"Yeah, well, the time for research is over. It's time to get back to basics."

Lori Inversato had split off from the rest of us early, pushing the edge of the envelope when it came to the definition of identity. Was Lori Inversato still herself when she was a grease monkey? A giggly manicurist? A black man who traded in used slaughterhouse equipment and secretly built slave ships in his basement? A homosexual Guatemalan peasant girl studying theology at the University of Chicago? Newton Pavlichuk? The question was significant because she *became* these people, she didn't just act like them. She was a serial multiple personality. So who was she? Who was I talking to?

"Are you wearing makeup?" I asked. "Why?"

She pursed her dark-red lipstick-covered lips. "I wanted to look my best, Peter. It's something to do. Just changing your face isn't enough, sometimes. You want to *do* something to yourself. For an event."

"What event?"

She smiled. I'd never seen her smile that way before. Not even with other faces. "It's been a long time since I've had anything, Peter. You know how that is. We gave it all away. Do you want to know something? Other people aren't any happier than you are. Believe me, I know. I've been all of them."

A line of trees appeared to parallel our walk. They tinkled against the crash of the waves and the roar of the traffic on Lake Shore Drive beyond, and gleamed ice in the sun, vestiges of last night's freezing rain, which had torn off most of their leaves. As the wind blew, fragments broke off from twigs and fell to the ground.

Led by Lori, we went through an underpass beneath Lake Shore Drive and left the lake behind us. Ahead were the high, old apartment buildings that fronted the park, and the lesser structures that jostled for a peek at the lake behind them.

"I brought something for you," I said, and pulled out the ratchet wrench I had long ago stolen from her.

She examined it in wonder. "It's my old half-inch S-K Wayne. You bastard. This is a great tool. I never managed to replace it." She clicked the head. "That was a good life. Cars make sense." She put it in her purse. "Not that I need it anymore. That's not who I am, now. You think I can repair a car in these nice pumps? Which you haven't even noticed, incidentally. . . ."

I grabbed her arm and turned her to face me. "What do you know about Charlie's death?"

"Charlie?" Her eyes widened. "*Our* Charlie? What happened to Charlie?" She didn't try to pull away from me. "Tell me, Peter."

"He was murdered. In his apartment. Under the name Morris Lanting. Two days ago."

She shook her head blankly. "I didn't know."

"How could you not—" I stopped myself and let go of her arm. There was no reason she had to know. It was partly chance that I knew myself. He'd died under another name, another face. "Anthony Watkins blew up his body."

A smile appeared at the corners of her mouth. "Ah, good old Tony. How is he?"

"A shithead." I was surprised at the surge of anger that I felt. "As always."

"Did he kill Charlie?"

I sighed. "I don't think so. Do you have any idea who might have killed him?"

"Oh, don't go on about poor Charlie. He didn't *accept*. I do." Suddenly, awfully, tears appeared in her eyes, glittering on the ends of her exaggeratedly long lashes. "We've been so stupid, all of us. I missed you, Theo. I missed all of you. I tried to be a family all by myself, and it didn't work, you can only fool yourself for so long . . . I broke my nose falling out of a tree house when I was little. I don't remember where it was, or if someone pushed me out. I don't remember if anyone took care of me afterward. It doesn't matter. That wasn't my real life, my real family. I know what my real family is. You. All of you. And I want you back. Don't you want that?"

"No," I said, involuntarily.

She looked sharply at me. "You're lying."

I remembered the house I had grown up in, a dry barracks building, the old boards peeling back from shiny nails. I'd practiced my piano in the room at the end of the hall. I'd lived at my grandmother's. The hall had smelled of burnt oil and licorice. The upstairs hall, the one I hadn't liked, with the dark stain on the wallpaper. You could see the Oregon desert from the window.

That was all the childhood I had. Nothing but the Group. But wait—I remembered my father, standing in a doorway, light streaming past him from the hall. He loomed over me, his head huge, huge, filling all I could see. He reached forward. His fingers held the arm of my wheelchair, the fingernails precisely manicured . . . damn it! That son of a bitch Straussman again. Not my father, whoever that might have been. It didn't matter if *that* father came back to life.

"All right, I'm lying," I said, realizing that, at least in part, I was. "Do you know where we all are?"

She looked crafty, like a child with a secret. "Oh, not all of us—though mostly I can guess. Like Hank. Where do you think he is?"

"By this time?" I thought about the implants, the mechanical body parts. "He could be an automated orbital factory. Or a fleet of netlinked vans speeding along highways across the continent. Anything but a human being."

"Very good. He isn't any of those things, but he's like that—I hear. He *is* a factory. An out-of-business factory, abandoned, weeds all over it. I don't remember what it used to make—paint, maybe. Bathtub ducks. Don't know. But he's inside of it, digging away at it, changing things."

"How do you know that?" I asked.

"Really, Peter, don't you read your alumni newsletter?"

"They must not have my new address. Anyone else?"

She shook her head slowly. "Karin's still doing the old work, I think, somewhere. Gene Michaud's at war. Somewhere, somehow, he's at war. You know that. Watkins you've met, I guess."

"Charlie's dead."

She paused for an instant, then nodded. "Charlie's dead."

"And—" I took a deep breath. "Linden Straussman?"

For a long time she didn't answer. We walked slowly up the street, morning traffic becoming thicker, the sidewalks more crowded. It was just a normal day in a normal city.

Lori brushed at her eyes. "You made my mascara run, Peter. It needs to be in good shape. Let me just—" She stopped us there, in the middle of pedestrian traffic, took my shoulders, and looked at me. "I'll tell you, Peter. Everything. I'll tell you. I just have to . . . it's my own thing, right now. Do you understand?"

"No."

She laughed, a little shakily. "We'll talk about it. Right now—mascara." She ducked into a storefront Bengali restaurant and vanished around a corner. The tubby man at the counter watched her, eyebrows ascending in elaborate annoyance. He gestured to the waitress who leaned, bored, against the wall by the kitchen door and she, reluctantly, took up one of the huge menus and followed Lori.

I did the same. The counterman looked even more appalled as I also ignored him and stuck my head around the corner. A men's and women's, a trash barrel, and no other exit. She would not be able to duck out and leave me. The waitress grumpily emerged from the ladies' room, still carrying the giant menu, which carried the image of a multiarmed Hindu god with plates of food in each hand, and returned to her station against the wall. Shrugging at the counterman, who returned my gaze stonily, I retreated and waited out on the street, watching the turn of the hall carefully.

She was in there a long time. I began to get fretful. Perhaps she had climbed out of a window in the bathroom and made her escape down the alley. I pictured her doing that in her dress and heels. It seemed an unlikely expedient....

A slender man in a short purple shirt that showed his stomach muscles emerged from around the corner, nodded to the man behind the counter, and brushed out past me, trailing some strong scent. I stared after him. He had elaborately curled and oiled black hair and yellow-brown skin. I had no idea of his race. His pants were extremely tight. He walked quickly up the street, moving easily to catch up with a city bus at the next stop, half a block up.

Damn her to hell. She thought I was an idiot, and was almost right. I sprinted after the insolently strutting figure, and caught him just as he was stepping up into the bus. I grabbed his elbow and pulled.

"Dammit—" It wasn't her. I could tell that immediately. No amount of shifting of zygomatic arches and cheek sacs could have changed her face into the wide-eye-set, skinny jut-chinned one that now glared at me, not without major surgery.

"I don't know you," he said, tense and angry, squeezing the words out.

"Sorry," I said, at a loss. "I thought you were—"

"Certainly, Mister Flat Man. But I'm not. Not at all. Hope you find her." He swung into the bus, wiggling his hips in lazy contempt.

He had gotten up the two steps, when I reached up and grabbed him by the collar.

"Hey—!" He hadn't been expecting the yank and fell backward. I took his weight in one arm, it wasn't much, and deposited him back out on the sidewalk.

I bared teeth up at the bus driver. "Sorry. He owes me money."

"Handle your finances somewheres else," she snarled, shut the bus door, and accelerated away from the curb.

"You son of a bitch, you're asking for it!" He reached for what I had thought was his bare stomach but was turned out to be sudoskin, probably for a knife concealed in that wonderfaux rectus abdominis. Little guys can be mean and tough but size definitely has its advantages. I elbowed him casually in the jaw and knocked him back against a concrete wall. His head thocked against it.

He oofed and bounced back. I grabbed him. "She planned this, the whole neat switch. Tell me about it."

"I don't—ow!" I was enjoying being a bully and hit him harder than circumstances required, one of those short-windup punches that don't look like anything from a few feet away. The fake stomach muscles were resilient under my knuckles but didn't seem to protect him much.

He doubled over and I straightened him up. Then I put my arm tight around his neck, forearm against his throat, and started walking him down the street, back toward the restaurant. "You know it was a woman I was looking for. Any reason I should mistake you for a woman?"

"Hey, that's not—"

"You know who it is. Talk."

He sighed. "Okay, Mister Beef. She said it was just a trick. On a friend. Shit, she didn't tell me you'd be pissed. Bet off then, I'd a said. I'm not poking at people I don't know. Ack?"

"Ack."

"A little fun time, is all. Ack?"

"Just tell me the story." I let my forearm tighten against his throat for a moment. I could imagine it cracking like an egg. . . .

"Not much to tell." He spoke quickly. "Lady came up to me a coupla days ago and asked me if I'd be willing to do a little job for her. Simple thing, just sit in a goddam bathroom for an hour, then run out and catch a bus. Simple shit, and she paid well. Didn't say when, then she calls me up at *six* of the clock ayem this morning, says 'I'll pay double, be there' and I go. Don't have nothing else on so I go. That's all. Said I'd get away clean when you saw your mistake. Lied, she did, after getting me up at *six*—"

"Where is she now?"

He shrugged as well as he could with my arm tight around his neck. "Slid out right after you took off after me. That was the plan. Didn't tell *me*. I'm just hired beauty, is all."

"Yeah, right. Gorgeous. Where'd she first see you? Where did you meet her?"

"Let go of me. Let go!" I did. He jumped away from me, looking wild-eyed. "You—!"

"Just tell me where you saw her."

"Why the hell should I?"

"I can find out who you are and call your mother and tell her where you are."

"My mother!" He spat and glared. I'd pegged him as a suburban runaway. Looked like I was right.

"Exactly. Just tell me. Then we can both fade."

"Up north a ways," he said, waving his arm. "Near Upton Village." He produced a wire-knife from his false stomach, then seemed unsure of what he was going to do with it.

I nodded slowly. "That's fine. You can be on your way now."

"On my way! On my way! You grab me, make me miss my bus, push me around—"

"I'm sorry," I said. "This was too important to waste time." Now that he was out of my hands I felt a little sick, ashamed of having enjoyed pushing him around so much.

"You can just say that, just do that and say that, and you can't just do and say things like that." He accented his speech with the knife as if it was a conductor's baton. "Ack that, Mister Oil Spot?"

"There is something in what you say. But quit waving that thing around, you might hurt somebody. Like, yourself." With a reflex I didn't know I had, I kicked up at his wrist. The wire-knife whirled through the air. We both dodged its spinning blade. It clattered on the sidewalk.

He looked at me. "I've got stuff to do," I said, and walked up the street in the direction he had indicated, toward the development named Upton Village.

"Don't you be wiggling your butt around here after this, Mister Cold Cut." He picked his knife off the street but did not try to follow me.

"Thanks for the help," I called over my shoulder. "Piece of advice: be more careful who you take money from."

-15-

UPTON VILLAGE WAS A LITTLE COLLECTION OF FORTRESSLIKE TOWN houses frowning at the street, their entrances thrusting out to the sidewalk like tunnels. I knew I had come to the right place when I saw the wind sculpture swooping around the forlorn little park across the street, making the clanking and tinkling sound I had heard in the background of Lori's telephone call. Articulated arms swung around, banging into what looked like enameled pots and pans. It was probably an endless affront to the inhabitants of Upton Village. Lori had had the windows open in the middle of a cold, stormy night, listening to the damn thing . . . for the fresh air, she said. Something tickled at my memory.

The town house windows were narrow on the lower floors, high-arched above. The walls looked like rough-hewn stone, though they were really some sort of foamed composite linked to a crystalline skeleton—I had seen a show about it on TV. The buildings were sturdy, anonymous, their entrances far separate from each other. It was the perfect place for Lori Inversato to live and change her identity. Neighbors were probably kept anonymous here by some sort of covenant, or had an electronic signal that told them when one of their neighbors was about, so that they could remain inside, shades drawn.

I was preparing to ring doorbells, from one end to the other, when inspiration struck me. I could see high, upper-floor windows open to the air above me. I pulled out my flexicard and contacted my home processor. It pulled out the source number for Lori's call and dialed it. In a few seconds I heard the shrilling of a phone, coming from the windows of—I dodged back and forth along the sidewalk, trying to hear the direct sound and ignore the echoes from the hard walls all around— the third house from the end.

I walked down the narrow passage to the front door and rang the bell. I couldn't hear anything and the door stayed solidly shut. "Lori!" I shouted, hoping for a voice-actuated response. "Lori. It's Peter." Nothing. I pushed on the door but it was as solid as a slab of rock. I pounded on it. No sound, and I hurt the side of my hand. I backed away from the door. "Lori!" I yelled up at the open windows above, not caring if I pissed off the neighbors. The windows stood silently open.

I rang the doorbell a couple of more times, just for the sake of thoroughness, then ran out and around the wall of houses. There was an arched entrance diving below street level, heading to parking and automobile access. The gate was closing slowly, a car just having exited. Before I could think, I dropped and rolled through it. The alley was dark, only a strip of sky overhead, the houses even more dominating from behind. I ran down the hexagon-patterned roadway to the back of Lori's house.

Next to the fermenter and the recycling chutes were two guest parking spaces, both empty, and a back door. It was not quite in the jamb. I walked up and, holding my breath, pushed. It swung open, and I ran through.

"Lori!" Around me in the half-darkness was an elaborate kitchen, single-crystal–bladed dinosaur-claw knives dangling above a cutting board the size of a tennis court, a bulging buddha-belly stove in gleaming brass. The floor was resilient, like a taut muscle under skin. I could almost feel it flexing beneath my feet. "Lori, dammit, where are you? Why did you scrape me like that?"

Beyond the kitchen, oddly shaped rooms climbed their way up around a central staircase. I walked up the stairs, saying her name softly, as if she was taking a nap and I wanted to wake her gently. I felt the cool outdoor breeze blowing from above. A door stood open, rocking gently. I pulled it aside and stepped through.

Lori lay dead on the white rug in the top bedroom, one of her legs twisted under her. A shoe stood on its heel next to her, as if ready to be put on. Blood had spattered across the rug like paint flicked from an artist's brush.

Her head was turned to one side, and I could see the cause of death: a blow to the back of the head. Blood pooled by her shoulder and soaked her dress. A small table had overturned next to her, scattering toiletries: emery board, clippers, a small file.

"Oh, Lori," I said. "Why did you run away from me?" I knelt next to her. I searched her dead, still face for a clue. Her skin, stretched and compressed too often, sagged like a deflated balloon on the deformed bones of her face, making her look as though she had been dead for centuries.

She'd been going to meet someone, and had spent the morning deciding whether I should come along. I had failed some test along the way, proved unworthy, untrustworthy, and so she had dumped me to go to her appointment alone. And so I was alive and she was dead.

"Who were you meeting?" I asked her. "*Who was it?*" I found myself angry with her, angry for her obtuseness, her refusal to reveal anything to me, her being lost to me forever. "Was it the same person who killed Charlie?" I spoke more softly now. "Did you let him in too, the same way?" But Charlie had been strangled, not struck with a blunt instrument. And there was only one connection between Charlie Geraldino and Lori Inversato, one that lay far in the past: the Nimbus Project, and the Group.

I touched her sagging face. The skin slid beneath the tips of my fingers. "Oh, Lori." Her dying brain had sent contradictory signals to her modifiable features, and now she didn't look like anyone. One cheekbone was high and sharp, the other thick. Even as I watched, her forehead darkened, melanin spreading through the dermis. "You couldn't even die with your own face on."

A sound came, like the whistling of wind through a crack in a distant rock face. It came a second time before I realized it was Lori's doorbell. Stepping gingerly over Lori's outstretched leg, I activated the front intercom.

"Ms. Inversato?" I recognized the voice instantly. It was Amanda TerAlst. "My name is Ku Bremmer. I'm with Laurentian Biosupplies, and I'm talking with all members of your neocultural community about the proposed changes in your block's waste ducting. Could I possibly have a few minutes of your time? Here is my ID." She slid a card into the slot and her identification appeared on a flatscreen, indicating that she was who she said she was. Icy lukes have a lot of access, a lot more than regular police. Or maybe it was just Amanda TerAlst who had access. . . .

I turned and ran down the stairs. I didn't know if TerAlst had the authorization, or the power, to get in through the front door, but I couldn't afford to wait to find out.

I ran quickly and quietly down the stairs, imagining sound sensors, motion detectors . . . a woman's figure suddenly appeared at the door of the kitchen in front of me, blocking my path to the back door. She leaned against the edge of the doorway, hip-slung, one boot crossed over the other.

"Now, Peter, you shouldn't be running around other people's houses like this."

It was Priscilla McThornly. The sleeve of her loose, high-collared jacket had fallen away from her slender wrist as it rested against the side of the doorway. Under the jacket she wore a heavy shirt and thick denim pants. She looked ready for a hunting expedition.

"What the hell are you doing here?" I said. My fear came out in my voice as anger.

She pursed her lips, put a long red fingernail to them. "That's not very polite." She sighed. "If you want to know the truth, I followed you here. You looked so wonderfully *furtive*. It was irresistible. What the hell are *you* doing here?"

I didn't believe her, but there wasn't time to argue. "There's someone out front that I don't want to run into," I said.

"Old girlfriend?" Her voice was lazy.

"No! Come on." The doorbell whistled again.

"Hot pursuit! How exciting." She followed me out past the hanging knives of the kitchen. Her relaxed unconcern annoyed me. I felt like taking her upstairs to see the murdered body of my friend. Did I really want to do that? Just to see her face change? Maybe I did.

"Their security systems don't have any idea I'm here," Priscilla said, when we came to her car. "Probably just as well, if the police are around. Come on, come on, get in. Let's go."

"How did—" The door opened and I did as she commanded.

"How does sweet Priscilla get around security barriers?" She put on a pair of cat's-eye sunglasses and tied a colored kerchief around her head. With a whine, the car backed out of the space. "It was all installed for me by a friend." She floored the accelerator and we drifted, in the hissing silence of a good electric, toward the closed alley gate. She tapped her thumbnail against the steering wheel and the gate opened for us.

"A friend?" I said.

She smiled slyly at me, then whipped the car around the corner and out onto the street. "I like Tom to be just suspicious enough—but not too much. But that's a technique question, and you're in an entirely different line of business. I don't suppose you're interested."

"I'm always interested in . . . technique."

"I'll bet you are."

Priscilla was just the sort of woman to have useful lovers, perhaps even lovers who did not have to pay for her services, snuck in under Farley's cash umbrella. Another secret life, several more. I blinked at her, wondering how I could become one too. I would love to be someone else's secret. Even if I was only one of many.

I turned my head to look at Upton Village as we sped away from it. I had left too many mysteries there. Who had Lori met? Why had TerAlst appeared there? It wasn't to investigate Lori's murder; as far as I knew no one was aware of it yet. Had she made it into the house? Was she even now looking into Lori's dead face, wondering how the poor woman had died? Or had she given up and gone home, checking Lori's name off some routine investigation? I should have stayed back there, hidden myself in a closet, something. No, that was insane.

"You still haven't explained what you were doing in that house," I said.

She pouted. "After I save you from the police like that? Not very gracious of you, Peter." She sighed. "But didn't I tell you already? I was following *you*." She laughed. "It was pretty easy—you don't seem to worry too much about being *pursued*." She arched her back and fluffed her short dark hair with her fingers.

"It's not something that usually happens to me," I answered, nettled. And, secretly, frightened. Was I really such a wide-open target?

"Oh, I'll bet it happens more often than you think."

"Why should you want to follow me?"

She glanced over at me, suddenly serious. "Do you really want to know?"

"That's pretty much why I asked."

She thought for a moment, pulling her lower lip between thumb and forefinger. "I don't know," she said finally. Then she thought of something. "Did you leave your car back there for the police to find?"

"No," I said. "I didn't. Where did you start following me?"

She gasped in exasperation. "You never give up, do you? 'How did you know I had a piano? What the hell are you doing here?' Come on, Peter, give a lady a break. I spotted you near the lake. You were just taking a stroll, I suppose. Come out from Downer's Grove to walk around with an old friend, that faded woman."

"Faded?"

"Well, worn out, anyway. Is that the old girlfriend?"

"Never mind."

"Oh, my life's supposed to be an open book. But his? 'Never mind.' That's okay. We can play it that way, if you want." She took a corner with squealing tires and headed for the lake. "You must be parked in one of the lots near the beach house. Want me to take you there?"

I was starting to feel contrite for interrogating her. She seemed genuinely hurt, hiding it with sarcasm. "Where else?" I said vacantly.

She grinned. "I was thinking I could take you to my house for some coffee. I haven't had mine yet, and morning's almost gone."

I looked at her, but she kept her eyes intently on the road. "Sounds great," I said.

-16-

PRISCILLA PAUSED JUST AFTER GOING THROUGH THE FRONT DOOR OF HER apartment and listened. I listened too but didn't hear anything.

With a barely audible sigh, she swept through to the kitchen. "You put cardamom in it, don't you?" she called. I heard a cabinet open, rummaging, the sound of a bag of coffee beans hitting the counter.

"How—"

"How did I know? You poured a quart of it into Thomas the other morning. If he hadn't told me about it, I could just have smelled it on his breath."

On a table the texture and color of a conch shell's interior crouched an insectoidal Bulgarian espresso machine in multisegmented metalochitin. Eastern Europeans used organiform in weird ways. Just the edge of lacy wings stuck out from under the green gleam of the carapace. Vestigial, I supposed. Espresso machines can't really fly. I'd have heard of it. Two espresso cups stood next to it, grounds trailing delicately down their sides. Her housekeeping was good enough that I didn't think they had been there for days.

"I'd rather have an espresso," I said. "If that's possible."

"Even very possible."

Before clearing the cups from the table, she stopped by the window and examined the street. She looked like a lonely child waiting for her mother to come home.

She turned and half sat on the sill. "Tom depends on me, he really does. I don't know how he got along before."

"Maybe his wife handled it."

To my surprise, she blushed. I didn't take it too seriously. It's easy enough to put that reflex under conscious control, giving an air of innocence to even the most jaded. "She called me once. Her name is Imelda.

115

I have no idea how she got my number. Tom might have given it to her. She . . . thanked me for getting him out of the house."

"If I were married to Tom Inman, I think I'd feel the same way."

"Then she called me a slut and hung up. I can see why men have trouble with women."

"Was he supposed to be here?" I asked. "When you came in?" I didn't question the entire bizarre scenario, the made-up wife, the undoubtedly false circumstantial detail. It was the first place Priscilla's ability to answer my every question perfectly had broken down, and it made me feel more comfortable. I would hold the knowledge that Thomas Inman was really a man named Gideon Farley, and married to my ex-wife Corinne, in reserve.

"I don't know." Her eyes were unfocused. "He could have been. He comes and goes."

"Where is he?"

"I told you, I don't know!" She turned and, with excessive energy, cleared the cups and started the espresso machine. As it heated its water it chirped like a cricket.

The apartment was a curling-edge organiform showroom. The chairs were modified cacti with rubbery, massaging spines. The liquor cabinet was a whale's baleen. The coffee table was a huge green leaf. The lamps were grotesquely swollen protozoans, their mitochondria fierce pinpoints of light. They changed shape slowly, organelles tumbling inside.

"Do you like it here?" I asked. The place looked like Priscilla had used a deranged ecologist rather than an interior designer.

"Hell, no! Every time I sit down on the couch to read a magazine I think the lamp is going to drop down and slurp up my head."

"So, why—"

"A woman of pleasure has to surf the curling edge of fashion. Otherwise, what is she for? If all you want is sex, go to one of those con-supped prostitutes they have at a suburban spurt house. They sell themselves by the hour. I know all about it. I make it my business to know. The system downloads dreams of death, calm home life, classes on how to become a legal secretary, whatever they want, right into their heads, the customer programs the body to do whatever *he* wants, and everyone's happy. Great system. Replaces universities. No need for fashion there." She vanished into the bathroom. "Besides, I have a ralfie hidden in the bedroom. When Tom's away, I have it make chintz. I ruffle up the whole bed, then have the poor thing eat it again before Tom comes back."

I walked around the apartment on the thick rug, not touching anything. A thick, black umbrella leaned in a stand near the door. Farley had come, last night, in the rain, and then left in the sunny morning. What had Corinne been doing all that time? Of course, the umbrella could have been there for weeks, have belonged to someone else entirely, even been some fashion fancy of Priscilla's.

A wide triple window opened out toward the lakeshore, with a view past a high apartment block. I could see the traffic on the Drive, and the thin line of trees indicating the path along the beach. Indeed, Priscilla didn't live far from where I had met Lori. She could have spotted me by accident, here in her neighborhood.

A bookshelf was filled with old books with lumpy spines covered with gold lettering, mostly poetry and—I leafed through a couple, their names being unfamiliar to me—elaborate literary essays, all on thick, solid paper. They all had the look of being read, not just stuck on the shelf for looks. Jammed in next to them were a variety of picture books: a photo history of Chicago factories, a big book about the Columbian Exposition, wildlife of northern Illinois, one on quilts.

On the shelf above—I felt a tingle. Lying in a row were elaborate fetishes—combinations of crystals, feathers, enamels, what looked very much like human skin. I hoped it was sudoskin. They strongly resembled the symbols used by Tigranes's Messengers.

"Aren't those interesting?" she said behind me. "An indigenous art form." The espresso machine burped as it forced coffee into the cups. "Completely unmediated."

"What are they? Where did you get them?"

She pursed her lips in disapproval of further random questions on my part. I felt as if I'd broken some agreement, though I couldn't recall making one. "They're becoming quite the collector's items. City and suburban gangs use them as formal challenges to combat. I have no idea where they might have picked up such style. I suppose soon imitations will be sold in boutiques."

She was barefoot now, her outdoor boots gone. We sat down together on the couch and sipped our espresso. She had tiny toes to match her fingers. I could feel the heat rising from her skin. And her scent, which had struck me so vividly in the still air in front of my house. It was sweet and dry at once, like bitter oranges in sunlight. She was pristine and butch-adorable in her outdoor gear, the heavy cloth of her shirt contrasting with the fineness of her skin.

"I followed you because I had to know who you were," Priscilla said softly. She reached over and gently ran her fingernails down my forearm to my hand. The soft pads of her fingers rested on my knuckles and the sharp

ends of the nails pricked the skin between my fingers. Then she picked up
my hand and licked the fingertips with the fine end of her tongue.

My heart strained at my chest and I found it hard to breathe. The
symptoms of lust are exactly those of fear. The apartment seemed unnaturally quiet, as if hung with thick cloth. It even seemed darker than it
had been.

"And who am I?" I managed.

"I'm still trying to find out. Give me some help."

Her lips tasted like her perfume, just a little citric. She kissed with the
same insistent softness as she touched. The fabric of her shirt was softer
than it looked, and its buttons slid from their buttonholes so easily that it
seemed they had never been holding anything at all.

Her belly was round, all her curves smooth, not at all like Corinne—
and why should I be thinking of her now? Priscilla pushed her hips up off
the couch and I helped her pull her pants down over her hips. She rested
her full bottom back down on the couch. Her skin was flushed.

My clothing was more difficult, not being designed to be easily removed,
and it was some soft, giggled time later that I was finally out of it. Even
the air of the apartment tingled on my skin, roiling across it like warm
flowing water.

Priscilla reclined on the couch and put her arms above her head. One
leg, knee up, rested against the couch back, the other dangled down over
the side to the floor. I slid my hips across the softness of her thighs, and
ran my tongue up the fine line of hair descending from her navel. She was
salty, her entire body already covered with a thin sheen of sweat.

She murmured deep within her throat, a silky sound, no words, nothing
understandable. Her fingers tangled in the hair at the back of my head and
she pulled me up to her. "Hold me hard," she said into my chest.

I put my arms around her, pinning her arms to her sides. Her stubby
fingers straightened out, then grabbed at mine. She pulled against the
confinement, but not strongly enough to escape.

Her heel fell against the small of my back as she urged me into
her.

"I KNOW YOU KNOW," SHE SAID, HER VOICE NOT AT ALL SLEEPY. HER HEAD
rested on my shoulder, her hips against mine, knees against my sides. She
seemed too light, as if she was just floating above me, barely touching. I
could smell the last traces of her perfume above her collarbone.

I had been half-asleep, but came awake. I knew she could feel the
tension in my muscles. "Know what?"

Her head was turned to the side. She looked wide-eyed at her own apartment. "Know that Thomas Inman is, under his other name, married to Corinne. Gideon Farley, his name is. Much more interesting than Tom, don't you think? You should have told me, instead of letting me prattle on about—what did I call her?—Imelda, and all that other shit. It's embarrassing."

"It's because you were so snotty and contractual when I asked you, back at my house."

"Contractual. I guess I was at that." She took a deep breath. I could feel her ribs push out against mine. "If I don't take what I do seriously, what can I be serious about?" Her hand rested on my hip, and I felt a surge of renewed desire. Feeling it, she twisted her hips off mine, slid off me, and sat up.

"I don't know, Priscilla. Look at me." She was a complete mystery, this woman. Had she murdered Lori, then waited in the darkness of the kitchen, in the china cupboard, wherever, for me to come back down the stairs? It seemed unlikely, but not impossible. "What are you doing? Why are you imprisoned here?"

"As soon here as anywhere else." Her voice had a weary flipness that grated.

"That's not an answer."

She gasped in annoyance. "You fuck me so you think you have a right to interrogate me about my life? What business is it of yours? Or is it because I sleep with your ex-wife's husband? A family thing, is that it?" She stood up and stretched, beautiful despite her peevishness. She had small breasts, full thighs, narrow shoulders. She shouldn't have been as sexy as she was. Her muscles shivered at the full extent of her stretch.

I winced. "Priscilla." I ran a finger up her thigh. "You know I have a piano. I don't know anything about you." I wondered if my voice sounded false. She was a mystery herself, but she was some part of a mystery outside herself. Farley, Corinne, Priscilla. The dead body of my friend Lori Inversato. Amanda TerAlst. I knew no one involved, least of all myself.

"I want you to play for me sometime," she said, softening.

"I will."

She disappeared into her bedroom. "You want a story, Peter? All right. Hear it and tell me what you think." I heard a closet door click open. "I was born when my mother was thirteen. She gave me away—sold me, really—to an adoption agency. I hope she got a good price. An adoption agency with an interesting program. They've since taken their profits and disbanded. I suppose I could track the individuals involved, but what would be the point?"

I felt a chill. It was something in her tone, a dispassionate hate. "What sort of adoption agency makes huge profits?"

"One that keeps close track of their clients and directs their . . . careers. I was adopted by a rich family, one that had three other children, all adopted also. I don't know what their lives were like. Sissy, Karl, Tara. They lived through something different. We never talked, not about that. For all I know, they lived out happy childhoods. Except for Karl, of course. I'd call them normal happy childhoods, but I don't know how many of those there are anymore. Was yours? Happy, I mean." Clothing rustled invisibly.

I had played the piano in a quiet room at the end of the barracks. My older brother, Anthony Watkins, had given me little plastic trophies he'd bought in town and had engraved with fake competitions. I always placed second or third. "You might say it was. I don't remember a thing about it."

"How lucky for you. That gives you a clean place to start from."

"It doesn't give me anywhere to start from."

She reemerged from the bedroom. The outdoorsman was gone, a city woman in her place. Priscilla now wore a long skirt and a low-cut crimson bustier, with a vest over it.

"My father was distant, threatening." As she spoke, she knelt and opened a panel in the base of a hairy black cabinet covered with red spider's eyes. "I always wanted to please him. If you think that's a cliche, you're right. An archetype, more like. I think they had a deliberate plan. I did some research later. Dad, who I knew as Dad, was a chemically controlled sex criminal who'd once made a small name for himself as the Crosby Hills Rapist. You can look him up in newspaper files. He'd been put through court-ordered treatment, but someone had created receptor site blockers that could temporarily release the control. The court monitors never caught it. When I was thirteen, I suspect, he was supposed to rape me.

I looked at her. Her dark face was intent as she felt inside the cabinet, like an archaeologist uncovering an artifact. She looked amazingly young, almost a child.

"He didn't. Something went wrong, or it was a more complicated plan . . . whatever. I was thirteen, hot, wound so tight I thought I was going to snap and spill guts all over the living room. I was pushing, hard, against the inside of my skin. It was a sweaty summer, and I barely wore anything, knowing men were looking at me. At night I would lie in bed with the window open and my legs spread, just to feel the breeze blow between them. The wind had a tongue. . . ."

She found whatever she was looking for and sat back on her heels. Her toes curled up under her butt. It seemed odd that she hadn't yet put on her stockings. "So did Karl. My dear brother. He was a beautiful boy. Long hair, wonderful chest. Played on the tennis team. Looked great in white. A couple of years older than me. One day, we were just wrestling on the floor in the living room. No one was home. It wasn't innocent, of course, though we pretended later it had been. He was much stronger than me. He got me in a half nelson and I could feel his breath hot on the side of my head and he was hard against me. Not really thinking about it, I reached back and touched it through his shorts. I could feel it press forward against the palm of my hand. It was something that belonged to me."

She sat back down on the couch next to me and spread her legs wide underneath her flowing skirt. She turned her back to me and held out her hands behind her. In one was a soft, self-tightening leather strap, the thing she had pulled out of the cabinet. It was elaborately tooled, some sort of folk art. Slowly and delicately, I wound it around her wrists and pulled it tight. She let out a shivering breath.

"He had a strap like that. He'd borrowed it from one of his friends. He tied it around my wrists, just like that. Just like that. Then he pulled my pants off and licked me. Slowly and gently, teasing, not like a fifteen-year-old boy would do at all. Totally in control."

I knelt in front of the couch and pulled her skirt up. She was naked underneath it, her legs smooth and open. My tongue ran slowly up the smooth insides of her thighs. Teasing was not just something for brother Karl. She breathed fast and tried to push herself onto my mouth. I didn't let her. For a long time, I didn't let her. She moaned. Finally, I tasted the musky sourness of her. She writhed above me. I was in the dark tent of her skirt.

"I still like it. I try not to, I try. But *God* I still do. Yes!" Her legs closed around my head as she bucked herself against me. She came with a convulsive shudder. I sat up. She lay on the couch, on the side of her face, looking at me, completely still.

"No, don't let me go," she said, when I reached for the strap. "Not yet. We ran away together. I think Karl was really part of the script, or one of the alternatives they had planned, depending on which way I jumped. I don't know if he educated Sissy and Tara the same way. We ran off downtown and lived together in an abandoned warehouse. It was a wild time. The Devo Wars were ripping the world apart, there were the riots here in Chicago, the burning of the Robert Taylor Homes, the Jackson Park Assembly, all that history. Karl dealt psychotropes with a burnt-out Yemeni War vet. One day he ran off. He hadn't been paying his debts, and his friends came to our place to find him. They found me instead, and extracted their payment. He must have owed them a lot."

My fingers trembled as I clumsily undid the strap. I half didn't want to do it. She looked so relaxed there, lying with her face pressed into the cushions, her legs curled up. It would have been comfortable to leave her that way.

"Afterward they left me out on some piles of discarded roof shingles in the pouring rain. One of them wadded up an old jacket he found and put it under my head. That pointless kindness just drove it all in deeper. I was too hurt to move. All I was able to do was to take that goddam jacket from under my head and throw it as far as I could. It wasn't a cold night but I think I would have died of exposure if I'd been out there for much longer. I wanted to. I was rescued by a man, a very handsome man, in a red sports car. Silvery gray hair. Heo type. Nice suit, gold-nugget-and-citrine-crystal neckpiece holder. I remember it, glittering in the street lights. I've never seen one like it."

"God," I said. "Another modern archetype? He look like your father?"

"Yeah, yeah. What else would he look like? He was kind, took me up, cleaned me and got me warm. Took me to a Hunan restaurant, a little dive out near Lake Calumet. The fortune in the cookie asked me 'Do you want a job?' "

"And you did."

"I did. What else was I good for? I've kept at it ever since." She ran her hand down her side, along the satin bustier. "And look at the great clothes I get to wear."

"Who did this?" I asked, feeling anger on her behalf, if she refused to express it herself. "Who did this all to you?"

"I told you—just some people. Evil people, performing their own actions. Are you expecting me to name some omnipotent, secret organization? Modron? Nimbus? Some Atman project? Those are just excuses, modern demons, things that live in the technological woods and steal children from inside locked high-rise apartments and turn them into cyberslaves. Bogeytech. Netwanks raised to the status of myth. So don't give me that shit, Ambrose. I won't stand for it."

There, the anger—directed at me. I didn't really mind. The mention of Nimbus didn't make me jump, even as I wondered about its possible complicity in her story. Someday, perhaps, her anger would find its proper object. But could it? Everyone who had done these things to her was long gone—or a victim himself. There was no one left to hate. Unless it was everyone.

She looked at me. "So, Peter, do you know me now?"

"I'm not sure I do," I said. "From the story, I would have expected someone different. Someone more afraid. I'm glad you are still able to live."

"Thank you, Peter." She reached over and, for an instant, stroked the back of my hand. "Terrible things were done to me, I suppose. But what was it that Sartre said? What's important is not what has been done to us, but what we do with what has been done to us."

"And what have you done with it?" I asked, uncertain of who Sartre was.

The corners of her mouth turned down. "Are you pointing out that, after it all, I'm exactly what they wanted me to be?"

"I didn't—"

"Oh, it's all right." She jumped up from the couch and walked over to a small, mirrored table. She sat down at it and began to pull tiny bottles and boxes out of a drawer. "Gideon's coming over soon. I guess I can call him that now." Grimacing at herself in the mirror, she began quickly and expertly to apply her makeup. I'd always liked watching women put on their makeup. It was like watching a cat wash itself. "He's taking me out. His wife has some sort of charity work tonight. Abandoned children, something like that. She works hard at it." She smeared some sort of shining crystals underneath her eyes, and they disappeared completely, without a trace.

She smiled at me in the mirror. "Style hint. This is IR makeup, invisible under normal frequencies. It shows up in surveillance images. There'll be a butterfly on my face, if you see me through an IR security camera."

I looked at her. What kind of woman was careful about makeup that was only visible to someone suspicious, afraid, or paranoid?

"Where are you guys going?" I asked.

She sighed, exasperated. "Some event. As a heo at Tran Two, Gideon gets invited to almost everything. He rarely goes, and when he does, he takes his wife. This is unusual." Swung around in her chair. "Please go, Peter. Get your clothes on and get out. I'll talk to you later."

I put my clothes on slowly and let myself out the door. I had night business myself, back at Sister Death.

Priscilla did not look at me as I left.

-17-

"**I** THINK IT WAS ALL A GAME TO HIM, AT FIRST." SLIP SANDERSON paused by a wall of metal shelving, corroded from generations of spilled lubricant and power-supply acid from the cleaning machines stacked there, and looked over them, as if searching for something he had misplaced. "An extension of some diet-modification routine, you know? Hasp took stuff like that seriously. I've never liked broccoli, just as an example. The texture, not the flavor. Flavor's okay, but you won't see me fucking my head up to eat it." Brightly colored pipes arborized over our heads, carrying hospital fluids: oxygen, nitrogen, water, vacuum.

"I feel that way about marmalade," I said. Slip unsealed a door and a cold, dank wind blew past us. We were in the deep corridors under Sister Death, the roots of Slip's domain. Slip's eyes glittered at me a moment, then he stepped through. I followed.

"Huh. I kind of like marmalade, myself. But you can do without that, right? Anyway, first thing, Hasp took to eating raw meat. Didn't matter much what kind, or even how fresh it was. Big slabs of it. Neolithic diet, he said. Made his breath smell something awful."

The endless bright-lit hallway smelled of bought-by-the-tanker-truck industrial disinfectant and the pattern in the floor was worn away by the shuffle of countless feet. I'd never wanted to come back here. "Slip, I need—"

"But he didn't stop there, oh no, not Hasp." Slip's voice was hurried. I looked at the back of his round head. He'd gotten even bigger over the years, and now resembled a large, cruel baby. "Turned the gain up, whatever. He started sneaking in *here*. He had authorization, programming responsibility. Used the gurneys as goddam tureens, *chafing dishes*. Tucked hospital linens under his chin and dug right in. Livers, hearts, pancreases, you name it. Tasted great to him. Ambrosia. Couldn't stomach regular food anymore. A burger would've made him upchuck. Hell, a carrot. Tofu. Whatever."

Slip's hysterical story was interesting because when I met him, years ago, he was a ghoul. I suppose that sounds like a loaded term. It's merely descriptive.

A mental prosthetic, a virt, is an incredibly expensive device, as well as often an illegal one. It doesn't cease to be worth a lot of money simply because the person whose brain it's boosting has died. Where a market exists, marketeers operate. Slip figured out early on in his career at Sister Death that if the body was delivered to the family with rings and gold fillings intact, they somehow didn't bother to check if the fine-proprioception processor Uncle Frank had black-installed in his cerebellum was still there. Particularly if Uncle Frank had never told them about it. Slip thought of himself as running a neural used-car lot.

I had been desperate when I met him, sole survivor of the wreck of my marriage and life, clinging desperately to the only support I had: my old neural-juggling skills. Slip and I had been useful to each other, him slipping virts out of dead skulls, me slipping them back into live ones.

Now I was back for a friendly visit and he knew damn well it wasn't for any good reason.

"Hasp only pulled stuff from closed investigations. Things no one would ever want to see again. He liked tumors particularly. Said they tasted like truffles." He glanced at me, seeing if I was disgusted.

"I don't know what truffles taste like, Slip."

He shrugged. "Who the hell does? I don't even know what they are. Anyway, someone finally caught him—called up an old autopsy file and got a liver with bites taken out of it. They tracked him, figured out what he was. Big chase through the halls here. Got it on video if you want to see it. Stabilized hand-held, not too bad to watch. A few copies hit the malls. Last thing was, he locked himself in one of the rooms down here, boosted the gain on his modifications even farther and . . . ate himself. Part of himself, anyway, starting at the bottom. Finally chewed his way through his own femoral artery, bled to death, gulping the whole while. Best dinner he ever had, I expect. Wasn't much left of him when they busted in." Slip grinned at me. There was a piece of lettuce on one of his front teeth.

"Poor Hasp."

"Poor old Hasp."

We found ourselves in front of an operating theater where an autopsy was in progress. The door was closed and two uniformed Chicago police stood in front of it. Slip jerked his head at them. "Another damn skein killer victim. Found her today in her apartment, head bashed in. Or so the police claim. *Someone* thinks it's a skein killer, anyway. Son of a bitch."

I felt a chill, as if Slip had just pointed me out to the police. "Which skein killer is that?"

"New one. But no standard MO. One strangled, one bashed. Have no idea why they think it's the same guy that did them both. But hell, I can never figure out why the cops do what they do. I just file the corpses."

He led me into a bleak, underground office with several battered old metal desks and filing cabinets. Water rumbled in the pipes rising through the damp floor. Half the room was filled with boxes of sterile swabs, some of them water damaged.

This, I knew, was not Slip's real office. The real one was high up in the Atman building, with wide windows and a dentiform desk with legs made of tangled boar's tusks. But the person who had that office was a different person than the one I had known. The one I had known had lived down here.

"Now, you know, Peter, there's not really a lot I can do for you here." He didn't look at me, instead opening and closing drawers in the desk. "Security's tight as a bug's ass, if you know what I mean."

"I know that," I said. "I also know that you have privileged access. You know how to slide in and out."

He shook his head. "Things aren't like the old days. Can't just K-Y that little bug's butt, you know. It's solid up there. Iron sky. No way through."

"You know what we're offering."

"I do, and I'm real grateful to you and your . . . principals, Peter, I really am, but I can't. . . ."

Slip was sticking, hard. I didn't know the reason for it, but it couldn't have been a good one. Because I *knew* that there were still ways into Atman. It was the way the place had been built, and Slip had been in on it.

A building is a complex system, too complex for any one human mind to comprehend. They are designed by squads of people using expert software assistants—softasses, in the trade. Plumbing and waste pipes snaked in between supporting members and heating ducts. Software-actuated security locks interacted with IR intrusion detectors. At Atman, someone had snuck in egress and ingress pathways through the system. Atman's security had never been as good as people thought—the damn place was too disorganized for that—but this was a deliberate gap in the shield.

Time for Plan B. I love having a Plan B. "I should tell you something, Slip. Security's not as tight around Sissy-Dee itself as it should be." I leaned back in my seat. "Not too long ago I found three mil-surplus aggression/attack modules for sale down at the Mysteries. It's kind of hard to find those old psychotomimetic virts, as you probably know. They're classics, neural Duesenbergs. Some people are still crazy enough to buy and sell them."

Slip Sanderson was suddenly still. "They sell all sorts of things down at the Mall of the Mysteries. From all sorts of places. Whose booth you see those in?"

"Never mind whose." I silently thanked Lemuel for having put himself in debt to me by exposing me to TerAlst. "Only a lunatic would install an aggatt unless someone put a gun to his head. They might be of interest to some neural hobbyist, the kind of person who tries mental evolutionary regression to lizard-brain at home on weekends. But it seems that they belonged to three drinking buddies, Yemeni vets. Original users, from one of the early projects. The driver piled the car into a bridge abutment on the Northwest Expressway. They'd overridden the masters on the car and were driving free. Aggatts eventually hit your motor control, you know that, Slip? Not to mention stressing your endocrine system until it falls apart. Those guys must have been wrecks, sitting in that car, shaking, sick from the effects of one beer. Damn shame. But you must know all that. After all, where do you suppose the bodies ended up for autopsy and organ distribution?"

Slip's face clamped tight. "I don't supervise every body that comes in here."

"Oh, I know that, Slip. I'm sure everybody knows that."

Someone had screwed up was my guess, done a little private business without cutting Slip in or letting him know. Stupid, if true. There weren't a lot of those old aggatt hypothalamus virts left and each of them had been a virtual brassboard. I remembered them. Easy to trace. It hadn't taken me much of a correlation search to figure out who they had once belonged to and where the bodies had ended up.

But the Feds were still touchy about anything to do with Yemen. If this came out, there would be a full-form investigation of the entire office. Slip couldn't afford that, no matter how many times he'd washed his hands to get the corpse smell off.

I'd like to say that sweat beaded up on his forehead, but he stayed as cool as marble. Like many executives, Slip had had his sweat glands suppressed in the interest of good corporate appearance. You can tell who they are: they're the ones dropping like flies during the softball game at the Fourth of July company picnic.

He'd been glad to see me, in a weird way. An old buddy, back from the past, ready to talk over old times. After our business was done, I suspected, he'd intended to ask me out for a beer. Just to have someone to talk to. As we get old, we all run out of people to talk to.

Instead, I'd gone for the weak point. Even an old turtle like Slip Sanderson had some chinks, and I sensed that I'd just slashed in through one. I almost held out my hand, told him to forget it. We could go have that beer. Something. None of this stuff was important.

Instead, I just watched the skin on his face tighten as if it was drying out in an invisible wind. I wondered where he lived when he wasn't here. I didn't even know if he had a wife, if he played golf on weekends, anything. It didn't matter, I told myself. It didn't matter.

"All right, Peter. All right. Just a second, we'll get it."

"You'll get your full payment—"

"Never mind. Just never mind."

He slumped out of the office, leaving me there in the fluorescent light that didn't seem like light at all, just like the back side of darkness. Would he take a stroll over to those police guarding the autopsy of poor Lori Inversato's body? I held onto the arms of my chair to keep from standing up. The water pipes rumbled and burbled.

A rattle in the hall and Slip wheeled in a terminal on a cart. It was a modern one, covered with pliablack. He hooked it into the port.

"They're worried he'll blow this one up too."

"Blow up?"

"Didn't you hear? This skein killer can do anything. He blew up his last body before they could autopsy it. How about that?" Diagrams appeared on the screen. "There are rumors that it's someone way high up, with a lot of contacts. Maybe even someone in the police itself. . . ."

I sat down at the screen and started sucking secure information off of it. Atman was a maze of interstitial spaces. The space occupied by human beings was the lesser half. I plotted a route through the postern gates set up by old corruption. Most of the people responsible were probably paid off and retired by now, but their legacy remained.

Tigranes had told me where we were going, but not who his contact was at Atman. As far as he was concerned, if I didn't need to know it, then I shouldn't know it. But I knew that person knew who I was, had sent those virts to me. I had to figure out who it was.

The level Tigranes and I were going to penetrate was completely occupied by one lab. Among a mass of other data, I got the staffing for the lab into Tigranes's datacrisp.

Once it was done, the terminal spit the datacrisp back into my hand. I curled my fingers around it like a child with a piece of candy.

Slip smiled blandly at me. "Get what you needed?" he asked.

"Don't know. We'll see." I didn't know what, but there was something wrong. Slip had balked when he shouldn't have and had given in when he shouldn't have. Now he was all solicitousness. And just like that, like a flash of unwelcome knowledge that comes while watching the languid way an unfaithful lover takes her coat off after running some mysterious and unnecessary errand, I knew that he had betrayed me. Most of the information on the datacrisp was undoubtedly correct, but somewhere on it was a trap.

"You need anything else?" Slip asked.

"No, Slip." I put the datacrisp in its case. "I think you've done more than enough."

"GOT WHAT YOU WANTED?" SHELDON'S LOVER ARNIE ALWAYS WORE HIS shirt open, even though his chest, frankly, was not so great. He shook his long hair and took a swig from his coffee mug, which had a winking picture of Hector del Annas dressed as a gaucho on it.

"Yeah, yeah." Sheldon's apartment was starting to get associated with not enough sleep. I rubbed my eyes.

"You don't look like it." He sat down at the breakfast table and pushed aside a stack of hand-notated music. The top sheet was an arrangement of "Why Do You Do" by Chester Donato, with his scrawled signature at the bottom.

"Well," I stared at the screen on the desk in front of me. "We don't always want what's best for us."

He stared. Arnie often didn't know what to make of me. He was too straightforward.

Sheldon came out of the bedroom. "You got what you wanted, Peter?"

"He got what he wanted, but don't know if it's best for him," Arnie explained. "If you understand that."

"Of course I understand it, Arnie." Early in the morning, Sheldon looked vulnerable, his thin face bonier than usual.

"And just what is that supposed to mean?" Arnie's voice developed teeth.

"No . . . nothing, honey. C'mon. You want more coffee?"

"Sure." Arnie was willing to be mollified, if some effort was put into it. He stared out of the window.

I watched Sheldon walk quickly into the kitchen. This was a side of him I didn't often see: the nervous and vulnerable lover. I didn't like it, but then I didn't like anything that seemed to detract from the music.

I looked back at the screen. One name showed there: Helena Mennaura. It was a familiar name. I'd seen it on papers about symbol manipulation and suchlike subjects, and never given it much thought.

That name now cut through my forehead like a scalpel. I knew that it had to be Karin Crawford.

I remembered her, as sharp and serious as the bone-handled scalpel I had stolen to represent her. She sat on a wood bench with one broken slat, sunning herself by the side of the industrial chicken coop the Group used as its Bessarabian headquarters, and drew a diagram in the dirt with a stick. A thick book sat on the bench next to her. She was working out a favored theory of Straussman's, about identification with the group.

"You can create artificial ethnic groups," she said, shaking her elaborately braided hair, letting silver loops glitter in the sun. "Tie their identity to simple speech accents and let all the other artificial ethnic groups identify them that way, and have an emotional reaction. We can calculate the reaction. Shibboleth. It's been done before. Simple. You know the story?"

"No," I admitted.

She shook her head. "All these educated men. We heard all these stories in church. You really should read the Bible more, Theo. You might learn something. In the time of Judges, two Israelite tribes, the Ephraimites and the Gileadites, were having a war. The Gileadites held the fords of the Jordan, and refugee Ephraimites tried to cross, denying they were Ephraimites. The Gileadites told them to say the word "Shibboleth." Ephraimites spoke a different dialect of Hebrew and could only say "Sibboleth," and so they were taken and slain."

"Does Shibboleth mean anything?" I asked.

She shook her head. "Nothing important. What was important was the pronunciation. We can fiddle with Rumanian pronunciation and create five different groups within the city of Kishinyov in a matter of weeks."

"In weeks?" I said. "All that burden of memory, lifted away? They won't remember who they were before?"

"That doesn't matter as much as it might. You know how groups are created, Theo. By the Army. In sports team. At summer camp. With the right stimuli, people perform in-group, out-group signification in a matter of minutes. Change the circumstances, the groups change."

"Some groups last much longer than that," I said. "It would take a major cataclysm to change them."

Sheldon nudged me. "You all right?"

I cleared Karin Crawford's new name, Helena Mennaura, off the screen. "Can you do something for me, Sheldon?"

"Name it."

"I want you to send a special invitation for me, to the Club Le Moustier tonight."

He looked dubious. "A music lover?"

I remembered Karin Crawford sitting and listening to me play. She'd loved it, though I had the impression it all frightened her somehow.

"A music lover," I said. "Please, Sheldon."

"No problem." He pulled out a gold-edged gray envelope.

I opened it and, at the base of the invitation, wrote, "Please come. I need to talk to you. Theo Bronkman."

"You ready to play tonight?" Sheldon folded the invitation back up.

"I've never been readier."

-18-

"**L**OOKIT THIS," SHELDON SAID. HE HELD OUT A COMPLEX BRASS INSTRU-
ment that looked like a tuba that had gone on a diet. The maker's seal
glowed silver on the bell. We stood in a relatively quiet corner in the
anteroom of the Club Le Moustier, leaning against the shattered remains
of an interior wall.

"What the hell is that?"

"Really, Peter. You'd think you didn't know musical history at all. *This*
is the B-flat ophicleide played by Barnabas Barabbas in the RKO picture
Dark Summer. Remember? He plays it in that Havana gambling casino
scene. Standard Afro-Cuban, with that oompah band twist they thought
was so clever, but he does a good job."

"It was made . . . what, 1978?" The room was getting crowded, with
a mass of new arrivals pouring off the huge freight elevator every minute or so.

"Yeah, I think so. He seduces Paidea Forza with this thing. Then she
sings that Bahian stuff and takes all her clothes off. Remember?"

"How could I forget?" He'd actually faked up clips from the movie.
Must have taken days of work.

Sheldon blew. The ophicleide had a deep, low bugle sound, sensuous,
in an odd way. More likely to attract a woolly mammoth than a woman,
but there seemed no reason to tell Sheldon that.

He collected a bit of an audience. The people coming into Le Moustier
were ready for music, and expected it to slide into their ears from some
unexpected direction. I could see the gold-edged gray envelopes in their
hands, emblems of our shared obsession. Getting an impromptu concert
while in the anteroom was an extra treat.

Sheldon stopped, bowed expressionlessly to the applause, and put the
instrument back in its fur-lined leather case. His self-consciously cool
demeanor couldn't conceal the gleam of joy in his eyes. I felt the shivering

133

tension of anticipation myself. The air felt thinner and colder, as if I had climbed to a great height and looked out over a familiar but mysterious landscape.

"Let's go," Sheldon said. "We gotta get warmed up onstage."

"Sure." I helped him pick up a couple of instrument cases he had with him. A pianist brings nothing with him but his fingers, and is thus at a disadvantage when subtly demonstrating his status. Hauling the oddly bulking leather cases gave me a visible definition, even if I wasn't quite sure what instruments were inside them.

Several circular doors cut their way through the wall ahead of us like the mouthparts of abyssal segmented worms. Their huge, brass-coated irises dilated and closed, allowing only the elect through.

"Hey, listen!" someone complained. "This is ridiculous. I'm with *her*." A large man in an expensive suit, his neckpiece holder a huge gold eagle, bent over to yell at one of the tiny Asian men who guarded the doors. "She's got an invitation."

"Sorry. You no can go."

He kept one hand on the elbow of a serious-faced woman with long dark hair, who looked like she would rather have been almost anywhere else.

"Why not?"

"You no have invitation."

"But I just told you, *she*—"

"She go. You no go."

She put a hand on the man's shoulder. "I warned you, honey. They don't allow—"

He shook her hand off. "Then why the hell do you want to go? Let's get out of here. We can get to L'Angoulême for dinner. They know me there."

Her eyebrows went up. "I'm going in. I'll see you after the concert." The two men at the door took her invitation, bowed, and swept her in. They then turned to the man with cheerfully deadpan faces, ready to bounce him out on his ass. Their heads barely came up to his shoulders.

"No you won't!" he yelled after her, then turned and stalked out. The crowd applauded him, almost as delighted by his performance as they had been by Sheldon's.

Le Moustier existed only as a temporary intersection of lives and music. People whose lives ordinarily did not come close to each other reacted here, in this separate event space. The gate guards, operating under Le Moustier policy, stripped the invited guests of allies, friends, associates, and forced them to enter as social ions. The music put them in an excited energy state and, interacting directly with others, they formed new bonds and alliances.

There was a time when Club Le Moustier became outrageously forward shock, and everyone was desperate for an invitation. Incensed, since he knew that only a small fraction of the people who wanted to get in were interested in the music, Sheldon let everyone in and then oppressed them with an endless concert of droning Tibetan chants performed by alcoholic alley nomads. The climax came when the white-bearded priest directing the choir puked noisily in the lap of a well-dressed woman sitting in the front row. Le Moustier did not stay forward shock for long.

The guards inclined their heads at us and waved us through. They were recent immigrants from various Chinese republics, kingdoms, domains, warlordships, commanderies, hegemonies. Most of them spoke no English. The other club employees communicated with them via a device which turned spoken English into flowing ideograms glowing in the air. Their dialects of Chinese were mutually unintelligible by sound so they used the same device to speak with each other, since the written form was always the same. Some of them sat on the floor in a corner, eating rice from small bowls, spinning ideograms in the air above them marking some fierce argument.

We climbed up on stage and looked out onto a stippled fabric made of countless faces. Segmented cherry pickers hauled tightly packed parties high up above, in lieu of normal balconies. The crane operators jockeyed for position, manipulating their delightedly shrieking payloads as if they were of no more account than video images. I searched for Karin Crawford's face, a task as futile as picking one particular jelly bean off a crowded conveyor belt.

The printed sheet music on the piano was, according to the information on the back, from a music publishing house called Aaron und Ismail in Beirut, The Lebanon. The text was in French, with Arabic and Hebrew addenda. On the back was a crescent moon with icicles hanging from it.

"Hey, Sheldon," I said, flipping through the sheet music. "This stuff looks a little like Cairene retro-hajj stuff. Egypto-Syriac Renascence. Like what the Topeka people played in the early Nineties, from all those Arabic immigrants in Kansas. You remember, Shara Shirkut, Aziz Mufuela, Bamboose the Turk, those guys." I loved Sheldon's universe, much more than I loved the real past. It was as lush as a rain forest.

Sheldon shook his head, smiling. "Not a bit of it, Peter. This here's Falafel. French-Jewish-Arabic stuff from the Lebanon hill country. Jewish settlers thought it up, Christians in the city picked it up, Moslems jazzed it up and brought it to the States. Mufuela *did* cut a couple of sides of Falafel-influenced stuff with that group, Lecompton Constitution."

"Yeah, right," I said, though I had no idea. He could always top me.

We started to play. It was weird, but not at all bad, with lots of sweetly intricate guitar work and tangled chord transitions that tied my fingers into knots. Forget blue notes, the brass section played Arabic quarter tones, shrieking and wailing. Sheldon stood up and soloed. He played an oddly shaped silver-valved trombone that didn't even seem to be tuned to a normal scale. I couldn't tell what it *was* tuned to, so maybe the claim that piano players ruin their ears by constantly listening to the well-tempered scales of their instrument is true. The twenty-two *srutis* of Indian music? Some hypothetical computer series?

So I sat there, on display, and played. I was giving Karin Crawford— now called Helena Mennaura—a choice. I sat before her, visible and vulnerable. I knew that if I had tracked her down, to her home, to her office at Atman, and confronted her, she would have frozen, closed in, become completely unresponsive. She'd always liked doing things her own way in her own time. I didn't know if she was out there in the audience, and if out there, whether she would stay or slip away without confrontation. So I played.

The night suspended itself while we sawed away at it with our music. At a head gesture, a waiter started bringing me raki, bitter aniseed liquor from the same mythical Mandated Lebanon the music came from, alternating with cups of thick Turkish coffee. As we played I could see the skeptical Wynans blowing his tenor sax for all he was worth. Whether or not he believed in Sheldon's alternate universe, he was obviously starting to believe in its music.

The breaks between sets were long, because it all went on all night and the music was just part of it. I slid off the stage into the crowd. The Club Le Moustier actually occupied what had, until a day or so ago, been the seventeenth through nineteenth floors of the office building. Passageways and rooms thrust their way out from the main concert space like vagrant pseudopodia. There was no trace of what business had once been there.

In a small circular room sat a man whose clothing was covered with colored spots of phosphorescent fungi—decayform, the latest trend, the logical and transcendent conclusion of organiform. His cheekbones were covered with a soft orange growth of dermal mold, and his hands were swollen and purple, like skin burned in the light of a supernova. He did not move but just hummed softly to himself.

"He looks exhumed, doesn't he, Theo?" a soft voice said at my shoulder. "Just like the rest of us."

"Helena," I said. "Is that you?"

A hand took my elbow and squeezed. "It is now." Her tone was slightly bitter. "My husband calls me Helena. So does my daughter. And I've never really gotten used to it."

"Too bad. I like Peter Ambrose a lot better than I ever liked . . . the other name."

I finally turned and looked at her. Her face, once merely sharp, was now severe. She had not bothered to change it much. The elaborate, silver-bound braids were gone, replaced by a short puff of curly hair, whitened by a flurry of age. She was off duty, but her high-collared dress still made her look medical, like a military nurse from some war known only from old movies.

"Peter. All right then." We walked down a hall, leaving the decomposing man behind. She glanced at me, eyes searching. "Why did you choose that face, of all faces?"

"Because it's really mine. I wasn't born with the right one."

"That's funny. When most people find their true faces, they're dazzlingly attractive. Yours isn't at all."

"You recognized me instantly, didn't you? Even though I don't look a bit the way I looked at Fitzwater." I was not offended by . . . Mennaura's famous bluntness. I *had* chosen this face myself, and it was mine, even if it looked like the face of a dull peasant who would be strained by any task more complex or interesting than sorting potatoes from rutabagas.

"That's only partly true. I recognized you more from the way you played. As I think you expected."

We climbed a narrow metal ladder to a hanging platform covered with cushions. From somewhere far away I could hear Sheldon's ophicleide again, like a wailing from the Pleistocene.

"I'm sorry," I said as we sat down. "I didn't mean to yank you out of your life, but—"

"I've already been yanked. So I've been waiting for someone else to show up. Almost six months ago, a man came to see me in my public office at Atman. Barney Winooski was his name. He shambled into my office. A tall, gangly man. I recognized him immediately, of course."

"'Barney Winooski.' Jesus, it's more ridiculous all the time. It was Anthony Watkins."

"The same. He looked like hell. His skin was dead, almost unconnected to his flesh. His corneas had that faint haze you get from excessive Elysion use."

"A nimbus, some people call it. Seeing a nimbus."

"Yes, that's right, they do." She seemed surprised, as if the connection had never occurred to her. "I asked him, right out, if he'd come to me for addiction recovery."

"And he laughed." I didn't even have to think about what his reaction would have been.

"That's right. He didn't get angry. He just laughed. You know him, Peter."

"We all do. He's our older brother."

"He did sit on all of our chests in turn, just to show who was boss, so I suppose that's right. He thanked me and said that he'd just quit on his own. 'Just took a little mental steel wool,' he said. 'Not hard at all, if you have to do it. Lost a few convolutions in the process, but there's more where those came from.'"

"Did he say why he quit?" I asked, expecting her to mention the paradoxical resurrection of Linden Straussman, our returning father, thus leading us naturally into the next subject I was interested in.

"He said we were being investigated, after years of being ignored. The Group, that is. Someone was after us. Someone from the government. A penetrating agent. A luke."

I felt a precise icy chill. Six months ago, long before Geraldino's death, someone had been investigating the Group. Amanda TerAlst? She seemed the most likely candidate. But what, then, had started her investigation if it hadn't been Geraldino's murder? Six months ago!

"Did he say who it was?"

She shook her head. "He was more interested in forcing me into action than in telling me anything. You know how he was. Is."

"What action, then?"

Her dark eyes were wide as she looked at me. "He wanted to find us. All of us. Every member of the Group. I was the easiest to find, after all. My face is almost the same, as is my career. I didn't really try to hide. I think I convinced myself no one would ever come looking. Or that if they did come looking, they'd find me, whatever my subterfuges. But the rest of you had disappeared, erasing and rewriting yourselves. For all I knew, you were all dead, or had forgotten everything that had made you what you were."

"To some extent," I said, "that was true. I removed a lot of myself in order to be able to live. All the edges and protrusions that kept bumping up against things."

She shook her head. "Then why live if that's all you have left?"

I grinned at her, a tight, tooth-drying rictus. "I also put away the inclination to ask that particular question. It's amazing how much easier living becomes if you stop caring about it."

"You care now, don't you?" She was tentative. "I heard it—when you played. I always liked the way you played."

"I *do* care now—though playing like you care is easier to fake than you might think. That's why I brought you here. I need to know. We all do. Charlie Geraldino and Lori Inversato have both been murdered—Lori just this morning."

The blood left her face, leaving the dark skin unsupported, loose on her bones. "What . . . how?" So there was more than one way to ignore that which was too painful to face. I had used twenty-first century techniques of memory modification and suppression. Helena Mennaura had used the old method of simply not turning her head.

I shrugged. "You must have eaten some of that news. Charlie . . . well, the police didn't release it, but I hear that he was strangled. I know how Lori died. I found her body myself. She'd been hit over the head. There was a lot of blood. She was going to meet someone. I got the impression that it was supposed to be . . . Daddy."

Surprisingly, her eyes flashed contempt. "Daddy. Isn't that just like her? She never knew who the hell she was—so she never knew who anybody else was, either."

"Helena," I said. "I'm trying to figure out what's going on. What's going on *now*. What happened in the past—"

"Is equally important. Why else did you expend all that effort to remember? It's all back there, Peter. It all means something. I knew *that* as soon as Anthony Watkins walked through my door and brought that past in with him."

"I hope so," I said bleakly. "I certainly hope it all means something."

She looked at me and shook her head. "You're still not remembering—thinking about—everything, are you? Even things that are important."

"Maybe. So what did Watkins—"

"You're not *listening* to me." Now that I had brought Karin Crawford back out from under her disguise as Helena Mennaura, she seemed intent on bringing everything else along with her, related and unrelated. "You have to take the connection. Do you remember that little girl, Tundra? The one who died at Fitzwater? She was an orphan, unadoptable. An orphan because her father had beaten her, then killed her mother and himself."

"What does . . ." The little girl's skull had been deformed from the violence she had suffered, squished out like an underinflated football. She'd been—stored, there is no other word for it—in a hospital several hundred miles away from Camp Fitzwater for some months, silent, drooling, her meaningless but oddly fluid motions like the swaying of undersea plants. She was a despair to the hospital staff—no longer human, but with a human appearance and pedigree, painful grit in the gears of definition, not alive but not to be permitted to die. No relatives came forward.

Aside from motor damage, she was severely aphasic, with great damage to the tracts connecting that part of the left hemisphere that understood language with that part able to produce speech. Damage to her occiput had left her essentially blind, though her eyes were undamaged. At a request from Straussman, she was transferred to Camp Fitzwater, which had, miraculously, become named "Fitzwater Rehabilitation Center."

Under an experimental protocol, Karin Crawford and I surgically implanted a replacement speech processor of Crawford's own design. It had extensions that reached through the corpus callosum to the right hemisphere, into the gyri cognate to the left-hemisphere Broca's area— only on the right side of the brain they deal with the creation and perception of music, rather than the creation and perception of speech. A pattern analyzer integrated what parts of her visual association cortex were still functional.

I remembered that little girl, her face hideously deformed, a pink ribbon clipped to what was left of her hair. Her name had originally been Tundra, but when she finally was able to communicate with us, it became a tuneful bird whistle. Patients with motor aphasia can often remember the words to songs while singing them, even when they are incapable of normal speech. Tundra, with the assistance of Karin's implant, carried this to an extreme, and communicated by sung words that carried tonal information, like Chinese. She could see things that moved, or "danced," but nothing that was motionless. Everything had to be rhythmic, tuned, in fluid patterns.

I, the musician, communicated with her, in some of the oddest duets I'd ever taken part in. Even so, I was only partway into her world. She was a nation of one. No one else in our world spoke or understood her language. That was probably why one day she tried to speak to the sun by flying out of a high window.

I was the one who found her tiny body, in its blue jumpsuit with the white bunny on the chest, lying sprawled on the ground, its broken limbs motionless in a hieroglyph with no meaning.

"I remember her," I said.

"You don't remember enough. The processor I made for her was an early type, but it was a type I've been working on ever since. I call them Kundalini devices. Kundalini yoga holds that there are six centers, or chakras, ascending the human spine. . . ."

With hallucinatory vividness, I finally remembered. A translucent virt lay in a humoral bath like a sprouting bean, ready for installation. On its back a tiny, precise symbol: six interlocked circles. It was a virt I had obtained from Sal Tigranes.

"You sent that virt to me," I said. "You knew that if I was out there, Tigranes would give that virt to me. But you made a mistake."

"What?"

"You thought that if I saw that pattern, I would remember your work on Kundalini devices, know that you had sent it, and get in contact with you. But I didn't remember anything, Helena. I had deliberately forgotten all of it, every bit of it."

"You found me, though. You found me anyway."

"Yeah. After two of us are dead."

"There's more to it than that, you know. Not just six interlocking rings. That could be the insignia on a kind of handbag. What's inside those virts . . . I learned a lot from Tundra, that poor girl." She sighed. "Too much, maybe. It got so that everything I saw was a symbol, a sign of something beyond what was in front of me. Everything represented something else."

"Speaking of which . . ." I reached into my jacket pocket and fingered what I carried there. "I have something of yours." I produced the antique bone-handled scalpel. "I took it."

She held it in her hand with wonder. "I don't have many of those things anymore, you know. They vanished over the years. The stethoscope. The patellar reflex hammer. All those things physicians once had to symbolize themselves. Thank you for returning it. You chose well, you know. For all of us." I must have looked startled, because she smiled. "Oh, I knew, Peter. I knew. You wanted to hold on to all of us. That made sense. Those little things you took . . . I thought that was good."

"And here I thought it was a secret."

She shook her head. "None of us have secrets, not really. Because there's always some other part of us that wants to tell."

I thought about that, but was starting to find her reasoning too oblique. Maybe it was just that it was late at night. "What did Watkins want from you?"

"He's a strange man. He always was, I guess. The thing he wanted— that he *said* he wanted—was simply that I understand. He wanted me to see the truth. That wasn't all, of course. He needed money, he needed contacts, he needed connection through the data I had available to me: deep data bases, not normally accessible. Money was the most important. He needed it for his 'project.'"

"Finding Linden Straussman."

"Or bringing him back to life."

-19-

IN THE SKIM-MILK HALF-LIGHT OF EARLY MORNING, EVERYTHING LOST its third dimension. We walked past the barely balanced-on-edge paper facades of buildings. The harsh metal El tracks that stood above us turned into an unwound paper ornament made by schoolchildren to decorate a ragged Christmas tree.

Helena Mennaura peered in through the display window of a fabric store at mountain ranges of patterned cloth. "I made Darlene a dress with cloth from here," she said. "The only dress I've ever made. Work takes so much time . . . and you know, Peter, I can't even remember what I do? I remember making the dress, pricking my fingers, hemming unevenly and having to pull it out, trying to figure out the damn patterns on that borrowed machine—whoever invented the damn thing could have done brain surgery—but work . . . it's like it all happened a million years ago and I don't even remember it. And I came straight from the lab to the concert. The dress wasn't even that good. Better suited to a clubfooted hunchback."

"I'm sure your daughter was happy to have it." Mennaura had shown me a picture of her daughter Darlene, a cute thing with pigtails. So she at least had time to fuss with her daughter's hair.

"That's the funny thing. She was. Even though it didn't really fit. She called it Mom's dress and acted like she was just borrowing it from me, an adult thing that she had. As if any adult would wear such a monstrosity."

A clatter of pounding metal and abrading buzz of some machining tool came from behind a chain link fence next to the fabric shop, the only sound on the early-morning street. The El tracks emerged from here, flanked by two blank, curving walls of brick. As Mennaura's sad mother's eyes picked out the brocades, taffetas, and fine silks that would never be made into dresses for her daughter, I looked into the junkyard under the tracks, beyond the screen of ailanthus branches that had woven themselves through the rusty fence, trying to see what was back there. The retina-searing glare of a welding torch danced through a mesh-reinforced window.

"I work in a high-security area at Atman." Mennaura's voice was dreamy, as if she was recalling a memory from her distant childhood. "So I have a secure-site personality there. When I get home I remember . . . I don't know, huge cliffs washed by waves, huge lurching dolls with no eyes, fire that slithers across the floor. It makes it so hard to take work home. . . . And sometimes I just remember what we did, way back then, when we were all in the Group, and it seems like I just left all of you there, just a few minutes before."

Hisec workers suffered from an artificially induced multiple personality disorder, accepted voluntarily for access to highest knowledge. Like Gideon Farley, his own thoughts encrypted, his name changed to Thomas Inman, they lived several lives, and only one of those lives, severe, serene, living exclusively within the white walls of a security lab, was able to know the secrets. It was enough for some people, it seemed, to lie in bed early on a silent morning after a snowfall, awakened by the crunch of rubber-booted feet on the walk outside and be aware that some part of their mind to which they had no conscious access knew a truth, though they themselves had no way of knowing what that truth was. I had never thought that Karin Crawford would become that kind of person.

"Maybe that's Karin Crawford in there, in that lab," I said, to Helena Mennaura. "Your old self, still alive."

She shuddered. "I hope not. That woman was terribly alone. I'm not alone anymore." She took my arm insistently. "I panicked when Watkins appeared. I didn't know what to do. I couldn't ask Mose, my husband, because he couldn't know the first thing about it. And he always thought he could protect me."

Just beyond the fence, in leaning rows, were ranks of automobile radiators, aging in Chicago's acid rain. I could see some of the enameled logos: Hupmobile, LaSalle, Mercer, Duryea. A huge mass of car parts was stacked behind them. They were classified by year and make. Had they really made Duesenbergs in 1957? Who needed cylinders from a 1973 Crossley? I looked farther, at a sleek, tarp-shrouded shape. Was that, perhaps, a 1979 Studebaker Regent, the car whose gull-wing door Brock Stolier had thwonked Leatherlips with? I could just see the hint of a gleaming hubcap.

This machine shop, Temporal Requisition, Inc., made the past. Not the real past, which had, after all, made itself, but instead artifacts from countless alternate pasts, to order. It was famous for its attention to historically correct alloys and manufacturing techniques, making everything from lost-wax bronze casting created in Shang Chinese–ruled Mexicos to single-crystal engine blocks. It was from here that Sheldon's B-flat ophicleide, his strange silver-valved trombone, and the other sinuous devices of his music had come. I held tightly onto the rough rust of the chain link fence. I think it left its marks on my face.

"Hank Rush must come here," Mennaura said, looking over my shoulder. "The way a woman would go to a jewelry store or a cosmetics counter."

"What do you know about Hank Rush?" I was suddenly alert. He was the one I had seen no sign of yet. Just a piece of ambiguous information from poor Lori, that he was a factory of some sort. Hank Rush and Gene Michaud, though I had no doubt Michaud would soon surface, in some unpleasant, probably violent way.

"Remember that military parking lot in Lvov? It was crammed with those old transport trucks, and Hank . . ." She started to laugh, an honest, head-thrown-back laugh. "And Hank . . ."

"I remember." I laughed myself. "I remember." Hank Rush had servoed his mind into a giant device made out of a crane on massive caterpillar treads. Two huge spherical fuel tanks had been welded to the base. He ran rampant in that parking lot, crushing those transports like egg cartons. It was only after a few moments of watching that you realized that his servo device was a gigantic technobaroque penis. Rush had shrieked in irresistible pleasure. Shattering glass, ripping steel, and wild laughter, amplified and played through huge speakers. In the end his gigantic device had collapsed across the remains of the last trucks, to be cleaned away by bewildered Byelorussian military police.

"It was an ecological thing, *he* said," Mennaura explained. "They were dumping toxic waste into south-flowing rivers, to poison the Magyar troops down there. The streams were full of dead fish. . . ." She shook her head. "It would have been better if he'd had no reason at all."

"Do you know where he is now, Helena? It's been a long time since I've heard of him."

"He was dedicated to our life on this Earth. In his own way. Always in his own way. Yes, Peter. I know where he is. He lives in Chicago. No surprise, we all seem to, don't we?"

It hadn't occurred to me as odd, but now I saw that it was.

"He's not quite . . . human any more. He's had a long time to work on it. We all have. He lives down near Lake Calumet, in those wetlands around where all the factories used to be."

"Does he have an address?"

She shook her head. "He doesn't live anywhere. Not like we do. He's just there. Go look for him if you want. Let's go. I should get home. Everyone should be gone now."

At the irregular, unbalanced intersection—three streets colliding like tipsy pedestrians in a fog—pavement had peeled away to reveal the El tracks' forgotten shadow, a double ribbon of streetcar tracks. Rough paving stones shouldering their way through evanescent asphalt implied that our world was just facile graffiti scrawled across a completely different reality. The El stalked the street like an aggressive steel centipede. Its ancient legs were held together by massive bolts, their edges softened by generations of paint. A train rumbled by overhead and threw a handful of sparks down at the street.

I smelled breakfast on the air: baking rolls and hot coffee. An illegible neon sign lit a steamed-up window red and blue. Morning denizens ran in and out through the door.

Mennaura looked in after them. "Darlene likes this place. She gets a roll here, sometimes, in the mornings on the way to school—an Armenian pastry, I think she says. I've never tried one. She loves them. I've never even gone here." Puffs of warm air came out every time the door opened.

"Looks good," I said, thinking of a bowl of café au lait. And an Armenian pastry. Hadn't she ever been curious enough to find out what it tasted like?

"It does, it does." She walked on, and we left the steamy window behind. I never did find out what the name of the place was. I wondered if Mennaura knew. And I wondered why she was looking for her daughter there, as if she was an old friend who had changed addresses and could only be run into by accident.

"He liked hot chocolate, you know," Mennaura said suddenly. "I used to watch him drink it. At night, he liked to have it."

"Who?" An ancient yellow-painted traffic signal with a Balinese cap winked at me from under its croupier's shades.

"Our . . ." She paused. "Linden Straussman. It was kind of a habit with him. You know he never drank, and I don't think he even understood what drugs were for. The idea of changing his consciousness made no sense to him."

"He was a man with no physical sins," I said, remembering something Watkins had said once. Though, to me, it had seemed more incomprehension than virtue. He had been simply unable to understand the pleasure others took in food, in sleep, in sex. From the point of view of the rest of us, this had made him strong. His sins lay elsewhere.

"Yes. He did dearly love that hot chocolate though." She spoke with the fondness of a daughter who no longer has to deal with her father.

"Watkins thinks Straussman killed Charlie. He probably thinks the same about Lori."

"I know. He's wrong. He's quite wrong."

"Then who—"

"Hush, Peter, we're almost home. I have no idea, you know. No idea."

We were on a peaceful Chicago street lined with brick and limestone single-family houses with small porches. Mennaura's home was a simple shoe box of yellowish brick, with a green tile roof and an autumn-empty flower box under the front windows.

"Come in, Peter," she said. "No one's home."

The house was silent and still. Everything was neatly in place, except for a few toys scattered on the living room rug: a doll with its arms twisted up above its head, a talking book, a sphere with stars inside it. The star sphere was covered with dust. A photograph of Mennaura's husband and daughter—he a huge Samoan man with an eruption of dark hair, she a slender, smiling ten-year-old on his lap—stood on the fireplace mantel. The room smelled shut up, as if no windows had been open in a long time. Outside, two women with bright turbans pushed baby carriages along the cracked sidewalk. They discussed something seriously, with many graceful arm gestures.

"Helena," I said urgently. "Leave. Leave now."

"What?" She turned to me, gently puzzled, as if I was a child with an eccentric request, a hot dog in his grape juice, or something.

"Get out. Take your family. You must have enough money. Leave this place, now, today. Get as far away as you can."

She shook her head. "That's impossible, Peter. You know that. I have a job . . . it's very responsible . . . I can't just leave. . . ."

"Helena." I took her arms. "Someone's out there." I found myself staring out of the window, as if I would see him, whoever it was, coming up the walk to ring the bell. "He's already killed two of us. Straussman, Watkins, whoever the hell he is, I don't know. You can't afford the risk. You have a family. They depend on you."

"They do," she said quietly. "They depend on me for their existence." She pulled herself away and walked into the kitchen. "Do you want some hot chocolate, Peter? I bought some yesterday. Just a whim, I don't know why I did it. It won't take long to make a cup. . . ."

"Helena—"

"It's too important. I can't go now. Don't worry. We'll all be fine. God, it's stuffy in here." She slid open a window in the kitchen. I felt a fresh breeze blow into the living room.

I wondered what Tigranes would have said if he knew what I was doing. Here I was, risking our entire expedition into Atman. If Mennaura left her position without warning, all security procedures would immediately be changed. We wouldn't stand a chance. But I really didn't have a choice. I had to convince her. . . .

The toys on the floor were really suitable for a much younger child than the one in the photograph. I looked more closely at the family picture on the mantel. With modern image-processing technology there is no way to tell if a photograph has been doctored, or created outright. Were these people real? Even if I went upstairs and found Mose's large underwear in the drawer, there would be no way of telling. Darlene's room could be filled with childish decorations, worn biographies of famous women, notes in curlicue handwriting from school friends. None of it meant anything, except what it said about need. If a false past can be created, so can a false present. We had the technology, if the need was there. I looked at the dusty star sphere and felt a prickling at the back of my neck.

A green school notebook lay on the coffee table, "Darlene Tatupu, Fifth Grade" written on it in careful letters that were shaded into the third dimension. What, if anything, was inside it?

"Do you want that chocolate?" Mennaura's voice was in my ear.

I jumped. "No, thank you." I looked at her. Her face was drawn, severe. Her mind had been pulled too far apart by the forces acting on it: Fitzwater, Atman, her life. Most of us fail miserably at even being one person. How could anyone manage more than that?

"Go ahead, look," she said. "Darlene works hard. I'm sure she wouldn't mind your seeing what she does."

"No, I—"

"Look, damn you!" She picked up the notebook and shoved it into my hands. "Look and see."

I opened the notebook up. On the first page was a drawing, a child's drawing, of a huge rising sun with reaching rays. A little girl in a dress was floating up to it. A big smile took up almost all of her face.

"Wasn't it amazing?" Mennaura said. "That she could fly like that? I would never have believed it."

When I had picked Tundra's body off the ground it had felt like a bundle of broken sticks. She hadn't weighed anything at all. Why shouldn't she have thought that she could fly? Why shouldn't Karin Crawford have believed it too?

I flipped farther. In perfect childish handwriting, in a variety of colors, were equations describing the states of neural circuitry. Drawings of nerves tangled on the pages, like seaweed around a drowned corpse. A multicolored diagram on one page was headed: CORONAL SECTION THROUGH FRONTAL LOBES AT LEVEL OF ANTERIOR COMMISSURE. An implanted virt extended processes into the corpus callosum. Part of it was labeled "grooby brain stuff," the rest "tapioca pudding."

In the margins were doodles and rhymes. "I like Tod," surrounded by hearts. "Darlene + Tod 4ever," under a tree labeled "under den linden." A list of Barclai's latest hit songs. Drawings of cats and horses. Content aside, it looked exactly like a ten-year-old's notebook.

Then a floor diagram of a building, headed MY SCHOOL. Various parts were labeled "Mrs. E's room," "Where I threw up last year," "Drinking fountain with sloobery stain," and "Boys fight here." The stain was large, growing from the cracked tiles above the drinking fountain. I saw why a little girl might be nervous about drinking from it.

I started to flip past, then noticed the legend "This is what's at, man." I blinked at it. After close examination, I realized that it was actually a careful drawing of the security concentrics guarding Mennaura's laboratory floor at Atman Medical. A dark ovoid sat in the middle, carefully crosshatched and labeled "Tar Baby Egg." A small figure with a frowny face seemed to have its hand stuck onto it. It was surrounded by jagged colored lines. Next to it was written "They changed this yesterday," and a date. Yesterday's date.

I looked at Helena. She was staring out of the window, and thin lines of tears came down her cheeks. "I can't leave, Theo," she said. "When I walk through those doors at Atman, they give me something back, and I'm real again. I do my work, and I'm real."

"Do you know that?"

"It has to be true," she whispered. "I can't remember it, but I know I'm real."

"Helena, please—"

"No! There's nothing to be afraid of. Charlie and Lori had their own problems. They don't have anything to do with us, with Mose and Darlene.

Please go, Theo . . . Peter. Please go. There's nothing for you here."

"All right, Helena. Is that offer still good? For the hot chocolate?"

She smiled through her tears. "Sure, Peter. I'll go make it."

While she was in the kitchen, I tore the Atman diagram page out of Darlene's notebook, mentally apologizing to her, whoever or whatever she was.

-20-

THE MASSIVE STONE CHESS PIECES STOOD IN THE SMALL PARK, HEMMED in by buildings. Dry flower beds surrounded the field of black and white squares, defining where the battle was, and where it could never be.

"C'mon Paula. C'mon, *whip that thing.*" The shouting boy, dashing in a gold-medaled red beret, dropped to the left of the slightly larger boy guarding him. A lanky girl, presumably Paula, threw a bright red, grapefruit-sized ball. It bounced off the stone forehead of a statue of a man with a skinny beard and a headdress, labeled Tuthmosis III, who served as a rook for the white side. As it bounced it made a sound like a crystal breaking.

The boy shrieked in delight, caught the ball, "Good *shot,* Paula," and dodged around one of the pieces opposing Tuthmosis's team, a looming figure of another mysterious bearded king, this one called Sennacherib. I couldn't even figure out how to pronounce it. The boy bounced the ball off the foreleg of a giant cow with a bearded human head, black's knight, then dodged back.

The ball continued in play, following incomprehensible rules that, for all I knew, changed with every crystal-shattering bounce. Children ran among the frowning statues of pharaohs and ancient kings from nations everyone had forgotten, or at least I had. A smaller boy, too young to play, had climbed up an ominous figure with gouged-out eyes, name of Sargon, and hung there, watching the game intently, swiveling his head like a lemur. A flying ball almost knocked him from his perch and his mother, patience exhausted, yelled at him to get down.

Standing on the other side of the playing field, gray hair flared out above a long black coat, was Amanda TerAlst. She stood behind the bench and watched the game, near several other mothers, a couple rocking the carriages of future contenders. She rested her elbows on the back of the bench and chatted amiably with a red-coated woman who held a squirming girl in her lap, trying vainly to correct some defect in her hair.

At that moment I saw her differently, as a mother, much like other mothers. Surely she didn't spend all of her time trying to excavate the dried-blood past. I looked among the laughing, screaming children, wondering if one or more were hers. Tigranes's information had indicated two, sexes and ages unknown. That tensely hunched girl with the backward antique White Sox cap, tactically hanging around another Egyptian pharaoh's legs in wait for the ball—did she inherit that intense gaze from her mother? But no—whatever her schemes, TerAlst would not bring her children along to a confrontation with a possible skein killer, even to further their educations. Besides, she lived far from here, somewhere on the North Side. She had suggested a rendezvous point far from any possible contamination of her home ground.

If Corinne and I had had a daughter, she would have wanted to name her Melissa. I imagined that girl in the White Sox cap as our daughter, Corinne's and mine. Suddenly, for no reason at all, save her pleasure in being there, the girl laughed, jumping from foot to foot. Then, responding to a flurry of action on the other side of the field, she darted behind the pharaoh and disappeared from my sight. I watched for her, but she did not reemerge. Perhaps her mother had called her and she had left the game, perhaps she had seen some other friends and had run over to talk to them. I hoped she would make it home all right.

I made my way around the perimeter of the chessboard toward TerAlst. The fall air was crisp as an apple, just a few roaming clouds defining the sky. Everything seemed articulate and solid in the sunlight. Even the eccentric ancient-seeming chess pieces seemed to make sense, as if interrupted in their millennial game by the mushroom growth of the city around them and patiently waiting for the damn thing to sink back into the lake.

For at least two days, everything had seemed a sign of Gene Michaud's approach, his reaction to my offering of the tsuba. Every unidentified figure was an agent of his. The constant vigilance was tiring. And that, I suddenly thought, must be the unidentified pain of paranoia: its weariness.

But TerAlst had picked a meeting place perfect from a defensive point of view. Context is everything. The two men who patrolled the edge of the square would have looked unexceptional anywhere in the city but here, amid these parents and children.

The stone heads of ancient tyrants and warriors had been domesticated and reduced to obstacles in a children's game. The two men, with their long, wide-shouldered coats and high gloves like gauntlets, revived something of the terror in those carved heavy faces. They affected to be strolling and chatting: a thin man with long blond hair and a balding black man with the look of a corporate accountant, scarred and street-dog mean.

Their discussion was animated and they did not look around them as they walked, but I still got the sense that they missed nothing. This suspicion was borne out when a bad bounce sent the ball off the forehead of a huge statue with the equally huge name of Tiglath-Pileser III directly at them. The children all paused and gasped, seeing their game world suddenly encompass rigid adults. Without even looking up from the point he was making, the bald man batted the ball with the back of his hand. It dropped back into play and the children immediately forgot everything but their game.

Michaud's men, I suspected. I had not seen either of them at the Mall of the Mysteries, so I couldn't know if they had been behind the bloodhound attack.

I looked at TerAlst, but nothing in her face indicated that she had noticed them. She straightened, bade good-bye to the other mother, and walked toward me.

"You're looking a little frazzled, Peter," she said, her tone gentle.

"I had a performance last night," I said, speaking the absolute truth. "I didn't get to bed. Came straight here."

"Why?" Her voice was arid. She didn't want to mess around.

I swallowed. "Because I'm afraid."

She looked at me, eyes sharp, but didn't say anything.

"I'm afraid someone's going to kill me."

We walked a few more steps, leaving the playground behind us. "Why are you afraid of that?" she said mildly. "Has someone threatened you? Who are you afraid of?"

I chose to answer the last question first. "I don't know who it is. I'm not even sure why I should be a target. But—to understand, it's hard." I thought about my approach. "There have been two murders in the past week."

"Chicago had several dozen murders last week." She clearly wasn't going to give me any help.

"Two that are important to my case." I didn't say, the only two *you* are investigating. I was still going to accept her disguise as a Chicago met cop. My knowledge that she was an icy luke could still come in handy. I needed any microscopic advantage I could hold on to. "A man named Morris Lanting killed in his apartment on the eighteenth, and a woman named Lori Inversato in hers on the twenty-third. The specific weapons haven't been mentioned."

"You don't eat the right news," TerAlst said. "If you did, you'd know that in a piece of macabre humor on the killer's part, Lanting was strangled with one of his own neckpieces. Apparently he had the hobby of painting them. There was quite a collection in his apartment. Careful, fine work, from what I could see. It looked like they were all unworn."

I felt a chill. "And has the news been revealed about the second death?"

"Nothing so interesting. Occiput fractured by a blunt object: an ordinary ratchet wrench. Since she was killed in her bedroom, it is presumed that the killer brought it with him. It was carefully cleaned off, well enough that it took the lab a while to determine that it actually was the weapon used."

"My God," I said involuntarily.

She eyed me. "Odd, certainly, but not startling. You might be surprised by what killers turn to. A cast-iron frying pan, shattered window glass, a porcelain bust of Lenin. This in a world with no shortage of decent weapons." She shook her head at the eternal fecklessness of murderers.

A neckpiece, a ratchet wrench. Death. And I had blithely given Helena Mennaura back her antique scalpel. Suddenly it seemed like a curse, an omen of doom. But that information tore it. Twist and turn as I might, someone in the Group was behind the deaths. Not any other coincidental agency.

"So, Peter. What is your connection with these people? I know you knew Lanting through your work, but the other . . ." Her voice had just a frosting of suspicion, enough to let me know I could easily be in trouble.

We passed through a large sandstone gate with castlelike crenellations on it. It looked like an old factory, one of those with the huge yellow-brick smokestacks that have the little, precarious metal steps all the way up so that you can climb and look into the smoke. On the other side was a different neighborhood, its mood subtly more drawn-up than the one we had just left.

"We were once musicians together. During the Devo Wars."

"A musical battalion?"

"Go ahead and laugh. We played together and worked for the Army. God knows what anyone was thinking back then."

"And soon it will only *be* God," she said. "Most of that history is already a goddam deliberate blank, like a bad drug experience. Records were wiped. Masses of them. You'd think there was a solar flare that stretched from the Mall in D.C. to Diego Garcia. And now we all pretend we don't remember a thing. Just a long nap, and we had a bit of a nightmare. That's all." Her voice seethed with anger. She'd been through those wars too, somehow, somewhere. She hated seeing it forgotten. "All right, then, you were musicians. I don't have any record that either of the victims even knew how to play a musical instrument, but that's not surprising. I don't even have birth records for them, school. Dental, for Christ's sake." She pressed her lips shut, reining herself in. "Go ahead."

I suspected her voluble revelation that she didn't know anything at all. "There really isn't much else. We played together, almost ten years ago. Under different names, of course. I can load them for you, if you want." I did have nice names ready for them, names no less real than the ones they had actually borne, since the real ones no longer existed either.

"Which theater?"

"Dniestr-Prut." The story, as I told it was fantastic, unbelievable. My only hope was the real and solid fact that it was all unbelievable, truth and fantasy together, a great mad ball where everyone wore disguises under their masquerade costumes. But this one was Sheldon's fault, all Sheldon's. Once you got started on something like this, there was no stopping.

"All right. So you played in a, a what, a jazz band?"

"That's right. Cloud of Witnesses was our name. Don't know who thought it up. Eight of us altogether." The phrase, cloud of witnesses, was one Karin Crawford had used. From the Bible, she had said. I had no idea what it meant or what it referred to, but it had stuck in my mind.

And I saw them: a clanky-pounding percussionist, almost a machine, Hank Rush; a low, almost subliminal bassist, Charlie Geraldino; a sweet clarinetist, Karin Crawford; a switch-hitting cornetist/trumpeter/flugelhorn player, Lori Inversato; a great, sardonic saxophonist, Anthony Watkins; me, the piano player; and the leader, a dark, huge man, Linden Straussman. The image, for an instant, was vivid, more vivid than truth could be.

"Any guess as to why anyone would want to kill any of you?"

I shrugged. This was where my story connected neatly into the real events of that time. It was nice, kind of like shading a drawing into the third dimension.

"We played the jolly cities of Bessarabia, Moldavia, eastern Rumania, even Odessa. And a lot of shit happened there, those years."

"And you think someone wants to kill you all because of some of that shit."

"Who knows?" It was hard, so hard. Getting even this close to the truth was making me sick. "All that stuff. The assassination of General Otatea in Odessa. The Declaration of Brasov. The Crimean Syndicate's push up the Danube. Pick something."

"All right. Do you know where the other members of your band are now?" She was brisk.

I looked at her carefully. Who was she, really? The Group had committed actions, not particularly unusual actions for that time, and then disbanded itself. Was someone indeed still after us? If so, why not this self-assured icy luke? Who better, to find us? I tried to picture her wrapping a hand-painted neckpiece around Charlie Geraldino's neck. Didn't work. She was too subtle for that, too precise. If she had to kill someone, she'd do it without a fuss, clipping neatly through the spinal cord below the foramen magnum and instantly sliding the body into a cooler with a time-and-date stamp on the forehead.

We were in an odd, newly built neighborhood. The buildings around us were brick, tall and narrow, facing us with snooty expressions in their multipaned windows. Above these burgherish mugs they had elaborate hairdos of enameled copper or explosive-flared aluminum: sunbursts, tiaras, leering loose-lipped faces wearing dented Roman helmets. I looked up at them, uncomprehending, not knowing where I was.

"Peter." Her tone was urgent. "If I'm going to protect you, I have to find you. All of you." The voice of a seducer. The voice of a wicked witch in the woods.

"I want you to find the killer," I said. "I want you to figure out who it is." My tongue felt swollen in my mouth.

"I *will*. But you have to give me help. Do you have any idea, any idea at all? Any suspects?"

"No! I only know who people *were*. I don't know who anyone is." I thought about it for a moment. Watkins. I could give her Watkins. Surely she'd be able to find him, somewhere under his piled mass of aliases. But I couldn't. He was still too close to me. And I didn't know. I didn't really think he was the killer. Just as I really didn't think Priscilla had anything to do with Lori's death. But what did I know?

All I knew was that I couldn't just turn anyone over to Amanda TerAlst. Not without being sure.

"All right," she said. "At least I can protect *you*. There's a safe location in West Virginia, in the mountains. It used to be a village, but no one lives there now. It's kind of a resort. I understand it's very beautiful."

"Very beautiful." I couldn't imagine it, this safe place in the mountains. I imagined it as Camp Fitzwater, plopped down somewhere with cliffs all around it.

"You'll be safe there, I guarantee it. The killer, *whoever* it is, will never get there."

"No, Amanda." I didn't even have to think about it. "If I go there, I'll never know."

"Never know what?"

"Never know! Anything. I'll just sit there in your resort, looking at old magazines. Maybe playing golf. I can't. . . ." The thought terrified me. It was like having someone put a pillow over my face.

We stopped at a brick-paved corner with a wrought-aluminum lamp overhead. An electric-powered delivery truck unloaded gleaming bulbous refrigerators with insane names: Crosley-Shelvador, Ben-Hur, Supremacy. Was the world made a better place by resurrecting obsolete lines of appliances? The coverall-wearing delivery men and women, with their patent-leather–billed caps and white gloves, looked like the usually invisible operators of the world revealed, overdressed bunraku puppeteers. The vividly colored refrigerators had clocks in the doors, radios, insolent voice boxes that told you your weight. They were all wheeled into a brand-new yellow-brick building that had been aged to look decayed. A bored woman with a pillbox cap and fishnet stockings stood in the doorway, checked invoices, and directed the iceboxes to the proper apartments. Her legs were OK, but only OK.

"I need you to talk," TerAlst said. "And I will have it. Do you understand me?" Her voice had developed teeth.

"I don't—"

Behind the refrigerator truck was another delivery van, this one called New Deal Moving, gold letters on red enamel, with a picture of some bespectacled guy with a long cigarette holder pushing what looked like a wheelchair full of boxes. I didn't get the joke, whatever it was.

"If you don't give me the information I want, I am empowered to take you into custody as a noncooperative witness." The rear doors of the delivery van swung open. Inside, rather than stacks of crates, was a mobile police lab.

"PETER ZACHARIAS AMBROSE." THE POLICE EXAMINER WAS A CRISP woman whose nameplate said "Glover." "This is a routine neuro exam. You are not being judged or punished. Do you understand?"

"Yes." I felt the exam chair snuggling around my naked skin.

"Though results are not admissible for final determination of your case, legal counsel may be present if requested. Do you so request?"

I could see TerAlst sitting at a table examining something on a soft display. She didn't look at me.

"My retained legal counsel is my home processor." I tried to match the police's crispness. "I wish to netlink and download the exam results. My emergent processor is registered with the Illinois Bar Association."

Glover peered intently at her screen. "Okay. Your home system accepts. Are you ready?"

I sighed. "Does it matter if I am?"

"We can wait a few minutes for you to prepare yourself, if you want. Do you need to go to the bathroom?"

"No, no, I'm all right. Go ahead."

I felt the cold shiver of microelectrodes sliding in between my vertebrae to tap into my spinal cord. A face mask slurped on to my skin and wormed infomycelia up the cranial nerves. A light started to build in my skull.

Then I was sitting and peacefully drinking a glass of orange juice, dressed in my own clothes, smiling at Glover. She was red-haired and really very pretty. I took a sip of juice and tried to see her breasts under her straight-planed and creased blue uniform. Her holo nameplate tilted back promisingly.

A colleague of hers appeared, a quizzical Asian man with a high, balding forehead. As he sat down, a screen flipped data. They both stared at it, ignoring me.

"Are you sure?" Glover said.

"Zero defect. That's straight." His nameplate said "Smith."

They both looked at me accusingly, as if I, unconscious, strapped to an exam chair, my personality as structurally unified as a box of kitty litter, had somehow jiggered their system.

"We were told—" they began simultaneously, then stopped and looked at each other.

"You are a known implanter," Glover said sternly. She leaned forward on her elbows. I became convinced that she had large breasts indeed, though I still couldn't see them. "But the scans show no modifications of any sort. We were told that you were heavily modified."

"You were told wrong. It wouldn't be the first time, right? People are always telling you what they want you to find. I know how that works."

They weren't interested in being buddies. They stared at me in resentful puzzlement. Police don't like surprises.

"If you conceal virts past this point you may be subject to additional criminal prosecution," Glover said.

"If you could explain it to us," said Smith, the reasonable one. "Why does an implanter have no implants of his own?"

"Why don't you arrest yourself?"

Glover glowered and Smith sighed. But there was really nothing they could do. The examination had been complete, even if it had not given them the results they had every reason to expect.

But now I started to get anxious. It had been a while since I'd had time to examine myself. Was there really no change in my brain, no self-generating modifications? The possibility was always there.

"Are you sure there were no mods?" I asked.

"None at all." Glover was crisp.

"Absolutely sure? Did you check for a parasitic plate embedded in the blood-brain barrier in the choroid plexus? Ripeno of Malta has one in experimental trials. It generates paracrine surges in the cerebrospinal fluid. Crude in its effects but almost invisible by standard scanning."

Startled, Smith called something up on his screen and stared at it. "No," he said finally. "Nothing in the choroid plexus."

"Huta Bowodowa, a Moravian firm, has an inductive visual pattern processor that fits into the lateral geniculate body and projects into the pulvinar of the thalamus. It's a distributed processor and its effects are large-scale emergent, so it's sometimes hard to—"

"Mr. Ambrose." The lovely Glover was getting irritated. "It's very gracious of you to help us do our job. Please stop."

"You don't understand. I have legitimate reason to be worried and you can give me independent confirmation. Have you ever thought about a sleeper prosthetic?"

Smith looked politely interested. Glover looked disgusted.

I spoke quickly, the words spilling over each other. *I'd* thought about it. "It would take the form of a modified oncogene that trips at some coded stimulus and creates a series of artificial, metastasizing tumors in the nervous system, or maybe the surrounding glia. These information-processing tumors might seize command of the tracts and completely change the functioning of the CNS. Don't you understand? That oncogene could be sitting there buried in the junk DNA of some innocent-looking cells. You wouldn't find it in a million years. But—a stimulus, and my brain's gone in a matter of hours."

"I'm not sure it hasn't happened already," Glover said nastily. "You're not modified. You're crazy." She flounced her red hair.

"Are you going to book me on a charge of malicious insanity?"

"We leave that up to the courts."

"The courts and, I assume, Amanda TerAlst."

She flinched and glanced over to where TerAlst was working. "Ms. TerAlst does not control our operations. Chicago Metro has provided its services as a courtesy."

"Hm. That's not what I hear."

Glover leaned forward, ready to bite my head off, as I intended. Later, that anger could be directed at IntraCranial, which was messing with their operations. It could be useful to me. Smith put a hand on her shoulder. "He hears nothing. Don't let him crawl up your ass."

And that was it. She sat back and smiled sunnily and it was all true. She could do whatever she wanted, and hide her breasts from me, and I was still a prisoner.

TerAlst came up and glanced at the report. If it surprised her, she didn't show it in her face. "There's a plane leaving O'Hare for Wheeling this evening. We can go to your house to pick up a few things. . . ."

"You're serious," I said, despairing. If she sent me away I would never understand. I would die gasping up there in the mountains.

"I'm always serious, Peter."

"I don't doubt that." I searched her face. It was as informative as a postage stamp. "I'm more useful to you free."

"And *I* don't doubt *that*. But only if you tell me something. Anything, Peter." She was intense. Hungry.

There was a long silence. "The killer," I said finally. "The killer is a dead man." She didn't react in any visible way. "Look for a man with—" The thoughts slid away from me as if on ice. What distinguished Straussman? His hat? I couldn't remember a hat, or even what his head looked like. I pushed my mind onto the point. "He likes . . . he likes hot chocolate. And having the windows open. And—what?—he's obsessively neat, always rearranging things, and has extremely clean fingernails."

There had been manicuring equipment lying all over Lori's bedroom. Clippers, an emery board, a small file. She'd been a manicurist once. It was in the picture. Her name had been Margie and she'd been black, with blond hair. I could remember it.

TerAlst, oddly, didn't respond as if I was crazy. "Anything else?"

"The . . . the next victim may be murdered by a scalpel. An antique one, with a bone handle. It's hard to kill someone with a scalpel. At least, if they don't want to die. The damn blade's just too small, no matter how sharp it is. It's my fault, that scalpel."

"I see."

Another long silence. "It's just a hunch," I said. I was babbling. "Just a guess. I'm not having visions. Voices aren't talking to me. There's a connection . . . the previous murder weapons. It's a pattern of objects. Maybe coincidence." I sucked air. "Helena Mennaura. The woman with the scalpel is named Helena Mennaura. She's a researcher at Atman Medical."

"Lieutenant Glover." TerAlst spoke sweetly. "Please return Mr. Ambrose's personal effects and release him."

"Yes, ma'am." Glover seemed surprised by the decision, but didn't argue with it.

We stepped back outside the police van. As soon as we were on the street, its doors closed and it drove silently away, to deliver its New Deal somewhere else. The day suddenly seemed cold, the bright sunlight unhelpful. The city around us, built to philosophical principles I did not understand, refused to pay me any attention.

Shockingly, TerAlst put her arm around my shoulder. She was shorter than I was, and felt harder, despite her motherly appearance.

"Don't worry, Peter," she said softly. "I won't betray your friend."

I only hoped it was true. I only hoped that I had not just condemned my old friend Karin Crawford to death.

-21-

THE PRAIRIE WAS A STRIKING VISION, TAKING UP AN ENTIRE CITY BLOCK in an otherwise densely populated neighborhood. The bare and exposed walls of buildings faced it with some puzzlement. It looked like a mirage, a preternaturally clear image of something that was really miles away. Cars were parked dense around it, having eaten the asphalt bare.

The prairie's high grass was dry and brown now, in the fall. I don't know my grasses, as Tigranes had pointed out, can't tell my bluestem from my wild rye, and it was kind of a popcult thing in the suburbs. I could learn it, if the Canyonites' version of reality ever got virtual and I had to. I stood and looked at it. TerAlst had left me there, knowing full well that something was waiting for me. She had the information she needed, and would let me run free to collect some more.

Two men walked past me without a glance. I recognized them from the chessboard park. Where had they been wandering all this time? They stopped nearby and looked across the prairie as if searching for buffalo. Their gaze was so intent that I found myself looking too. The grass was certainly high enough to hide a herd. A small one, fed out of a paper bag by a crazy blue-haired lady in a housedress.

"Don't you ever want to park there?" the long-haired blond asked. "I mean, doesn't it tempt you?"

"Tempt me? You crazy? Having my ass plowed under for fertilizer don't tempt me."

"They won't use a plow. Wrong tech. Just drop you, let the birds get you."

"What, pigeons'll eat me? They'll throw up." The bald man chortled. "Get sick and die."

"Carrion fowl." The blond used the term with relish. "Big stinky things, razor beaks. Ecologically correct."

The black man looked up at the roofs of the buildings across the prairie as if expecting buzzards to be roosting there, waiting patiently for him to drop dead. "Yeah, sure, wrong tech. They used vavoom to blow up these buildings, didn't they? Real native."

A few charred remnants of the old buildings were piled up along the cracked sidewalk. There were some dozen sites like this in Chicagoland. Fires, explosions, weirdly localized earthquakes—whatever, blocks of abandoned buildings came down and prairies grew up in their place.

"Vapor-vortex, sure." Blondie ran his hands through his long hair and swayed as if he'd just named his favorite band. "Wrong tech devours itself from the tail, not the head. You ever hear that, Leslie?"

"Yeah, I've heard it. Never made sense."

"Doesn't make sense? Okay, park your car." The blond pointed out into the grass. "Nice spot, right there. Who'll know?"

"Get virtual. You know who'll know."

"Who? Who?" Teasing voice.

"The Sons of Glen Canyon, fart brain." Leslie spoke loudly, proving his bravado. "As far as they're concerned, you're just fertilizer that moves around too much."

A wind whipped off the lake and the grass rustled. Virgin and undisturbed, it stayed that way because everyone feared the Sons of the Canyon. Radical deep ecologists, they had nasty tempers and immense, mysterious resources. Their Chicago branch actually had some innocuous name like Friends of the Lake, but no one used it. Their version of Chicago was a nice, clean prairie, fading into swamp at the lake's edge. Oak and hickory forests would cover higher ground, and the skies would darken with flocks of passenger pigeons grown from restarted genes implanted in common pigeon ova. Canyonites argued about whether some version of nomadic Amerindian would even be allowed to exist. It was someone else's version of paradise. But then, we were all already living in someone else's version of paradise.

The two men started shoving each other toward the grass, laughing. As far as anyone knew, the Sons of the Canyon didn't mind people just *walking* on the grass, but who wanted to take a chance?

"C'mon, go out there, take a dump, make something grow," the bald man said.

"Bend your head over then."

"You—" They scuffled more violently.

These men were clearly artists, but it was cold, I was tired, and I didn't feel like waiting for them to put the finishing touches on their work—my kidnapping from the city street.

"Hey!" I said. They froze in their tussle and looked at me. "I want to see Gene Michaud. Can we get on with it?" I sounded more irritated than I meant to.

That made the bald black man angry. His face tightened. "What the hell—"

His companion put a hand on his shoulder. "This guy's known the boss a long time. You've got to expect—"

"I've got to expect *shit,* Myron." Leslie started toward me.

Myron grinned at me and shrugged, as if to say that matters were now beyond his control. He put his hands into the pockets of his long coat and swung it back and forth in a little dance. I stepped off the sidewalk, feeling the crunch of dried seed pods under my feet, and half turned, ready to run into the high grass. Startled crows flew up out of the tangled dry stalks, squawking in irritation, perhaps taking report of my trespass to the proper authorities. I would have to deal with the Canyonites at some other time. Leslie stopped, watchful, balanced on the balls of his feet.

"Listen," I said. "I want to see Gene Michaud. You want to take me to Gene Michaud. Doesn't it seem like we could reach some sort of arrangement?"

Leslie looked stubborn. "Don't know no Gene Michaud. Don't *want* to know no Gene Michaud. Our boss is Aylmer Brandt, ManPower. Right? He wants to talk to you. Real bad."

"Okay, great, wonderful." My fear of him was heady, like a drug. "Can we get on with it?" I had known that Michaud—Aylmer Brandt, in the double naming traditional in my family—would be unable to resist trying to retrieve his tsuba. *That* would be the only way I could get in touch with him. Gene Michaud had always been such a security maniac that there was no way that I, with my limited resources, could have found him without his cooperation. I wouldn't have even been able to discover his new, ridiculous name, Aylmer Brandt.

I would have liked to make a clever deal with Myron and Leslie and guarantee my safety, but I had no leverage, despite my ability to lose myself in the high grass like a small boy. To get what I wanted I had to stick my head in the lion's mouth and there was no way I could persuade it to even use a breath mint.

HALF AN HOUR LATER, AFTER A PERILOUS RIDE IN A WHEEZY OLD METHANE-powered utility van, we stood in a vast windswept space under a high apartment tower. The tower was a crumbling mess, half its windows boarded up, black streaks from apartment fires feathering up its sides.

At its rear were immense moraines of years-uncollected trash. Similar apartment blocks stretched off in either direction. Most were uninhabited now, their elevators out of order, their water and power turned off. In the cold late-afternoon light, the building in front of me was more terrifying than any of those black towers of fantasy novels, which at least had the merit of being picturesque.

I was glad my kidnappers were with me. I wouldn't have wanted to go in there alone.

They walked me into the lobby, white spots of caulk on the concrete walls indicating vanished tiles, and shoved me into an elevator. They were turning away from me even as the doors closed. The elevator control panel had been ripped out, leaving a tangle of loose wires. The elevator rose, slowly, rumblingly, to some unspecified floor and let me out.

In place of the narrow, peeling-paint hallways of public housing, I stood in a wide foyer facing two huge, elaborately chased suits of armor. Standing between them was a strong, unsmiling man in a silk house robe, a domestic uniform of one of the hyphenates. The corporate logo, one I did not recognize right off, was woven subtly into the pattern. His face was completely unfamiliar to me, his shoulders unnaturally wide, as if uniform epaulets had been built into his bone structure.

"Gene?" I said. "Gene Michaud?" I stepped forward, hand extended. "It's been a long time."

He shook his head. "The name's Aylmer Brandt. I am head of Man-Power, a subsidiary of Hyundai-Chunkoju. We need to talk—"

"I need to talk, but not to Aylmer Brandt, whatever his fine corporate affiliation. I need Gene Michaud. Come on. Charlie's dead. Lori's dead. Watkins is off the deep end. And Straussman is . . . whatever he is."

"Quite right." He finally took my hand. "Whatever he is."

"We never had a secret handshake, Gene," I said. "The Group. Why is that?"

I realized that his eyes, at least, were still the same: fierce, hawk eyes, green stippled with brown. People not born with them have to pay a lot of money for eyes like that.

"We never knew what the hell we were doing," he said softly. "Whatever and whoever we were. And my name, as I think I told you, is Aylmer Brandt, Mr. Peter Ambrose."

"Hell, call me Theo, if it makes you feel any better."

"I'd rather not. I'd rather remember who we *are*."

Since I'd spent a lot of time and trouble recovering who I had been, rather than who I was now, his complacence irritated me.

I grinned. "Your security precautions are very . . . picturesque, but not particularly thorough. Lack of corporate effort at Hyundai-Chunkoju? And I've heard of ManPower—you're supposed to be good. How do you know I don't have a folded-tube IR laser in my left eye taking your retina print and feeding it to a slushware ID data base microcortex in my third ventricle? The eyes, I think, are still yours. Gene."

That made him blink. "But you don't, do you, Mr. Ambrose?"

"No, I don't. And if I linked into any current ID data base, I'm sure I'd come up with the name Aylmer Brandt. You would have remapped all the cross-links. But who knows if you missed one?" I had wanted to dent his complacence, which was as heavy and smooth as a piece of machined weapons-grade U235, but had failed, as I always had.

"Please come this way." Michaud, who called himself Brandt, led me between the two suits of armor. One held a wildly spiked mace resembling a magnified radiolarian, and seemed to be made out of grotesquely swollen insect parts, all shining metalochitin. It had a samurai look, with that snarling whiskered face they liked to use. The other was gleaming streamlined steel, with a wide, stylized chest—Art Deco armor, suitable for crowning the top of a skyscraper. I imagined it as a high-altitude lawn jockey, holding on to zeppelin mooring lines with one hand.

ManPower. It was an organization I'd heard of. It recruited from the South Side gangs, black, white, Bengali, Afrikaner, Eritrean, Albanian, Berber, Jewish, Moslem, for the world's military forces. Society had figured out how to manipulate the innermost aspects of human personalities, but hadn't a clue as to how to make a city a livable place for normal human beings. So societal engineers had taken advantage of the situation, subverting cute gang cultic practices to their personal ends, figuring that if lives were to be ruined, they should at least be ruined in a useful way.

"How's business?" I asked. The building's internal walls had been removed, making a vast space out of the warren of cramped apartments that had once filled it.

Michaud didn't turn around. "Better than ever. You know that."

The gangs ruled the streets in their neighborhoods and believed in their own independence, but were actually as well-organized and co-opted as Cub Scout troops. They fought a continual vicious urban war, putting them in great demand worldwide as urban assault troops, much as Vikings had been hired everywhere in the Middle Ages. The gangs were military farm teams. Aylmer Brandt managed the organization, and traded them to counterparts in other nations, less settled than our own.

I was worried about that insect-machine samurai. I wouldn't count myself a connoisseur, but having seen a number of his best works at close hand, I judged it to be an original Hank Rush. Why was Michaud crazy enough to have it in his own house? Rush always put a lot of himself into his work.

The large room beyond would have told me who he was if nothing else had. Crammed with old military memorabilia, Gene Michaud's collecting passion, it was a complete mess, as always, and the density was so great that there was barely room to move.

I sat down on the cordovan leather couch. Around me dangled swords, colored maps of Gettysburg and Austerlitz, brass helmets topped with plumes of horsehair, and wheel lock dueling pistols. Back at Camp Fitzwater he'd been able to cram his collection into one wooden case left over from some WWII proximity fuzes. I thought I recognized one of the original pieces, an evil-looking eighteenth-century bayonet with what he claimed were bloodstains on the blade. He kept the bayonet clean but wouldn't polish the stains off.

"I put out that query about the tsuba because I knew you would see it," I said. "Hide as you might, I knew you couldn't ignore that. Get me a cup of coffee and we can talk. About Straussman and Watkins. About everything we have to talk about."

Michaud stared at me for a long moment. His new dark and handsome face looked remotely descended from some Caribbean island. He still had star-shaped scars at his temples, like tribal cicatrices, the remnants of direct weapons-control linkages. It was interesting that he'd kept such a dangerous piece of evidence on his face. Pride was behind it, misplaced pride in the professional marks of a military past. The effect was somewhat undercut by the recent habit among the young for artificial scars mimicking those old necessary ones from the Devo Wars. To a newer generation, Michaud looked like he was vainly aping youthful fashions.

I looked back into the foyer. The two visored helmets of the armor had been facing the elevator door when I entered. They had swiveled and now faced me. I swallowed. There was too much going on here. Those suits contained complex internal robotics. More and more dangerous, from Michaud's point of view. Saying that Hank Rush put a lot of himself into his work was not metaphorical. Having turned himself into something approaching machine, he netlinked across to his various creations. Some part of Rush's mind resided in that insect armor. A part of his mind that was completely inside Gene Michaud's elaborate defenses.

"How about some of your famous java, Gene?" I said, to take my mind off my disquiet.

It is sometimes the stupidest lines that resonate in memory. He stared at me for a long moment. "No one's called me Gene in ten years."

"For God's sake, do you really prefer Aylmer? Charlie Geraldino called himself Morris—Morris Lanting. Did you guys get issued those handles when you mustered out? Poor joke."

"We never mustered out, Theo."

"I know. That's one of the things I want to talk about."

He made a crisp military turn on his heel. "Cup of joe coming right up."

He knew right where it was, though he probably hadn't looked at it in ten years. A minute later Michaud emerged with a dented mud-green cylinder and set it on a kilim in the center of the floor.

"Aylmer Brandt exists, you know," he murmured, as he poured water into the coffeemaker from a grass-stained canteen. "Solid dovetailed, all the way back. Get into hisec backcheck files and you'll find his first grade report cards. A quiet kid. A's in penmanship, of all things. Not the kind of little boy suitable for war."

"Except for the fact that Aylmer Brandt *doesn't* exist."

"You're looking at him. It's Gene Michaud who doesn't exist." He even had trouble saying his old name.

"Aylmer Brandt, good penmanship or not, wouldn't even be talking to me. You should have gone whole hog, Gene, had your original identity suppressed. It's easy enough. Just cross-correlate modified versions of as many real memories as you can. Who's to say that that tenth birthday party with the Pin The Tail On The Donkey game happened to Gene Michaud or Aylmer Brandt? In your memory, all you'd have to do is tweak the racial composition of the kids a little, change a mother or two. You'd be set."

"Some people commit suicide that way. Core their memories out, just leave the body."

I shrugged. "A lot of people don't see it as suicide. If excising nonconforming memories make them someone else, well, why not? You're too softhearted. But then, some people get sentimental about their old personalities the way they do about their college letter sweaters."

He stared at me, unblinkingly attentive. "You're talking around the subject. Whatever it is."

"The subject is something of interest to Gene Michaud." I reached into my jacket and pulled out the Kanieye tsuba. I placed it on the table in front of me, between an ashtray made of a shell casing and a Victorian paperweight commemorating the relief of Mafeking.

He stared down at it. "That's mine, you know." His voice was mild.

"It's Gene Michaud's. I stole it from him when we broke up. Just after Straussman's death in the Canadian Rockies." Just as I had stolen one thing from everyone else, going through their stuff as we got ready to flee. Charlie Geraldino would never get his painted neckpiece back, and Lori Inversato would never remove another nut with her socket wrench. I wondered what Karin Crawford was going to do with her bone-handled scalpel. And she had known, known that I had done that. What had she done with the information?

"Why did you take it?"

"I wanted a souvenir. Something tangible. A handle on each of you, so that I could get a *hold* of you when I needed to. You know how unreliable memories can be."

He looked down at it, not reaching for it. It was a lovely object, its edges precise, the shining texture of the patina catching the light just right. "I could have used this, those early years after the wars. I almost starved. A collector would have paid a fortune for it. I could have lived in comfort, not in fear of my life."

"You'd never have sold this, Gene. Never."

"You're right." He reached out and picked it up. "Come here." The coffeemaker was gurgling and hissing, reluctantly making coffee after a decade of well-earned retirement. I stood up. Just around a partition was a Javanese cannon shaped like a snarling basilisk. Behind it was a lacquered stand with two swords on it, one longer than the other, each in an enameled scabbard.

"A *katana* and a matching *tachi*," Michaud said. "One for fighting, the other for ceremony." He picked up the shorter sword. "This *tachi* has its original decoration. It's taken me years to find it. The *kashira*," he pointed at the pommel, "the *fuchi*," a ring at the hilt, "and the *menuki*," some gold clouds in the hilt itself. Where the sword guard should have been was a disk of clear plastic. He slid it off. "At last I have it all, by getting the piece I had originally started with." He slid the tsuba I had brought onto the sword. Its decorations matched the others. "They haven't been together since the end of the eighteenth century." He looked at me, familiar eyes in an unfamiliar face. "You're not going to tell me you suddenly felt guilty about having stolen it, are you?"

"Of course not. I needed to talk to you, and knew that that was the only way I had to get you. You *are* too sentimental, you know. The Brandt identity is perfect otherwise. But you wanted to remain yourself. A weakness nowadays, Gene. You should have reattached your collector's interest to something else. Postage due stamps. Fat-Elvis memorabilia. Toby jugs. But you didn't."

"No, I didn't." His face was suddenly fierce. Save for the eyes it had always been rather gentle, before. "What do you want from me, Peter Ambrose? I have a life here, a world. I don't need you in it."

"You're a military man, Mr. Brandt. You cannot ignore a threat."

"Damn right, Petey boy," a voice came from behind me. "Nice of you to haul yourself up here for us."

Anthony Watkins stepped from behind a partition.

-22-

I SHOULDN'T HAVE BEEN SURPRISED, BUT I WAS, AND HE COULD SEE IT.
I jerked at his voice.

He grinned. "A bit of a jack-in-the-box, eh, Petey boy? Or like one of those peanut brittle cans they have in the old cartoons. Hey, Gene, got any peanut brittle?" Michaud did not reply.

Watkins put a rangy arm around my neck and squeezed me with his elbow in a half-hostile big-brother hug. I looked at him. He looked better than the last time I had seen him, back in that bar. His gray-blue eyes were bright and clear. His personality had swelled and filled his entire face. All signs of the hell he'd lived in for the last ten years were gone. At least Straussman's reappearance had benefited someone.

"Gene . . . I'm sorry, *Aylmer*'s made quite a place for himself in this world we made for him, hasn't he?" Michaud's face tightened at Watkins's praise, which, as always, contained a barb. Watkins strolled over to a window. "ManPower runs military training and recruitment for the whole city, did you know that? And surrounding areas, but the suburbs have never been good sources of warriors. South Side's a particularly good training ground, makes Kishinyov look like a playground." He turned and sparked his eyes at me. He was genuinely angry about something. "We should throw you out there, Peter, give them a little sport."

Michaud, ever-aware that anger had nothing to do with the workman-like business of war, was wearily irritated by his colleague's histrionics. "Bernard," he said. "He's right. We have business to discuss."

"Bernard?" I said.

"Bernard Bolcolme," Watkins said, and bowed ironically. "Don't call me Bernie. But really, Pete's a vet, trained. He could give your boys a run for their money. What do you say, Aylmer?"

"I say, calm down, Bernard. My troops aren't toys for you to play with."

"Bernard," I said. "Jesus. Can't any of you pick a normal-sounding name?" I turned to Michaud. "Where's that coffee you promised me? We need to talk."

I sat back down in the cordovan couch, hoping that it would not reveal gleaming spots of terrified sweat when I got back up again. Michaud sat on his haunches in front of me, for all the world as if he was outside somewhere, on a clear and sensible field of battle.

Watkins plopped himself down in a perforated metal swivel seat that had been ripped out of some obsolete naval destroyer and bolted to Aylmer Brandt's floor. "Still think Straussman doesn't exist, Peter? He got Lori too, out from under whoever she thought she was. And no one could ever figure that out, because she didn't know herself."

"That's why I'm here, for God's—"

"And then . . . poor Karin Crawford. Helena Mennaura, as I think she became." He watched me carefully, gauging my reaction.

"What happened to Karin?" I leaned forward. "Tell me." I remembered Helena Mennaura standing in the middle of her living room, telling me about her nonexistent daughter. What emotion is love when it is directed at a phantom? Our language had not evolved to deal with our new states. She wouldn't run. Wouldn't run despite the fact that she knew what was coming for her. . . .

Watkins shrugged. "She met Straussman, just like Charlie and Lori did. Let him right in. Sat with him, chatted over old times. In her kitchen. She made hot chocolate for him. Imagine that. After all this time she still remembered what he liked. There were two mugs on her table. His was finished, standing on the table in front of his empty chair. Hers was still half-full."

I imagined her body spread across her kitchen floor, blood spattered on the cabinets. "He cut her up with a scalpel."

Watkins was startled. "Jesus, what an idea." He rubbed his chin thoughtfully. "Maybe he did, later, but there's no way of knowing."

"Quit playing around."

"Don't be such a sorehead. I don't know how she died, if she's dead, because there wasn't any body. I was sure there would be, though I didn't have a nice death proposal like you. A scalpel! I broke into her place, more goddam security devices than a mall-drug warehouse, took me an hour, even with Gene's help, and there wasn't anyone there. Empty. And I don't think anyone's ever coming back."

"So what—"

"Straussman killed her family. Every toy in the place was smashed. The photographic emulsions had been bleached so that every photograph, still neatly in its frame, was blank, except for her, standing there alone with nothing around her. In the fireplace—the whole thing is very traditional, like an old novel or something—were the ashes of a child's notebooks. He'd deprogrammed her. Vicious. He's still the sophisticated bastard we always knew. Why strangle people or whap them on the head when there are so many better ways of destroying them?"

I felt sick. "And Karin?"

Watkins shrugged. "Didn't I say I don't know?" And not knowing bothered him, I could see it. He hated admitting it, even when there was no way he *could* know. "Maybe she just dissolved. Poof! Funny, isn't it? The only thing that existed for her was something that didn't really . . . exist."

"Hilarious," I said. Had I fingered her? I pictured Amanda TerAlst coolly tracking her down and taking her away for questioning. My fault.

Michaud handed me a collapsible insulating cup full of coffee. It was field coffee, hot, black, and as pleasant as discarded crankcase oil. It had been a long time since I'd tasted it and now I wondered why I'd missed it.

"Remember the siege of Dubossary?" Michaud asked. "The night they blew the dam and sent the entire goddam Dubossary Reservoir down the Dniestr?" His eyes flashed and his face came alive. Darkness, roar, and in the morning bent and broken bodies in the upper branches of trees. Was that his version of nostalgia?

Karin Crawford had been in Kriulany that night, just downstream from Dubossary, with some reprogrammed terrorists released from our project. All of her companions had drowned, and she'd spent the night on a crumbling tile roof. It had taken sedation and treatment to get her fingers to unclaw. I was sure she still had nightmares about it.

"I'd rather remember the morning walk we took, along upper Trajan's wall." The frost had still been on the grass. Most of the wall had been used as a quarry, what was left was just a green-covered hump, but Michaud had lectured enthusiastically on Roman Imperial grand strategy. I'd had no idea the Romans had ever gotten that far, much less built something that size there. But then, I'd never understood any of the history of that tawdry area, Bessarabia, or why we were there in the first place.

"Yes," Michaud said. "That was a long time ago."

"Two thousand years ago, Gene." For a moment I felt close to that distant man. He'd always wanted to be a soldier, and the Group was anything but soldiers. He'd finally, in his afterlife, achieved his desires.

"It was all those crazy fuckers we created," Watkins said. "In our labs there in that chicken coop. What the hell did they end up thinking they were? Some kind of ancient tribe that fought with the Romans. Dacians? Some damn thing."

"I believe that they had some theory about being descended from a tribe related to the Sarmatians," Michaud murmured. "Costoboci, I think they said."

"Costoboci. Sounds like some game old men play in the park." Watkins turned his eyes on me. "So tell me, Peter old son, what the hell are you doing hanging around with Amanda TerAlst, the iciest luke of all?"

The atmosphere in the room jelled immediately into hostility. Michaud and Watkins both stared at me. I'd already forgotten Watkins's new name.

"I could scarcely avoid 'hanging around' with her after you made me a major witness to your destruction of Charlie Geraldino's body. Or have you forgotten that? You took off and left me as a potential suspect. Flames and body parts all over the place and me standing there with my thumb up my butt."

"And why were you there in the first place?" Watkins looked supercilious, one of his most annoying facial expressions.

"Dammit, because someone had murdered Charlie, and that was the only way I could find out anything about it." I was getting irritated. "You *know* that."

"And you've met with her twice since." Watkins spoke with the careful precision of a prosecutor. Michaud just sat back and watched, the military content to watch civilian authority operate until they screwed something up.

"And what if I have?" The clear anger I felt toward Watkins blew away some of the clouds on my reasoning. "What do you think she's after?"

"She's after us," Watkins said. "The Group. She wants us."

"Does she? What for?"

For a moment, indignation silenced Watkins. "What *for*? What, are you out of your mind? She wants *us*. The Group disappeared, we escaped, got away from them. And now they want us back."

"I have to ask it again, Tony. What for? Our technical knowledge? I've been working in the field since, and I can tell you that knowledge has moved on. What was important when we knew it isn't important anymore.

Classified military information? We never really knew what was going on in the first place—"

"Speak for yourself," Michaud said. His voice, quieter than Watkins's, carried the snap of authority.

"What I'm saying is that there is no reason for IntraCranial, or anyone, to be pursuing the Group. Or do you know something I don't?"

It was hard for me to say, because I *knew,* knew deep down in my bones, below any logic checking or intellectual coherence, that they were *after* us. Not so much for anything we had done or anything we knew, but simply for who we were. But my reasoned conclusions did not match that emotional understanding.

I had read once that, once the proper temperature is reached, anyone can walk across a bed of coals. The feet will be insulated from the coals by a nonconducting layer of superheated steam. It's supposed to be a final exam for physicists—if they can bring themselves to accept their intellectual understanding of heat content as having more validity than their atavistic fear of burning their feet off in the fire, then they will step out on the coals without another thought. And the feet have to be bare, so the sweat can turn into insulating steam. Shoes will burn and leave the wearer with burned stumps for legs.

My conclusions were taking me off onto the coals barefoot. Would my old colleagues be willing to follow?

"What the hell are you talking about?" Watkins was so angry he could barely talk.

"Gene." I turned to Michaud. "You were so worried about TerAlst's finding something out that you tried to kill her with that bloodhound. You must know what you're afraid of. What is it?"

"It was a simple security precaution." His voice was clipped.

"To prevent—?"

"People are forever killing detectives just before the detectives find something out." Watkins had decided on a breezy cheeriness as a defense against me. "Even if the detective is looking for something else completely. Then someone else comes along, duplicates the detective's conclusions—bang-o. Gene decided to get rid of her before she got anywhere *near* the truth."

"You've gotten to the point where you can murder someone, just like that, just because she might find something out about you, even by accident?" Despite myself, I was startled. The Devo Wars were long gone and thank God for that. I didn't want them back. "Why not massacre all of IntraCranial then? And Chicago Homicide, while you're at it."

"We have to take things one at a time." Watkins was impervious. "Since you're buddies with her, you'd be the best one to kill her." He grinned at me. "Just to prove we're still friends."

I was back home. Michaud and Watkins talked past me, not listening at all to anything I might have to say. They exchanged a look over my head. What a baby, it said. Upset over the death of one stupid detective.

"Why are you so sure she's against us?" I said. "Maybe she's after the killer herself, whoever it is. The same person we're all afraid of."

"We're not afraid," Michaud said. "We're . . . concerned."

"Pissed off, more like," Watkins added. "Forget it, Pete. IC's not out to save our tender asses, whatever else they may be after." He looked thoughtful. "Though they *could* be using the killer for their own purposes. To scare us out into the open. Keeps their hands clean, gives them deniability."

"Let me get this straight," I said. "You think Amanda TerAlst killed Charlie Geraldino and Lori Inversato and made Karin Crawford disappear. Do I have that right? Or encouraged someone else to do it. Hauled him there on a leash and let him go. Who, then? Or are we talking complete nonsense, blasting away at her just because we can see her? What the hell kind of game are we playing here? If we aren't going to help her, what are *we* going to do about . . . the killer?"

"You mean Straussman, our old bastard?" Watkins leaned forward.

"If that's who it really is."

"Oh, believe me, that's who it really is." Watkins was serenely certain.

"Well, then, who the hell *is* Straussman?" I felt like we were playing basketball in the fog. The orange ball would occasionally whiz by, but no one knew the score. "Unless he crawled out from under the loam, collected his bones, and lurched on over to Chicago, he's been somewhere for ten years. Who has he been? Who is he now? Have you really given this any thought at all?"

"He's come back, somehow." His voice was tight. "I don't know how. His death in Alberta was clearly faked. He popped out of the world by becoming a dead man."

"And then back in by becoming . . . *who?*"

"What are you getting at?" Michaud's voice was lazily annoyed. His posture was superficially relaxed, but I could see that he was as tight as a spring. He wanted something to happen. If it didn't, he would make it happen.

"There's a real world out there, remember? It's not just a backdrop for the Group. Charlie, Lori, and Karin let *someone* in close to them. You think it was Linden Straussman. Maybe. But how did he get so close? Consider this: he appeared as someone they recognized, someone they did business with. Maybe Straussman set things up that way, planning for years. It was someone they knew."

"Okay," Watkins said. "You asked a question. Any answers?"

"It could be one of us, one of the Group, acting as Straussman's agent." The thoughts came to me as I spoke. "Or, if Straussman has become someone else, why not one of us? Who would he be best at impersonating? Maybe you, Tony."

"Bullshit."

"You may not even know it, consciously." I was warming to my own absurd theory. "Site-specific personalities are common. Why not a situation-specific personality? Straussman doesn't exist—unless he has to. The rest of the time he's the irritating and self-centered Anthony Watkins, not even knowing he's centered on the wrong self."

Watkins grinned at me. "Now Peter's being the Theo Bronkman I remember. Full of the most absurd theories. Do you really believe this? I don't resemble him at all, physically."

"Really? Think about him. Think hard. Are you taller or shorter than Linden Straussman, Tony?" The image of the man looming in the light expanded and contracted in my memory. The light was in my eyes and it was so hard to _see_. "Sure he looked different than you. Not so . . . wide."

"I don't remember Straussman as being particularly _wide_," Michaud said. "Whatever that means. I just remember his ears. Silly, right? Shell-like ears, real clean. No hair in them, nothing. I don't think they really worked, though. I don't think he ever heard anything any of us ever said."

Watkins looked irritated. "His ears? Get a clue, Gene. You never paid any attention to him, did you? You should have. He was the most important thing in our lives. Still is, looks like. He had those ridges in his scalp, kind of like a turtle. And his nose. He had a long, straight . . . nose." He paused, puzzled. "Dammit."

"What's wrong, Tony?" I asked. I already knew.

He rubbed his forehead. "I've lost him. I had him right here." He tapped his temple. "Swear. Now he's just . . . mist with a nose and neck."

Michaud's head swiveled at the sound of a distant trumpet. "Excuse me for a moment." He walked out of the room, treading solidly, like a brick with legs.

"Now all that's left is finding Hank," Tony said.

"He's probably shot himself into orbit by now," I said. "Building himself a body up there." I knew that wasn't true, but I wanted to see what Watkins would say.

Watkins looked sly. "Not enough waste up there for him. You know how funny he got on that subject, near the end. He's sucking up those toxics, you can bet."

Michaud returned. His face was carefully expressionless, but I could sense something. Anger, frustration, fury. Whatever message he had just gotten was setting him on fire.

"The house I grew up in had a big chimney," he said without preamble. "Brick, swelling up near the top. I think it was really old. It seemed that way to me, anyway. My Dad burned things in the fireplace. I don't know what. Railroad ties. Tires. Ancient mummies. He never let me see. Whatever it was, the smoke it made was always black. Dead black. It hung up against the sky and threw a shadow over the front lawn. You couldn't even *see* through it. Black, black, big and black. I remember playing with my toy soldiers on the lawn, looking up at it, wondering where the sun went."

"You don't remember any such goddam thing," Watkins said sharply. "None of us do. We don't have childhoods. None of us do. What are you trying to pull, Gene?"

Michaud looked startled. "Nothing. It's just—"

"It's just a false memory. An implant. You have to be careful of those. We've all had to learn. Maybe you've forgotten that."

"I haven't forgotten anything. But we've been challenged. The bastard. He's laughing at us, *daring* us. Why do you think he operates so openly?"

"Aylmer." Watkins looked, for the first time, worried. "We have a plan."

"A plan! We'll meet him on his own ground and beat him. After all these years. Then we'll see who's laughing." He had signaled somehow, though I hadn't noticed. Leslie and Myron, the bald black man and the blond tall one, appeared behind me, one to either side. "Sorry about this, Peter, but I can't trust you, not right now. Maybe later we'll be able to work together again."

"But, Gene, what about—" I started to get up, then felt an iron hand on each shoulder, forcing me down.

His eyes were hooded. "Everything you say about the Group might be true. Maybe we didn't do anything at all wrong. Maybe they're waiting to give us all medals, take us on a parade down State Street. Doesn't matter, does it? We've all done a lot since then. A lot we don't really want to shove into people's faces. Don't we?"

I could tell that Watkins was surprised by this sudden display of force. It had clearly not been in their original plan. Whatever message Michaud had received had just changed his mind. Watkins, however, was not about to protest. He just watched me sardonically, one eyebrow raised.

I twisted my body and the side of my head exploded into agony. Leslie pulled his fist back and let me look more closely at it. His interphalangeal joints had been armored with sharp-edged steel bands. I drew in a breath. Cooling blood tickled down my temple.

"Thanks for bringing that tsuba back to me, finally," Michaud said. "We can discuss the rest later."

-23-

THEY FROG-MARCHED ME DOWN A HALL, THREW ME INTO A ROOM, AND locked the door. The place was full of more military souvenirs, more leather, a man's room, like something my ralfies would have produced on a bad day. One wall displayed a computer-generated political map of Bessarabia and Moldavia, tinted in pale greens and yellows so that it looked antique, complete to water stains and signs of wear. Scenes of Group operations during the late wars were marked in black ink. I wasn't interested in looking at them. I stood for a moment, feeling with my fingertips at the blood on the side of my head.

I was in there alone, with only a set of bound leather copies of Freeman's *Lee's Lieutenants,* each volume signed by the author, to keep me company. After waiting a moment, I tried the door. Solid as if welded into the frame. The handle wouldn't even rattle. I couldn't hear what was going on beyond it. The rest of the apartment might as well have been completely empty. I ran my hand across the smooth cordovan leather of the couch, feeling the button dimples.

I crossed the room to the window. Night had fallen since I had entered. A tightly organized group jogtrotted across the floodlit open ground in front of the building. They didn't wear uniforms, but they might well have: long, dark, ominous coats and dark hats with crests of bright metal. From my height I couldn't even tell their race. There was something hunched and feral about their motion, as if they were weasels that had learned to walk erect. I pressed my forehead to the cold glass and watched them move purposefully out of sight.

There was some sort of activity directly below me, at the base of the building, but I couldn't see what it was. A converted school minibus painted with the insignia of some community group bumped across the bare earth in front of the building and came to a halt, doors open.

Following it was an elaborately decorated blue-and-silver Korean car, much too expensive for the neighborhood, with huge nonaerodynamic headlights. Two men got out of it and conferred briefly.

Blue gleams winked at me from the broken windows of the building opposite. A room was illuminated, the shadows of human shapes twisting across the walls and ceiling. They gathered around a fire, a mil-surplus bivy stove from the looks of it, with the light screen gone. I watched them for a long time, trying to puzzle out their actions from their distorted shadows. They were cooking dinner, I realized, frying something over the bivy. When it was finished they all slumped down, their shadows turning into featureless lumps, and communed with dinner. It must have been cold in that room with all the windows blown out. They'd probably climbed all the way up there, up the black stairways of that abandoned building, to evade the well-trained gangs that ruled the ground below. I wished I could have walked over and joined them in their supper.

A group of figures emerged from the entrance of Michaud's building. A light behind them, at the building's entrance, cast their monstrous shadows up at the crumbled buildings around. Their mouths puffed mist. In their midst I recognized the blocky figure of Gene Michaud himself. He brandished, improbably, a sword. The two men from the Korean car met him. They must have been heos of ManPower, or perhaps the parent corporation, Hyundai-Chunkoju: nervous global suburbanites, their pseudomilitary greatcoats hanging insincerely from their shoulders. One of them tried to argue with Michaud, but Michaud turned away dismissively and climbed into the van. The rest of his team followed him.

In the distance, behind a line of apartment blocks, a building burned. I could barely see it, but flaming orange seeped into the low overcast. Was that the distant rattle of small-arms fire? It was hard to hear through the thick glass. And far off, like the irritating whine of a fly caught in a window, the sound of police sirens. The minibus drove off, leaving the two heos by their car with the night. After a moment, they got in and drove off. On the opposite side of the field, another gang trotted past.

Damn them all. I was locked in this high cell, hemmed in from all sides, trapped. Those bastards, Michaud and Watkins, were going to keep me from finding out what I needed to know. I fought down a feeling of almost claustrophobic panic. Black ignorance boiled around me.

I turned and pounded on the solid door. "Watkins!" I yelled, as loud as I could. "Damn it, Tony, open the door. Watkins!" I was about to turn and find a heavier object to hit the door with when the lock unsealed and it opened.

Watkins stood in the hall. He wore one of those razorslick wrist holsters where a crook of the little finger would slide the decorative pistol right into the waiting fingers, otherwise leaving them free for shaking hands or eating sushi. In his other hand he held a thick book, finger between the pages to keep his place.

"What's the problem, Peter? Need to go to the bathroom? Gene told me that there's a nice brass chamber pot under the couch. Belonged to some general, I'm sure he knows which one. You should be honored to shit with greatness—"

"Tony, do you know where Gene went?"

He frowned, irritated. "You dragged me up from a comfortable chair to ask me stuff I can't tell you? Get back in the room, Peter, there's a good boy. We can discuss this all later." His mildness was ominous. Michaud's sudden departure had left him angry, and if I wasn't careful, he would take it out on me.

"You don't understand! Are we really all such easy victims? When we think we're so smart? Where the hell do you think he had to go in such a hurry?"

"Petey—"

"Let me put it another way. This place is a fortress, armored up the bunghole. It would take an army to get in here. If someone wanted to get Gene Michaud—Aylmer Brandt, if you please—what would be a good first move?"

"Get him out of here," Watkins said unwillingly. "But—" Watkins wasn't stupid. He looked at me for a moment longer. "You're saying that Straussman—"

"Decoyed him out." I wasn't sure it *was* Straussman, but that wasn't the point right now. "Where does he think he's going, Tony?"

"He didn't say!" Watkins was agitated.

"Do you suppose it's *there?*" My arm gesture was needlessly melodramatic, but it got Watkins to look. He stared out at the distant, burning building.

"Son of a bitch. *That* will be on the news for damn sure. People bet on these things." He ran down the hall and through a Moorish-arched door. I followed. It was Michaud's bedroom. As I might have expected, he slept on a folding military cot. He'd hung draperies from the ceiling, so that we seemed to be in a large tent, thick, gold-fibered ropes holding it up. The floor was made from wood pallets which would have left splinters in bare feet. Though Michaud was the sort of person to sheathe his feet in bulletproof composite. In one corner stood a traveling secretary, military knickknacks covering its writing surface.

Watkins set down his book, whose foreign-looking title was *Quo Vadis,* then sat on the cot and fiddled with a control. "Damn it, you're right." He rubbed his jaw vigorously. "It's some damn border thing—two gang areas rubbing up against each other, nothing too important. A war game, I guess it would be. Hell, maybe it's a graduating exercise for the new officers of the Macedonian, Sichuanese, and Yoruban armies."

A vivid holographic image of the burning building appeared in the center of the room. A roar went up as the roof caved in. Just above the thunder you could hear yelling human voices, punctuated by the occasional gunshot. Two fire trucks sprayed flame-retardant foam. Without the parallel scale-altering channel feeding into the visual cortex, the image seemed like a burning dollhouse.

" . . . a gang dispute that seems to have got out of hand," the announcer was saying. "Local crisis containment units have moved into position." A couple of police bubble cars slid down the street. Flames reflected in their mirror spheres.

"Training stuff, I thought," Watkins said. "A daily thing for him. But there was something specific that Michaud was worried about. He said some gang leader was confronting him. *Challenging* him."

"Straussman?"

"Well, not right out like that, for crissakes. There's got to be some subtlety involved, right? Got to give Gene a chance to delude himself. It was some local punk-warlord type, from what Gene said. 'He does it in perfect artistic form,' Gene told me, whatever the hell that means. 'Just the right formal challenge.' Somewhere in there was a nice little button push . . . 'come punch Daddy in the face, you little bastard'." He laughed. "Michaud never could resist the urge to prove how tough he was. To anyone."

"But you guys had an arrangement."

He rounded on me. "Damn straight we had an arrangement. Neither of us was going to go crazy. Should have gotten it in writing."

"The battle is so hot they're going into the building," the announcer said. Excitement vibrated in his voice, pushing its way past his professional detachment. "The place is burning and they're *going in*." Indeed you could see people jumping across the fire lines and heading into the building, their heat-wavering figures silhouetted against the flames. Once they vanished the camera panned up to show the gravid black smoke, red-lit from below, as it shouldered its way into the overcast.

"Bucking for a goddam graduation *cum laude,*" Watkins said bitterly. "Michaud's teacher's pets. The bastard. He promised me he wouldn't *lose it.* So, I—" He paused, staring at Michaud's secretary.

The objects—elaborate silver spurs like undersea creatures, a couple of WWII hand grenades, a hooked Asian knife, a few unidentifiable gun parts—were lined up neatly on the desk's surface, as if for inventory check. This was a recent arrangement. The pattern in the dust showed that they had once been thrown every which way.

Watkins bounced off the cot and strode out past me as if he had forgotten my existence. I followed.

Ahead of him, the elevator rumbled on its way up.

"He's been here, Tony," I said. "Isn't that what you're thinking? While you two have been laying your little plans, Gene Michaud went and invited Straussman up into his rooms for a little chat. And while they talked, Straussman sat there and, like he always did, rearranged everything on the desk. He always was obsessively neat. Isn't that right?"

Watkins looked back at me, his face tight, terrified. "Yeah, right. They must have had a little chat. People are in and out of here all the time, right? After he got the notification and we locked you up, Gene went in there to get ready. It took him about ten minutes. Then he came out and left, closing the door behind him."

"What are you saying?"

"Did you see Straussman hiding under the cot?" The elevator doors opened. "Gene did it himself." He shook his head. "He goddam did it himself."

As he stepped into the elevator, Leslie and Myron stepped out. They eyed him, wondering, but obviously recognized him as someone permitted to act as a free agent.

"Tony!" I said. He didn't turn to look at me as the doors closed on him.

Without another thought, I turned and ran down the hallway. It caught them by surprise, since they had expected me to act like a good little boy and get taken back to my cell so that they could get about their business.

There had to be, somewhere in this mess of military memorabilia, something that I could use as a weapon against them. But even as they moved after me, calmly self-confident in their own space, I knew I was trapped. They were armed with real weapons, not silver-chased halberd blades, and they knew what they were doing.

Which I certainly didn't. I ran softly, pulling my feet up like a character in a farce. I paused in the partitioned area by the Malaysian basilisk cannon. I blinked at the Japanese sword stand. The long one was still there, but the short one, the one to which Michaud had just attached the tsuba, was gone. I felt like swearing out loud.

I was listening so hard my ears were echoing. There was a hiss of indrawn breath. Kneeling, I poked my head around the edge of the partition. Leslie stood, facing away from me, in a relaxed, legs-spread posture. Without another thought, I launched myself at his legs. "Son of a bitch!" he shouted, as we fell with a crash. If I could take him out, that would leave only—

With incredible strength he rolled and smashed my face with his built-in brass knuckles. I fell back, slamming into the basilisk cannon. He got to his feet and, in a cautious crouch, started for me, his face dark with rage.

"Leslie!" Myron shouted from another room. "Goddamit, it's *moving*."

Leslie's head swiveled like a turtle's. "The shit's in here, Myron. Come on." With a sudden, surreal flicker, a yellow-and-black butterfly flew into the room.

"Fuck that—Jesus!" There was a loud crash from the front room. And a strange noise, a squealing chittering like a poorly oiled and loosely bolted machine running without a flywheel. Myron ran into the room, eyes flicking nervously. "Let's roll, pard. Now!"

Leslie straightened up. A gun appeared in his hand—I guess I hadn't rated one. "Report."

"It's that armor, Leslie. The damn thing . . . it's, it's *alive*."

Leslie didn't look impressed. "It's always been operationally servoed. A display thing. The boss liked it. It was mostly for—"

With heavy crashing footsteps, the massive insectoidal armor from the front room stomped in and raised its knife-spiked mace. Some kind of colored tassels now hung from it, as if it was trying out for a job as an exotic dancer.

"Huh," Leslie said, his voice amazingly calm. "Must be part of the defenses. We should just stand back and let it take care of this guy."

Myron looked dubious. "Well, if you're sure that—"

With blinding speed, the armor flicked out an arm and knocked Myron across the room. He toppled into an arrangement of halberds and pikes and fell to the floor in a noisy clatter. He lay there gasping for a moment, then pushed himself to his hands and knees. "What, Leslie?" he managed. "What did you say?"

Leslie stared at the massive armor as if mesmerized. I looked at it too, and blinked. Tendrils of green grew, even as we watched, around the edges of the armor plates. And the insect-pod lumps were cracking open. The tassels were revealed to be butterflies with still-damp wings newly out of their pupae, hanging on, getting ready for flight.

"Goddam," he said reverently. "Goddam. It's the Canyonites. Right up here. Right in the boss's own bailiwick. It's the Sons of Glen Canyon, Myron!"

Roots grew out of the armor's legs and spread across the floor. Leaves began to open out and cover it with green, even as the butterflies began to take off, filling the air with their colored, looping flight.

"I'm clicked out of here," Myron said calmly. He stood up and ran out of the room. I looked after him, wondering at such a sensible action.

The armor's massive helm turned toward Leslie. Flowers sprouted out through the snarling samurai face. The arm holding the spiked mace started lowering itself at him. "The Sons!" he said, with a strangled cry, and ran out after Myron. I heard the elevator doors open.

"Hank?" I said. "Hank Rush? Are you in there?" The armor did not reply, but it didn't make a move either. It was almost invisible beneath a writhing mat of growth. Those plants growing out of it had to be high-end organiform synthetics, mimicking the growth of real plants. No one knew how to make real organic plants do that. The butterflies were probably real, kept in some state of biological suspension in preparation for a moment like this one. The walls were now covered with fluttering masses of them, all different colors from electric blue to white.

It was probably a symbol kept in store to tell something to Gene Michaud when the moment was ripe. But Gene Michaud wasn't here, he was out assaulting a burning building in pursuit of the chimera of Linden Straussman, carrying a short sword with the tsuba I had given him, so only I saw it, even if I was incapable of understanding it.

I straightened up, feeling the agony in my side from where I had slammed against the cannon. No matter how spooked Leslie and Myron were by the image of vengeful Canyonites, they would be back up here soon with reinforcements. I couldn't go down the elevator: that was a trap. So was there anything else I could do? Not daring to hope anything, I left the room with the armor and began to search the apartment. It let me go.

More doorways, equipment, armaments from various eras . . . and a blank door with a glowing blue light over it. A push panel allowed for it to be opened outward.

Of course. As the burning image in Michaud's bedroom showed, no matter what kind of security system you had, you still needed a way to escape in case of fire. Technology would never completely eliminate that most primitive of terrors. Michaud and his men could squat impregnably on the tenth floor of this abandoned, hulking tower and then be burned out, cooked like squab, screaming, falling flaming from shattered windows. So—a fire escape.

I hit the panel and pushed the door open. Alarms could well have been wailing somewhere. There wasn't anything I could do about that. I ran through the door and down the open-grid stairway. Its high-friction surface gripped my feet, edges outlined in glowing light. I ran down, almost tripping and rolling down the unforgiving stairs, as fast as I could. And I listened, desperately, above the sound of my feet and my own breath.

I heard an almost subliminal click and felt a change in the air pressure. Someone had opened a door, probably somewhere above. The fire door immediately in front of me, built to let people into the stairwell but to let no one out, had an emergency self-illuminated override switch next to it. Without further thought I hit the switch and tumbled through the door.

Just as I did so, the lights in the stairwell died. The door swung shut and locked firmly behind me. Someone had finally activated a fire-escape override system, sealing what had been my escape route. But I was out of it . . . somewhere.

The floor I was on was a deserted mess. The hallway in front of me was piled with shattered furniture, the walls were scrawled with graffiti in a dozen languages, the most prominent being a phosphorescent exhortation in Armenian. Light filtered through the shattered windows from the security lights outside.

I ran into an apartment and looked out the window. A cold wind blew past me. The ground was two stories below me, looking impossibly hard in the bright lights. It was empty of people. They were all inside here, trying to find me.

I jumped back into the hallway and ran toward what I thought was the rear of the building. I was operating on sheer lower brainstem reflexes at this point and had no idea why it was so important for me to get back there.

I realized what it was as soon as I got there. Piled behind the building, as I had noticed on our approach, was a mountain range of unrecycled garbage. It covered what had once been a children's playground, and the top of a high swing set still protruded through the topmost layer, like the spine of some fossilized dinosaur.

I grabbed the window frame, swung myself out above the shattered glass of the window, and let myself drop. The city blew past me, then slapped into me as partially frozen garbage. I scrambled down the mound, expecting to hear bullets slapping around me, and ran off into the night.

-24-

ENOUGH LIGHT FINALLY FORCED ITS WAY THROUGH THE CLOUDY SKY for me to be able to define it as morning. With a desperate creaking of joints, I pushed my way from my place of concealment, ripping my way out of my cocoon of newspapers, garbage bags, and dried leaves, and bore myself out into the uncaring world.

I stood on the edge of a gray-mud–lined slough. The ground around me was dense with dead branches. The still surface of the water gleamed through a layer of new-fallen leaves. Visible in the dense undergrowth around me were pieces of cars, washing machines, and radios. The roof of another car protruded through the leaves and water of the slough.

Blood forced its way back into my legs with a searing hurt. I leaned against the trunk of a dead elm and tried not to howl. I felt like someone had snuck up in the night and snipped my toes off with bolt-cutters.

What the hell was Farley? That was the thought that had occupied my cold night hours, not careful plans as to how I was going to survive. He had married my wife, and had a beautiful mistress to boot. Why did it suddenly seem that that made even less sense than anything else? The thought of Priscilla actually made me warm for a moment. I thought of Gideon Farley, authoritarian and uncomfortable at the same time, sitting in my living room. He made love to both those women. I'd installed those virts in his head. . . .

I had jerked, there in the frozen darkness, startling the irritatingly curious raccoon that had been sniffing around me all night, incredulous that I hadn't brought any food. Farley had Karin Crawford's Kundalini virts installed in his nervous system. And what had she said? Something about the virts and the symbols inside of them. Damn it! The cargo my ex-wife's husband was carrying was in some way significant to my plight. My old colleague Karin Crawford had hidden something inside those virts, some symbol-parsing algorithm, some series of connections, that had something to do with Linden Straussman. And I had just installed them, good workmanlike, without thinking about what lay within, and sent the carrier off to live his life.

I had hoped to forget all about that, about Corinne, about Gideon Farley. Even about Priscilla, if that was possible. But it wasn't. Now, irritatingly, I had to find him again. I had to see if he could help lead to Straussman. And the way to Farley led through Priscilla.

I made my way around the slough's edge, wary of the slick gray mud, which could send me sliding into the stinking water. I came to an abandoned ore barge, sunk down in the mud, bent and rusted a gentle orange. A few mallards swam placidly past it, not paying me any attention. On the slough's opposite side rose a low hill of slag from the steel mills that had once operated in the area. It was all abandoned now, and plants had even started making a foothold on the toxic soil. What I thought was a leaning dead tree turned out to be an abandoned crane, red-leafed vines having already climbed halfway up its length. A cable dangled from its end, holding a gaily decorated artificial Christmas tree.

I could hear cars on a highway somewhere, but nothing was happening here. This was unprettied marshland, the original land of Chicago, and no one was interested in coming here to get their feet wet.

I knew he was here, somewhere. All the hints I'd gotten, from Helena Mennaura's nonexistent daughter's notebook, from Lori's description of Hank's factory, put Hank Rush somewhere down here, in the sodden mass of toxic waste dumps, marshes, and industrial junkyards that marked the southern reaches of the city. Maybe I had been under surveillance the entire time by his sensors. I looked for the tiny fisheyes in tree knots, the microphones under fallen logs. I couldn't find anything. For all I knew, I had been under surveillance by his sensors for my entire life since Camp Fitzwater.

I cursed my previous inattention to matters right-ecological, because I knew that the life around me was sufficient clue to Rush's physical whereabouts, if I had but the wit to see and understand it. There were enough leaves still clinging to branches for me to identify trees. That had to be a skill from my forever-forgotten real childhood. I certainly hadn't learned it at Fitzwater. That compound-leafed ailanthus for example, favorite of vacant lots: even I knew it was native to China. This wasn't Rush's territory, then. That would never have been permitted.

But over there, past a water-filled ditch, was a stand of white-green-brown-mottle-barked sycamores, little fuzzy brown fruit hanging from the branches. A solid Illinois tree. Gritting my teeth, I sloshed through the muddy water, feeling the cold hungry for my bones.

I trudged up a low rise of land on the other side, away from the water. No visibly out-of-place trees, no mangroves or sequoias, but what did I know about it? The undergrowth was dense, filled with bushes, vines, and fallen branches. I fought my way through it.

I climbed across a toppled chain link fence. The concentration of abandoned machinery was much higher here. Traces of massive foundations were visible through the growth. Beyond was the twisted ruin of an automated factory. It couldn't have become this overgrown in a couple of decades without a lot of help. Occasional tilted sections of concrete thrust out of the dried ferns and leaves like rock outcrops.

The understory opened out a little, and there was a stand of young, straight-trunked trees with yellow, toothed leaves, sort of like elm leaves, but longer and narrower. Spiny burs hung from the branches. I stopped and blinked at them. I knew them, not because I was a tree expert, but because they were a fabulous myth, a holy grail of original-intent home ecologists. Its image, rather than its reality, was familiar to everyone. I pulled a bur off and split it open. Inside, nestled together, were three chestnuts. I flipped them off my thumbnail, one by one, into the leaves.

The American chestnut had been extinct in the wild since the early twentieth century, victim of some blight from some damn place or other. It looked like the Canyonites were hoping to have it return to the forests. Of course, various factions had their disagreements about the importance of this. I had heard that debates had turned violent, somewhere out in the Utah canyons where they held their jamborees.

I cleared my throat. "Hank Rush?" I said, feeling like an idiot. No one answered me, not even the trees, since the air was still. The sun above the clouds hadn't seemed to make it any warmer.

A little beyond the stand of American chestnuts was the abandoned housing of some sort of steel furnace. It had sunk into the soft earth and a Liberty Bell–like crack ran up its side. The crack had been sewn shut by a fine silver wire anchored by shining bolts. I grinned to myself. If that wasn't Hank Rush, then nothing was.

"Hank! You home?"

Silently, the old furnace tilted back like an armor helm. It obviously wasn't sunk into the earth at all. "What is it?" a calm and weary voice asked from the darkness within.

"It's me. Theo Bronkman."

"Peter Ambrose, now. It's all right, Peter. I can handle it."

With a cracking noise in the fallen wood around me, dozens of segmented metal pipes emerged from the ground, to wave around me like grotesquely magnified cilia. Each of them was twice my height and any one of them could have pinned me down in an instant. I didn't know if Hank was threatening me or just stretching.

I knelt and peered into the blackness under the furnace, but I couldn't see anything. "You in there, Hank?"

"I'm not *in* any one place." As he spoke, I could hear revving, rumbling machinery in several different directions through the underbrush. Through my feet I felt the vibration of things moving beneath the surface of the ground. "You know that. It's so *confining*." Point made, the sounds ceased.

"It is, Hank. But being in one place at a time is just a bad habit I've gotten into."

"Oh, Peter." He sighed. "That's because you still use that old makeshift brain you were born with. Evolution's a terrible way to achieve good design."

"So you've uploaded your consciousness into hardware? I didn't know—"

"I haven't, no." His voice was straight, but I sensed that I had managed to annoy him. "You still lose something when you do that."

"Yeah. Like yourself." Despite all effort, human consciousness still clung fiercely to the human brain, with all its faults and deficiencies. Our minds were messy, as our evolutionarily kludged brains were messy, and uploading tended to straighten the kinks out.

"Tech'll be here for it eventually."

"God, I hope not."

He chuckled. "You've become a real conservative, Peter."

"Yeah. I long for the days when men were men and machines were machines."

"Come on, come on." His voice was amused. "Take a walk, let's talk."

"Something's been happening with the Group," I said. "Charlie Geraldino and Lori Inversato are dead. Karin Crawford is missing and Gene Michaud—"

"Move on. We're on my private land—I own this entire factory and its property—but I hate being obvious. If I hadn't expected you, you wouldn't have gotten anywhere near here. So take a walk."

I trudged through the underbrush. "You bought an abandoned automated factory?"

"Well, who else would have wanted it? No one wants anything in this whole area. It's an economic and ecological wreck. A lot of war work was done here, and you know the standards *that* sort of thing works under. I bought it under several cover organizations. The city thinks I'm a toxic-waste disposal firm. I suck up organometallics, biohazards, PCBs, whatever, get grants from the government, everybody's happy. Who'd want to check more closely?"

"And you work with the Sons of Glen Canyon."

"Well, of course I do, Peter. We're an ecology ourselves. We all fit together in what we do."

I strolled along, past huge flanged pipes clamped by massive hex nuts, past the ruins of conveyors and reaction vats.

"You can stop here for a moment." I sat down on a rock and looked around for the source of the voice. It came from a mechanical face in a row of similar faces that lined the inside of a tumbled I beam. Some of the faces were rubberized masks with stepper motors to push on them, some were discrete schematics, one was a focus of ionization inside an evacuated hemisphere. As Rush spoke, his voice bounced from one to another. None of them looked like what I remembered of him, all those years ago.

"What are you now, Hank?" I said.

"Oh, pretty much the same, you know. I've packed my spine with nanodevices that manufacture foamed copper-based erythrocyte analogs built to my own specs. They're a bit of an improvement over those dimpled hemoglobin things you depend on. I—use—these—faces—" his voice switched from one to another with every word, "though they're not anywhere near my processor, because, let's face it, that cranial nerve of yours doesn't work too quick and I can get the same speed of response over a distance of kilometers. Think about that. And *your* face is plastered right over your brain."

"Great, Hank," I said. "Great."

Aside from the occasional huge piece of industrial detritus, all around was grassland, patches of trees, and clear ponds. Concrete had been broken slowly and methodically; probably, in orthodox Canyonite fashion, by drilling holes, filling them with water, and letting them freeze, using a real phase change to symbolize a metaphorical one.

"God," one of the faces said, expression despairing, "I want to get out of this place."

"Where would you like to go?" I asked.

"Away from here," he whispered. "It's our ultimate doctrine." The speaking face slumped into despair. "To leave this globe so that it can actually live. It's the only way, you know. It's a logical conclusion. We have proved that we cannot coexist with it."

Perhaps, despite all of his modifications and extra processors, all presumably well-supplied with feedback checks and redundancies, Hank Rush was crazy. The faces, with their constantly shifting expressions, seemed to belong to a schizophrenic.

"Is Straussman alive?" I asked. "Is he out there, Hank? Do you know anything about it?"

"I *don't* know anything about it. I'm leaving, Peter. The main goal of the Sons is to remove human beings from the equation. Humans act like a zero term in the denominator. Nonanalytical. Humans cause things to reach infinity, so none of the other terms matter. Factor them out, and the world will be safe. . . . We can remove human beings from the record like an unconformity."

"Hank!" I felt like I was shouting into the wind. I had found my oracle but its prophetic heads gabbled nonsense. "I need to know."

"What do you need to know?" The voice was suddenly reasonable.

"Straussman—"

"Dead. Fertilizer."

I waited a moment, but he didn't say anything more. "How do you—"

"You want forensic evidence? Mossy bones? Don't have them. He crashed on Mt. May, in Alberta. Just an accident. That's all. It happens. If accidents didn't happen, then nothing would. That ever occur to you? Determinism is stasis. Look back through the history of Earth. Mass extinctions, selection for absolutely no reason, fortune and doom have no care, and that's where our life comes from. Without that, life would be a perfectly symmetrical crystal. If Straussman hadn't died . . . well, maybe nothing would be different, since you guys all act like he's *still* alive. You'd better think about that one a bit. Take a look at that rock you're sitting on."

I peered down between my legs. It was a chunk of some fossil-bearing stratum, lousy with sea worms. But—I looked closer. They had elaborate mouthparts, some so well preserved that I could see the gears that opened and closed them. Another rock nearby, with a metallic sheen, had preserved the remnants of some weird creatures that propelled themselves with miniature paddle wheels. Inside their shells were the controlling circuit boards.

"That's *my* history," Rush said proudly. "I trace my descent back to the Cambrian era, you know."

"And where are we in these layers, Hank?" I said. "Where is Fitzwater? Where's the Group?"

"Gone, washed out. Rocks build up, layer by layer, over millions of years. Then they erode. A few million years of that, and they start to build up again. The result, when you look at a highway cut, is called an unconformity, a gap of missing time. The fossils above the unconformity are wildly different from those below it. Early geologists thought unconformities were the result of vast cataclysms that utterly transformed the world in the space of a few years. They didn't understand that the stratigraphic record was deceptive, that it wasn't continuous. The world makes connected sense, if you know how to look at it right, and the discontinuities are just continuities concealed."

"You're not as unconnected from what's going on as you claim," I said. "You know something's going on, you know someone's . . . killing us. Removing us. You put that armor in Michaud's place. . . ."

"You liked that?" Rush sounded pleased with himself. "Gene was always so greedy—he didn't bother to try to figure out what it was. He investigated it closely, of course, found that it was completely inert, concluded it was some failed experiment in military automation. Who knows what alternate line it was supposed to have come from. And, when he looked, it *was* inert. No way it could have acted independently in that state. But he ignored the fact that things can grow, things can change from one thing to another, changing as much as a caterpillar does when turning into a butterfly . . . nice touch, the butterflies, didn't you think?"

"You saved my ass, Hank, that's a fact. And the butterflies were sweet." And that had always been a characteristic of Rush's: a strange sort of sweetness that came from behind the multiple-element lenses and wideband photomultiplier circuits through which he viewed the world.

"Well, I needed to talk. The thing had been sitting there for long enough, gathering dust. It was about time something happened."

"But something's *been* happening. Straussman—"

"It's *not* Straussman." He sounded petulant, annoyed that I wasn't listening to him. "It's just your memories of him. He bounces around, propagates . . . get rid of him. Refuse to understand him, don't accept what's being said to you. Rearrange him. Bit by bit. Take him away, one piece at a time, and after a while it will look like he was torn away by a thermonuclear explosion. A nonexistent cataclysm."

An unconformity, he'd called it. The Fitzwater Unconformity. That was as good a way of describing that part of my life as I had heard, even if it came from a semielectronic brain case.

"Hank, you have to give me more information."

"No, I *don't*. The whole thing really doesn't interest me very much, you know. I have other things on my mind. Lots of other things. The fate of the earth. Things like that."

"So why did you let me come here?" I asked.

There was a long period of silence. I thought he had finally withdrawn from me, pulled in his sensors, retreated into darkness. A wind blew the trees, sending their bright leaves fluttering over me. Some ducklike bird, a loon maybe, swam around in the water of a pond, sticking its head into the water and its tail into the air.

"Because I wanted to see you, Theo," he said, finally. The faces whispered together, like the hisster of cicadas on a hot summer night. "I wanted to talk to you."

"Sure, Hank," I said. The loon's head emerged from the water with something—a fish. A flicker of silver and it was gone. "It's been a long time. It's good to see you again."

"A long time. I'm linked into some fast processors. It seems even longer."

"Remember when you were the pot-and-pan man of Kishinyov?" I said. "I think you were the most popular man in town then."

"It was something to do." Despite the coolness of his tone, I realized that I'd managed to get to somewhere important to him.

"You did a good job. I'm sure they still remember you."

"Yeah, well. I never thought I'd make a living repairing samovars."

At one time in his career of self-modification, Hank Rush had installed a laser welding apparatus in his left hand. This, like most of what he did to himself, had no real purpose. However, once he had the welder installed, he realized that he could repair small objects for the impoverished people of Bessarabia, who were suffering under the myriad small wars that percolated through the area like weather fronts.

I had found an old music school in a peeling–stucco-covered building near the old center of town. I would play there, days we were free from our work up on the Byk River, on a stage facing an auditorium that was being used as a supply room. The ranks of seats had been removed and replaced by a complex of metal shelving filled with anonymous wooden boxes that never seemed to be moved. I couldn't even figure out how anyone would get in among the shelves to retrieve anything if it was ever needed. The old silver-star-patterned curtains still hung down, partially hiding this bureaucratically symbolic scene from where I sat at the old concert grand.

I convinced Rush to set up a small stand in front of the building. Every morning that he was able to come, a long line would form, snaking around the corner of the building and out into the public square. They brought their old washbasins, their pots, their pans, their hot water heaters, and their samovars. The samovars were most noticeable from the upper window past which I would walk when taking a break from practicing: huge brass cylinders with legs and spigots, often supported by several generations like an offering to a god. Rush sat patiently, fixing and patching, the lightning-glow of his hand lighting up his only half-human face. War had so disrupted life that no one much noticed his modifications. And if they did, they probably assumed that they were due to war wounds.

At the end of the day, Rush would come up and hear me play. I could never figure out if he actually enjoyed it, or just did it in gratitude for the new career I had found for him. I was just glad to have someone listen to me. It convinced me that I was actually making an audible sound, rather than just imagining everything.

Watkins ended it, in his cleverly malicious way. He snuck in, God-only-knew how, a fake saucepan made out of magnesium alloy. Rush's welder set it into bright, flaring flame, which immediately consumed the makeshift wooden stand and the crown of one of the square's trees. I heard the shouts and sirens even in my isolated chamber and ran to the window, to see Rush standing, all alone, with what looked like a miniature nova in his hand. If you looked at it directly, glaring blue afterimages made you blind. I almost fell down the stairs afterward. His hair seemed to be streaming back from it, as if it was actually spilling out solar flares, but that must have been the wind. Burning fragments of wood lay around him, and his clothes were scorched. He himself was expressionless, as if nothing was going on around him, not the yelling crowd, not the pathetic municipal fire engine, broken down from months of fighting incendiary-lit apartment fires and barely able to muster a thin stream of water from the broken pipes, not the fire he held in his hand, meant anything to him. The police closed down his operation as a public safety hazard, a ludicrous judgment in the middle of a modern war, but inarguable without bribes Rush was unwilling to pay.

"Tony shouldn't have done that," I said. "It was pointlessly nasty."

"Ah, well." Rush was unconcerned. "It's the fault of the body, you know, Peter. It's not worth keeping when it goes through such things. Not when it can be replaced by elements that are so much better."

It was time. I reached into my pocket and pulled out Hank's wadded up, spike-lined glove. He'd worn it on the hand that replaced the one with which he'd held the saucepan.

"Here," I said. "This is yours."

"Drop it on the ground," he said. "My scavengers will pick it up."

"It's Watkins, isn't it, Hank?" I said. "He's the reason you don't want to have anything to do with it. With finding the killer."

"Watkins doesn't matter. He doesn't matter at all."

"It's all right to hate him, Hank. You have good enough reason to."

"You'd never hate him," Hank said. "You kind of like him. Always have."

I thought about it. "I suppose I do."

"Oh, I don't mind. You just have to be careful of that, that's all."

I sighed. I wasn't going to get anything out of him, not on the subject that interested me. But still . . . he was alone here, alone despite his interconnections in the world of ecological rewind. I had an appointment later, with Tigranes, that I didn't really want to keep. I didn't have a choice. Tigranes, in his unorthodox, symbol-oriented way, had set our meeting for when the evening star of Venus set, about half an hour after sunset. And I was sitting in one of the few places in metropolitan Chicago where I would be able to see it. So I did have a couple of hours I could spend with an old . . . sibling. It had been years since we had talked.

"So, Hank, what do you want the world to look like?" I said.

He told me. We talked about how the western parts of Nebraska and Kansas were once again a vast prairie covered by herds of buffalo, the water-parasitic wheat farms long since dried up and blown away. Alligators belly flopped in abandoned Jacuzzis in tumbled-down retirement condo complexes in southern Florida. He told me how they would edit Chicago from the pristine shore of Lake Michigan.

I envied him his connection with these purposeful, if insane, people. They wanted something very badly, and were willing to do almost anything to see that it came to be. And they did it together. The way the Group once had.

"And where are we?" I asked. "What happens to those of us who happen to live in this world?"

"You'll go the same way I'm going. It's the only choice left. Those bioreactors you call bodies are hideously inefficient. That's the real problem. Join me, and billions of people can live right in the middle of the life of this world without disturbing it in the slightest. A little solar radiation, a few geothermal gradients, a bit of wind—and life can go on without our infected footprints all over it."

"You hate us," I said with wonder. "You hate us all."

"No! No, I—" There was a long pause. "I don't hate you, Peter." His voice was quiet. "I want you to live. You *will* live. All I can do is offer my own solution. My own."

"You want to disappear," I said. "You want to go away."

"What other choice is there?"

There were a million other choices, but I didn't feel like arguing the point with him. For him, maybe, there wasn't any other choice. For me, there was.

I yawned. The cold dampness of the mud still clung to my legs. The afternoon sun, though autumn-pale, was warm by comparison to my memories of the night before.

"Hank," I said. "Is there somewhere I could lie down and take a nap?"

"A nap?" For a second I thought he was going to claim that he didn't remember what that was. "You're tired."

I yawned again. Now that he said it, I felt it, like weights tied to every particle of my being. "Yes. I need to sleep."

"I don't have a house, Peter." Hank was plaintive. "I don't have a bedroom for you. I wish I did." As he spoke, I pictured a sturdy old brass bedstead, solemn lace curtains, darkened pictures of family ancestors on the striped wallpaper, a sink in the corner. If Hank had stayed a human being, he would have had a guest bedroom like that, I was sure. But it was too cold for me to just lay myself down outside. The cold earth and stiff breeze would suck the heat out of me, leaving me shivering and miserable.

"Wait!" Excitement caught in his voice. "I know. I know. Come around to the left."

In response to his instructions, I circled the I beam and worked my way down a narrow passage between two ruined walls. Around a corner was a shoulder-high stretch of glazed cinder block that had once been one wall of an employee rest room. On the other side of it was a patch of vibrant flowers, their bright-green leaves still thick, in defiance of the weather. The toilets were gone, though I could see the curved rim of one sticking coyly up through a patch of clover.

"Lie down, Peter." Hank's voice was soft. "Lie down."

"I—" Staring wide-eyed at me, head just poking out of the flower, was a doe. She flicked her ears, levitated, and bounded away, so quickly that, after a second, I wasn't sure if I had seen her at all.

The glazed wall broke the wind and retained the heat of the afternoon sun. Still, when I lowered myself down on the bed of lush growth, the ground seemed warmer than it had any right to be, in October.

"Why is it so warm here, Hank?" Even as I spoke, my eyes were drifting shut.

"I pipe heat." Hank spoke eagerly, as if anxious for praise for his cleverness. "I have a section of matte-black piping. Some old solar heating experiment. Must not have been economic. Maybe that's why the factory went out of business. I've never found out. But it ducts enough heat that I can keep this area warm. Animals like to come here and rest. It's warmer than anywhere else."

"I'm sorry, Hank," I murmured. "I haven't seen you for so long, and here I'm just going to sleep on you."

"That's all right. You have a lot to do."

"Too much." My eyes closed. "Too much to do." I slept.

-25-

THE NORTH BRANCH OF THE CHICAGO RIVER FLOWED DARKLY SOME-where below us. Confined by concrete bulwarks for centuries, it was too depressed to make a sound, visible only as a line of black beyond the rusted concertina wire that marked the end of the junkyard where I stood with Tigranes. He had not remarked on the fact that I was covered with dried mud and seedpods.

"What are you eating?" he asked instead.

I swallowed. "A hot dog. A Vienna frank. Want a bite?" I held it out to him.

Tigranes looked down at the proffered dog and suddenly looked hungry. "I haven't had one of those in years."

"Go ahead. This is my fourth. I ate the other three in two bites each. Come on." I'd circled the nervous vendor like a hawk, each time trying to convince myself that I was done.

Gingerly, afraid of getting mustard on his beard, he nipped off a bite. "God, that's good."

"I bought them when I realized that I couldn't remember the last time I'd eaten. And my memory's better than it ever was. I spent the day talking with an old friend." Hank had woken me, gently, when time came for me to go. I wondered if I would see him again. "Sal—I'm learning too much. That ever happen to you? I don't understand anything anymore. Everything I thought I knew . . ."

"It'll fall into place. You know how to think."

"Thanks for the vote of confidence. Will I like what I figure out?"

"Why should you? If you liked it, you'd probably understand it already."

"Hah. Coffee?" I held out the insulated cup.

Tigranes laughed. "Here I've got all my breaking-and-entering gear, and you show me how ill prepared I actually am. Thank you."

We strolled for a moment and he briefed me on our assault plan. I licked ketchup from my fingers. Abandoned automobiles were piled high around us. No late–twentieth century Hupmobiles or Hispano-Suizas—it looked like we were stuck with the real past. The cars in the lowest levels had corroded and been crushed by the increasing weight above. I could see the ornate wheel covers and door panels of the late Nineties, the baroque extravagances of the last decade of cheap oil. Above them were the stolid cars of the early twenty-first century, with their glumly purposeful streamlining. Some still had instruments glowing, powered by solar panels. Above were the high-impact resistant resin cars of later years.

"And how's your old friend the icy luke? Meet her children yet?"

And that was a subject Tigranes couldn't be casual about. From Tigranes's point of view, Amanda TerAlst was a free radical in a cell, ready to rip complex enzyme pathways to shreds. I didn't want to think about what would happen if my interests happened to collide with his.

"No. But she's been strangely . . . helpful."

"They do that sometimes. It's odd, a defect in the system. These Inherent Potential types . . . well, they start to want to be useful. A systemic problem. Train people to think and, by God, they start to do it even when it's inconvenient."

"Maybe," I said.

He nodded in approval. "That's it. She's smarter than you, Peter. Just remember that. Nothing personal, mind you. She's trained to be intelligent, not just skilled. And she's her own woman. Neither her bureaucratic employers nor you will ever be able to twist her in a direction she doesn't want to go."

"You haven't met her." It was half a question.

"No, I haven't met her. But am I wrong?"

"No, Sal," I said. "You aren't wrong."

Most of the useful car parts had been combed. What was left of the cars had been fastened together and served as complicated gopher-hole homes for some of the many refugees from the global chaos of the Devo Wars. They dug their way through the piled vehicles, making their nests. The blue glow of bootleg fuel-cell heating units came through windshields and reflected off rearview mirrors. I could hear the faint sound of a radio playing wailing Arab-Brazilian fava salsa.

Looming over us on the other side of the river was our destination, the Atman Medical Center. Sixty stories high, it occupied what had once been several city blocks and had sucked up the intervening streets into its bulk. Its skeleton glowed.

The shadowy figure of a woman appeared atop a Verkoep hovercraft whose elaborate tail fins had been bent into spirals by some unusually patient teenagers. The woman reached into her coat and released a bird, which flapped off into the night. Tigranes solemnly pulled a multifaceted crystal out of a compression box and tossed it up. It flickered with internal light through a piezoelectric effect. A moment later the bird, having made a circuit of the area, returned to the woman and perched on her shoulder.

"We have safe passage through this area," Tigranes whispered to me. "We're actually inside Atman's outer defensive perimeter. If she knew what we were after, she'd never let us past. These people exist at the sufferance of the hospital because they provide symbiotic support. The trading path for used and spoiled medical goods goes through here. Syringes, clamps, tubes, drugs, all sorts of things. Instead of being dumped in expensive regulated sites, they come here. A nasty toxic waste problem for Atman is turned into a source of profit for low-level operatives."

I pierce the millions-of-years-evolved protections of the brain on a regular basis, the meninges and endothelial layers. I couldn't afford to take any chances like using spoiled equipment. I must have looked disgusted.

Tigranes chuckled. "Don't be so disapproving, Peter. Sterilize the stuff with a little bleach, give it a dose of radiation—poof, good as new. The hospital can't afford to mess with that. And these people are immigrants; they need a leg up. Capitalism. Remember capitalism? Economic system dominant before corporate syndicalism."

"I'm a capitalist," I protested. "An entrepreneur."

He shook his head. "Sorry, Peter. You're a criminal. Not quite the same thing."

"Outlaw capitalism and only outlaws will—"

"Oh, hush up. Let's go."

Our guide was a tall woman with a shaved head who looked like she might be a Maori. Her bird, I saw when we got closer, was a dove. Some virts kept it docile on her shoulder. It probably saw her as a cross between a tree and its mother. She opened the door of an old Mercedes and we stepped in. The seats had been removed and the roof pounded up into a high ovoid. A scintillant light gleamed at its apex. Under our guide's unspeaking supervision we washed our shoes with a spray nozzle. A quick dry with a quartz heater and we walked through into a long, twisting tunnel lit by maintenance lights. Distant motors pumped air through the hallway. Fiber-optic cables snaked in and out of various holes in the wall. Faces peered out at us through smoky glass. Through one wide windshield we saw an Asian family gathered around a large bowl of soup, all sitting comfortably in bucket seats. The smallest child, a little girl in a neat blue dress, was strapped in with a seat belt. She held a ladle like a staff of office.

"*Amanita muscaria*," Tigranes said, "the fly agaric mushroom, is toxic, and is used as a hallucinatory intoxicant in Siberia. It's not a benign drug, makes you sick, puking. The urine of an amanita-intoxicated person is also hallucinogenic, but much less toxic. One of the active ingredients, muscimole, is excreted unchanged from the body, while some more toxic fractions are metabolized. The Chukchi of Siberia drink the urine of an intoxicated shaman and, under his magical supervision, have their own visions."

"That's fascinating, Sal," I said. "Not to mention disgusting."

"The body's an interesting thing, my friend. There was once a rich trade in urine from Atman, right through here. A variety of expensive proprietary treatment drugs likewise pass unchanged into the urine. A simple fractionating procedure can profitably extract them. Put them back into gel capsules and syringes: real money. For some reason Atman thought this went too far. They cracked down and started inventory controlling piss." He cackled, to our guide's unconcealed irritation.

We climbed down through some older vehicles, including an ancient yellow school bus, its windows opening out on the steaming pools of a bathhouse. The pools were sliced and welded sections of a tank truck. Dozens of people frolicked in the steaming water, lit from above by banks of fog lights. It made me want to take off my clothes and stay.

Our guide pulled a massive lever and, with our help, slid open a metal security door. We stepped out onto a foot-wide lip of crumbling concrete just above the water and listened to the door thud solidly shut behind us. Our guide had never spoken a single word.

Atman looked even more intimidating from here. It was completely surrounded by black water, cut off from the city around it. A couple of high-arching bridges carried the flashing lights of ambulances and police cars. A distant, tinny wail of sirens came across the water. Helicopters swept by overhead. Against the featureless overcast sky, they looked as if they were instead far below us, in the depths of the water.

Balanced precariously on the ledge, we pulled on our mil-surplus insuits and breathing gear. My suit held me warm and snug. I looked up at the looming pangolin back of Atman. Somewhere in there, my old friend Slip Sanderson expected me to be caught. He had known about the security changes hinted at in Darlene's notebook, and fully expected me to walk into them unwarned. Somehow that didn't bother me as much as it might have. One should never complain about the quality of extorted information.

I was looking forward to finding what was there. This operation, at least, was clear. It made sense. Succeed or fail, I knew what I was doing. I was tired of trying to reconstruct a well-forgotten past from the burnt ends of old bones. I felt a sudden surge of energy. I was starting to have fun.

Our packs contained integrated equipment for a dozen contingencies: a rhodopsin-inactivating gas that caused temporary blindness, doctors' gowns and IDs, an inflatable raft, IR confounders, focused–electromagnetic-pulse packets to scramble integrated circuitry. I hoped we wouldn't need any of them.

Tigranes and I put on our goggles and slipped into the cold, silent waters of the river.

Our point of ingress was the water inlet to Atman's own water treatment plant. We swam slowly upstream, almost blind, counting piers. Ten minutes after we started, we passed the rising ridge of concrete that indicated Atman's proprietary water flow. We crawled over it and, now sliding with the current, came to the heavy bars of the weir that caught any heavy objects in the river's current. Tigranes squeezed my shoulder and went to work. He'd showed me the devices before we started: two simple metal jacks. Inserted between the bars and cranked, they forced a space wide enough for us to slide through sideways. He left them there, to irritate and confound some future security inspector.

The inlet narrowed and the flow increased. According to plan, Tigranes pulled back and held onto the weir. I swept past him, much faster than I had intended. I grabbed at the walls but they allowed no purchase. The water churned and I tumbled. I bounced off an obstruction, losing my sense of direction. I was breathing, but having a childhood drowning nightmare. An instant later I slammed painfully to a halt.

I was pinned against a metal grate. Hints of light were visible beyond it. Great. Now I could just stay there, flattened like a road kill, until the maintenance crew came in the spring and scraped me off. I pulled my arms and legs in slowly, afraid of ripping my suit apart. Then I rolled across the sharp grating, fighting the flow, and managing to bruise every square inch of my body. I got my arm around the edge and pulled myself off.

A few shaky breaths through my miraculously still-functioning breathing apparatus, and I could reach into the tool kit strapped across my kidneys and crotch. I felt through the tools. They were texture-and-vibration coded by some scheme of Tigranes's, the handle of each one responding to my touch with tactile data I had trouble understanding. I finally pulled out the proper ratchet wrench.

Atman must have had some creative lunatics with a lot of time on their hands to create the many layers of their security system. The water inlet grating was held in place by a variety of asymmetrical socket bolts. No standard tool had a prayer of undoing it. Atman knew that the sort of datadorks that busted their network security software were probably incapable of pounding a nail straight, much less muscling their way through such physical obstacles. The ratchet head pulled itself into the sockets. A squirt of debond and I began to unbolt the grate, trying to keep as much of my body out of the frantic flow as I could lest I be slammed against the grate again and lose my wrench. It took at least fifteen minutes, by which time I felt like a pounded cutlet.

Tigranes appeared beside me. Together we pried up a section of grate and swept through into the light of the filtration plant. A glance around the empty room and we climbed a maintenance ladder out of the water.

Pools swirled mysteriously below us in the bright overhead light. A huge pump thundered behind a wall, sending potable water to patients on the upper floors. A massive heat exchanger dumped the hospital's waste heat into the Chicago River. We stripped off our insuits and shoved them, dripping, into our packs.

Using an antique patellar reflex hammer, Tigranes thumped the wall near the pump, listening with a stethoscope. What he could hear over the violent din I couldn't imagine. I kept my hands over my own ears. He waved me over.

"Nothing is ever simple around here." He pulled out a three-pronged tool, probed with it, and turned. A wall panel, seamlessly invisible, cracked open.

"After you." Tigranes gestured gracefully.

A moment's hesitation, and I was through, climbing the rungs of the access ladder in the wall. Tigranes followed. As we rose, the noise of the water plant vanished.

We were in the interstitial space that ran between the human-occupied areas of the hospital and contained support systems: optical cables, snaking ventilation ducts, backup power subsystems, plumbing. The worker's access ladders snaked through mazes of equipment which opened out beyond our vision every time we came to the space between floors. We inched along, invisible, internal mountaineers, striving to be silent, only a hand's reach away from the life and death of Atman. The hospital was in its night phase, silent, twisted in sheets and wet with night sweat. We could hear what went

on in every room we passed, the sound of hoarse breathing, the beeping of
life-support equipment, the rattle of gurneys.

"Is that morning?" asked a plaintive voice.

"No, honey," a nurse answered. "That's the Moon. It's just rising."

"I wish it was the Sun."

"It will be, soon enough."

"Not soon enough for me."

We heard nurses gossiping at their stations, idly discussing husbands,
lovers, children, changes in hospital administration. At one point Tigranes
turned incautiously and slammed his head into a stair rung with a thunk.

"...and I swear Connors doesn't wear anything under his gown.
No, really, don't laugh. When he's not a doctor he's nothing—did you
hear that?"

"What, Susan?"

A third voice. "Dr. Connors dropping his balls?"

"No, really, I thought—" Tigranes and I held our breath. "Oh God,
maybe this hospital's haunted after all."

"Only by doctors."

"No ghost could afford the insurance premiums."

As we moved on, Tigranes snaked alarms in among the hospital's circuitry. He detected orders to the elevators, monitored heat-and-movement
signals from secure floors, and found signal lines leading to electronic
locks. We passed through a maintenance hatch, Tigranes using one of
his electronic keys to open it. This was the hole in the defenses, created
and kept open by the eternal low-level corruption that keeps technological
civilization from locking up solid.

It was dark beyond. We left the access ladder and began to work our
way, hunched over like miners working a narrow seam, in the space
between the floors. Tigranes found what seemed to be the correct point
and knelt down, but paused for a long time, his head cocked thoughtfully.
"See like a mosquito," he'd told me. "Heat, moisture, carbon dioxide.
What distinguishes a human being from a machine."

Then he shrugged, hooked a line to an overhead stanchion and, after
motioning me to remove my goggles, levered up a ceiling panel. Light
streamed up. A moment to light-adapt and we swung through and lowered
ourselves into Helena Mennaura's secure office.

-26-

"**I** THOUGHT THERE MIGHT BE SOMEONE IN HERE," TIGRANES SAID. "But it must be some lab animal. Not enough trace for a human being." Nevertheless, he strolled around, checking carefully.

It took us a few moments to orient ourselves to the lab, a complex of incurving spaces, like vortices spinning off the leading edge of a hypersonic wing. The place was forward shock, consoles covered in sensuous pliablack, table legs with iridescent lizard scales, bookshelves like delicate traceries of hyaline bone. Organiform now implied curling-edge tech, even though it had nothing to do with function. Why should sitting at a lemniscate-curved screen and pushing a warm button with the feel and resistance of a woman's excited nipple imply control over technology? Don't ask me; I can't even use all the controls in my car.

"It could be someone hiding," I suggested. "Shielded."

He shrugged. "There could be an entire army in lo-met hibernation hanging somewhere above the ceiling, ready to get heart-started and drop on our heads."

Despite myself, I looked up, imagining their feet crashing through the ceiling panels. "Well, you can't worry about everything."

"You can't worry about everything."

Our goal sat in the still middle of a vortex, a spot of calm in chaos. It was a dull black cylinder, half sunk into the floor, and looked like some sort of weapon. In a sense, it was. If weapons are the ultimate tools of politics, then mental prosthetics are the ultimate tools of philosophy.

"Our contact couldn't tell me anything about access," Tigranes said. "She was actually able to give me its location, and something about what it looked like, but that was about it. She honestly couldn't remember much. Normal activation was need and presence, you know the drill. And I couldn't yank it out, not that she would have sat still for it. Interference would have left traces, and she was subject to random check."

The cylinder *felt* heavy somehow, as if it had been hauled up out of the depths of the earth and still wanted to get back. Subtle perceptual clues—and for no good reason. Who the hell cared how heavy it seemed? I thought about it. The site-secure–personality design staff must have used that sense of mass as a mental imprint releaser. To the Mennaura personality that worked here every day, it was a simple secure storage device. Did it loom in the domestic personality's dreams, a heavy, hanging threat?

What had happened to her after her family was killed? I imagined her throwing herself into the Chicago River; I wasn't sure why. Like a character in an old play I'd heard about once, picking flowers on the edge and falling in, not caring anymore. Maybe.

I looked at Tigranes. He leaned over the cylinder with a small box the incongruous yellow of something waterproof, one side of it shiny with switched molecular adhesive. It was a high-density dedicated esemplastic processor, its attention now turned to secure penetration. He grinned at me, a little nervous. Atman had a reputation for clever security booby traps. "Holographic spillover copy. I searched everything from her memory of a day at the park to her knowledge of numerical methods. Memories adhere oddly sometimes. There are association paths . . . misfilings. I narrowed down the list of possible accesses. Some magnetic induction probing—"

"Don't." My voice was sharp. "It's not in there."

He looked startled, waving bushy eyebrows. "Why do you say that, Peter?"

Good question. But the feeling of dread was strong, so strong I wanted to back away from that poisonous egg before it exploded. I felt a cold wind blowing out of me.

Suddenly I wanted to ask Tigranes if Mennaura had remembered being alone that day in the park. Or had she had a little girl with her? What did she remember of her life? What did I—

"I talked to her," I said suddenly.

"What?" He dragged the word out, looking almost frightened.

"I talked to Helena Mennaura . . . at her house." My words tumbled out in rushed confession. "I had to—it was something I needed to know—something totally separate from this. Separate, but connected underground . . . oh, damn, Sal, I'm not making any sense. But I wasn't betraying you . . . it was something . . . ."

"Peter." His strong hand took my shoulder. He looked at me as if I was his son confessing tearfully to having put a dent in the bumper of the family car. "All this may be really important. We'll talk. But just now we're standing inside some of the tightest security in the country, and we have a reason for being here. If you could—"

"Right." I caught my breath. This was no time to convince him to absolve me of my sins. "This is a hollow egg. Holographic spillover . . . you found the memory a lot of places, didn't you? In the park, in the mental techniques, in the skills. Stuck on like boilerplate, coating everything like black grease."

"Yes," he said reluctantly. "It *was* all over the place. But it's important, dammit. It loomed in her mind. Ominous. Dark. Atman's security is tough. She never got used to it."

I shook my head. "You, of all people, should know that you can get used to anything. Were her memories routinized? Habituated?"

"No, they—" He stared at the cylinder as if he'd just tripped over it. "An embossed memory. An installed security suck, to yank us right in. She didn't have a single real memory of using this thing."

"She used a term . . . I read it. In some of her notes. I'll explain that later. They're probably gone now, destroyed, but I read them. It sounded like a reference to something. She called it a tar baby egg."

He barked a laugh. "Well, it looks like ol' Brer Atman is smarter than I thought. Ain't sayin' nuthin', but there's no way *we* can lay low. I'll explain that to *you,* later." He put the yellow code reader away, the precision of his movements showing his anger at himself. "A tar baby. Son of a bitch. There's a secure storage in this facility, but this isn't it. It's a booby trap. A fucking tar baby."

"We can find it, Sal."

"The schedule . . . go!"

We searched the lab carefully. It was full of research equipment, some of it clearly hauled in recently and not yet worked into the elaborate organiform decor. Desks had been moved from their precise vortex foci to accommodate the new gear.

Tigranes was actually showing his nervousness, realizing that he wasn't as much in control of the situation as he had thought. For some reason, that calmed me down. At least there was a good reason he had brought me along.

This complex place was where Helena Mennaura had felt most herself. Here she had probed the secret functions of the human brain, even as large sections of her own personality were off-limits to her. And when Straussman, or whoever, had destroyed her life outside, where would she have come?

"Here it is," Tigranes whispered. "Damn it."

The devices we had come to get were within an armored suspension box that formed the base of a microfocus PET scanner. The base didn't look like it had enough room in it to contain anything, but that was a clever optical illusion. There was actually a storage volume of at least a cubic foot.

"Here embossed memory—that damn tar baby over there—was of a relatively simple coded security box." Tigranes stared off into space as he spoke. "This is a milsec security vault. An EternArk. It can survive a fusion explosion."

We were a good match as a team. The tenser he got, the more relaxed I was, the way a good marriage is supposed to work. "Too bad. Did you make me carry the thermonuclear device? No wonder my pack was so heavy."

"Huh?" He did a slight double take. "This isn't funny. The decoding linkages are in quantum spin-state form."

"Can we carry the whole thing out with us? It's not too big, not like the fake egg."

He shook his head vigorously. "Look more closely. It's part of the crystal structure of the building itself." I did. He was right. "Damn, damn, damn. Peter. I don't have the computing power for this." He held the yellow processor as if he wanted to throw it across the room. "But if we leave, we'll never get back in."

I sat back on my haunches and thought about everything we had seen in the lab. The new equipment had been hauled in hastily, no doubt for some important, emergency research work. "I'm beginning to think that Mennaura set things up for us. She knew there'd be a security bolix and wanted to get us past it. The security on this EternArk's too high for us to get over." I pointed at the lacy-mayfly-wing–covered thorax of a Moravian dense processor. "But I bet you can get into that thing. And we have means for manipulating electron spin states—that quantum harmonic scanner isn't even turned off." Mennaura had clout. The lab was full of the most sophisticated equipment available. I, of course, had absolutely no idea of how to do what I had just blithely suggested. I was just shooting off my mouth in the hope that Tigranes would be able to figure something out.

Tigranes looked around and grinned. "What do you know? Looks like they haven't had systems security in here lately to check for synergistic security cracks. Ha! Let's go."

A surprisingly shrewd security compromise by Mennaura, if she had planned it. Atman had even more problems than I had originally thought.

But then, Mennaura had once been Karin Crawford, one of the Group. We'd learned a few skills in our time.

The Moravian computer opened to his esemplastic processor in about five minutes. "No sensitive info in the data files, so no one bothered to lock it up. Now, all we have to do is link the processor through a driver to the quantum harmonic scanner. The damn thing's here to do statistical analysis of synaptic transmission, not to penetrate milsec quantum state locks, but it will do just fine."

I grabbed my head. "Don't try to get me to understand it, Sal. You'll just confuse me. I prefer that magic datacrisp you gave me to get into the computer system."

"Right." Tigranes hunched over his devices. "While I'm at this, could you check our egress route?" And after that my presence was forgotten. I grabbed some of his security scanning gear and walked past the rank of high windows, looking out at the floating lights of Chicago. City of the big butt, shrugged shoulders, where the fog leaves bloody little paw prints on the cracked concrete . . . and there's not a hog to be seen that isn't in the form of chops in a biodegradable package. Tigranes had said that once, quoting someone. He'd had me read the original so I could understand what he was making fun of. I couldn't remember the poet— Sanders, I thought. Colonel? Or was that someone else? The guy who had managed Elvis . . . Twentieth-century culture was a big trash dump, most of it smelling pretty bad by this point. I usually didn't bother to pick through it. No wonder Sheldon wanted to hose it out and start over.

An antique phrenological head stood on Mennaura's desk, its various regions marked: amativeness, philoprogenitiveness, love of approbation. And knowing Mennaura—Karin Crawford—I was sure that it was an antique, not a reproduction. I tapped a spot on the side of the head near the top. It looked like about the location of the central sensory area of the parietal lobe, but here it was labeled "Hope."

Next to the head was a picture of Mennaura and her family. I picked it up. The heavy, Samoan husband, the pretty little daughter. And Mennaura, looking quietly happy.

Her family was gone, destroyed, lying in fragments on the floor of her house. Where, then, had she gone? I looked around the office, back of my neck prickling. Her diplomas hung on the walls in curved frames, like wet leaves plastered there by the wind. A glass case held a bone saw and an ivory Chinese diagnostic figurine, with meridians marked and annotated by ideograms. Tiny jade-stoppered jars held mysterious herbal remedies.

What had she said? When she walked through the doors of Atman, then she became real. Not anywhere else. Where else would she have come when everything else ceased to exist?

I walked past a storage area into the back part of the laboratory, into a large office. There was a new area here, marked in Mennaura's daughter's notebook in brightly colored pencils. It looked like a positive-pressure clean facility. I could hear the whisper of blowers.

The route of egress we had worked out with Slip Sanderson started in a corner of the office, just above an anatomic-expert–assisted laser surgery drill. A spherical skull clamp, like some old astronomical device with metal lines of longitude and latitude, gleamed right under it. It was studded with countless tiny adjustment motors. The control screen and panel had been yanked from their usual location at the operator's station and rested precariously on a makeshift assembly made of two stacked optical-storage modules. The silver cranial globe examined its own reflection in the control screen.

According to our information, there was a clean cutout route that ran parallel to a waste pipe from an upper floor. We could rodent our way down and out into a public corridor near the cardiac ORs. We had clearance chips for our hospital greens that would get us through to an exterior pedestrian access way. From there we would run as fast as a Vaselined tort case in a room full of lawyers and evaporate into the night. But before we could get to the waste pipe we had to climb through a ventilation duct that twisted through a narrow, birth-canal type of arrangement that started just above my head, ducking under the bulk of a fire-sprinkler reservoir.

If anyone wanted to lay a trap, that was a great place.

I climbed up on a desk covered with a mess of datacrisps, papers, and abandoned coffee cups full of mold. I sent cascades of notes to the floor, and silently apologized to the desk's occupant, who probably wouldn't notice a thing. I wondered who it was. It seemed like someone I could probably get along with.

I reached up for the ceiling—and stopped, looking down at the laser surgery setup. Under what circumstances would someone clamped into the operating harness want to send commands to the laser surgical drill? It didn't make any sense.

I jumped to the floor, followed by another blizzard of papers, and examined the laser drill. Attached to one of its struts with windings of surgical tape was an antique bone-handled scalpel. Its clean blade was a flash of silver in the half-light.

The answer was hiding somewhere near me. I could almost hear it breathing. And when I put Tigranes's mosquito scanning gear on, I could see it, just a thin stream of wet, warm air from the vent nearest me like a bit of ghostly ectoplasm.

I didn't have a weapon—there was no way we could get into a violent tangle with Atman security and come out the better for it. That reasoning didn't stop me from feeling utterly exposed.

I must have stood there, frozen, for a good part of a minute. Then I put my palm on the door plate and pushed. A click, a snuck of air as the pressure seal was broken, and it swung open. I paused again. Tigranes had been past here, in his quick security check. The door had been security sealed. But the touch of my palm had opened it. . . .

I almost didn't see her at first. It was dark, most of the light provided by the city beyond the high windows. The room was unfinished, with exposed ceiling pipes, loose wiring, and stacks of modular snap panels. From the looks of things, this was going to be a sealed clean room when they got done with it. I felt a breath as the door swung shut behind me.

Helena Mennaura was a dark figure sitting by the windows. Her head was bent over, and she didn't look up as I entered. Her once-braided hair was long, and fell around her face. I felt on the wall for a light switch, but there didn't seem to be one. The lights hadn't yet been installed.

"Helena?" I said, hearing nervousness in my voice. She did not stir. I flicked on my temple light. I angled it away, so that she was not spotlit like a suspect, but was instead illuminated by reflected light from the wall. She straightened up then, slowly, like one of those stop-motion movies of plants tilting toward sunlight.

I stepped over to her and took her chin in my hand. She looked at me, but didn't give the impression of seeing me. A puzzled look crossed her face, as if she knew that she *should* be able to see something. She wore a simple coverall, perhaps one left behind by a worker.

Her hair was long, but parts of it had been crudely hacked off. I flipped up a handful of hair and found myself looking at a shaved spot on her left temporal lobe. Several red, puckered, swollen craters in the skin, were covered over by a transparent bandage. I blinked at them. They were drilled straight down through the speech areas of the left hemisphere, as well as the auditory association area. With the destruction of Wernicke's area, Mennaura was no longer able to understand the meaning of spoken words. I wasn't even sure she would be able to hear them as words. By this point, wind through the trees or firecrackers exploded in garbage cans would contain as much meaning as anything I could say.

Not that that stopped me from trying. "Why?" I yelled, shaking her. "What the hell do you think you're doing? Karin! Are you in there?"

The shaking, at least, seemed to annoy her. She shrugged out of my grasp and turned away. I relaxed my hands and stroked her, ran my fingers through her hair. Touch, at least, still meant something to her. She had not burned holes in her postcentral gyrus. The hair was still thick over the top of her head.

I tilted her head slowly. There was a tiny, puckered hole on the left of her occiput, through the visual cortex. She didn't seem to be blind. I couldn't be sure, but from the character of the rest of the damage, I hypothesized that it was specific damage to the part of the occipital lobe that processed visual data, particularly written words. With a single programmed burst from the surgical laser, she had given herself a total dyslexia in which no symbolic representation would ever again make any sense.

She had probably vaporized no more than a couple of grams of tissue in total, and completely removed her ability to relate to the human world. I held her hands in mine and looked into her eyes. She looked back, pupils so dilated that they were just holes in her face.

"Oh, Karin." I slumped down on the floor in front of her. "Oh, Karin." No one had done this to her but herself. She had shaved the proper portions of her scalp, fitted herself into the skull clamp, pulled the control panel to her, and programmed a series of laser bursts, probably not lasting more than a few seconds, which burned her bridges to the outside world. The clamp had sprayed quickseal on her wounds, then let her go.

"We'll take you with us," I told her, though she had no way of understanding me. "I can give you virts . . . you can speak again." Her face was blank. She had no desire to speak again, or to understand any of my words. She wouldn't thank me for hauling her back out of the pit of silence. Well, damn it, we could argue that out later.

I turned her chair so that it faced outward, toward the lights of Chicago, and sat her back down. She didn't react, but just stared forward. Were even those colored lights now meaningless to her? She was now an evolutionary enigma. All of her ability to reason, to think, to feel emotion, were intact. All ability to communicate any thought or emotion was gone.

"I'll be right back. You'll be all right." And I pretended to myself that the tilt of her head was an answer.

-27

I GOT BACK UP ON THE DESK. THE CEILING PANEL FLIPPED UP EASILY, AS if this was a regular path out of the office for a cigarette break. I reached to pull myself up into the gap above—and found myself dangling, kicking my feet, like one of those manacled prisoners that are a staple of philosophically minded cartoons. I lowered my feet back to the desk and drew a breath. Pull-ups. If I put in a bar in the basement, near the entrance to my OR, and exercised diligently, maybe in a couple–six months I could get enough upper-body strength to haul myself up smoothly from an extended hang . . . but just now I was a cow carcass hung up for evisceration.

I stacked a desk chair on top of the documentation dunes and teetered myself atop that. I put my elbows on either side of the ceiling gap and levered myself up, gasping, a weary fish hauled from the sea. I resolved to get to those pull-ups as soon as I could. After this all was over I would dedicate my life to them.

My face was pressed against the rough fibers of an air filter. A moment's work with a screwdriver and I was able to lay it aside. If I accomplished nothing else, I had already made our escape more efficient. The narrow passage snaked ahead of me, dipping under the smooth bulk of the water reservoir, which pressed down on it like a swelling tumor on a blood vessel, and vanished from my view.

With exaggerated care, I attached a line anchor to the side of the duct. We weren't carrying internal climbing equipment, since we couldn't afford the weight and bulk, but Tigranes had added a lightweight support harness to what I was wearing as an extra piece of insurance. The double support line linked to the harness just above my shoulder blades. The duct ahead of me looked steep, and I didn't want to find myself sliding down it face first, to slam into another filter grate and turn my face into a waffle.

I slid my way slowly down the duct in the spirit of thoroughness. I had to see what was beyond the curve. I could feel the line paying out from my harness. The light clipped on one side of my head flickered—a glowing, scampering rodent ahead. I pulled myself down to the lowest part of the curve, where a wide segment of grating and filter sucked air downward, and looked up ahead.

Disaster was immediately obvious. Where Tigranes's plan showed the duct curving back up, to meet the descending waste tube, there was nothing but a wall of gleaming metal. The duct had been rerouted. And recently: I could see a few loose glittering filings from where metal had been cut and bent, and the edges of the metal were rough and shiny. I tapped the new blockage with my fingers. It didn't thud emptily. It was heavily reinforced. This was the trap Slip Sanderson had vengefully let me crawl my way into.

With a couple of barely audible pops, the grating under me gave way. For one surreal instant I floated above it, watching it tumble down the shaft, spinning and getting smaller. It sounded like a pebble rattling around a metal garbage can.

Then I was falling. One blinding instant of complete terror, and I slammed into the side of the vertical shaft, caught by my support lines. I hung there, dazed, my right eye blinded by blood, and had only one thought: no life had flashed in front of my eyes, not even the one I actually remembered.

The thin lines vanished over the edge a few feet above me. My face was pressed against the side of the shaft. I pushed myself away. My feet dangled below me. I peeked between them, down the endless shaft. The filter grating had made a hell of a noise as it bounced down. It had probably woken up everyone on the level where it had finally landed. Someone would put in a call, to maintenance, if no one else.

For a moment I ran in idiotic slow motion, trying to gain purchase on the shaft side with my feet. There was none. All I succeeded in doing was banging up my knees. The lines were too thin to grab on to with my hands, and the edge of the shaft was just out of reach. The safety lines had saved my life, only to hang me up to dry like the victim of a spider.

Like the victim of . . . I suddenly felt as if cold air were pouring down the shaft. It roiled past me and its eddies caught under my stinking, sweating arms. It chilled but did not cool me. What kind of vengeance, what kind of anger is there in the world? Our anger is refracted through our lives and our circumstances at strange angles, not readily calculable. Karin Crawford had tried to save a mute, battered little girl, in vain. Sal Tigranes had tried to save his mute, battered daughter, also in vain. Who was Sal Tigranes? I didn't really know. His life, as befitted his profession, was dark, echoing silence. All I knew was that, for some unknown reason, he communicated with symbols. Symbols very much like a neckpiece, a ratchet wrench, a tsuba, and a scalpel.

I cursed myself for an idiot. I couldn't trust my own thoughts any more. I had lost all authority over them. Sal was my friend. Even given the limitations of his position, no one had been kinder to me. Still, I felt suddenly as if Sal Tigranes was a whirlpool, one that I had circled safely for a long time but was now, with increasing speed, sucking me under. He had sent me here.

Damn it! He had also provided the lines that kept me alive. And that might yet save me. I plucked at them. They vibrated like piano strings in an untuned chord. The shaft edge was only a couple of feet above my outstretched hands. I had to get out of my harness. It was the only way.

I felt around my body. There was a quick-release latch just at the base of my sternum. It was intended for use only in emergencies, if the belt pack became a dangerous encumbrance. Well, it had. I gritted my teeth and yanked the latch.

I had expected it to part gently, letting me get a grip on the loosening belt. But it was an emergency device, intended to free me if I was stuck. The latch blew open with a bang of compressed carbon dioxide, slapping me painfully on the forearms, and I dropped out of the belt pack.

I scrabbled for it like a falling cat and managed to hook an elbow over it. I dangled there for a moment, feeling the sucking depth under my feet, then managed to pull myself up and get the belt under my armpit. I swung to and fro, hanging at an angle. It was a situation in which nothing was going to improve by waiting. Kicking my legs, as if I could swim up the shaft, I hauled myself up, painfully and slowly. After long, agonized minutes, I stood up on the pack, like a kid in a tire swing. From that position I was able to reach over the shaft edge and pull myself up on my elbows. The effort seared through my shoulders and upper back. I suspected that it would be a week before I could reach my arms up over my head. I rolled over onto my back and lay there on the floor of the ventilation duct, barely able to breathe. I was safe.

And we weren't. The falling grate would start alarms. I pulled the pack up by the safety lines, snapped it around my hips, and, lying on my back, heel-pushed my way back up the duct.

I dropped down out of the ceiling, hitting the desk with my ass. We'd have to use the other route, the one hinted at in Mennaura's childish notes.

"Sal!" I yelped.

"Come in here." His voice was calm. "Come in and look."

I ran out into the other room. He was still hunched over the EternArk, seemingly not having moved the entire time I was almost killing myself. Nothing seemed different. His back was wide and serene. Who exactly was I afraid he was?

"Sal—" He raised a hand and I shut up.

The plasma screen on the quantum harmonic scanner displayed a complex, slowly growing form, a representation of the spin-state patterns it was modifying in the lock. The pattern crystallized.

Suddenly, in total silence, the suspension box drifted open. It was crammed with a complex of tiny devices, vastly magnified for view, their images floating above. I recognized the logos of all the major prosthetics companies: Fulger, Paralogix, Hesseman AG, Cephalik, Xinhua of Sichuan. And, sitting among these neurodesigner jewels, were five tiny devices marked with six interlocked circles in a line.

These were the rest of the Kundalini devices. But . . . I looked more closely. These were neat, compact devices, the product of a small-run industrial operation, undoubtedly somewhere in this lab. All were microcoded with identification numbers, part of the bureaucratic inventory control common to all such facilities. I could make out, on some of them, the symbols for various experimental runs.

But none of Farley's virts had borne inventory numbers, or experimental designations. But more than one of them had undergone repairs or modifications. I remembered noting the microscopic flaws. I would never have installed an experimental device in one of my clients. A few things were starting to make more sense. What focused design had Mennaura slid off on me? Those virts had contained specific functions. What had she said? Everything had started to appear to her as a symbol of something else.

Tigranes stared down at them with some sort of dawning knowledge in his own eyes.

"We have a problem, Sal," I said finally. "In the next room—"

He whipped his head around in response to some internal signal. "Damn right we do. Someone's coming to this floor."

AS HE SCOOPED UP THE KUNDALINI DEVICES AND RESEALED THE SUS-pension box, I explained the situation: our key escape route was cut off. My exploration of it was probably what had called the dogs down on us. Helena Mennaura, brain damaged, speechless, sat in a sealed room.

I unfolded the multicolored sheet from Darlene's notebook and pointed out the new route, feeling like an idiot. The page, I now noticed, had little smily faces in the corners.

"All right, all right," Tigranes said. "I don't care where it came from."

"I got it from Mennaura herself, although I don't think the personality I was talking to knew what was being given away. Let's go."

Tigranes preceded me and pushed the palm plate. Nothing happened. He turned to me. "I thought you said—"

I brushed past him and did the same. The door clicked open. "It's for me. She wanted me to find her."

Mennaura had gotten down from her chair and was sitting on the floor, head thrown back so the remnants of her hair dangled down. She looked like she was taking the sun at the beach. Tigranes knelt and commenced undoing a floor panel. I should have helped him, we didn't have much time, but instead I tried to pick Mennaura up.

She twisted away and fled from me on her hands and knees. I wasn't anything she recognized, just a force to be evaded, like a cold draft or a stinging insect.

"Peter!" Tigranes said behind me. "Let's go!"

I turned to him. "We have to take her. We can't leave her." It was obvious. There was nothing else I could do.

He stared at me, wide-eyed, uncomprehending. Alarms rang through the building, security forces were heading for our floor, and Tigranes didn't find it obvious at all.

"What's wrong with her?" he asked.

I grabbed her under the arms and pulled her up. Caught, she sagged against me. She smelled of talcum and mild soap, like a baby.

"She can't talk, Sal. She's burned the speech centers out of her brain. I can't just leave her here. I *can't*."

He had been on the verge of authoritarian rage, something I had never seen but knew he was fully capable of. His mouth had opened to snap an order at me. Then he shut it. He reached out and gently touched her face with the tips of his fingers. She turned toward the pressure but her eyes did not focus on him. His eyes widened in some sort of realization.

"All right," he said. "We'll bring her. That means we get caught." He looked at me. "You know that?"

"All right," I said. "We get caught. Let's go then."

We descended through the floor into another maintenance way. Atman's systems were so complex, and so subject to malfunction and breakdown, that it was lousy with accesses that must have driven the security people nuts. A few levels down we lateraled, again inching through a low passage between floors. Then down the metal rungs of another access way. By this point I was completely disoriented, feeling that I was doomed to spend the rest of my life wandering within the interstices of Atman like a lost soul. Mennaura was amazingly compliant, following the pressure of my hand on her arm. The neural damage had not affected her balance or coordination, and she was still capable of complex intentional movement.

"Here," Tigranes said quietly. He cracked an access box and attached clips to several of the wires. He then undid several bolts and slid a panel aside.

We found ourselves staring down an elevator shaft, the support cables sliding past like serpents.

I felt sick. "I don't want to go through this again," I said. "Sal, I can't." I had visions of clipping on to the cables and sliding down, infinitely down, into some pit.

"Don't worry." He was cheery. "This'll be a breeze." He glanced at Mennaura and his face became solemn.

Suddenly, with a dull rumble, the elevator slid past us, inches from our noses.

"What—"

"Wait for it." Tigranes manipulated a small control box. "The damn thing has to be empty first. We have enough trouble without subduing innocent hospital employees."

A few minutes later the elevator descended again. It slowed when it neared us, and stopped with its top even with the bottom of the open panel. Tigranes stepped off onto it. After a moment's hesitation, I did the same, tugging Mennaura after me.

"Help me with this," Tigranes grunted. Together, we wrestled the wall panel back into place and attached it. Then we tore open the access hatch on top of the elevator. Tigranes jumped in. I took the unprotesting Mennaura and lowered her in by her hands. Tigranes took her and set her gently on the floor. I came in after.

Tigranes grinned at me. "Hey, look, an actual normal way to get around."

"I don't know," I said, looking around. "Looks kind of dangerous to me."

Tigranes just grunted and slipped into the hospital greens we had brought. When I had done the same, and adjusted my photo ID on my chest, he tapped the combination of buttons that released the elevator from its between-floors confinement. The doors opened and we stepped out into a hospital corridor like some chemical crossing the blood-brain barrier. We were back in the world of human beings.

"Look arrogant," I advised Tigranes. "Otherwise they'll be on to us for sure."

He snorted, his eyes scanning the situation. The place was as disturbed as a nest of hornets just knocked off the eaves. The normally sleepy night routine was disturbed, and the hum of conversation was everywhere.

Despite our gowns, we carried our equipment with us. While medicine had become more and more like engineering, it still did not require climbing equipment and sophisticated lock-breaking tools. In addition, Mennaura, walking placidly between us, did not look anything like a patient.

"We need a prop," Tigranes said. He poked his head into several darkened rooms and finally came up with a wheelchair. It was a semi-intelligent device that could take direction from a direct link into the patient's spinal cord.

"I belong to Wally Melnick," the wheelchair said. "Please show authorization."

We paused and Tigranes inserted a false authorization key into the wheelchair's slot. Its security interlocks were not sophisticated, mostly intended to foil joyriding teenagers.

"Thank you," it said.

"Shut up," I said.

We concealed our equipment in its undercarriage.

"That is not a safe stowage area," the wheelchair said.

"Shut up," I said.

We sat Mennaura down in the wheelchair and put a blanket over her legs.

"Has Wally Melnick been informed of my reallocation?" it asked.

"Shut up!" I said.

Tigranes looked at me in wonder. "Why are you yelling at the thing? It's just a machine."

"If it's just a machine, then why is it arguing with us?" I was suddenly furious. "I hate these goddam things." I put a shaking hand on Mennaura's brutally half-shorn head and willed myself to relax. I felt like my muscles were going to snap and rip themselves out like overstressed bridge cables.

"Wally has lost the use of his legs," the wheelchair said plaintively. "He is not ambulatory without artificial aid."

"Damn you," I said. "If you don't shut up, I'll install a new voice chip and you won't be able to talk anything but ungrammatical Finnish with a Cantonese accent."

"I am to be serviced only in a registered maintenance facility. Unauthorized repairs will invalidate the warranty. Do not attempt to service—"

I grabbed a screwdriver out of my kit and shorted out its voice box. A blast of static, and it was silent.

"Damn smug gadgets," I muttered. "If some people had their way, our toilets would chortle and thank us for shitting in them. It's because human beings have nothing to say to each other anymore. Nothing! Better to shut the fuck up."

"I had no idea you were such a cultural critic."

"Yeah, well, I can think too, you know."

And so, at a sedate pace, escorting a wheelchair, we slid out of the hospital and into the night.

ONCE AGAIN WE STOOD ABOVE THE SWIRLING INKY WATER, THOUGH ON THE other side of the Atman buildings from where we had started. This was a canal, actually a creek resurrected from the concrete that had covered it for a century in order that it isolate Atman from the city around it. It joined the river just below us.

A quick modification, and I was able to release the wheelchair, its tiny memory completely wiped. I watched it whiz eagerly away along the catwalk, back to its home. Human memories were not so neat. There were always traces left, like dust in the cracks of a wood floor, impossible to vacuum out completely.

"Get down and inflate the raft," Tigranes said, "so that we can cross the Lethe."

"What's that, Sal?" I was tired, and hated the little verbal traps he always set for me. There was always something I didn't understand, didn't know. . . .

"The River of Forgetfulness. It flows through Hades. You drink it after you die, so that you are not tormented by memories of what you once were."

"Sure, Sal. Sure." I climbed down the slippery ladder. It was poorly maintained, and rusted bolts were coming out of the crumbling, substandard concrete of the wall. I settled myself slowly into the water, feeling its pressure climb my insuit, and released the raft. With a quick hiss, it ballooned out. I held on to the bottom of the ladder with one hand, to the raft with the other.

"Lower her down, Sal. I'll help her in." I tilted my head back, looking up at the lights of Atman. Which floor had we come from? What was going on there now? I couldn't tell.

A few seconds later, I saw Sal coming down the ladder, Mennaura held easily in his arms. She was almost limp and stared blankly out at the meaningless city stretched out before her. She slipped a little in his grasp and her feet touched the water.

"Damn it!" Mennaura squirmed vigorously in Tigranes's grasp as soon as the cold water touched her. "Peter!"

It was too late. Before I could juggle the raft, the ladder, and my own weight, Mennaura had worked her way free of Tigranes's arms and toppled into the river with a splash. I released the raft, figuring to catch it later, and grabbed for her.

She floated on her back, hair billowing out around her head. Her eyes were wide open. She gasped and exhaled noisily. The water closed over her face and she sank from sight with eerie suddenness.

"Karin!" I dived after her and swept my arms through the water, hoping to touch some part of her otherwise invisible body. I thought I might have grabbed a handful of her hair, I was never sure afterward, but that pulled free and she was gone. I gasped to the surface, put in my breathing gear, and dived back after her. Even with my temple light, I could see nothing in the thick darkness of the river. She had vanished, caught by the quick current here and sucked away from me. And she was dead. She had drowned, long minutes ago, probably immediately after I last saw her. Her body was jammed under a piling, or would float up at Wolf's Point to be pointed at by commuters on the bridges tomorrow.

My head broke the surface. It took a moment to reorient myself. I finally saw the dark vertical trace of the ladder. Tigranes stood a few rungs up, peering down into the water. His bulk occluded the lights of the Atman Medical Center behind him. He loomed over me. I pulled the breather from my mouth, feeling like it was choking me. I couldn't breathe any easier in the open air.

"Peter." His voice seemed calm, as if he was just calling out the front door to see if I'd unlocked the car. "What happened?"

I pulled myself away from the sound of his voice, away from where he stood above me.

"You . . ." I managed. "You killed . . ."

"Peter!" His voice was concerned. I heard him slide into the water. "She fell. You saw that." He began to stroke after me. "We were taking that chance."

"No!" I fled, splashing desperately in the water, feeling nightmarishly that I wasn't going anywhere. The water impeded me, grabbed at me, tried to suck me down into its depths the same way it had sucked Karin Crawford.

And behind me came Linden Straussman, in the guise of my old friend, someone I had trusted, someone I had believed in. I would meet him on the far bank.

-28-

THE OTHER SIDE OF THE RIVER WAS AN EMPTY, WEED-GROWN PARKING lot surrounded by a half-toppled chain link fence. Only half the overhead lights were still operational. Still, someone had seen fit to turn them on, and they illuminated the torn asphalt in irregular blotches, like some mysterious binary code intended to be seen only from the air.

I pulled myself from the water. The river sucked at me. I hauled myself through a low hole in the fence by my elbows, dragging my legs behind me. A predator lurked in the water behind me. I wasn't ready for him. I would never be ready.

"Peter! Damn it, what's your problem?" Tigranes puffed after me. I could hear him dragging himself through the cans, bottles, and broken furniture at the parking lot's edge.

A fuzzy black couch stood abandoned, facing the river, probably a place local teenagers came to have sex with the gleaming, rippling bulk of Atman looking over them. Younger kids came to watch the helicopters swirl overhead. Beer cans duned on the asphalt around the couch.

I was set to run across the lot into the night but it was like trying to get away from the back of your head. There was no point to it. I sat down on the couch. It sagged limply under me. I sneezed the dust that rose from it.

Tigranes stopped a few feet away from me. His dark, heavily creased face was solemn. "What's happening, Peter?"

"Why don't you call me by my real name?" My voice was high and cracked. "Theo Bronkman."

He frowned. "Do I know Theo Bronkman?"

"You know you do."

"Peter—is it okay if I call you that? That's how I know you. I don't know . . . that other. Peter, I didn't murder your friend. She pulled herself from my hands." He looked down at them, loose on the ends of his wrists, as if they had some answer, some explanation, for him. "She was terrified. Of the water. As soon as it touched her." He did not come a step closer to me, but I could see him slump down inside himself, as if some crucial piece of interior scaffolding was being removed. "She's dead now. But I didn't kill her. You must know that."

"Why should I believe that?"

"I needed her too. Isn't that terrible, to feel sorry about someone's death because they might have been useful to you? But that's the way of our business, isn't it? I didn't haul her all the way out through Atman security just to throw her in the river. That's absurd, Peter. You know it." His voice grew sharper. "She might have been able to swim, she might have gotten out. . . . There are too many practical objections to your accusations, if what you know about me isn't enough to convince you."

He sounded hurt. No, more than that—deeply injured. Despite myself, I felt regret. Tigranes had been my friend for a long time.

"You knew she was afraid of the water," I said. "After what happened at Dubossary."

"What are you talking about, Peter?"

I peered into his eyes and remembered my rant to Watkins and Michaud about situation-specific personalities. Did he really not remember who he was?

"Do you remember your childhood?" I asked.

He crinkled the corners of his eyes. "I should say I do. I've been thinking lately. I'm getting old. My memoirs . . . I was born in 1960. I remember everything from Little League practice to my first kiss. What do you want?"

This wasn't going to get me anywhere. "I don't—"

"How can I persuade you that I am who I say I am?"

If Straussman had concealed himself under another personality, how could I find it? When did he reemerge? The answer was simple. He reemerged when he needed to murder a member of the Group.

I willed myself to relax and smile. Lowering my shoulders was like settling myself into a pot of boiling water. "I'm sorry, Sal. I don't know . . . I've been under too much stress. Not enough sleep. You know. There are things about the past . . . but they don't matter now. Forgive me. I didn't mean to . . . accuse you of anything." My smile must have looked like the bared teeth of a fish drying on the beach. It was the hardest thing I had ever done.

Tigranes came closer to me, step by step. I kept my gaze on his eyes, waiting for someone else to crawl out of the interstices of his brain, waiting for Linden Straussman to reappear. I thought Tigranes would swell up like a balloon as Straussman's personality roared into him. What method of death would he choose for me? What symbol would be found with my corpse? The air congealed around me.

Tigranes put a hand on my shoulder. I managed not to jerk in terror. "Peter." His voice was barely audible. "I don't know what's wrong. I may never know. But if you want to tell me . . . I'm sorry your friend is dead." He smelled the same, that leathery, mossy smell. He was the man I had always known. I could see every smile and worry line in his well-worn face. His beard was mostly gray. He'd never bothered to readjust the follicles.

I grabbed his garden-roughed hand in mine. I tried to see him strangling Geraldino, smashing Inversato's skull in, taunting Michaud out into the flames, destroying Crawford's imaginary family. I couldn't. The hand on my shoulder grew heavier, pushing me down into the sagging couch.

"I'm sorry too," I said. "I never saw her much, but I'll miss her." As I would miss the rest of them.

He sighed deeply. "You have to tell me what you're thinking, Peter."

I looked at him. Something tugged at my soul. I wished I had a piano at my fingers. There were things I needed to say, but had no way to say them. The language I was able to produce with my larynx was not the one I wanted to use.

"Sal.˙ Why did you open that window?" Cool breeze always blew through wherever Straussman was. He loved that fresh air.

He frowned, puzzled. "What window?"

"In your kitchen. When we were talking. Planning this goddam operation in the first place." I held my breath, as if I was going to trap him.

"Peter. You're the one who opened the window. Don't you remember?"

"I opened—"

With a high whine, like a mosquito reconnoitering an ear, two sharp-prowed boats whizzed up the river, scanning the banks with powerful searchlights. Other, smaller lights clambered up and down the far bank.

Without another word, we flew off the couch and ran for a toppled stretch of the parking lot fence. "Put your hood up," Tigranes managed. "It'll shield you from IR sensors." We cleared the tangled remnants of the chain link fence and ran off into the surrounding neighborhood. There may have been shouts from the searchers at the base of Atman. The blood was pounding too hard in my ears for me to be sure.

After several minutes of ducking, twirling run, in the process of which we knocked over at least two garbage cans and drove a chained dog into an insane frenzy, we found ourselves in a neighborhood of ancient brick apartment buildings and limestone three-flats. It was still the twentieth century as far as they were concerned. The gleaming, wrinkle-skinned Atman buildings still loomed overhead like the promises of a nightmare, over the broken-bulbed lampposts, replacement halogens clipped to them like parasites, over the night-empty front stoops, over the careful, tiny front gardens, rosebushes already trimmed and hidden under insulation. It was just before dawn and few lights were on in the houses around us.

Tigranes and I stood in an alley and divested ourselves of our insuits. In a few minutes we were nothing more than normal pedestrians, men strolling home from a night shift. We crossed a street and I could hear the whoosh-whoosh of fast-moving cars on some busier street, their sound constrained by the old brick buildings that guarded the street's exit.

Garbage lay in the gutter and phosphorescent graffiti covered a brick wall. I found myself laughing. The air I drew in to do it tingled in my lungs.

"Peter!" Tigranes took my shoulder, nervous about my hysteria. "Think!"

"I am thinking!" I shouted. I stopped laughing, though. It seemed to make him nervous. The laugh had cleared my head like a jet of cold water. I was dizzy, as if I was breathing the sun-filled air of the first warm day of spring.

"Will you shut the fuck up?" someone yelled at us from somewhere above.

"Okay!" I yelled back. "Do you have a beer for us?"

My only answer was a slammed window.

"Peter—"

"Don't worry, Sal. First I threaten your life, act like a nutcase, then I get hysterical, is that how you see it?"

"You have a better version?"

"I do. I'm alive. That's the best version I got. I'm alive, and I'm going to stay that way, no matter what anyone else's plan is, do you understand me?"

"No."

"Sal." I stopped him and held on to both his shoulders. Tigranes was starting to look genuinely nervous. "Sal. Someone's trying to kill me. He's out there somewhere." I gestured broadly, taking in the city. "He's killed four people already. Four people who were close to me. He's after the rest of us. Members of my . . . family, you might say. That started as a metaphor. It's something more now."

"Does that family include Helena Mennaura?"

"It does. That's why I blamed you when she died."

He thought about that. "You think that I'm trying to kill you?"

"I did, Sal. I did. Sorry about that."

"Sorry, he says." Tigranes looked only mildly offended, as if it was a common misunderstanding, one he encountered daily.

"I am." I put my arms around him and squeezed. He had a barrel chest. His bushy beard rustled against my face. "You don't know how sorry I am, Sal."

"Sure." He hugged me back. "Sure thing, Peter." There was still an undertone of puzzlement in his voice.

I pulled away then, embarrassed by the sudden vehemence of my affection. Where had that come from? My ... love for Tigranes, if that was the right word for it, had always been somewhat hidden, before. It seemed that the death around me had excavated it.

"We were a special project group, during the Wars of Devolution," I said, keeping my voice carefully neutral. I tried to order my thoughts. They squirmed like overtired children. "Our manager died, we thought, and we demobbed. Now it seems that he, or someone acting for him, is back, alive. And killing us. Mennaura sold you those virts and told you to sell them to a jazz musician. She was trying to contact me, to warn me."

"Ah." He waited, but I stayed silent. Instead of asking me to go on, he was silent too, and we walked next to each other along the night street.

What was I doing? I wanted to tell someone, I wanted to tell *him*. But I had told TerAlst about Mennaura, and a day later Mennaura was insane, then dead. Now I wanted to talk to Tigranes. What did I really know about anyone? The world was conspiring to pull out what I had so carefully husbanded in my head, and then to use it.

"There was something in those virts, Sal. Some sort of information." I tried to remember exactly what she had said. "It's something important, something to do with all of us. She hoped that I would figure it out ... but I was blind, then. I didn't see it."

"You installed them in a client."

"Yes, yes I did. I wouldn't have if I had known. . . ."

"And where is this client now?" His voice was harsh, clipped.

"Where?" I felt vague. Where would Gideon Farley be, now? In bed with Corinne? In bed with Priscilla? Commuting somewhere between the two? "I don't know." I found myself whispering, as if everyone wanted to know, and I was afraid of being overheard.

"Peter." Tigranes was patient. "You're telling me this for a reason."

I thought about that. "I suppose I am."

"You've lost your client, and you've lost your virts with him. They are important to you. Do you want me to find them for you?"

"I don't know. . . ." There were glimmerings of dawn on the shop fronts. Did I indeed want Tigranes to pursue Corinne's husband for me, while I sat back and took a well-deserved nap? "No. No, Sal. He's my problem. Entirely mine."

"Then you'd better get on it. Now." His voice snapped with authority. "If you value your life, as you say that you do. And if I can help you . . ."

"Thank you, Sal. I know where to go." I looked ahead, through the stacks of buildings, for Priscilla's, and smiled at myself. What a wonderful thing, that I had a practical reason to see her again.

"Excellent." He slapped my shoulder. Why was he so cheery, all of a sudden? He mirrored my, entirely senseless, mood. "Let me tell you something, Peter. Something that may help explain. A few weeks before my daughter Shira was in her accident I gave her a present: a little windup dog. Completely mechanical, no electronics. An antique I'd found in some dusty store. If you wound it up, it played a tune. She had it with her when the truck killed her mother and injured her. Afterward, it was bent and would no longer play . . . I think it was 'How Much Is That Doggy in the Window?' Some terrible old thing. She had lost the ability to recognize anyone, to respond to anyone. But she knew what that dog was—it was my love for her. She knew that, you see. That was her symbol for it. That offbeat virt I installed seized on it." He shook his head. "The technologies we create are just more and more elaborate mazes for our emotions to run through. So don't be surprised what happens when you finally find your client. Don't be surprised by anything. I'll leave you here."

We stood on a corner just like any other in the city. A few pedestrians had appeared on the sidewalks with the approach of morning. The city was speeding up.

"I won't force my help on you," Tigranes said. "But if you need it, let me know. Use this." He handed me an old, worn coin with an eagle on it. "Place it in any regular drop. *Don't* try to contact me in any other way. You won't reach me."

"Thank you, Sal." We embraced, and I watched him stump slowly and ponderously down the street, his head bowed in thought, until he turned a corner and disappeared. I didn't know how he was going to get home, but imagined Messengers arriving to pick him up, on unicycles, in a dual-torque electric car, in a Conestoga wagon. Who knew?

I started to look for a phone to call Priscilla.

-29-

"**W**HEN I ASKED YOU TO GIVE ME A CALL, I DIDN'T KNOW IT WOULD take you this long." Priscilla tilted her hips and sat down on the couch next to me.

I blinked at her. That couch. Its texture was soft on my skin, like a lover's breath. It was an erotic couch. I loved that couch.

"But you're not here just to pass the time, are you, Peter? You have something to say."

"I do. Give me a few minutes to figure out what it is." I felt like I had reached a safe haven. The knife-edges outside could not reach in here. And there wasn't even any real reason to feel that way.

"Okay." She smiled at me. I liked that.

"What do you feel for me, Priscilla?" I found myself asking, though that wasn't what I had come to find out at all.

"Feel?" Her smile grew uncertain. "Should I feel something for you, Peter Ambrose?"

That was sharp and cold. I should have expected it. "No . . . no . . . of course not. It's just that . . . I like it when you smile at me. That's all."

"Most men do. But be careful. A smile's no realer than makeup. Less real, actually, since it takes some effort to put makeup on, and that might be considered somewhat honest."

She hadn't moved away from me. I could feel her warmth, leg against leg, and smell her. She wore the same perfume. It tugged at my memory. Not a memory of her. Of something, someone else. It was a dry smell, like desert blooms, like orange flowers blowing in a breeze from the hills. It had the desired effect of a woman's perfume—it opened up the pores of my desire. I knew she felt it. But she still did not move away from me.

"Smiles can be real," I said, feeling a little like a child who claims to have seen an elephant in the backyard.

She eyed me, just a little contemptuous, maybe disappointed. "You, a man in your business, are telling me that? Isn't there some kind of smirk circuit in your brain that you can flip on and off like a switch?"

"More complicated than that," I said. "But not much. Hypothalamus to brainstem motor centers to facial muscles. You're right. Still, I stick with what I said. There are smiles that are real. They may not look any different. But they *are* different." I yawned, feeling the night I had spent with Tigranes weighing on my bones.

She looked at me in wonder. "What's been happening to you, my friend?"

"A lot. A hell of a lot. Are you going to make me a cup of coffee or are you just going to sit there harassing me?"

She grinned, then wiped it. "That was a real one, I think. Okay, okay. I'll crank up the bug." She leaned over the insectoid espresso machine and turned it on. She wore a ribbed wool dress that clung to her curves. "Be careful when you ask someone like me what she feels." She fussed with the machine, not looking at me. "If you get the truth, you may not like it. What do you know about love, Peter?"

"Not a goddamn thing."

She laughed trillingly. "Have I struck a nerve, or what? Don't be so angry. None of us know much, after all."

"Some know more than others. What do you know?"

The espresso machine cricket-chirped and she turned away from it, leaned her round butt against the conch-interior table, and looked seriously at me. "Fluids and mechanics, plenty. I can even call myself an expert. Love? People talk too much about love, that's all. There's no way to mention it that doesn't take used lumber. Are you asking me if I love Mr. Gideon Farley?"

I hadn't been, but I nodded.

"Yes, of course I do." Her tone was breezy. "It's in my contract. So I'm hooked on Gideon Farley. Love the hell out of him. Follow him everywhere. I even like it." She sucked air through her nostrils. "Does his wife love him too, do you know?" She sounded vulnerable, jealous. That bothered me a lot more than the breeziness.

"Seems to." I felt like something was being knocked away bit by bit from under me.

She shook her head. "Amazing. And she doesn't even have to." She hissed coffee into demitasses, handed me one. "You can get rid of it for me, can't you? That feeling. No one would ever be the wiser."

"Do you want to?"

"Hell, yes!" She glared at me. "It leaves a woman defenseless, to feel that way. That's the hell of this profession in this day and age. It used to be that you could call your feelings your own, filthy though they were. Not any more. Not at all."

"Priscilla. I need Gideon Farley."

She regarded me with half-lowered lids. "What for?"

"He has something I need. Something in his head. I have to get it."

"Something in his head? Something you put there?"

"Yes."

"Ha! Are you crazy? You think he's going to let you anywhere near that precious skull of his? He's linked in, he's hot, his brain's flaring across the universe. It may be some weird kind of malfunction, I don't know, but I know that he loves it."

"What are you talking about?" What she was saying was making me nervous. God only knew how much Mennaura had modified that virt, or what it did now.

"That's most of what I know. You think I can analyze his net interfaces and see what sparks are shooting across them? That's your job." She considered. "You gave him something, though. Something special. Of course, I don't know all about this stuff, what the *level* of technology is, all that bullshit, but I know that you've done something to him."

She tugged her lower lip thoughtfully. I wiggled my ass on the soft couch as she did it. It was her skill that she could turn thinking into an erotic action.

"He's found something. Something important. The promised land, maybe. And here he'd thought, like the rest of us, that he'd have to stand and stare over the river at it . . . no, sorry, that doesn't make any sense. Moses was actually looking for the damn place. For forty years. I don't think Gideon ever was. But now he's there, feeding on honeydew and drinking the milk of paradise."

"I still don't understand." I didn't even get her references, which were probably from the Bible, or something.

"Oh, I don't know." Light came from beneath her skin. "I just know that it frees me. He doesn't need me any more. He doesn't need anyone. When he has sex, it's no longer with me. I'm just a place to put it while he fucks the universe."

"I'd like some specific behavioral—"

"Never the fuck mind!" Her face was flushed. She reached behind herself and unzipped her dress. It fell down around her ankles. Her underwear was red lace under it, so sheer it seemed to be written right on her skin, and her flush went all the way down her chest. She turned away and looked at me over her shoulder.

"Coming?" she said.

I WOKE UP WITH A START. THE BEDROOM WAS SOFTLY LIT. THE RALFIE had been working overtime here. The lace and frills tumbled around me like surf. I turned my head. Priscilla leaned on one elbow and regarded me with amusement. She still wore her red lace. I tried to remember—

"You fell asleep," she said in wonder. "I brought you here into my bedroom to make love to me and you fell asleep."

I thought about that. "I was tired."

She laughed happily. "You were tired. You were tired!" She squirmed over to me across the lacy pillows and multiple sheets and laid her head on my shoulder. "Thank you, Peter."

"What for?" I ran my fingers through her hair.

"For falling asleep."

I yawned, trying to clear my head. "I assume you'll explain that."

She shook her head. "Maybe I shouldn't. You dozed right off. I have my own techniques for making men feel . . . more men than they are. They're not very complicated. But I wanted to see what you would do, here, now. And you curled up against me and went to sleep, like some big, friendly animal."

"Well," I said. "I felt safe here. I don't know why."

"Maybe because you are. You made me feel safe too."

"Maybe." Her fingers were soft on my forehead. "But I didn't come here . . . I didn't come here for this." I was erect, hot. I wanted her. But I knew that it was too late now, that there were other things I had to do. Had she just now stimulated me to make that point? I didn't know what she was capable of.

"What if I told you that of all the men I've met, you are the one I would most hope to love? What would you do then?"

I breathed shallowly, trying to move as little as possible, so that I wouldn't disturb the idea, as little sense as it made. "I don't know. Is your smile real? Do you know yourself if it is?"

"You think I should lie down in a cool dark room and try to get over it?" She smiled. "Tell you what, Peter. If you don't trust it, if you think it's a manipulated illusion, like everything else in this world, like what I have for Farley, then do something for me. Put me down on that table in your mad scientist's lab and get rid of it. You can do that, can't you? It's like taking out a phobia, or putting in the ability to juggle. Let me say I love you." Her eyes glowed, not with a painful, girlish sincerity, but with a hot fire that was all any man could ask from a woman. "Let me say it, then lay me down to sleep and scrub it away. You won't have to worry about it then. You won't have to fear it. You will be positive it doesn't exist. I'll consent. Like a front-end alignment. Okay? You're the best, I've heard. If anyone can do it, you can."

The thought gave me a chill. "I don't want that. You know I don't want that."

"What do you want?"

"Right now? Don't get angry with me."

"I won't be angry."

"I want Gideon Farley."

"You son of a bitch!"

She jumped up from the bed. I took her hands. She pulled free of my grasp and moved back a step. Only a step, but it opened up a gap between us.

"I need him," I said. "Four people have died in the past couple of weeks. And I might be next. And that virt I stuck into him might provide a key. You tell me something has happened inside of him. I have to find out what."

"Died? You mean murdered, don't you?"

"I do."

"Okay." She was cool. "Do you know who's doing it?"

"I don't *know* who the killer is." I drew myself out of bed and put my arms around her. "Please help me, Priscilla. That virt in Gideon's head may hold part of the answer. I can't know, not from this distance. I have to see him." I was startled by her lack of reaction to the idea of murder.

But my touch got her to respond. "Let me go! Let me . . . Is this why you . . . everything? Why you came to me?"

She tried to pull away from me but I held her. Late-afternoon sunlight spilled through the bedroom window. Her bureau, the waxy yellow posterior of a five-foot-high human skull with drawers in it, was covered with clean white lace. As lace slid off the overhanging curve of the occiput, revealing the squiggly sutures of the cranial bones, the ralfie made more. The skull's base was hidden by drifts of lace snow.

"No, Priscilla." I turned her so that I could feel the beating of her heart against my chest. "No." Her questions had been so plaintive that I didn't know what to say. I could feel her ribs expand and contract under my hand.

She turned her head and looked into my eyes. "You slept so hard you have sheet wrinkles imprinted on your cheek." She rubbed them with her fingertips. "They'll be gone soon."

"I want to stay alive. We may have love, we may have some more-or-less okay substitute for it, we may have shit, but I want to stay *alive*. Can you understand that?"

"I can understand it, but I don't really believe it, Peter. Here, get your clothes on."

I had thrown them off onto the floor, but they now hung neatly on the back of a bentwood chair. As I reached for them, I caught a look at myself in the huge, heavy mirror near her dresser. I saw the same hulking, overweight man I had always seen. But there were new lines in his face, a new furtiveness in his movement. I looked like a victim. Straining against automatic reflexes, I dropped my shoulders, straightened my spine, relaxed my hands. I also sucked in my stomach, not that that made any sense. Priscilla must have seen it already.

"Why don't you—"

"Because if staying alive was all that mattered to you, you'd cooperate with that nice police, Amanda TerAlst."

I kept pulling on my pants, nice and easy. "You talked to her?"

"She didn't give me much of a choice. We drank tea together, out in the living room. Had quite a nice chat, actually. All about you and Farley and how you weren't really helping her get anywhere in her investigation. And about how one or the other of you could well be the killer's next victim."

So that was why my news about murder hadn't startled her. It made sense. I kept thinking that TerAlst would just sit around and wait for things to happen, but of course that was complete nonsense. She was on this case, for whatever reason, and wanted to solve it. My contact with Priscilla had become known to TerAlst, so it was natural that she should be questioned.

But why did TerAlst think that Farley was a likely victim? He'd never been a member of the Group. The only things he'd ever done that were even remotely connected were marry Corinne . . . and pick up some cargo from me.

"So you don't care much about staying alive, it seems. Otherwise you'd cooperate. She'd protect you. You know that. It's something else you want, Peter. What is it?"

"I want to *know*, dammit. Is your life open to you, Priscilla? Do you understand it? You don't even know who acted on you. You have no idea why any of it happened."

"It happened! I'm supposed to go back and check out the petty, twisted little motivations of everyone involved? And what more would I know when I was done? Not a damn thing that's important." She flashed her eyes at me. "But that's not it for you, is it? You want to dig around in the muck just in case you dropped something important in there, right?"

"If I have to."

She looked at me for a long moment longer, then turned and started to get dressed. She pulled her clothes on with efficient briskness.

"I'm sorry, Priscilla."

"What for?"

I thought about that. "I'm not sure. Because I've pissed you off. I didn't mean to. I just wanted to—"

"I know, I know." She softened. "Finish getting dressed. We've got work to do."

"Are we—"

"I'm going to listen to you play. That's the deal. You promised me that, before. Or was that just to get me into bed?"

"Ha. We'd already made love when I told you that."

"Fancy that. You must have meant it, then."

"I did." I put my hands on her shoulders. She relaxed, just a little, enough that I felt the curve of her bottom against my crotch. I considered making love to her now and just letting the rest of the world go to hell. Maybe there were things that made forgetting worthwhile.

"All right." She pulled away. "You set something up. Some musical thing, a small one. Can you do that?"

"Yes," I said slowly. "I have friends. We can put together a small, impromptu concert. Why?"

"Do that, and I'll bring Gideon. He likes it when I find odd little things like that for him. It's one of the things he pays me for. Do it tonight. Then we'll see."

"Thank you, Priscilla."

"Wait and see what happens. Then you can thank me."

-30-

PRISCILLA SLID ONTO THE BENCH ON THE OPPOSITE SIDE OF THE BOOTH and smiled at me. "Is this somewhere you like to hang out?" Without even looking for a waiter, she lifted a finger and produced, through some feminine alchemy, two large red bowls of cafe au lait.

"No," I said. "I've never been here before. It's in memory of a friend."

"I like it here. I'm glad the future doesn't happen everywhere at once. That would be too tedious."

We sat in the cafe that Helena Mennaura had pointed out to me as her daughter Darlene's favorite place. The bustle and steam of early morning were gone, replaced by subdued plate-fork click and conversation. It was a symbol, of sorts, and I should have grown wary of symbols, which lately had been becoming all too real, but something in my soul demanded it. Mennaura had never come here herself, at least not consciously. I should have liked to sit down and share a cup of coffee with her here.

I had called Sheldon and told him what I wanted. Then I had described the place, vague as my information about it was. His response was immediate.

"Amalik's! Know the place. Do their uniforms, sometimes. Bunch of Somalians, desert guys, sleep out on the roof when the weather's nice, which it never is. One of them plays some flute, pretty good. He can play with us. Okay?"

"Okay," I had said, feeling a relief that had nothing to do with luring Gideon Farley out of hiding. I missed Sheldon, the only dependable thing in my entire universe. I was afraid that he would prove to be a complete illusion.

Priscilla ran her stubby-fingered hand across the dark-lacquered slats of the booth, feeling the ancient graffiti carved there. "But do you suppose that this is really old? Or is it just a simulation of it? These names, 'Hector and Luisa,' might have been carved by a computer-operated burin."

"No one simulates the real past anymore," I said. "Find some evidence that it comes from a past that's more interesting than our own, and you'll know it's a fake."

Sheldon, the apostle of nonexistent reality, appeared at the door, trombone case under his arm, and waved to me. I signaled him over.

"Well howdy-do," he said. "I'm finally getting some good work out of you, Mr. Am*brose*. Seems like the music's seeping out of your little brain and right into your blood." He plopped down next to me and grinned at Priscilla. She grinned back. "This lady the cause of the event? You should bring her around more. For the music to get *into* it, the blood's gotta *move*."

I introduced them. He shook her hand and winked at her. Then he elbowed me.

"How come you never *tell* me anything?"

"You never give me a chance."

"Not true, friend, not true. I give you space, let you *play*. Not my fault you screw your solos right back into your own navel. Speaking of which, I got what you want righ*cheer*." He unrolled a piano keyboard on the table in front of me. I ran my fingers across the silent keys. They didn't have quite the resistance of real keys, but it was pretty close.

"You always carry that thing around with you?" Priscilla said. "Just in case you run into Peter somewhere?"

"Well, you know, honey, it's not most of these bars that have pianos in them anymore. Used to be a big upright in every dark corner, I hear. That, or a pool table. But at least, nowadays, I can carry one around with me, so's if I find a friend who can tell it from a computer tickler, well, he can play up with me. No place for a lady to recline on top and display her legs, maybe sing a little ditty, truth, but progress leaves as many things behind as it gets to. So I hear, anyway. Myself, I ride backwards, looking at the tracks we leave."

"That's too bad," she said, with a practiced pout. "I'd have liked to sing something."

"You a torch singer, then?" Sheldon peered at her, as if he was trying to place her in some dark club.

"You *are* looking backward. What do you want me to sing? Something Gershwin would have written if he hadn't died in 1938?"

Sheldon looked at me and nodded, impressed. "You got a live one here, Peter, you hear?"

"I hear. Are we going to make a racket, annoy the other customers?"

"Hell no. We're going to make a racket, make them happy to be alive. If only to beat us up and throw us out." He winked at Priscilla. "We please them one way or another. Peter called me about Amalik's, I was surprised. They let us play here, once in a long donkey while. Kind of a whim of Amalik, who propriets here and sticks his name on it." He nodded in the direction of an empty corner that looked like it was missing a table. "I *think* that's where we're supposed to set up. Not sure, have to ask."

"I'll ask," Priscilla said. "I'll be right back."

We both watched her sashay away. "Boy," Sheldon said. "Looks kinda ridiculous, but sometimes it makes a little sense, you stay het like that."

"Yeah," I said. "Old habits die hard."

There was a bustle as a couple of other musicians came through the doors: Swandown, a young music student with custom glass fingernails matched to his piezoelectric guitar, and the grumpy Wynans with his sax, still unconvinced that the music he played really existed. They were joined by the flute-playing waiter.

It was a working session, with an audience. We worked on a few pieces of Sheldon's, parts of repertoires of nonexistent jazz combos. I wasn't at my best. My fingers felt like wood. Every swing of the door heralded Farley's arrival. And God only knew what would happen after that.

"Hey," Sheldon said in my ear. "Let's let girlfriend sing. Relax you, hey?"

"Sure," I said. "Sure thing, Sheldon."

He signaled to her and she came up. They bent heads together like conspirators. Sheldon then spoke to Swandown who looked irritated. Sheldon hummed something. Swandown fiddled with his strings, then shrugged, okay.

Sheldon slapped my shoulder. "Gershwin. While he was alive, fact. 'Lady Be Good.' You okay with that, good lady?"

"I'll do my best," Priscilla said.

We played quiet, as instruments sound far away, and she sang low. She had a smooth, dark voice when she sang, like dark chocolate that's just barely sweet, and has been warmed to body temperature.

" 'Oh please have some pity, I'm all alone in this big city'," she sang. She knew all the words. Musicians seldom do.

The front door swung open and slapped against the stop. I looked up. But, instead of Gideon Farley, the person who walked in was his wife, Corinne.

*   *   *

MY OLD WIFE KNEW HOW TO HOLD A STAGE. SHE STOOD THERE FOR A LONG moment, a mixture of night and streetlight defining her figure against the warm light of Amalik's. Her long hair swirled around her shoulders. She wore a bulky, floor-length coat slashed with bright red. She walked in slowly, regal, straight backed, and pulled off her gloves. Her silky hair caught the light as she fluffed it back with her fingers. A waiter, completely against his usual habit with customers, helped her off with her coat. His reward was a grateful nod. She sat down.

Priscilla finished the last few words of the song, though her voice was suddenly full of sand. She looked at me, eyes frightened.

"We'd better take a break," I told Sheldon.

He raised his eyebrows, nodded. "Sure thing. You guys going to mix it up? I don't want to pay for the furniture." He signaled the rest of the band, who dispersed.

"Don't worry, Sheldon. I'll handle it."

He shook his head, muttered "hets," and turned to clear the spit out of his trombone.

I pushed my keyboard aside and walked over to her. She sat erect in her chair, wearing a blue silk dress and a braided necklace of freshwater pearls. She looked like she was dressed for one of those charity functions Priscilla had told me Gideon often took Corinne to.

She had ordered a beer and now poured it, slowly, into her glass, concentrating as if it was the most important thing in the world. The neck of the bottle clattered against the rim of the cup. She set it down on the table, appalled by her body's betrayal.

"Hello, Corinne," I said.

She didn't look at me. "You. You too. Goddamit, what the hell is going on around here?"

I sat down opposite. "I thought you had come here to see me."

"I didn't come here to see you. I came to see *her*." She glared up at Priscilla, who leaned over Sheldon, chatting with him about something, with every appearance of casualness. "You're a special bonus."

I had to ask. "Where's Gideon?"

"Gideon?" She looked around vaguely, as if expecting to find him sitting in a booth. "I don't know where Gideon is. I don't think you'll find it odd if I say I don't care." She spoke precisely, each word discrete.

I didn't want to be here, caught in the middle of this. This, of all things, didn't have anything to do with me.

"Corinne." I pushed myself right into the mess. "I *have* to know where Gideon is. It's important."

"*I don't know.*" She opened her purse, rummaged, and, having found nothing, closed it again. "Get her over here, Peter. She can't pretend I'm invisible forever."

"Okay." I stood up. I could smell her perfume, a smell that sometimes wafted out of a forgotten drawer opened after a sleep of years: desert flowers, a warm wind sliding between the leaves of lemon and orange trees, dry spices and open hillsides. Some of those associations, of course, came from the image, as precise and vivid as an old orange-crate label, that had adorned the blown-glass perfume bottle standing on her bureau. We fill in, in our dull way, everything in between the shivered shining fragments that are all of the universe that we actually perceive.

Before I had gone two steps, Priscilla came forward. As she did, I smelled her too, and realized that she wore exactly the same perfume, smelled exactly the same. I stopped, shocked by how I had been manipulated. Smells dive right into that old limbic system and root out our most basic emotions.

Priscilla brushed past me and stood in front of Corinne. Her posture was not as exact, her features not so finely made, and even her dark, wild hair seemed crude by comparison to Corinne's light, silky brown.

"Corinne, I—"

"I didn't come here to chat with you." Corinne leaned slowly back in her chair, as if uncertain of whether it had a back, and was nervous about toppling back onto the floor. Her spine touched and she relaxed. "I don't think we have anything to say to each other."

"Maybe we don't. But I'm not the one who came here not to say it."

"Oh my." Corinne was sardonic.

"So why did you come here?"

"Just to see you. Not to have you tell me how he always mentions my name when he comes, or to commiserate together about what a scum we both love. Just to see what you are."

Corinne's hate blazed from her. Priscilla did not shrink from it, but she wasn't interested in quenching it either. The hatred of wives was an occupational hazard for her.

"You must be what he wanted, though. He changed so much for you. Became someone else. Just for you."

"How?" I found myself saying. "Tell me how. I need to know."

Corinne's head turned. "And you, Peter. I didn't think you liked it all under control like that. All that trained *passion.*"

I squeezed Priscilla's hand. She had manipulated me—but I had been all too willing to be manipulated. I was tangled in a knot. But I was about to cut through it. The one thing, the only thing, I wanted to do was to find Gideon Farley.

"Corinne," I said. "I need a ride home. I don't have a car. Can you take me?"

I felt Priscilla stiffen next to me.

Corinne pushed her chair back and stood. "Sure, Peter. Why not? That will give you equal standing with Gideon, won't it?"

I could feel the skin prickle as I blushed. It startled me. "That's not what I want, Corinne. I need a ride. And I need to talk to you."

"You're a madman," Priscilla said in my ear.

"Maybe. I have to know."

"You have to know. Well, know, you son of a bitch. *Know.*"

Corinne put her coat back on. "Come on."

I tried to catch Sheldon's eye, but he wouldn't look at me. He was packing his trombone back in its case, ignoring Swandown's frenzied objections. I followed Corinne's forceful back out of the restaurant.

-31-

My house was cold and still. I hadn't been in it for a long time.

"It looks just the same," Corinne said. "Do you really live here?"

"I do."

"Don't you keep bumping into the past? I would." She rapped her knuckles on an arm of a Solar Mission chair. "The corners are too sharp on these things. Dancers are clumsy, you know. I always had black-and-blue marks from them. I'd have gotten rid of them a long time ago."

She took off her coat, folded it, and sat down. "You know why I came here with you, don't you?"

"Corinne, I—"

"Not to sleep with you. You don't really want to do that, do you?" Her tone was weary, as if she'd do it without objection if I asked, as a tedious duty.

"No, of course not." I sank into the chair opposite. "I brought you here to critique my furniture."

She smiled tightly. "I want to talk to you about Gideon. About what's happened to him."

"Okay. That's what I want to talk about too."

She took a deep breath. "In all the years I've known you I never thought you would be capable of such a grotesque and petty vengeance." She had to have practiced that line on the way over to say it without stumbling.

"What do you mean?"

"Have you managed to remember anything?" she said.

"Yes, I have. Thank you for what you did. I know it wasn't easy."

Her jaw tightened. "All right, then, Peter. I'm here because of what you did to my husband, Gideon Farley. You operated on him, put things in his head. Is that sufficient information for you to answer my questions? *What did you do to him?*"

"I . . . I did just what his contract called for." My cracking voice sounded false, even to myself. I *had* done what the contract called for—but in the process had inserted a black box of Mennaura's design, and had no idea what it did.

"Contract!" Tears appeared in her eyes. I was deliberately wary. Voluntary crying didn't even take a virt. It could be done by a few minutes of training. Tears now were symbols, nothing real. Nothing to feel sorry for. "You're so damned clever, Peter. However did you think of it? To turn him into something I so desperately wanted, and then make sure I couldn't have it."

I spoke with stupid reflex. "If he wasn't what you wanted to begin with, why did you marry him?"

"That's none of your business. You weren't what I wanted either, and I married you. I even loved you." She wiped her eyes.

I tried to relax. "All right. Let's run it back. Why did he come to me? Did you know what cargo he'd be carrying?"

She shrugged, suddenly uncomfortable. "Oh, I don't know exactly. He wanted some circuitry for network interface, data analysis . . . stuff that's standard for his business. He couldn't compete without it. I may have mentioned your name, I don't know, but that was what he wanted. You, Peter Ambrose. He came back, pleased as anything, and told me he'd been to you. I was even proud of you, a little."

"Corinne." I leaned forward. "What's wrong with Gideon? Why are you here? Tell me."

Suddenly she wouldn't meet my gaze. "Gideon was always a . . . good man. Understand that, Peter."

"I do." And the funny thing was, I did. I didn't like him, but he was not an evil man.

"But when he came back from you, he was different. Not just the fact that he could taste stock quotes on his tongue, but—"

"Did he say that?"

"He said all sorts of things. He felt the power, he said. He felt minds linked together across the net. I thought it was kind of silly. You always hear people talking like that, on those dumb shows about net hackers, datadorks, those people. I've met them, he works with a lot of them. They twitch and pick their noses . . . not like Gideon at all. But he seemed to mean it."

"Anything else?"

"Yes." Her eyes sparked at me. "That was where your trick came in. You know more about these reflexes, these circuits, whatever, than I do, so

I can't figure out what you did. I tried to do some research—the enervation of the bulbospongiosus muscle, the prostatic plexus of the parasympathetic autonomic nervous system, the posterior-superior cingulate gyrus—" she stumbled over the syllables. "But none of it had anything to do with me. Do you see the world through that broken mosaic, Peter?"

"Yes." I tried to remain judicious, though I felt like I had been kicked in the stomach. "So that's it? Sex?" She'd listed the muscle responsible for ejaculation, the nerve that controlled erection, and the brain center behind sexual drive. Not normal nighttime reading for her, as far as I remembered.

"Yes, Peter. Sex. Nice short word, isn't it, for something we don't understand? Gideon was . . . you made him a better lover. In almost every way. Not just physically . . . though that was there. It's always there, no matter how we talk around it."

Was that what had been inside the slick virtual of Mennaura's device? Some sort of priapos virt? I didn't think so—it had to be a side effect, the same way a tumor in the posterior superior part of the cingulate gyrus could lead to nymphomania or satyriasis. Some side effect.

"Is that a problem for you?" I spoke like a therapist.

Surprisingly, it didn't irritate her. Maybe she was too tired. Or too angry.

"*That* is not a problem." I looked at her, curled up on the couch. I remembered the graceful absurdity of the physical side of our love. I breathed in. She must have entrained me with that citrus-and-sun smell she wore, sliding it up into my limbic system as we made love. I wanted Corinne, and she knew it. And Priscilla knew it too.

"But it looks like our friend Priscilla gets to enjoy it all too, doesn't it?" She slid her legs out in front of her, leaving them bare for most of their length. "But it is a joke. Isn't it, my sweet?" Her voice dripped sarcasm. "Because you sneaked something else in under it. He's linked in. His mind touches everything, like an ocean, he says. He's happy. You should see the glow on his face. It's as if he drew on a power beyond the rest of us."

"Corinne, I'm sorry. I didn't know . . . but I did something. I don't make those virts, those devices I put into people's heads. I depend on companies, Cephalik, Xinhua, you've heard of them. At least one of the virts I put into Gideon's head has turned out to be some type of experimental model. Refracted. I didn't know when I put it in. I didn't do it deliberately. I'm sorry."

I reached out and took her hand. It was cool in mine. She did not hold me, but she didn't pull away either. "I don't know what's happening," I said. "But what's in his head somehow links to everything I need to know. I need to figure him out as much as you do."

There was, I had read once, a parasite that lived part of its life in a snail. Its next phase required it to release its eggs in the excretory tract of a bird. To get from snail to bird, the parasite infested the snail's eye stalks and made them swell and turn bright red, mimicking the appearance of the caterpillars that were the bird's favorite prey. The parasite-modified eye stalks screamed EAT in neon letters. Farley had a parasite in him, the virt I had installed. What advantage did that parasite derive from the changes in Farley's behavior?

Corinne looked startled. "I . . . I didn't expect this, Peter. I don't know . . . I thought you would deny it, suppress it. Be dark, the way you always were when something was important."

"Was I . . . is that how you see me?"

"How else? You acted like you told everything just the way it was. But you didn't. Your eyes would go blank, and when I asked you why, you would get mad. Not normal mad, not like you did when we were lost in the car and you thought it was my fault, but defensive mad, as if I'd asked something you'd *told* me not to bring up."

I'd always tried to blame most of our failure on her. Corinne had wanted me to make more money, to live a better, more secure life, and I, for one reason or another, was unable to provide it for her. But maybe all she'd really wanted was a husband who did not carry the banked fires of the Nimbus Project within himself, constantly brushing against the iron box containing it and getting burned all over his body, bit by bit, until there was nothing to do but huddle in the farthest corner, hoping it would someday cool off.

"This is not time to discuss our personal . . ." I trailed off. It *was* our personal problem, inextricably intertwined through everyone else's like wisteria weaving its way through the palisades of a garden fence. "All right. I hid it, all of it, and by hiding it allowed it to destroy what we had between us. Back during the Devo Wars . . ." And again I told the story, revealing the Group. It had grown easier, but I still felt a tug of . . . I had to call it conscience, at exposing all of us. Perhaps it had grown easier simply because there were that many fewer of us left.

"It will never come back," I said. "What was between us. We have to move on from here. But four members of the Group are now dead."

Her eyes widened. "Dead. How?"

"The methods don't matter. They were killed, all by something we had tried to forget."

"And you think Gideon is somehow involved. How? Do you think whatever you put into his head has turned him into a killer? Is that what you did to him?" Her voice rose, whether in anger or fear I didn't think she knew herself.

"I don't—How did you find us? There at the coffeehouse?"

"My God, Peter, does that matter now?" She looked at me. "I found a note. A little scribbled note, written on the back of a receipt from the grocery store. Gideon started doing that recently, I don't know why."

"Oh. And where did he go?"

She shook her head. "I don't know. He's been wandering around lately. Going to see that damn mistress of his, I now know. When I got up this morning, he was gone. No note, nothing. Just the goddam windows, open. I was freezing. I'd had nightmares of . . . I don't know, glaciers, icicles. Maybe he climbed right out of that window and swam down the river. I don't know who the hell he is any more."

I thought that I might now know. "Corinne. You have to talk to me, be honest with me. This affects all of us."

For a moment she looked ready to spring up from her deceptively relaxed posture on the couch and run out the door to her car. If she chose to do that, I wouldn't stop her.

"What are you talking about, Peter?"

I think your husband is a killer. I think that, somehow, through the link Mennaura installed in his head, he is carrying out the will, dead or alive, of Linden Straussman. I think that, before he gets into bed to make love to you, he has to clean blood out from under his fingernails.

"Has Gideon developed a taste for hot chocolate?" was what I said instead.

-32-

I WOKE UP SLOWLY. STRONG LIGHT, MORNING ALREADY GONE, CAME through the dusty slats of the window blinds. The acoustic-panel ceiling was stained brown from years of water leakage. The wall panels were springing away from their indifferently driven nails, revealing the aluminum framework of the barracks building. I began to sweat immediately, a cold sticky sweat like that collected off the bodies of gibbeted prisoners by alchemists with long, rough swabs, to be squeezed into desperate concoctions.

I sat up and sucked in air. I was on a metal-frame bed. The wall panels were painted a military drab green, a color, Michaud had once assured me, that had been invented by Roman legions on garrison duty. I'd never been able to check that.

The room was my barracks room at Fitzwater. I recognized the books on the shelves, the old parallel-processor computer with its piles of datacrisps, the spongy model brain on little motorized wheels that we let whiz down the hallways at night. Those damn bastard ralfies. This time they'd gone too far. Just wait until I got my hands on them—

"A security system isn't much use if you don't turn it on."

It was Anthony Watkins, sitting, pretty much as he always had, slouched in the beat-up wingback chair in the corner. That had been his favored spot during the endless bull sessions that made up Fitzwater's evening entertainment and helped form the civilization in which we now lived.

"These things are clever, though. They're a lot like people. You can convince them to do almost anything." Watkins held a ralfie in his hand. It was wearing a sharpcut American military uniform from the time of the Wars of Devolution. He turned it toward me. It had Gene Michaud's dead face, complete to the cicatrices on the temples. Watkins dropped it and it lay sprawled on the floor.

"What do you want, Tony?" Watkins wasn't the killer. He was obnoxious, overbearing, but he'd also hated Linden Straussman more than anyone. Still, I felt a shiver of fear. The victims had let the killer in, and I had gone to sleep without turning my security system back on after Corinne left in the morning. I'd almost invited him in.

"I never thought it would be you," Watkins said in a sudden rage. "Of all of us. Not you, Theo." His stupid little razorslick wrist holster dropped the pistol into his hand and he waved it at me. But he hadn't shot me while I lay there, snoring innocently, so he obviously had other plans. "Daddy's little fair-haired boy, eh? Jesus!"

"What? Tony, you don't think—"

"I *do* think, Petey boy. You may be a crackerjack skein killer, but you suck as a liar. And the name's Martin—Martin Schaeffer."

He had the gun, he was in control, but the accusation was so absurd that I had trouble taking it seriously. "Expecting me to just fess up?" I sat up and grabbed a pair of underwear from the floor, not checking to see if they were clean. The ME who examined my body on a slab at Sister Death could worry about it. "Get virtual, Tony—Martin, if you want it that way. I haven't killed anyone. Although I'm starting to wonder if you have."

He made an irritated raspberry. "Cut the crap. It's got your fingerprints all over it. Nice delayed action device. You subtle bastard. You always hated us, didn't you? All of us. The Group. All you ever wanted to do was play that stupid piano and let the rest of us go to hell."

I pulled my jeans on. I couldn't tell if this was one of his loony hypotheses, which he only half believed himself. Watkins took even the craziest things dead seriously. "You're just rambling," I said. "You have no idea of anything . . . Martin. You're just swinging your fists in the dark, hoping to connect with something."

Watkins sighed, as he always had, at the suddenly revealed abyss of my stupidity. I sat back on the tangled bed sheets and felt the years fall away. Strips of light sliced across Watkins's bony face. Some large vehicle ground down the street outside, and it sounded like a five-ton, blandly rolling on some unguessable military errand. Despite my situation, it relaxed me. When I had been in the Group I had at least known where I stood.

"Well, I have then. I've connected with your fat jaw."

I shrugged. "Have it your way. What happened to Gene?"

"The famous Aylmer Brandt? They're going to have to carve his portrait in a wall with needle-gun fire as a memorial. He's dead. He never came out of that building. He burned in there."

"And you think that I—what, Tony, what? What did I do to kill him?"

"The name's Martin," he said peevishly. "And I don't know what you did. All I know is that you're Straussman's stalking horse. You find us, he kills us. I never thought of you as Daddy's little darling, but nothing's ever clear, even in the best run of dysfunctional families." He got up and started pacing, kicking laundry around. "He's got control of us all. There's no arguing with him. All we can do is remove him. Destroy him. Kill him."

"Straussman? Straussman's dead."

"*He's not dead!*" Watkins waved his gun at me. "He's around, somewhere."

"No, Martin." I felt tired. I hadn't had enough sleep. "It was all over a long long time ago. We are the only ones responsible."

"Over, eh? Why do you live near Chicago, Peter? Why did everyone else, before they died? The Group originally came from all over the country. I've seen the records. Maine, California, North Dakota. Why here? Because Linden Straussman grew up here. The suburbs of course, like any normal white boy, he lived on Near North Side later. Can you imagine that, Petey? Linden Straussman living somewhere like a normal person? I can't. But that's why we all came here, after we demobbed and went our separate ways. To be right next to the memory of dear old Dad. His hand is on all of us. It will stay there until we pull it off. But it's his hand that's pushing you, isn't it Peter? The dutiful son. The *good* boy." His voice rose.

"I don't know what you're talking about."

"You've killed most of us, but that's not going to stop me. Hear me, Straussman?" He yelled at the ceiling, his skinny body galvanized.

"Did you know you were crazy, Tony?"

There was a weak cough, as from a toy, and window frame shattered near my face, spearing me with glass fragments. "Jesus!" Reflex flung me back, against the wall. Blood poured across my face. I rubbed at it, and brought my hand back scarlet.

"Ha." Watkins smirked. "Use your sheets, idiot. You won't be needing them for anything else."

I pulled off a pillow case and rubbed my face with it. Blood smeared. I needed a mirror and tweezers to get the glass fragments out. I was well and truly screwed. I'd sent Corinne out with the coin, a signal to Tigranes. By the time he got back to me, it would be too late.

"Let's go," he said.

"You're an idiot." I kept my tone harsh, despite my fear. "I didn't kill the others. If you get rid of me . . . Farley's got the secret. Gideon Farley. I installed a virt in his head that Karin—"

"Oh, spare me." Watkins threw his hands up theatrically. "I'm not making red-herring bouillabaisse. Move it!"

I stepped out ahead of him. "Dammit, listen to me—"

"Daddy's errand boy," he taunted. "Geraldino at the hospital. Then you met with Inversato, and she turned up dead. Little hobby, eh, like mushroom hunting. Then you had a little breakfast with Crawford—and she vanished. You get to Michaud—and he runs out to burn himself to death. I bet you've found Hank Rush now too, haven't you? Spotting him for Straussman."

I felt a chill as I walked down the stairs in front of him, even though it was absurd. God knew what implanted programs we all had, and what I had done without knowing. For example, how had we all gotten back in contact? Each of our independently motivated actions had had essentially the same effect: it had made our paths cross.

"I didn't know Geraldino was dead until the news appeared on the TV," I said. "My TV demon picked up my old face in the picture hanging on his wall and displayed the murder for me without me even asking."

"Sure you didn't. You never went to his apartment. You never saw him."

"That's right. I never even got a chance to see his corpse. You blew it up to conceal the incriminating cargo he carried."

"Never saw him." Watkins's voice was distracted. "Then why, I wonder, did you have one of his famous hand-painted neckpieces lying in your dresser drawer?"

I caught its blue-green flicker at the corner of my eye, and then he hit me, hard, knocking me the rest of the way down the stairs. I hit the bottom landing, rolled, and found myself facing his gun. He threw the neckpiece down at me like a football ref marking a penalty. I looked at the Indonesian figures on it. My souvenir of Charlie Geraldino.

"You're not much of a murderer if you leave stuff like this around," Watkins said. "An investigation—"

"Would show that that thing is at least ten years old. It's from the old days. Fitzwater. You might even remember him wearing it, walking through those happy streets of Kishinyov."

He sat down on the steps, feet near my head. I didn't try to get up. "And this." In his fingers he held a vivid blue-green marble. "This is mine, isn't it?"

"Yes, Tony. It's yours. I took it when we demobbed. A souvenir."

He rolled it down his fingers and rested it in the palm of his hand. I stared at it, feeling as if I had never seen it before. Charlie Geraldino, strangled with a painted neckpiece. Lori Inversato, skull staved in by her ratchet wrench. Gene Michaud, grabbing his tsuba before disappearing in the flames. Karin Crawford, her soul imprisoned by a laser with her bone-handled scalpel tied to it. What had happened to Hank Rush, since he had his spike-lined glove back?

And Tony Watkins held his marble. The box was empty, and the Group was almost all dead. What had I done? Where had I been?

"Come on," Watkins said with weary contempt. He helped me to my feet. "Let's go." We walked out into the cold, sunlit front yard.

HE TOOK ME OUT TO THE SAME BATTERED UTILITY VAN HE HAD USED FOR blowing up Geraldino's body and apartment. The car seat automatically restrained me when I got in it. Must have been an extra-cost option on the van. Watkins drove out to the industrial area where he had parked his van the first time I had pursued him, all those psychological years ago, a place full of hulking electromagnets, water-filled clay pits, humming electric-arc smelters. Brutish matter manipulation. And I had thought that in our world we had forgotten all that.

"Think about what you're doing," I said, trotting out an argument I'd thought up on the way over. "*You're* the one who's killing *me*."

"That's right, Petey. Good guess."

"Well, what does that mean? What evidence do you have that *you* aren't the killer, Tony? Maybe you killed everyone else, and convinced yourself it was necessary to get Straussman. That's the way these things work, isn't it? It's all self-justified."

Watkins backed the van into a cracked, weed-overgrown parking lot next to a dramatically corroded metal-sided warehouse. "I didn't."

"All right. So why did you talk to Karin about getting the Group back together, long before Charlie was murdered?"

That one actually gave him pause. "I *was* trying to get the Group back together. It was the only way—all of us at once. You wouldn't join me, remember? Karin wasn't sure she could deal with it. Lori really wanted to. But she was killed before she could."

"If she wanted to join you, it was because she thought she could find Daddy if she did."

"Maybe." He no longer seemed interested in my arguments.

"But *why*, Tony?"

"Never mind. There's no Group to get back together anymore. Thanks to you."

"If you kill me, the police will settle on *you* as the suspect."

"They won't. They'll know it's you."

"That ancient neckpiece is scarcely enough evidence—"

He chuckled. "You think I'm an idiot, don't you, Ambrose? You always did, secretly. I have a PhD from Johns Hopkins but you think my brain's full of nothing but connective tissue."

"So this is why you want to kill me? Because I don't respect you enough?"

"I don't need a reason even that good. I am a god. I have whims of iron." The seat released me and, at a gesture from his pistol, I got out of the car. He directed me into the battered warehouse, muttering under his breath as we walked. "It's going to look like you killed yourself, Ambrose. The final stupid end to a pointless life. A demonstration of how meaningless life really is. An ungrammatical existential statement."

"It's bad enough to be killed without having to endure your sophomoric philosophical ranting."

He stopped for a moment, then barked a laugh. "You know, now I remember why I liked having you around, Theo. That was before you became a crazed skein killer, or yarn holder for a skein killer, or whatever the hell you are. 'He was such a nice guy,' they always say. That's why I've never trusted nice guys. Hate 'em. Capable of almost anything because they're so fucking boring. And they *want* to be interesting. They taste it so bad they choke on their own saliva. They bugger infants and rip their mom's tongues out with needle-nose pliers, all to be interesting to someone, anyone, even if it's just a bored precinct investigator who mispronounces their name."

"I haven't killed anyone, Tony. There's no evidence tying me to any-thing."

"You may have been smart enough not to leave any, I don't know. But you know that virtual is real. Right? The net's got a mass of requests from you for information about your victims' cover identities. Quite a complete little search you did, and you covered your tracks well. It'll probably take the police a few weeks to get all the details straight, figure out what psycho scheme you were hatching in your deranged brain. The Nimbus Project had hi-pry access—and I still do. System somehow keeps forgetting to eliminate it, probably because it's forgotten the Group ever existed. It can't seem to resolve to forget something it can't recall in the first place."

I looked at him. "So you put these requests in when—just after Geraldino's death?"

"Yeah, that's right. I got that feeling, that little lumpy turds were going to start hitting the fan, one by one."

"So," I said musingly. "You put in for-info requests about the cover identities of everyone who has now turned up dead."

He stared at me, doubting himself for a moment. "Sit down here."

A small partitioned area in the huge warehouse, once a dispatcher's office, had obviously served as some sort of hidey-hole for Watkins. The office had no separate ceiling, revealing the sagging trusses of the warehouse roof high above. It contained a cot with crisply folded blankets, a self-powered mil-surplus cooler, and a hard wooden chair with a curved back, relic of a library or schoolroom. I sat down on the chair as directed, knees weak. As I watched, he set a few of my possessions in the room, giving evidence of my occupancy. He'd taken them from my house. A half-eaten tray of lasagna went in the cooler. I tried to remember how old it was. He put a stack of piano music under the cot. An ancient, battered ballet slipper, a vestige of Corinne I'd never thrown out, got hung over a nail on the wall. I stared at it. Corinne had left my house sad and alone. I hoped she had taken my warning to heart, and not gone home to lie in bed waiting for a skein killer. That is, if Farley really *was* the skein killer, and not Watkins. Or me.

I didn't know what he was going to do, but my only choice now was to refuse to let my death look like a suicide. If I got up and ran, charged at him, forced him to blow me away like a target in a shooting gallery, then the marks would be inconsistent with a self-inflicted death. It wouldn't save my life, but at least it would prevent the investigation of my death from detouring into the purely fictional. But I couldn't get my body to respond. It sat inactivated in the chair.

He grinned at me. "You know, Peter, I've spent a little bit of time trying to figure out how an installer and skein killer like you would kill himself. Some sort of simultaneous neurotransmitter chelation? A flechette through the soft palate? Self-infection with fast kuru? Heart depolarization with potassium chloride?"

"Well, Tony, I have no idea. Have you written me a note?"

"Fewer than one in five suicides leave a note, even an electronic one. Courts are always sorting through last network messages to figure out what the motives were. No, you mysterious and inarticulate bastard, you haven't left a note. But you've killed yourself in an extremely interesting way." The muzzle of his gun rested against the lid of my left eye. What the hell was so interesting about that? I felt a moment of annoyance at the way he was patting himself on the back.

Watkins pulled the gun back and grinned at me, now half-obscured by a blue pressure phosphene. I blinked, which didn't do a damn bit of good. A slap to the back of my neck, and he hit me with a spinal. I lost feeling from the neck down and almost fell off the chair. He propped me back up with gentle gestures, like someone taking care of an aged parent.

Then he dropped an oddly shaped box on the cot, just in my field of view. I couldn't move my head, only my eyes. Its case was crudely welded, but an organiform soft coral had grown over it, turning the welds into miniature pink reefs. I looked at it and felt as if I was underwater along with Helena Mennaura. Data lines led from the box to an infomycelia insertion mask, a full-access field device. Clamped to the face, it snaked infomycelia in through the foramina in the facial bones along the cranial nerves and blood vessels that passed out through those openings, contacting the brain in hundreds of locations. As complete as you could get without actually opening the cranium. And sticking the thing over my head and turning it on was something I could easily have done by myself. Total sensory addicts did it all the time.

"It's a contraevolutionary thing," Watkins said. "A descent into the neural swamp." He swung the mask on his finger. "An experiment. I've programmed this little esemplastic gizmo to selectively deoxygenate later-formed connections in the CNS. It'll start with your labile short-term memory of the last few minutes. Then it'll wander around your long-term memory, trying to decide which linkages were formed more recently, and then eliminating them. Hell of an integration problem, wouldn't you say? It's going to be recording the results, so someone will get to see them. Nice touch, you as self-sacrificing scientist as well as brutal skein killer. The news channels will have a field day."

If my heart was pounding with terror, responding to signals from the sympathetic nervous system, I couldn't feel it. My body felt swathed in cotton batting, like an heirloom stored on a high shelf in a closet. My vocal system worked, though I would have trouble controlling my breathing, but I wasn't going to give him the pleasure of discussing the matter with him.

"After that, we'll accelerate the scale." My lack of response didn't faze him, not that I had expected it would. "Next it'll eliminate the most evolutionarily recent parts of the neocortex: things like symbolic communication skills, voluntary movements, visuo-constructive skills, a host of other schematic processes. You'll be a lower mammal then, operating on everything below the basal ganglia. Then the limbic system'll go, losing you your basic behaviors: dominance-submission, sexual courtship—"

"Enough." I didn't want him to give me a toneless lecture on my reversion to primal therapsid, then down to the loss of brainstem functions and the eventual cessation of heart and lung function, even if it meant I would live a few minutes longer while I listened to it.

Watkins looked hurt. "Peter. I always thought you had a basic intellectual curiosity."

"Fuck you."

"Oh, well. When your neocortex is gone, you can respond on a more basic level. Perhaps you'll be more pleasant then. Hope you enjoy your little stroll down evolutionary lane."

"Farley," I managed. "Check Farley out. For God's sake, Tony, even if I'm dead." It was an effort to try to convince him to save himself even as he was trying to kill me. "Watch out for him. He's some kind of link back to the old guy. He has all the signs, the hot chocolate, the windows, the notes—"

"Thanks, Peter. I'll give it the thought it deserves."

He clamped the mask over my face and the world went completely dark.

SOMEONE RIPPED THE MASK FROM MY FACE. I FOUND MYSELF STARING AT a few square feet of unswept concrete. I could feel its roughness on my cheek, though the rest of my body was numb.

After a few minutes I felt the pin prickles of returning feeling in my fingers and toes. The spinal was quickly metabolized, so that it would be gone and undetectable by the time Watkins's neural time machine had reduced me to inanimate matter. Suicides do not usually paralyze themselves before doing their business.

I finally had enough muscle control to push my chest off the floor. I found myself staring at two pairs of polished shoes, their owners sitting primly next to each other on Watkins's cot. I pushed myself up farther.

Sitting on the cot were two of Tigranes's foppish operatives, a man and a woman. The man wore a turban but the woman's elaborately twisted skull was exposed, the bone ridges highlighted by some light-blue makeup devised for the purpose. Each of them held a device resting on his knees, something that looked like a lyre made of human bone. The woman stroked hers with impossibly long fingers. She smiled and dropped a gene-spliced dark-blue rose in front of me. Dew clung to its petals.

The flower freed me. I could feel it, somewhere inside. But I couldn't speak. I tried, but no words came.

Supporting myself on the wall, I pushed myself slowly to my feet. The cold outside breeze whistled through a pair of holes punched in the thin metal wall. I looked up at them in uncomprehending wonder.

Words were starting to come, but they were the wrong ones. They didn't tell me anything important. I grabbed at the man's arm and stared into his face.

I could see Tigranes, see his face, his gestures, smell his mossy smell, but I couldn't think of his name, not right then, right when I needed it. Tears came with the effort. Before I knew it, they were streaming down my face, stinging bitter in my eyes, and I had no idea of what I was crying about.

-33-

ONE OF MY RESCUERS HANDED ME A WRINKLE-SURFACED BLOWN-glass bulb. Inside of it was an angrily wing-beating beetle with an irides-cent green carapace. After a moment it settled to the bottom of the bulb and folded its wing casings. With stubby, stubborn legs it forged its way up the curving side, slid back, and started over.

It was a special-made symbol, not one they usually carried. A com-munications system whose morphemes have actual physical weight does have distinct drawbacks. I looked at them, the silent man and woman. Their faces were expressionless, another communications modality disregarded. The meaning of their symbol was not too obscure—they had rescued me, and thus possessed me.

They moved closer to me, their posture ominous. Each of the lyre-like objects held a bone arrow. With that as evidence I recognized what they were: supersonic crossbows, which accelerated their arrows through an incredibly fast analomycin contraction. This mating of sophisticated bio-logical analogs with primitive technology was common among alternate presents. Supersonic pseudorganic crossbows were something overevolved australopithecines might have used to settle quarrels. They had blown holes in the wall during their assault on Watkins's headquarters, an attack I had missed in the process of having my mind stripped. The sound of the arrows smashing through the metal wall must have been shockingly loud. I wished I could have seen Watkins's face when it happened.

I checked myself quickly to see if I had suffered any damage while under the spinal. Lying on the floor in front of me were a blue-green marble and a soft leather glove, my last two symbols. I knelt and picked them up. Then I held the bulb out to the Messengers. They waved their refusal.

Without another thought, I flicked the bulb onto the concrete floor. It shattered in a fine spray of fragments. The beetle sat on the floor for a moment, considering the additions to its personal space, then pushed its wing casings forward and flew off.

They didn't react to my predictable symbology and escorted me out of the silent, echoing warehouse.

TIGRANES'S HOUSE WHISPERED WITH INTENT ACTIVITY. HIS STRANGE agents moved swiftly, opening wall panels and removing equipment, punching commands into consoles, removing and neatly folding flowered window drapes. No one looked at me or acknowledged my presence.

Tigranes's body lay sprawled on the living room rug at the base of the sharkskin clock. His limbs were twisted at unnatural angles and I felt an urge to straighten them, to give his corpse at least the appearance of comfort. I knelt down next to him and, in defiance of all police procedure, cradled his head. It was frighteningly loose, coming free of his neck.

His throat had been ripped out by his own antique Victorian pruning hook, which lay bloody on the floor next to him, yet another symbol, the very one I would have chosen to put in my box to represent him. His beard had fallen back and concealed most of the ruin of his throat, but blood pooled on the rug next to his head. He had died not more than an hour ago. I took his hand, which was already cold, and sat with him there. The tears had never really stopped flowing from my eyes, and I let them continue to drip. All around me his empire, no doubt according to previous arrangement, was being dismantled. In a few minutes the house would show no evidence of ever having been anything but a normal suburban dwelling.

I grabbed one of his men as he passed, wanting to ask what had happened, how, but couldn't think of what to say.

He looked past me, not seeing me, but reached into his bag and pulled out an old, solid-core key. Then he slapped my chest and turned away to his business. It was obviously up to me. I held the key tightly in my hand, uncertain of whether it was just a symbol, or actually opened some real door in the house.

No one paid any visible attention to me but they had set up lines of resistance, like the walls of an invisible maze it was my task to penetrate. If it was a puzzle Tigranes had designed for me before he died, I wasn't sure I wanted to have anything to do with it. But anything was better than sitting there with his huddled corpse. I patted Tigranes's shoulder, as if it would comfort him, and set out to look for signs and symbols. A glance, a gesture, a vicious, subliminal line of violet, almost-UV laser, each was enough to turn me in another direction. I heard a door lock electronically behind me after I walked through it. Another swung open at my approach, exhaling warm, wet air.

I wandered through the long greenhouse at the back of the house. The orangery, Tigranes had called it, and there were indeed two dwarf orange trees near one window, sagging with unpicked, normal-sized fruit. I pulled a blood orange off a branch, rubbed it under my nose to smell the aromatic oils, and peeled it messily, getting red juice all over my hands. I spit the seeds on the floor. Maybe they would grow there, their swelling branches knocking over the flower boxes.

The rest of the orangery was filled with lush, dense plants—fleshy orchids, bromeliads, delicate multicolored anemones. Here was the source of the symbols used by his people, the bright flowers that served as introductions and declarations. A garden of terms, the place where symbols grew. Who would take care of them now that Tigranes was gone? The mad cyclone of deconstruction had not yet visited this place, so perhaps they had suborbital shuttles squatting on the ground at O'Hare, launch engines spun up, ready to whip them back to their native jungles.

As I stood there like a sunstruck tropical explorer, the tall woman came in, the one who had, long ago, made me a miserable lunch. She pressed her thumb against a huge mahogany bole covered with hanging orchids and it opened. It contained a suspension box. Out of it she pulled the spongy, vitreous container of Kundalini devices and displayed it to me like a magician showing me that the hat is empty. She then produced a vial of red liquid and poured it over the top of the container. It flowed thickly. Blood. Tigranes's blood, I had no doubt. That was the nearest available source. The woman packed the container, turned, and walked away.

I wanted to run after her, to demand clarity, information, but I stood rooted where I was, staring at her retreating back.

To my left was a wooden door, brought from some house much older than this one. The key in my hand fit into the ancient keyhole. On the other side were carpeted stairs that led up to what looked like Tigranes's personal office, a room that existed in each of his houses, and which I had never seen.

It was an austere room, almost empty of objects, though perhaps most of them had already been packed up.

I sat down at the only piece of furniture, a beat-up wooden desk with a torn leather writing surface. There were dozens, maybe hundreds of drawers in it, so perhaps it had once served for specimen storage in some laboratory. It was covered with balls of dust picked up by moving furniture, broken pencils, bent paper clips, scraps of paper, all the mess left by a quick move. On it also stood a photograph in a silver frame. I picked it up and looked at it.

It showed a much-younger Tigranes and his family. They sat on a stone wall by an orchard somewhere: you could see out-of-focus fruit on the trees. Tigranes's wife, a slender woman in a high-collared white blouse, rested her head on his shoulder. On his lap sat his daughter, a cute, pigtailed girl of three or four. This was something he had always kept with him, for all the years since their deaths beneath the snow-sliding wheels of a truck. It was left here, because he no longer had any need for it.

I looked at the scraps of paper, the receipts, the notes, the junk mail. Lying face down were a couple of photographs. I picked them up. The first was unclear, a tangle of leaves in the orangery—I recognized the mahogany bole suspension box—with vague shadows behind them. In the second, the shadows had clarified, to become the face of Gideon Farley. He was looking thoughtfully down at something out of the camera's field of view. A data stamp in the corner had yesterday's date.

Corinne told me that Gideon had disappeared. He had told Priscilla he would come to our little impromptu concert. He had never made it. Tigranes had persuaded him, or taken him, and brought him here. But why? It made no sense. What would Tigranes want with Gideon Farley? And why would Gideon Farley, skein killer, agree to come?

Light spilled on me from my right. I blinked into the sudden brightness. What had seemed to be a solid wall, complete with an oil painting of some sailing ship avoiding a windswept shore, had split open. The light was blindingly bright.

A glass sphere rolled across the floor and came to rest at my foot. I bent over and picked it up. It was one of those old snow scenes, with the plastic flakes that swirled when you turned it over. But—I looked more closely. Instead of the usual house like they don't build any more, with icicles hanging from its eaves, the scene showed an automobile accident, a small car crushed by a huge segmented truck, the desperate skid marks of the car's tires visible in the slick snow just covering the street. I shook it and watched the swirling snow obscure the accident where Tigranes's daughter Shira had lost her ability to speak, and her mother had lost her life. Then I looked up.

She stood in the doorway, as well as she could with the left part of her body only partly functional. Her head was hidden by a colored turban. The light behind her slowly died, bringing detail to what had at first been only a silhouette. In an attempt to be kind, the medicos striving to save her life after the car accident had given her a high-cheekboned, smooth-skinned face. It didn't look much like the little girl's in the photograph.

I raised my hand in greeting. The beautiful face was expressionless, the right eye still dark and alive, the left a featureless translucent marble the vivid blue of glacial ice. Neither of us said anything. Her speech centers had been destroyed beyond repair and the experimental, eccentric communications processor her father had acquired from the smoldering remains of the Nimbus Project communicated through the means of other, less comprehensible symbols. That had been one of Karin Crawford's lines of investigation, back during the Nimbus Project.

She stepped forward into the room from that forever obscure part of the Tigranes house, the space that had always been hers, the space I had never been allowed to know. Every place he had ever lived had contained this area of darkness. I craned my head to see what was there, what decorated a space where every object and every relation of objects had specific meaning but the wall drifted shut and left it a mystery.

Her left leg dragged behind her. I frowned. Why, when we had the power to repair everything from the level of the premotor cortex down to the neuromuscular junction, was she disabled? Her left hand moved through an elaborate gesture and she dropped thoughts on the desk top: a gnarled piece of red coral, a glassy tektite, the bright feather of some tropical bird, a tiny pair of old brass watch gears. Some spilled essential oil filled the air with a pungent perfume, one just on the edge of decay. She moved the objects delicately, showing me their relations, and revealing herself and her query.

At a questioning look from me, she pulled open narrow, wide drawers in the desk, revealing endless ranks of objects arranged, I now realized, by the peculiar grammatical rules imposed by the interaction of her mind with the eccentric comm processor Karin Crawford had once designed, not knowing its ultimate fate. And that, of course, was why Shira was still maimed, still moved stiffly, dragging her leg behind her. The person in front of me was a mating of that processor and that brain. And it was a person who wanted to live. Tigranes had no doubt feared destroying that individual in an attempt, doomed to failure, to recover the daughter he had once known, the graceful daughter his wife had been driving to ballet class when she died.

I thought of the little girl, Tundra, whose life we had saved for no good purpose. No, not saved. It was not possible to save a life. Only to prolong it. She had talked with music, as Shira talked with concrete symbols. As Helena Mennaura had, at the end of her life, been unable to talk at all, every possible communications link destroyed by automatic laser surgery.

Seeing her and her work, and then hearing me describe the life and fate of the Group, Tigranes must finally have understood the origins of what dwelled inside his daughter's head.

And he had brought Gideon Farley here, a man who also had a virt in his head that had been designed by Karin Crawford, now called Helena Mennaura. Tigranes had teased the information out of me, the last time we spoke. I hadn't had any idea of what he was doing. He must have followed me, seen my contact with Priscilla, and backtracked, figuring out who I must have installed the critical virts in.

The language of the Messengers, the language, I saw now, of Shira Tigranes, was not one I was fluent in. I pulled open drawers morosely, seeing ranks of incomprehensible symbols, ready to be imbued with meaning. I slumped over them in despair.

There was one thing I had to say. I found a withered, dead, blue parakeet and leaned it against Tigranes's photograph, to tell her "Your father is dead." There was little explanation I could make beyond that.

She stared down at the bird, quartz crystal resting on its breast, and nodded, tears streaming from her one living eye. The other just stared blankly. She didn't ask me questions—how, when, why—but just rearranged her coral, tektite, feather, and gears, asking me something else, a question I only gradually puzzled out as "When did you first understand who you were?"

I looked at Shira. She stood, attentive, ready to accept my words. I shook my head at her, then reached out and put my arms around her. She was startled, and stared at me for a long moment. Then, with stiff and uncertain movements, she laid her head on my shoulder.

It was too much. Too much. Too much death, too much destruction, too much despair. I had nothing to say to her, nothing to tell her, nothing to give her save the pain we already shared.

I don't know how long we held on to each other that way. It made no sense, none at all. There were things that needed to be done. Violent events would not stop with the death of Sal Tigranes. It was hard to let her go, to let her stand again, still and alone, on the floor of her father's house.

Shira examined my face for at least a solid minute, perhaps more. I stayed perfectly still, as if posing for a portrait. Then, she pointed back at her query: "When did you first understand who you were?"

With a piece of broken glass, I was finally able to answer, stammeringly: "Right at this instant."

We talked. I suppose it was that. In my still-wordless state, it was more like something else I was familiar with. It was like a jam session with a solid-balanced musician, one much better than I was. If I said I had no idea what we said, I wouldn't be lying, but if I said I understood it, I wouldn't be much closer to the truth. Crystals of galena, yellowed carpal bones, splashes of aromatic benzoin, networks of spider web preserved by tensile plastic, seed pods of tropical plants—the morphemes were expressive of so much that it was almost superfluous to communicate staid human ideas with them. Or such is my excuse. I'm afraid that trying to communicate with me was extremely frustrating for her.

There was one thing I did want to know. What was to be her fate? Where was she going? Where did she *want* to go?

With the Messengers, she replied. Her life was with the Messengers. She was emphatic.

I shrugged. OK. Then, with a sense that I was violating the dictates of her entire world system, I handed her a business card. I always kept a few for those people who didn't use flexicards. She held it in her hand and stared at it as if she didn't even know what it was.

"My phone number." My voice rang oddly in my ears. I couldn't remember the last time I had heard it. "My address." With the return of my speech, the symbols that now covered the surface of the old desk meant even less than they had before. I felt despair. I did manage, finally, to pull out a cockleshell, symbol of safety, of home, and indicated with it that, if she wanted, she could come to me. She could come to me, and I would welcome her. Shira scooped up the cockleshell and held it in her fist.

With an emphatic rattle of hard-shod feet on the stairs, the Messengers appeared. There was nothing more that could be said. I looked at them as they shepherded Shira out of the room, with their covered heads, their robes, their mysterious symbologies. Tigranes had invented them so that his daughter would have someone to talk to. They had developed their own momentum, their influence spilling out into the world at large. She was still the focus of their attention, the creator and maintainer of their language. I watched her leave. She did not look back at me. The last Messenger, also not looking at me, closed and locked the door behind her.

In the sudden echoing silence I heard a tiny mechanical tune. An old tune, a cliched cultural artifact: "How Much Is That Doggy In The Window?" I looked down. Sitting on the floor, bent and creased by what it had gone through, was a tiny windup toy, a dog, its head down, its spiral tail turning around and around as it played. The first and final symbol of a father's love, the beginning of Shira's view of the world. It finally uttered a few last strangled notes and stopped. I left it where it was.

-34-

THE FURNITURE WAS GONE AND THE FLOORS WERE BARE OF RUGS. Several of the walls had been torn down to the studs, to remove whatever gear had once hidden there. The windows stood open to the cold October air. Not a speck of dust remained to indicate that anyone had ever lived here. Even the garden—I stared out the open-swinging French door—was gone before it could begin, now nothing but a wilderness of turned earth. Only one thing was left to indicate Tigranes's past existence. An oak sapling now stood, hunched slightly against approaching winter, its leaves tinged with copper, by the corner of the garage. Its newly planted roots were insulated by a layer of white foamed plastic.

I was trapped here, far out in the suburbs, far from transportation, and I had no doubt that the no-doubt-overpaid security of this privileged enclave would soon be here to expel me beyond the walls or arrest me for trespassing. I would be a sitting duck, for Watkins as well as for Gideon Farley.

But Tigranes, or his Messengers, had done me one final courtesy. My own car, battered but still functional, stood in the brick parking spot under the hedge, and the gate behind it was locked open. Panic tingling my fingers, I jumped into it and hit the highway to the south and east, in the direction of Hank Rush.

The car's map showed me the roads around Lake Calumet, but had no way of telling me where I had wandered in the swamps and woods of Rush's domain. In between neighborhoods of tight little houses were stretches littered with abandoned factories, toxic waste dumps, and great piles of garbage covered with the flickering burn of vented methane. And all the time I searched, Farley, our killer, was no doubt forging to his next target. Hank Rush was mostly mechanical and electronic, but he could certainly still be killed.

Then I saw it, far away: a long crane, rusted brown, with a decorated artificial Christmas tree dangling from it. I immediately cut the car to the shoulder, almost dumping it off the embankment to join a battered refrigerator and stove that leaned against each other cozily in the underbrush, thrown there by some frenzied, redecorating householder.

I ran, slashed by low branches, torn by pricker bushes. If there had been a defensive perimeter, it was now gone. Nothing impeded my mad scramble.

"Hank!" I shouted as I ran. "Hank Rush!" He didn't even rustle the remaining oak leaves to answer.

I cleared the fallen chain link fence with a mighty leap, only narrowly avoiding tangling my feet in it. Beyond it was the clearing with the smelting-furnace housing. It was tilted back. In front of it stood trees that I did not remember, twisted, branchless things like palm trees that had been through a hurricane. It took a moment for me to recognize them as the segmented pipes that had come out of the ground to frighten me during my interview with Rush. They were now dead, frozen in their death throes. As I passed through them, I saw that the silver wire that had bound the shattered furnace housing together had parted, and the top had slid down, tilted crazily like an alley nomad's hat.

The once-cool autumn air was now hot pain in my lungs, but I forced myself forward at speed. The forest cleared away, and I found myself in the open area where Rush's rubber and ionization-field faces had once spoken to me. Sitting placidly in a rocking chair was Gideon Farley.

He rocked gently back and forth on an as-yet-undigested plane of concrete with the air of a man on his own porch. The rocking chair was old and beat, one rocker covered with mud and torn grass, so he had probably pulled it, orphaned and abandoned, out of a slough. His head was bent in contemplation and he didn't look up, even though I was gasping like a whale.

There was a rumbling that I could feel through the soles of my feet. A few yards away, the ground shifted, just slightly, as if something, a huge mole maybe, was digging just under the surface.

"Hank!" I yelled. Nothing, not even the wind, answered me.

Farley's head turned slowly toward me. He smiled. "Peter! What a wonderful surprise. I never expected to see you here."

He wore one of Tigranes's house robes, red silk, neatly strapped up. He looked like he was ready to sit down to tea. He put neatly manicured fingers on the chair arms and turned it to face me. I could see now that the robe was not neat at all, that it was torn and slashed by the thorny underbrush surrounding Rush. That didn't seem to bother Farley, who leaned back casually in his seat.

"What the hell are you doing, Farley?"

He didn't seem startled by the harshness of my tone. He shrugged, as if we were old friends and he knew I was in a mood. "Taking care of a few loose ends." He spread his hands out to me, as if offering something. The soil roiled behind him and clods of dirt bounced into the air. "Making sure it's all neat and clean." He smiled. "Doesn't that make sense to you?" He noticed my stare over his shoulder and gestured. "Hank's devices. He had a lot of them. Some of them are quite clever, really. They dig. Some secrete their own piping as they go. Big ones, little ones—some are tiny grubs that pull optical fibers through the dirt behind them. Well, they're as useful for taking things apart as they are for putting things together."

A nightmarish giant worm head with three spinning sets of grinding teeth emerged from the dirt, flailed back and forth for a few seconds, then dived back underground. A loop of its long body remained above the ground as it moved. The shining metallic segments succeeded each other for the better part of a minute.

"I can control them. But only with your help, Peter. Only because of what you did to me. I owe you something for that." Farley tugged a handkerchief out of a breast pocket with two fingers and dabbed at his forehead with it.

The air got thicker in my throat. It was a familiar gesture. Farley was someone I had known long ago. Someone I had missed. Someone I had—

"Pull up a seat, Theo." His voice was quiet. "I don't think anyone will disturb us. By this point, Hank has been transferred . . . elsewhere. I don't think we need worry about him." He patted a rock nearby, one dense with some kind of mechanical trilobites.

I took a couple of steps, then stopped, balancing on one foot. The world was suddenly torn into two images, leaving ragged edges. In one, a skein killer sat placidly, waiting for me to sidle up next to him so that he could add me to his tally of victims. In the other—I felt the rug on my knees as I crawled quickly across it to the door, where I could pull myself up and look out through the lowest pane of glass at where Daddy was just getting out of his car his long legs with the big brown shoes precise oxfords all I could see and I giggled and smeared at the glass with my fingers because I couldn't wait for him to come in and pick me up under my arms and throw me up into the air so that I would float for just a second under the hall light looking down at his face as he smiled up at me my father—

"Director Straussman," I said, my voice the barest whisper.

"You know me. Don't you?"

I licked my lips. They were spiky dry. "Yes." And I did. Everything, from the way he sat, the way he held his head, the way he smiled to the way he was pulling me in closer to him told me who he was.

His smile got a little sad. "I've missed you, Theo. I've missed all of you. It's been such a long time. What have you been up to?"

"Oh, stuff. Nothing much." I took a step closer, and teetered again.

He nodded sympathetically. "I know how it must be. Boring. Civilian life . . . well, it doesn't *challenge* much, does it?" He looked off across the clearing toward the abandoned factory. "It all slows down like thick blood. Sluggish. Am I right?"

"It's not so bad. If you've got the music."

"Ah." A warm smile suffused his face. "You're still playing, then. That's good. I gave that to you, you know. You needed it. And you still have it."

"I still have it." He cared for me. He cared what happened to me. That was all I had wanted to know, and I had been afraid, afraid that he had lost all interest in me. But he still cared.

"I'd like to play for you," I said. "I'd like to play . . .what you always liked to listen to."

He nodded gently. "Beethoven's Seventeenth Sonata. I don't know much about music, Theo, you know that. Never did. Don't know why I settled on that piece. Do you? Some of those sonatas have names, don't they? Moonlight. Appassionata—Lenin's favorite, I hear. The Seventeenth's called . . . what?"

"Some people call it The Tempest."

"I knew you'd remember. I like it a lot. I hope you can play it for me. I always liked the way you played it."

I wasn't going to get next to him. I wasn't going to offer to buff his nails, or make him hot chocolate, or challenge him to single combat in a burning building, all those things my sibs had decided to do to welcome their daddy back.

I wasn't. I wasn't. I took another step forward.

He leaned forward. "Did you miss me, Theo?"

I nodded. And finally remembered what it had been like when we had lost him.

They'd stuck us back in Camp Fitzwater after it was all over, after we'd done our Bessarabian business and learned our lessons. I didn't think they'd had any special plan, either nefarious or kind. That was the only place they could think to put us. It was just the same as it had been, already so old when we found it that a few more years didn't make any difference. But it didn't feel right, too small, as if we had come back to sit at our old fifth grade desks and stare at a poorly erased chalkboard.

The world was tangled. Cities burned, and there were threats to communication from the Aryans in the Idaho mountains. Then Linden Straussman took his plane flight north, across the mountains of Alberta and British Columbia.

I cried when I heard. Harder than I could ever remember having cried before. I know I haven't cried that hard since.

I lay down on my bed with my face in the worn fabric of my pillow. He'd never be there again. I'd never see him again. I would never play for him again. I couldn't imagine what life would be like.

The others were in their rooms, facing his absence in their own way. Even Tony Watkins, I was sure, was slumped miserably in his bed, feeling that something had been ripped right out of him and the cold wind was blowing through. That was why none of us wanted to look each other in the face after that day, once we felt ourselves to be free.

And now Linden Straussman was back.

I'd lost the heat of my run through the woods and the swamps and was starting to feel the cold, despite the high sun. I shivered. *Think,* dammit. This man murdered Charlie, Lori, Gene, and made Karin kill herself. This man tore out the throat of my friend Sal Tigranes. It didn't matter one goddamn that I loved him.

"Why?" I said, feeling dust sliding off the word as I forced it from my throat. "Why did you do it?"

He shook his head, not understanding. "I came back to see you, Theo."

"Not me. Not just me." I heard a distant scream of rending metal. "What are you doing to Hank?"

He shrugged delicately. "Pruning him down a little. He always needed it, didn't he? He liked to spread all over. It got a little annoying sometimes. Not knowing which of the objects around was really him."

"Yeah," I said. "Annoying."

"I mean, look at this nonsense." He gestured at the I beam that held Hank's faces. They were all frozen. As I watched, they all changed, growing slowly into expressions of terror.

"Stop it!" I said.

"All right." His voice was calm. "Let's—but you have something for me, don't you, Peter?"

"What? I don't know...."

"What is it, now? Hank. Try to think. How do I hold on to him?"

He thought a moment, then held up a soft leather glove lined with sharp spikes.

Farley smiled. "That's it. That's what I need. Now we can eliminate the rest of it all."

Two digging claws emerged from the soil, trailing lines of cabling. A few snips, and the cabling fell from them to the ground, where it lay in a tangled mass. The claws reached up to the first face, a flexible one painted with Japanese–theatrical-mask colors, and ripped it from the beam. The mouths of the other faces opened wide, screaming in silent agony.

I found myself, finally, moving, but not toward Gideon Farley. It would have been just like Hank Rush to build a vast, complex structure, stretching over miles, deep into the earth, and still leave the whole capable of feeling pain. Pain was something he could never escape. I jumped to the digging claws.

It was stupid, as stupid as anything I'd ever done. The claws, armored and shielded, were as easy to wrestle as an engine block. They shrugged me off and went on with their business, ripping Hank's faces off and shredding them. With mechanical casualness, one of the claws flicked me off onto the ground.

"You always were too symbol oriented," Farley said, his voice sad. He shook his head. "Then there's Tony. We have to find him, talk to him. He's been out of hand. Have you seen him? Do you have his object with you too? Of course you do."

"No, I—" I took a breath. My ribs hurt where the claw had struck me. "Where have you been?"

He frowned, furrow between his brows. "Been? Theo, I'm right here in front of you. What else do you need to know? You always pried into things, a bad habit, really. That's okay, though. I can work with it."

I pushed myself to my feet. I was useless, helpless.

"You killed them," I said. "All of them."

"Now, Theo, don't be unreasonable. They brought me back. Bit by bit, they called me. And I came. With your help, I came."

"Damn you! I don't want you. Don't want you here." I managed a couple of steps back. My feet felt as if they were dragging through setting concrete.

"Theo," he said. "Don't try to go. We have a lot to talk about."

"We don't have anything—"

He stood up suddenly, his eyes wide. He looked around himself as if he had no idea where he was. Then he grabbed his head in both hands and screamed.

It was a scream like a shaman would use for breaking rocks, or killing a distant enemy. Blood must have been drawn from his throat. It rattled its way between the plates of my skull and tore at the innermost parts of my brain. Involuntarily, I dived to the ground, as if to escape it.

He drew a breath, a short instant of silence, and screamed again. "Oh, God! Where are they? Where is everyone?" He fell to his knees, hands on his head.

The digging claws had frozen in their motion. The underground rumbling had ceased. All around was stillness.

Farley closed his eyes, shook his head, and opened them again. When he looked at me, I found myself looking into the eyes of a sane man. Gideon Farley, and no one else. I felt silly being so certain, but it was as clear as anything I had ever seen.

"You're all right now, Gideon," I said. "You're all right."

"I'm not all right. I'm crazy." His voice was dispassionate.

"That remains to be seen."

He got to his feet. "Right."

What had happened to him? He still had the deviant Kundalini device in his brain. Karin Crawford had filled it with symbolic links to the Group, links that somehow had resurrected Linden Straussman, by means I didn't yet understand. Whatever had happened, that virt was still in there. Linden Straussman could come back at any time.

"Do you know who you are?" I asked.

"Yes." He seemed mildly surprised at the question. "My name is Gideon Farley. I'm a heo at Transcendental Transition. I am married to Corinne Zamm. She used to be married to you."

I waited for him to apologize for not having told me when we last met, but he didn't say anything more. In fact, he had spoken the last sentence with a hint of reproach, as if I had sullied Corinne for him. He was once again Gideon Farley, all of his personality flaws intact. I suppose that should have reassured me.

"Do you remember who you just were?" I asked.

He stared at me as if I had just asked an impertinent question. "I remember what you did to me."

"And what was that?"

"You killed me. I remember that. You all killed me. And that made me angry. So _pissed off_. After all I had done . . . the love I had given you. You fucking _killed_ me. And each of you had a piece of me. I had to get it back. So I . . . killed you all." He looked puzzled at his own memory. "One at a time. It made me stronger."

"That wasn't you, Gideon. That was someone else."

"Someone else? There's no one else here. Just you and me."

"That's right, he's gone now. He was an artifact of your connection to the network. He doesn't exist now."

"Neither do all those people I killed. Or are they alive now, gone home, sitting in front of the TV?"

"No," I said. "They're dead."

"Yeah, including that buddy of yours, the one with the daughter. I miss her, you know? She didn't talk, but she had more to say than anyone I've ever known. It was too bad to kill him, but I had to go, had to say good-bye; I had things to do, and it seemed right." He took a deep breath.

I felt a surge of hate for this man who had killed my friend so casually. I suppressed it—I had to deal with him, make sure it didn't happen again—but it was still there. I knew he could see it.

"You have to come with me," I said. "The virt I installed is defective. It's still under warranty—"

"Like hell." He looked commanding. "I'm not letting you back in there. It's my brain, after all. I like it. There's no way." He looked down at the torn house robe he wore. "I should be getting home, anyway. Thanks for helping me out, Peter."

I sweated in desperation. Linden Straussman was still there, somewhere. This was just a temporary remission. I had to make it permanent. "Gideon. You don't understand—"

"I understand perfectly well. You're pissed because I have your wife. Well, I'm really sorry about that, but that's the way the world works."

There is a great deal of difference between hating your ex-wife's current husband and hating the man who has murdered your friends. I tried to keep the two feelings separate. I moved a little closer to him. It was against all the rules, against the way I ran my business, but I was going to have to tackle him and subdue him like some sort of animal on a wildlife show, then take him to my lab and open his head up against his will.

"You be careful, Peter Ambrose," he said, moving back. "I took your friend here completely apart with his own tools." He gestured around at the invisible Hank Rush. "Just think what could happen to—"

"*Wrong!*" a voice thundered around us. "You strip a piece of chrome off my side and think you've eliminated me? You're stupid, as well as a murderer, Linden Straussman. You have instead freed me for my next task."

I looked around at the still-living Hank Rush. "He's not Linden Straussman, Hank. Straussman is dead. You told me that yourself."

"I know." The only face left on the I beam laughed. "That's why I killed him again."

"*You* cut him from the net?"

"He's on my territory here, Peter. He opened himself up to control my working tools. So I slipped in and cut him off when he was done doing what I needed done. There's a flaw in that device of Karin's. Sometimes I think she put them in on purpose. Because everything valuable always has a flaw."

"Can you help me with Farley?" I asked.

"I'm not interested in him."

Farley, who had been looking terrified at the booming voice around him, laughed. "See, Ambrose? No one's on your side."

"You'll just be yourself," I said. "Isn't that who you want to be?"

"How the hell should you know who I am? I am whatever it takes. That's why I run Tran^2, and you eat pizza in that miserable suburb of yours."

He was addicted to the power. I could see that. Even being someone else, even being the murdering Linden Straussman, was not too high a price to pay for the power. Connection to the net, strength, will, he wanted all of those. Perhaps Gideon Farley had never existed, save as an empty receptacle waiting for Linden Straussman.

There was a heavy, gale-force sigh from all around us. "Is it really worth it, Peter?"

"It is, Hank."

"I have to go. It's been too long that I've stayed here."

"You're ready to leave? That's too—"

Right in the middle of my sentence, I turned, sprinted and tackled Gideon Farley. Completely surprised, he went down hard, bouncing on the ground like a sack of potatoes. He fought back viciously, pounding at my face with his hands, his elbows, his forehead. I rolled back and smashed my heel into the side of his head. He oof!ed and stopped struggling.

I slapped my shirt as if I had a sedating dermspray, but there was nothing there. My OR was far away.

"I'll still be around, Peter. But not conscious, not the way you understand it. It's the only way to keep this world clean for the life that should be here. We turn ourselves into machines and leave it, descend below its living surface. The ultimate end of my evolution. I'm leaving this fecund and lush Earth behind. I will stay below, trying to repair some of the damage we have done to it. Someday it will regrow, and forgive us. Perhaps I will see you someday, Peter Ambrose. I would like that. I will miss our talks."

"Hank—"

The ground rumbled, much more strongly than it had when Farley was trying to destroy Hank with his own machines. Was he diving just below the surface to feast on pools of toxics and radioactives, or was he digging down through the crust to permit the upwelling of magma? Was he going to leave his own electromechanical fossils throughout the rock layers of the Earth? I had no way of knowing.

I waved. "Bye, Hank!"

"Bye, Peter."

The I beam with the last face on it fell to the ground. The abandoned factory crumbled in on itself with a distant crash. Between me and it, smoke rose from the ground. I squinted to see what was causing it.

Farley, taking advantage of my distraction, snapped under me and slid from my grip.

He ran across the field toward the ruined factory. I chased for a few steps, then stopped. "Gideon!" I yelled. "Stop!" He didn't slow.

Flames rose up from the dry grass of the prairie, once a natural occurrence every fall. The heat blasted almost instantly. There were sloughs and wet areas to prevent the spread of the flames to the forests around, but the clearing we stood in was going to go up. I watched the black smoke rise up into the sky.

Farley slowed and stumbled. Flames spread around him, flowing like some spilled, flaringly bright liquid. In a few seconds it was so hot that I had to turn my face away. The heat tore at my skin. Chasing him would have been like jumping off the top of a building to catch at the feet of someone who had fallen.

Farley screamed once, a high sound almost like a laugh, and then was silent. I peered into the heat, light, and smoke, and couldn't see anything. Linden Straussman had claimed his last victim.

-35-

TIGRANES HAD ONCE TOLD ME ABOUT SOME ANCIENT PHILOSOPHER WHO thought that the fundamental element underlying everything around us is fire. At one time that old Greek must have been through a prairie fire. Dry branches and grass exploded into flames as if that was what they had wished for all along, to reveal what they really were, fire held calm and green through spring and summer. Waves of heat swirled everything I could see as if it was underwater. My skin felt like it was blistering, but I didn't flee. I just retreated step-by-step, staring into the fire, as if I could see something important there, the blackening skeleton of Linden Straussman in Hell maybe. I couldn't even see the remains of Gideon Farley.

After a few minutes, a gust of wind carried the fire's roar away from me, and I heard a voice calling for help. I had been pushed back into the mud of the swamp. I turned and ran toward the voice with nightmare slogging slowness. The fabric of my pants seared my knees as it pressed against them. It seemed impossible that Farley could have run through that hell and survived, but then it seemed impossible that he could have done anything that he had done. . . .

"Theo!" the voice shouted. "Damn it, where the hell are you?"

I stopped, mucky water swirling around my knees like chocolate being stirred into milk. "Here, Tony," I said. "Here I am."

Watkins huddled on a small knoll under some oak trees. Flames licked up the knoll and the remaining leaves were flaring up, first one by one, then in masses.

Watkins's face was black, his clothes scorched. Flames had spread around the knoll, leaving it an island surrounded by heat and light. A temporary island. Burning flecks that had once been oak leaves floated down on him like incandescent snow flakes.

"Hank, that damn saucepan was just a joke!" he yelled, in long-delayed apology for the trick he had played on Rush in Kishinyov. "I didn't know—damn it, Theo, what the hell. . . ." He squinted into the light all around him and rubbed the blackened back of his hand across his eyes. I didn't think he could see anything. He was yelling my name out of faith, or hope. If I wanted to, I could just turn away and leave him there to burn, and forget any of the questions whose answers he might know.

I lowered myself into the slough like an amphibian. The water flowed heavily along my skin, cool and viscous, ignoring the hectic flames that burned along its edge. When I stood, my clothes were heavy with mud and water.

"Peter Ambrose!" He switched names, as if to conjure me. "Are you there?" He listened to the snapping flames for a moment, but I didn't answer. "I just came here to talk to Hank, shoot the shit over old times, try to get a handle on what was happening. Then that lunatic . . ." The flames whipped his words away. " . . . the hell he is. Or was. So I know it wasn't you. That damn Crawford laid a booby trap for all of us. Peter!"

I lumbered up the slope, dripping, as if I really was some primitive lungfish lunging for dry land, desperate to cremate myself, having blinked with undersea eyes for years at the fascinating hot glow from above. My soaking clothes held off the heat of the flames for the few instants I needed.

I hit Watkins hard. He never saw it coming. We toppled down the slope, through the burning grass, Watkins yelping, and dropped together into the water.

"Peter?" He still couldn't see me, blinded now by mud and decaying weeds rather than fire. He wiped his face with his hands. "There you—"

With desperate rage, I slam-dunked his head into the water with both hands.

He came up spitting. "Hey—"

I dunked him again, putting my entire body weight into it. His head popped up and I gave him half a breath before elbowing him in the face and shoving him underneath again.

I moved fast enough that he couldn't figure out where I was coming from next. He scrabbled beneath me like a crab, but went down again.

I would gladly have drowned him then and there, and left his body floating mysteriously for the police to finally find and puzzle over—one man burned to ashes, one drowned, one vanished into the depths of the earth. Draw one line through these points without lifting your pencil from the paper.

But—I couldn't. He was the only one of us left, the last of our distinguished dysfunctional family. The only one who could still understand me. I didn't want to become an only child by my own hand.

I put my knee between his shoulder blades and shoved his face into the mud while I yanked his right arm back and ripped his pistol out of its biceps holster. Then, at long last, I allowed him to pull his face out of the water and feel the muzzle of his own pistol against his eye.

He grabbed at it. "No, no, Tony. That's not the way to do it." I pushed a knee into his solar plexus.

"What the hell is this?" He stared up at the pistol, looking betrayed.

"Have you forgotten that you tried to kill me, Tony?"

"I already explained that." He was annoyed at my obtuseness. "It was a mistake. I didn't know about Farley. . . ."

"What a relief, to be murdered because of a flaw in your logic rather than because I was really guilty. That makes me feel so much better."

He shrugged, managing to be calm now that he had his breath back, despite the fact that he lay on his back in the mud, hot ashes blowing across and sticking to his face. "*You're* the one who operated on the son of a bitch, not me. And you didn't bother to inform me, give me any information. How the hell was I supposed to keep from aliasing?" His blue-gray eyes flashed contemptuously, daring me to shoot him.

I felt a surge of anger and almost obliged him. It's so much easier to squeeze a trigger than to hold someone's head underwater while he struggles.

His cockiness flickered, just a bit, as he watched my face. "Let's go," I said. "Farley's dead and we have things to talk about."

"Where are you taking me?" The hint of nervousness in his voice was reward enough for all I had gone through.

"Home," I said. "I think I need to go home."

WE STUMBLED, CAKED IN DRYING MUD LIKE ONLY PARTIALLY ANIMATED statues, into my basement studio. Watkins glanced up, then sat beneath the stain in the cracked concrete. I looked up at it. How the hell had that gotten cracked, anyway? It had been poured well, as far as I could tell. And the acoustic baffles had just fallen off. Poor glue, bad work, it depressed me. I sat down on the bench and leaned my elbows on the piano behind me.

"She was looking for us," Watkins said. "That damn icy luke, TerAlst. I don't know why. I don't know how she found out anything at all about us, but that was what set me off. She was . . . digging, rooting it out. You can't stop someone like that once they've gotten started."

"So you tried to find the rest of us."

"Yeah, I did. You know, it was funny. Once I started, I realized what I had been missing. You. All of you. It was like there was never anything else. And I'd let you all go, wander away, vanish." He sat, legs spread, long hands dangling loose between.

"Didn't it occur to you that without your searching, TerAlst wouldn't have been able to find anyone?"

Watkins's head jerked. "What are you saying?"

"You know damn well what I'm saying. If anyone was a cat's paw, it was you. You were the only one with enough knowledge to find the rest of us. How did you find out that IC was after us? They didn't send you a mail message."

"No, they didn't send me a mail message." He was annoyed. "I always kept my ears open, even when I was swacked out on a couch at the mall. And I heard. Someone was asking about the Group. Someone was looking for us. We'd done a good job of turning Nimbus into just another netwank, but I could feel the real questions burbling around back there somewhere. Someone wanted to know."

"So you went to Karin Crawford—Helena Mennaura."

"She was easy enough to find. She was doing exactly what she had always done. Almost as if she didn't care whether anyone found her or not."

"Maybe she didn't. Maybe none of us should have cared. Maybe then all of us would still be alive."

His eyes narrowed. "Yeah, maybe. And for what? What am I now?"

"You? You're what you've always been, Tony. Whatever you want yourself to be."

"Right." He reached into his breast pocket and pulled something out. I tensed, wondering if it was some weapon that I hadn't discovered while searching him, but it was just a pill box I had already examined. He pulled out a capsule and rested it on his palm. I relaxed. Unless he was going to overpower me and force poison down my throat, it was nothing to worry about. "But I have to say, Peter, that I've had more fun in the past couple weeks than I ever have . . . at least since we left Fitzwater for the last time."

"No reason to stop."

"No, there isn't. But we'll need someone to answer all the questions, someone up front. After all, our murderer is dead, burned up in a fire. The virts you stuck into him boiled right out of his skull. Lucky for you, I guess. But what sort of thing is that to present to the cops? It's just shit, Pete, and you know it. You know how they get when they get hungry. They'll want us, want our sweet asses. We've got to *give* them something. And that TerAlst babe's a hungry one. I can hear her belly rumbling from here."

"It's what we have." Despite myself, I was getting nervous. Watkins had a sort of serene confidence, as if, once again, he knew exactly what he was doing.

"Yeah, yeah. It's what we have." He looked meditative. "Linden Straussman. Where was he? Where is he?"

"Dead." My voice was harsh. "I'm tired of discussing it."

"So am I. Bones or no bones, wherever they are, it's time we had a talk with him, isn't it?" He grinned at me. "Interesting story, wasn't it, the one Michaud told us about the smoke over his father's house. I had a story too. I didn't tell it, because I understood something. I wonder if you do? My mom would always leave the teakettle on. It was a big cast-iron thing, much bigger than I was, and she'd always turn it on and go away and forget it. It would scream and scream, like one of those factory whistles they have in cartoons. And the steam . . . A huge cloud of it, Peter. A cumulus cloud, there in that green kitchen with the yellow flowered curtains. Refrigerator covered with magnets shaped like fruit. And a big black thunderhead, spurting out of that damn kettle, hanging right over me where I played with my trucks on the linoleum. I'd scream for my mom, but she couldn't hear me over the howling of that damn teakettle. . . ." His face twisted with the memory, as if it was exquisitely painful. He looked at me. "It was a chalky smell, kind of like vinegar and burning hair. I can still smell it. That's why I never drink tea."

"Tony, that doesn't make any sense."

"You're right. It doesn't make a goddam bit of sense." He popped the capsule between his fingers. I smelled a pungent, complex smell. Harsh hot oil and licorice. It was strong enough that I could taste it on the back of my tongue. It was the smell of my grandmother's house, of the upstairs hall. The smell, I suddenly realized, that made no sense at all. My grandmother, whoever she might have been, hadn't lived in a combination auto repair shop and candy store. I remembered that hallway, and the kink it made just before the . . . dry piano room at Camp Fitzwater. It didn't go anywhere, anywhere at all. There was no hallway, no grandmother, no stain.

I swung my legs around to face the piano. The cover seemed to slam up of its own accord and I felt my fingers lightly on the rough synthetic ivory of the keys. I needed it, needed the music like a drug. If I didn't play now, I wouldn't be able to breathe. It had kept me alive, through Fitzwater, Bessarabia, the years after Corinne. Nothing else was important.

Except Linden Straussman. He loomed over me darkly on the wall, where he had been standing all those years I thought I had escaped him. I felt his shadow fall over me.

"You weren't a musician when you came to Fitzwater," Watkins said as he sat down next to me on the bench. "Not at all. No family background, no training. But he found the latent control hook, gave you the skill, and let you loose. But the hook was always there, waiting, waiting for you."

The keys were clear lights under my fingers. Music sat on the piano, already open: Beethoven's Seventeenth Sonata in D-minor. His favorite. He had asked me to play it. The notes flew out into the silence of the world. It was a powerfully physical feeling, as if I was gathering the notes up, vibrating, in my hands, and flinging them up at the clouds.

"Is he there?" Watkins's voice was tense. "Do you see him?" I didn't answer. He grabbed my arm, making me flub a chord. The wrong notes cut. "Where is he? Is he there?"

Straussman reached for me and I almost flinched back. He'd been watching me all along. He was like that, quiet, sly, always there when you didn't expect him. Except that I'd learned to always expect him, hadn't I? I guess I had forgotten that.

"No," I said above the music. "I don't see him. He's dead, Tony."

Despite myself, my shoulders tightened as I spoke, because I knew the depth of Straussman's rage. He leaned forward over me, clean fingernails shining in the dark.

"You're lying!" Watkins yelled. "Damn it, he's there. You can see him. Tell me what he says!"

Tentatively, I started to add ornamentation to the music. Baroque ornamentation, as if I was playing Bach or Scarlatti. Beethoven would have booted me right the hell off stage, bellowing, hair wild, but he was deader than Straussman. I found myself sticking in grace notes, mordents, trills. It made a mess of things, of course. Beethoven had meant every note to stay where it was, and they were close enough together that they were almost stepping on each other's toes as it was. If Watkins had known the Seventeenth, he'd have known something was wrong, but he'd always had a tin ear.

"I don't see a goddam thing, Tony."

Air swirled, and the room was packed with faces. They shifted and melted and made no sense to me. Just features, no connection, like poorly put-up wallpaper. And blades, and knives, and blood, and hair . . . the world tottered around me, nonsensical. Only the music I made with my fingers was solid. Only that could hold me up.

As I played, I saw the band I had created for Amanda TerAlst—the Group. Hank Rush pounding out the percussion on his own multiplated body, Charlie Geraldino grunting out the low notes on the bass, Karin Crawford sliding sweetly on the clarinet, Lori Inversato switching from cornet to flugelhorn between notes, Anthony Watkins implying unspeakable acts with his saxophone, and Linden Straussman looming over all of it.

We were all Nonexistent Jazz Greats. Music seems solid until you try to pick it up and the notes squirm out from between your fingers and sink into the ground like swollen sperm cells. I had to tell Sheldon about it, I had to. It fit in with his world. The damn Group. Bandleader died in a plane crash, and the Group kept playing along exactly as if he had never died at all. They could see him, up there in front, throwing shadows in the spots.

Cloud of Witnesses, that played Bessarabia. Not a bunch of datadorks fiddling people's brains. That was right, that was what made sense. I imagined it that way, saw it as the past that I had. No one would ever be interested in murdering or arresting people who just played good music, would they?

I still couldn't get away, try as I might. Even pulling my fingers off the keys was impossible. Instead, I warped Ludwig van's theme. I played a series of variations based on some notes in the left hand, going through key and rhythmic changes, until the original melody had completely vanished. I didn't even know what I was playing.

Then, a whole block of notes down at the low end of the keyboard vanished. Hitting the keys got me nothing but silence. I bobbled, sucking air, and pulled back.

The silence pursued, up through the octaves, slowly chasing me up the keyboard, covering the music and putting it away. Thematic complexity vanished along with it. What I was playing got more and more pared down, harmonics simpler and simpler, until I found myself playing Tigranes's piece, "How Much Is That Doggy In The Window?" and mimicking the distortions of Shira's dented windup toy, all on the upper range of notes, tinkly and tiny. I cried for him because I missed him and for his silent daughter, wherever she was now. Then those notes vanished too and I found myself sitting at a completely voiceless piano.

I looked up. I had to blink my eyes to see anything. Standing at the foot of the open grand was Priscilla McThornly. Her hair was crudely shorn, like wood chipped by a chisel. In her hand she held a pair of wire clippers.

-36-

PRISCILLA STARED AT ME AS IF SHE HAD TROUBLE RECOGNIZING ME. "I . . . waited," she said. "That's what she told me. Wait and see. But I couldn't wait any more. There was something wrong . . . something in the way you played. I'm sorry I ruined your piano. It looks like . . . it . . . was . . . a . . . nice . . . one." She dropped the wire clippers and slid down to the floor.

I shook the dream off and stood up from the piano bench. The stain on the wall was now nothing more than that, just poor construction. Had I cracked that wall myself, so that Straussman would reappear above me? I couldn't know, now. Straussman had impressed himself into clouds, into the smoke rising from a chimney, into steam above a whistling teakettle, receding like a god into the world around us, the world inside our own heads.

Long hair lay on the floor all around Priscilla. She knelt and slowly picked up handfuls of it. She looked up at me. The shorn hair made her eyes look larger. "I hear that if you take your hair and throw it outside on the grass the birds will gather it up and work it into their nests to raise their children. Do you suppose it's true?"

"It's true." I dropped to my knees by her side to help her. "I'm sure it's true." The dark hair was long, spilled on the floor, and soft in my hands.

"We do that, you know," she said, voice confiding. "Women. When we want to make a point of our lives. We cut our hair. That's why we spend so much time growing it out and taking care of it. So we can make a point."

I ran the loose hair through my fingers and smelled its delicate perfume. It was no longer Corinne's perfume, I realized. This was a darker, stronger scent.

"What point?" I said, my voice sharper than I had intended.

She sat down on the floor, despite the fact that she wore a nice pleated skirt, and put her arms around her knees like a child sitting in the grass. "I didn't want to come here, at first."

I plopped down next to her. The strain of what she was doing showed on her face. "Tell me, Priscilla."

"Sheldon talked me into it." She didn't look at me, but leaned so that the warmth of her shoulder worked its way into mine. "'Peter's an idiot,' he said. 'He *looks* smart, sure, but spends so much time *looking* that he sometimes forgets to *be* smart, fact. He's a musician, forgive him.'"

A musician. I felt a chill. Now I knew why that was. "Thanks, Sheldon."

"You're still suspicious. Why?"

I turned and sniffed her neck. Still the winy, resinous scent, thick and primitive. "You changed your perfume."

Her eyes widened. "Ha! And here we put the stuff on, knowing men never notice it, just like they never pay the slightest attention to great shoes, and you *smelled* it. That's why! That's why you looked at me that way, back in Amalik's. Oh, Peter. Women always smell perfume. Particularly wives. If I had worn any scent other than that one, the one Corinne always wore, she would have smelled me on Gideon when he got home. She would have known immediately. She *would*."

"Ah." I drew in a jerking breath. I wanted to believe her. I wanted to have faith in her. "Then, I have to ask . . . that day I met you at that apartment . . ."

"Oh, God . . . what was upstairs, Peter? What had you just seen, that made your skin tighten up like that?"

I decided to play it her way. "A body, Priscilla. The murdered body of my friend, the woman who lived in the apartment."

"So that's what he was doing. A skein killer!" She laughed. "My lover was a murderer." Her fingernails dug into my upper arm. "How, Peter? He wasn't that. He wasn't a murderer when he hired me, when we . . . fell in love. He wasn't!"

No, Priscilla, I wanted to say. He wasn't one until I turned him into one. "Then why . . . ?"

"Why was I there? I was following Gideon. I was worried. No, no, not about another woman. Well, maybe a little. But really about him. Something was happening to him . . . I didn't know what. How many people did he kill?"

I counted in my head, and added Karin Crawford, drowned in the Chicago River, to the number. "Five. But it wasn't—"

"Wait, wait." She gestured fiercely. "Let me *think*." And I did, as she sat there in concentrated silence. "Was one of his victims a member of one of those military gangs?"

"Not exactly. But one did die in gang combat. In a burning building."

She shook herself. "Those damn challenges. It wasn't like him, I knew that. To collect stuff like that." I remembered the detailed symbolic fetishes lying on her bookshelf. Just collectibles, I had thought. "He was calling someone out. He was getting ready. I remember one . . . that damn fake human skin, with things sewn in it. A chess piece, pieces of a uniform . . . all sorts of little junk. Gideon! I can hardly believe it."

That was what had been delivered to Michaud that night, a detailed challenge based on Straussman's knowledge of his relationship with Michaud, just the thing to pull him outside his defenses. I wonder if it still lay in his headquarters on the South Side. I would have liked to get a look at it, to see, in symbolic form, how Straussman saw Gene Michaud.

Now that I thought of it, lying next to the fetishes had been a history of Chicago factories, a book on wildlife, a book about the far south of Chicago . . . research on how to find Hank Rush. It had all been there, right in front of me. I had just made love to Priscilla. I hadn't cared.

"Where . . ." Her voice was soft. "Where is Gideon? What happened to him?"

"Dead." There was no way to soften the word, and I didn't even try. "He tried to kill one more of us. And in the process . . . he died."

"Oh." She sat there, arms around her knees, and stared off at the great stain on the wall. "Oh." And tears appeared in her eyes. She wiped them away with bitter shame. "Oh, Peter, it's so st-st-stupid. . . ."

I held her. "Yes. It's stupid. Don't worry about it." She rested her head on my shoulder and hid her tears there.

"I never figured out what he was doing. That was stupid too." She wiped her nose. "I shouldn't—Peter. You scared me when you popped out of that house. I didn't know what you were doing there, what Gideon was doing there . . . but I knew I had to protect him. Until I could understand."

"That's why you slept with me," I said, breathing shallowly because my stomach hurt. "To distract me."

"Yes! I mean no . . . I suppose it was true, in part. It was easy enough to get you not to think."

"Yes. Real easy."

"Don't! I said, in part. But the rest . . . I'm not here to protect Gideon Farley, Peter. I'm here . . ."

"You're here. I don't think I could have escaped without your help. Escaped from," I nodded at the piano, "that."

Her wet eyes glinted at me. "Did you sleep with her? Your dear ex-wife, when you dumped me at the coffeehouse and brought her here. That night."

I would never have expected someone else's jealousy to make me so happy. It was like a charge at the base of my spine. "No, Priscilla." And then I thought—I'll have to tell Corinne. I have to go to her to tell her her husband is dead. No one else should do it. No one else should speak those words.

"Good answer."

I didn't want to let her go, but there were questions to be answered. There were always questions to be answered. It seemed that my life would never again be free of them, after so many years of having no questions or answers at all.

"How did you get in here?" I finally managed to ask.

She looked at me, surprised. I half expected her to tell me that I had let her in myself. In my mad musical state I could have done anything. But no, I couldn't have let Priscilla in without taking my fingers from the keys of that piano, and that was one thing my conditioning would not have let me do.

"That woman friend of yours let me in," Priscilla said. "That lady with the gray hair. She's up in your living room, drinking coffee."

"Oh." I thought a moment. Had I told Amanda TerAlst where I kept my coffee? Perhaps I had. Perhaps all of her interrogations had had that as their only object. "She let you in?"

"Yes. I don't know what I would have done otherwise. Frozen on your porch, maybe. But she answered the door and told me to go on down."

"How many other people up there?" My house was probably swarming with cops.

"Just her and one other guy. Tall man, gray eyes. He seemed kind of nervous. I didn't have time to look, Peter. I was worried about you."

I stood up. "Did they really seem like friends?"

She grinned. "No, of course not. She's a cop. You can tell them by the way they sit: looks like they live there but don't like it much. He was a prisoner—but not under arrest, I don't think. Not yet. He was talking real fast. I don't think he was doing too well. He'll be telling that story in court."

I stood there at the base of the stairs for a moment, lost, and she kissed me. Afterward, she looked at me and laughed. "Don't look so startled, Peter."

I just shook my head. "Nothing makes sense anymore. It seems I'm starting to like it." And I went up the stairs.

TINY IR RANGE FINDER NUMBERS FLICKERED AT THE EDGES OF MY VISION, correlating to various objects in the recorded visual field.

"I found them in the summer," TerAlst said. "What summer there is at that latitude and altitude. Late July. But I didn't want to leave evidence of my search by digging through the growth."

My living room was full of snow. It loomed on all sides, obscuring the walls. The thick, straight trunks of . . . pines, I guess, firs, some damn mountain thing, stuck out of it and thrust out through the ceiling.

"Why not?"

I felt rather than saw her shrug. "At that point I didn't know what implication the information had. I wanted to clear it up before I involved anyone else."

"And have you?"

She sighed. "You are a real pain in the ass, Peter Ambrose. No. I haven't cleared up a damn thing. Except managing to arrest . . . what did he claim his name was? Thorfinn Nurmi?"

The powder snow had been blown off by some jet and the densely packed lower snow melted by quartz infrared heaters. The mountainside was unnaturally clear in a rough circle about three meters in radius, revealing tumbled branches and dead, crushed plants.

"Thorfinn?"

"Anthony Watkins, as far as you're concerned, Peter . . . and I'll stick with that name, all right? Peter Ambrose. Not . . . the other."

"That's fine, Amanda." Corinne's Solar Mission armchair was as uncomfortable as ever. I shifted in it. "What charge did you arrest him on?" I held my breath. Membership in the Group? The murder of Linden Straussman? Would my own arrest follow?

"Blowing up an ambulance and killing a hospital orderly in the process. Not to mention seriously wounding a police in the course of her duty. What did you think?"

"I didn't know what to think. There are many reasons for arrest. . . ."

"There are crimes, there are laws." TerAlst looked impatient. "You can look them up. We know what they are. Murder is a crime. Do you think I'm some sort of arbitrary force?"

"IC has a certain reputation."

"Yes, and it helps me do my job. Just don't take mallside rumors for fact." She clicked her tongue. "He tried to kill me too, didn't he? Back at the Mysteries, with that crawling bug thing."

"I don't—"

She raised a hand. "No need for you to tell me now. We may not need it. I'll chalk it up to professional hazards. I don't even know why I take it so personally when suspects try to kill me. It's just a quirk."

The image grew around us. A huge lichen-covered rock loomed overhead. There was a dark hole under it.

"They'd rolled much farther down the slope than the search parties had expected, in the first place," TerAlst said. "Then a fox dragged most of them into its lair, looks like. The explosion must have shredded him."

Arranged neatly in front of the dark hole were human bones, sorted by size. The one whole femur was most recognizably human. Hand and foot bones were just loose stacks of bone chunks. Many of the long bones were cracked and broken. The holographic image of the dismantled skeleton moved past me and numbers flickered on the bones.

"Computerized Bertillon," TerAlst said. "Dozens of parameters. There's no doubt of the ID. And if there were . . ." A skull loomed at me, its black sockets staring blankly. X-rays of fillings, from several angles, flipped above it, overlapped and flashed, indicating a match. "There's the dental work. It matches his records perfectly. Pretty good teeth, actually." A whisper, and the computer did a calculated muscle-and-skin overlay on the facial bones of the skull. A face appeared, lying grotesquely on the bare Canadian earth. The eyes were featureless marbles, and there was no hair or facial expression, but I found myself staring into the long-dead face of Linden Straussman. I gripped the arms of my chair. I couldn't breathe. "No, there's really not much question. Right now, bucko, you're looking at the earthly remains of your old colleague, Linden Timothy Straussman, born Rush-Presbyterian-St. Luke's Medical Center, Chicago, Illinois, December 12, 1960, and died on the slopes of Mt. May, Alberta, Canada, March 27, 2021."

It could have been fake, of course. A complete fiction, like everything else. An alternate world where Linden Straussman was actually dead. But I knew it was true. He *was* dead. That was *this* world, little though any of us had wanted to believe it.

The mountain winter scene vanished and my living room reappeared. TerAlst looked at me. She wore a dark dress and her silver hair gleamed in the half-darkness.

"Now, Peter," she said. "I want something from you. I need to know a few things." I could see her need in her tense posture.

"But how?" I said, not able to help myself. "Why did you start this?" I gestured, trying to take in the now-vanished bones of Straussman, and all of it, all of it.

"No, I didn't just trip over them while on a hike." She steepled her fingers. "We have discretionary research time at IntraCranial. Sounds ridiculous, doesn't it? We're so overworked. But someone worked out a good policy. Often disparate things become unified when you look at them from another angle. Camouflage is intended to distract predators looking for something specific. And it all might just be a way of keeping us happy and entertained. At any rate, I found a reference, a piece of information, that indicated that the Nimbus Project was real—I, like everyone else, had always thought it was just a stupid netwank."

"Not by accident. What piece of information?"

"It was strange." TerAlst leaned back slightly, but kept her back straight. "But my job is full of strange. It was a bulletin board message referencing another, nonexistent, message, with a connection to military operations in the Dniestr-Prut region during the Wars of Devolution. I checked the military ops records and found conceptual gaps, though the records themselves were seamless. That put me on it. I never found out who placed that bulletin board message."

"I know," I said. "Linden Straussman."

A line appeared between her eyes. "Straussman is dead."

"So everyone keeps telling me. And that's the problem. For him. Because he never expected to be dead."

"What do you mean?"

"He expected us to demob. Maybe he even planned for it. That bulletin board message was a deadman switch, sitting deep in some memory, somewhere, anywhere. If he was alive, he would have deactivated it before it appeared. It would only appear if he was dead. He implanted operating behavioral routines in each of us for the day when he would use us again. I don't think he knew what he was to use us for. To overthrow the government maybe. To run his private household. I don't know. But I know that he never meant for us to wander apart." I thought about the incidents of the past few weeks. "He put some sort of tropism in us. That's clear. The rule seemed to be: if you can possibly involve a former Group member in something, do so. That simple tropism brought us out into the open, reconnected us, made us visible for whatever fate was determined for us."

"And all this operated despite the fact that he wasn't around. So why—"

"If he wasn't around, he felt there must be a good reason for it—that we had somehow killed him."

"And did you?"

"Not as far as I know. It was an accident. He just crashed on that stupid mountain all on his own. Randomness, the source of our evolution, according to Hank Rush. He was dead, but bits and pieces of his personality, his needs, his angers, still existed. There were functional schemata in propagating data bases. There were—"

"He hated you," she said. "Why shouldn't he? As far as he knew, you had killed him."

"Oh, God." I slumped in my seat. "This is ridiculous. He's not a ghost."

"No, and he's not the Commander stomping toward you from the graveyard. But he is a collection of beliefs, routines, habits, points of view. Some are, or were, in the minds of former members of the Group."

"Just the idea of Straussman," I said. "It existed on its own. And we brought it back to life."

"Just so. An idea parasitic on the members of Group. But, as I said, he hated you, a hate that transcended his death and found its expression through that virt you installed in Gideon Farley's head."

"Of course," I said, tired and sick. "It was always that way. We did it all. We didn't even need Linden Straussman. We just went merrily along as if he was still alive. Just like those Bessarabian revolutionaries who wanted to become someone else. We *let* it be done to us. We weren't victims. Straussman just provided an opportunity for our crimes. Maybe he never existed at all, save as an excuse." I shook my head. "It's all a loop."

"More even than you think." TerAlst's voice was calm. "As far as any information would show, Linden Straussman had been nothing but a small-time technological subcontractor during the Devolution Wars. I found his bones and confirmed the ID. So what? I almost gave up on it. But I found that I lived right where he had grown up, lived, and operated for many years—Chicago. So I started asking questions."

I looked at her. "Of course. And the news of your search reached the ears of Anthony Watkins. He moved, calling into operation his own long-dormant links. He squeezed Helena Mennaura . . . damn! And she sent the virt out, for me to install—to get out from under Tony's gritty thumb. That virt contained the symbologies and connections that mapped Straussman and the Group. It allowed him to exist. She never intended that. She certainly didn't intend for him to kill us all."

She nodded. "As I closed in on the Group, the Group came back to life . . . and died, one by one, before I could get to its members. God *damn* it, Peter."

"*You* brought us to life. We were the answer to your question." I felt like giggling. "If you hadn't wanted to find out, to satisfy your curiosity, they'd still be alive and I'd still be . . . dead."

She stood, smoothing down her dress. "That's it, then. Nothing. Everything I looked for vanished as I saw it, and the only arrest I've made is someone who was driven to his actions by my search. Nothing at all is left." She shook her head. "I have to get home now. Thank you for the coffee." She walked out the door and shut it definitely behind her.

"Peter," Priscilla called from the kitchen, where she had been waiting out my interview with Amanda TerAlst. "Come here. Do you know her?"

Frowning, I went out to look out the kitchen window with her. A small figure limped slowly through the fallen leaves in the yard, looking up at the house. A long dark coat covered her distorted shape. She was alone, her escort of Messengers gone.

"I know her," I said. "Open the door and let her in."

-37-

CORINNE'S APARTMENT HAD A SMALL BALCONY OVERHANGING THE river. She sat there on a wooden chair, bundled head to foot against the cold of oncoming winter. Her posture was huddled, like that of an old woman.

"Corinne, I—"

"Close the door behind you. You're letting the heat out."

I turned and pulled the porch door shut. The puddles at the base of the old warehouse had turned to hollow, frost-filled ice. The twin green-copper domes of the Catholic church were vivid against the cold blue sky.

"I would rather have done anything else than come here."

"Then why did you?" All I could see were her eyes, and they didn't even look at me. She stared off at the river, as if expecting an important boat to float down it to her.

"Because I had to talk to you. To tell you."

"You had to come to my house to tell me my husband is dead? You could have dropped a note. Taken out a classified."

"Corinne—" I made a slight movement toward her, instantly suppressed, and she hunched up further.

"It's not *right*. We had it—it made sense. That's all I'd ever wanted out of it. But it didn't even make that, did it? You know all about it. He hired that woman . . . and now he's dead. I suppose I should be glad."

"No, you shouldn't be glad. My past destroyed him. I've tried to explain it . . . all that I understand myself. I was too slow to know."

"He killed those people," she said musingly. "And the police never connected them together. Just a bunch of random murders, they thought. And Gideon did it."

"I tried to explain that. Gideon didn't do it. Linden Straussman, a dead man, was responsible."

"Responsible. Gideon never was, you know. Did he commit suicide?"

"No!"

She shook her head. "That at least would have been respectable, wouldn't it? To accept some responsibility for what happened."

Corinne would have, I suddenly realized. Virt or no virt, she would have accepted her role in the crimes. Even if that wasn't fair.

"That wouldn't have made sense," I said.

"Not logically, maybe. Emotionally? I think so. How could he live with himself? How did he die? Tell me! That's why you're here, isn't it?"

"He escaped me and ran. He ran right into a prairie fire. He couldn't have lived long there. I can't tell you he died painlessly, quietly, all those things. He didn't. He died screaming."

She shuddered. "I asked for that, didn't I? Wouldn't you say that running right into a fire was a stupid thing to do?"

"I don't think—"

"Peter. You just told me my husband died screaming in agony. I asked for it and you told me. Do you think running into a blazing fire is stupid?"

Michaud had done the same thing, I reflected. "Not stupid, exactly. Driven. They—he wanted something."

"He wanted to die." Her tone was final. "Whatever else Gideon was, Peter, he was not a stupid man. If he died, it was because he wanted to."

I thought of the figure of the desperately running Farley. Had he indeed killed himself, disgusted with his crimes, despite his brave words to me? I didn't think so. But it was possible.

"You may well be right," I told Corinne.

"I think I am." She peered at me. "You're with her now, aren't you? How do you afford her?"

I sighed. "I don't own her."

"Getting it for free, Peter?" She turned and resumed her contemplation of the river. "You always were a sly one."

"Don't get nasty, Corinne. Scream at me or be polite to me. Nothing else can match what has happened to us."

"She won't stay with you, you know. Not for long. She's not the type."

"Maybe not." I thought of Priscilla McThornly, well-paid mistress, sitting in my house, trying, patiently, to communicate with the desperately wounded girl who had once been Tigranes's daughter. I couldn't tell what she actually wanted her life to be like. "Maybe not."

Corinne rolled to her feet. With that gesture, her hooded robe changed from widow's weeds to the discreet garb of a highborn lady. She pulled the hood back and tossed her hair. She was beautiful. "We should have had that daughter, you know. Melissa. Whatever we would have called her. I wanted to, in a way I never did with Gideon. With him I was . . . afraid. I never knew why."

"I know," I said. "We should have."

"Good-bye, Peter." She pulled off a glove and rested her fingers on my face. "I don't think I will see you again."

"Good-bye, Corinne."

She led me through the darkness of the house and out the front door. I stepped through into the sunlight, squinting at the world, and walked off down the street toward the house where Priscilla and Shira were waiting.